Miss Adventure

by

Geralyn Corcillo

Cover by Sue Traynor
suetraynor.com

Published by Blackbird Press at KDP

ISBN: 978-1-62678-007-1
Previously published as *She Likes It Rough* and *She Likes It Tough* by GVR Corcillo

Corcillo, Geralyn
Miss Adventure
by Geralyn Corcillo
1st Edition
ISBN-13: 978-1-62678-007-1
1. Fiction I. Corcillo, Geralyn

Awards for *Miss Adventure*

Best Humor Book Rebecca's Reads Choice Awards

Best Indie Book Rebecca's Reads Choice Awards

Book Buyer's Best Finalist

Amazon Breakthrough Novel Award Quarter Finalist

For Ron and Doug

CHAPTER 1

Six months ago I woke up rich, famous, and thin. Every woman's dream, right?

Believe me, it's not all it's cracked up to be. Not by a long shot. If it were, I wouldn't be speed hiking up a mountain in what's left of my Dolce and Gabbana power suit. Chasing a man I don't know, no less.

I wish he would slow down! What was I thinking, following Jack Hawkins into the woods?

I'm charging after him through endless trees and shrubbery, clawing leaves and sticks out of my face as I go. What kind of hike is this, anyway? I didn't bring a machete, let alone hiking boots. I am not prepared for this.

I should stop.

In fact, I should've stopped chasing Jack twenty minutes ago. That's when he veered off the trail and disappeared into the forest. But I didn't stop. I kept after Jack. I'd pulled into the lot just in time to see him lope off the path and vanish into the green mess of a mountain. Without stopping to consider for even a second, I put my car in park, popped the trunk, grabbed my workout bag, and jammed on my running shoes. Then I stripped off my jacket and followed Jack into the wild.

How could I have been so desperately impulsive? Into the Wild is the name of his company, for Pete's sake! *Everyone* at USC talks about how he spends half his life in the great outdoors testing his designs. It's like he's the king of the eco-MBA or something. And I thought I'd be able to keep up with him? Big surprise, ab workouts in front of my TV haven't transformed me into a game mountaineer. My calves feel like pool balls and I'm huffing like an asthmatic Snuffleupagus. Jack *must* hear me following him. So why doesn't he just let me catch up?

I hate him.

God, I wish I could be more like him. So capable, so focused, so in control. It's like whatever he does is no big deal because he knows it'll turn out awesome. I can barely stand to look at the guy.

Wait—where is he? All I can see is wilderness. And no Jack. But I need him!

I pump my legs harder, ignoring all the branches snagging at me. I have to find him. Jack Hawkins is the key to everything. It's time to seize the moment. I can't be scared anymore. I just can't. I have to catch him and make him listen. Not to mention, I'll never find my way back to the car without him.

I lurch forward so fast that I stumble. And there he is! Jack Hawkins, a few hundred feet ahead of me. I haven't lost him. I'll get the chance to tell him my plan.

He has to agree. He just has to. It makes perfect sense.

Doesn't it?

Maybe not. But I got this feeling in class this morning that I *had* to talk to him. Talk to him right now, *today*, or I would lose my nerve forever.

Uh-oh. Uber-Hiker has slowed down to about the speed limit. But I'm not ready to see him yet. I pull back, keeping him in my sights through all the leaves and bark. He reaches under his windbreaker—he's also wearing these windbreakery pants that look intensely comfortable—and takes something out of the pack strapped around his waist. He quickly bends up each leg at the knee and slips something onto each shoe. He looks at his watch, slips the things off, zips them back into his pack, and runs back toward me.

Oh! I duck, but he isn't looking my way. He stops, turns, races back to the same spot, and repeats the entire process.

He came all the way up here to test some shoe-thing? Well, good. Now I'll have time to catch my breath and think about what to say to him.

How can I present my idea so that he can see how much sense it makes? Then again, maybe it makes sense only to me. I have been spending a lot of time alone since I got out of the hospital. Is it possible that my wits haven't fully recovered since the coma? Or maybe I just need to think before I crash ahead with an idea. But then again, I've been doing nothing but thinking for thirty-four years, and that's been no great shakes.

Oh, damn! He's gone! Jack just disappeared before my very eyes! Wait … he must have crested a hill.

I dash forward, frantic not to lose him. My legs throb and my feet lose traction as I push up an incline, but I keep going. Up and up and—it's not a hill. It's a cliff!

A CLIFF!

I teeter on the brink like Wile E. Coyote. Then gravity yanks me over.

CHAPTER 2

He keeps looking at me. Jack Hawkins is settling me onto a patch of loose dirt at the bottom of the jagged slope, but he could do this without looking at me, couldn't he? It's all so embarrassing. I mean, we've never even spoken to one another, and I just *fell* on him.

I try to remember that I'm a rich and famous survivor who's a lot skinnier than I used to be, but it doesn't make me feel any better. Seriously, what good are all the millions from the settlement if I've got no sense to go with them? And the fame is no better. I thought all the media attention was some sort of cruel anomaly that wasn't my fault, but here I am, voluntarily getting myself into one train wreck of a fix. And sure, I'm six sizes smaller than I used to be, if I go by numbers and not actual sizes, but I'm not nearly as in shape as I thought. How am I EVER going to get this topsy-turvy life of mine to make sense and count for something? Especially if I keep going off the deep end ... or over the cliff, as it were.

I look back up the slope I just hurtled down. From here it doesn't look so high. Eight feet maybe. And not that steep. Or jagged. But it looked A LOT scarier from up top. I really thought I was plummeting to my demise until Jack caught me. Well, body-checked me, really. But as titanium-tough as he's supposed to be, my momentum still sent us tumbling. And if that weren't mortifying enough, there was that awful yelp I made as we collided. Not an athletic *Oof!* or a ladylike *Ah!* or even a witty *Hey there!* Instead, I gulped down a gasp, sounding like a cat fighting to hack up a hairball.

I can feel myself blush as the humiliation of the past five minutes washes over me. Jeepers! I was half on top of Jack—and remember, this is a guy I barely know—when we finally rolled to a stop at the bottom of the hill. Naturally, I scrambled to get off him. But things only got worse.

* * * * *

"Ach!" he grunted.

Quickly, I shifted my knee out of his gut. But I couldn't move it very far. My left foot had somehow gotten itself caught in the cuff of his pants, and we were stuck together like two dim-witted turtles on a first date. So, I twisted around, trying to extricate my running shoe from his pants. That's when I noticed my skirt was pushed up around my waist, exposing to the world —and, more importantly, to Jack Hawkins—my now-filthy white undies and a garter belt holding up only one stocking.

And before you think I'm one of those secret sex goddesses who wears Victoria's Secret lingerie everyday—as if I'm that organized—let me just say that pantyhose give me a stomachache. And I'm not going to wear those thigh highs with the sticky elastic on top. Please. They will totally fall down. And over the past few months, I've learned a thing or two about my talent for embarrassing myself, and have adapted accordingly.

Present situation excepted.

I rushed to pull my skirt down over my butt. Of course, to do that, I needed the hands that were keeping me levered up off Jack. So, as soon as I made my move, I came crashing down onto him, giving him a smack in the face with my head and an even better look at my caboose.

I shut my eyes and began muttering. “Etylf Asil. Etylf Asil. Etylf Asil.”

I felt a jerk and shift beneath me, like the beginnings of an earthquake. But my chanting wasn't transporting me to a parallel universe as I’d hoped. Jack was merely freeing himself from my pinning girth. In one fluid move, he stood up and set me well away from him. We became disentangled just like that. But I still hadn’t opened my eyes or stopped repeating my name backwards.

“Stop it,” he commanded. “You’re not going back to the fifth dimension. At least, not until you tell me what you’re doing. Then, I just might send you there myself.”

I opened my eyes. “That’s not very nice.”

I was surprised to find that Jack Hawkins is only a handful of inches taller than I am. Maybe 5’10 or 5’11. I thought he’d totally block out the sun if I ever stood this close to him.

“Lisa Flyte,” he said, looking straight at me. “You’re a mess.”

* * * * *

That’s when he brought me over here and sat me down like I needed a time-out or something.

Man, I thought I was coming so far in my plan to straighten up my life and make it matter. Joining the MBA program, getting in shape, dying my hair back ... but now this. I’ve just completely humiliated myself on top of Jack Hawkins. The man I need so desperately.

I close my eyes as if I could make this scene fade away. Suddenly, I jerk my head back as my eyes fly open. He’s trying to touch my face!

“This would be easier,” he says in a low voice, one

calmer and less gruff than I would expect from such a Snake Plissken-type, "if you would stay still. Your face looks pretty bad." He catches my chin with his fingers.

"Hey—" I start to say. I'm about to slap his hand away when I realize he isn't staring me down, trying to make me wither with shame. Instead, his grayish-blue eyes skip around, searching my face.

As he examines my scratches, I notice that he's not the brawny man-hero type at all. For one thing, he doesn't scowl all the time, making a big furrow down the center of his forehead, like Hugh Jackman does when he's Wolverine.

And Jack's not super huge—he's not even as buff as stupid Rick, the useless ex-bodyguard. Jack's not that much bigger than Keith, actually. And I used to wear Keith's sweatshirts and boxers all the time and they weren't even that big on me. I study Jack. I suppose he could be hiding a lot of taut, lean muscle under his clothes. His long-sleeved jacket and windbreakery pants cover most of his body, so not much is exposed for me to check out. Still, all in all, The Great Jack Hawkins looks kind of like a normal guy.

But I'm still scared of him up this close.

"These cuts might get infected." He leans back from me, resting on his heels as he gets some stuff out of the pack around his waist.

He rips open a small packet and starts swabbing my face with one of those wipes like the ones you get when you order hot wings. But I think this one is medicated. Because IT HURTS!

But all I make is one startled sound, as though someone just woke me up and stabbed me. Then I clench my jaw. Hard. Despite my Spartan resolve, though, tears spring to my eyes.

But I have to give Jack credit. He works quickly and doesn't say anything to make me feel like a big baby or like someone who's getting what she richly deserves.

"Hold on," he says when he finishes.

Like, where'm I gonna go?

He puts down the wipe, opens a small tube, and squeezes a daub of white cream onto three fingers. "Hypericum and calendula," he explains. "It'll help the scratches heal."

I feel like such a dork just looking at him as he rubs goo into my cuts. I want to close my eyes, but that'll make it so obvious that I feel like a dork. It's not until he's twisting the cap back onto the tube that I remember the Agatha Christie book where the old lady is murdered with poison administered through her ointment.

Oh, my God.

But wait. Even if Jack does want to kill me for being so intrusive, what are the chances he hikes around carrying poison cream?

Jack looks up from zipping the tube back into his pack and catches me staring at him. "So," he says. "Does your face feel okay?"

I barely even register what he said. And I'm certainly in no shape to respond. Because pretty soon, I'm going to have to tell him my plan.

"Lisa? You okay?" he asks.

"Uh–" I flash on a crunched up plastic water bottle I saw in his pack before he zipped it. "Do you recycle?"

He leans back and sits against a boulder facing me. His movements seem cautious, making me wince.

"Sorry if I hurt you," I offer.

He just kind of shakes me off. "What about you? Other than the scratches, are you hurt?"

"I'm okay," I say. I hope it's true. I didn't really get much of a chance to test my ankles or anything when he hoisted me off the ground and moved me away from the rocky slope.

"Yes," he says, closing his eyes, "I recycle." He sounds

tired. "It's your turn."

My turn? *Quid pro quo, Doctor*. My hand flies to my face. "Did you poison me?"

He opens his eyes, and he's got this wolfish smile. Okay, maybe not wolfish. And maybe he's not even smiling. But I'm pretty sure one corner of his lip tilts up a fraction.

"Lisa," he says, "I want some answers. It *is* all right if I call you Lisa?"

His nod to propriety after everything I've done to him this afternoon makes me lower my eyes. Where do I get off *not* giving him an explanation?

I breathe in deeply and exhale a shaky breath. I can do this. I can tell him my plan.

"Why were you chasing me?" he asks.

Oh, thank heavens! I don't have to explain. All I have to do is answer questions. "You knew I was chasing you?" I toss back at him. "Then why—"

"I didn't know it was *you,*" he clarifies. "I thought you were another fast-packer."

"Me?" I say on a laugh. "You thought *I* was a fast-packer?" I have no idea what a fast-packer is, but I'm sure I would never intentionally be one.

He shrugs. "Generally, people from class don't chase me up mountains."

"But fast-packers do?" I counter.

Jack shrugs. "Some fast-packers'll challenge any fast-packer they run into."

"Oh," I say. "So that's why you were going so fast? You thought it was a race?"

Pause. "Yeah," he says.

But he hesitated for a second. I heard him do it. My scalp gets hot. "You weren't really going that fast, were you? For you, it was a leisurely pace, wasn't it?"

"It's my turn to ask a question," he says instead. "I think I'll ask the same one since you haven't answered it yet. Why were you chasing me?" Jack's voice is quiet, almost bored-sounding, but his sharp look pins me like a butterfly.

I swallow. "I wanted to talk to you."

"About?"

I know I just have to say it. Quick with my eyes closed, like when I had to take cough medicine as a kid. I know I have to. I do. I know.

"Lisa?" he prompts.

I know, I know. I just need a sec.

"Lisa," he says, "just tell me."

Okay. Okay.

"Lisa?"

I suck in a breath, then just blurt it out. The whole stupid truth. "I want to get brave."

There. I said it. But just like with the cough medicine, I have that yucky taste in the back of my throat, threatening to make me gag. Jack stares at me like I'm ... pathetic.

"It makes perfect sense," I rush to explain. "You leap tall mountains and jump off high ledges into raging rivers. You sleep hanging from cliffs and race big vehicles at incredibly dangerous speeds. You don't give a damn what anyone else thinks. You even told your rich family to kiss off. Can you deny it? Then you started your very own company from scratch. No family money at all!"

"What the—" He looks confused. Angry, even. "How do you—where do you—"

"I, on the other hand, have no problem with free money. Don't you get it?"

"What?" he squawks. "No, I—"

"I'm afraid of everything!" I cry. "Heights and deep water. Fast cars and big animals and loud noises. How to dress, walking into strange stores, grinding my own coffee beans, what my mother thinks of me! You can fix me. I'm sure of it."

Jack shoots to his feet. "Fix you?"

He looks so appalled, but I know I'm onto something. Something big.

I stand up, too, facing him head on. "You do scary stuff all the time. You can help me get brave."

He takes a step back and speaks softly, like I'm a rabid bobcat or something. "Lisa … Lisa … look …"

My heart pounds so wildly I can hardly speak, but I have to do this. I have his attention. This is my chance. I stand tall, feeling the steel snap into my spine. "I know it's a crazy idea, but I think it can work. We could help each other out."

His gaze narrows. "How could *you* help *me*?

I lift my chin. "You have your own company. I have money to invest."

"Into the Wild is employee owned. It doesn't work like that."

"I thought you were adding a charitable donation facet," I counter, unable to give up. "I thought that's why we're in the same non-profit classes."

Jack raises a brow.

Holy bravado, Batman! I think I've made a point he's considering!

"Into the Wild doesn't need your Burger Barn money."

His voice is so flat and unyielding that my temper flares, on principle. "Are you mad at me for getting money because their drive-thru fell on me?" I demand.

His jaw tightens. I actually see the muscles clench and wonder if I should warn him about TMJ. But he's looking at me with this blistering intensity, so I don't say anything.

"Into the Wild doesn't operate on corporate money."

His tone sends chills down my back, but I manage to

speak. "My money *isn't* corporate money. Yes, I *got* it from a corporation, but it's mine now, and I'm not a company. I'm a *person*."

He looks at me. "It doesn't matter anyway. We aren't going to take donations. We're going to make them."

"Then why didn't you just say that?" I shout. "Or did you feel that you just had to make a point about how my money is from Burger Barn and I was just an out-of-control fattie who got what she deserved because she wasn't slim and petite enough to fit into a wedding dress?"

I can tell from the way he looks away that he knows what I'm talking about. He saw the tabloids—he read the stories. *Comfort Food Almost Kills Her: Burger Barn's hayloft-style drive-thru nearly crushes a distressed bride-to-be on a binge*. Once I woke up from the coma, the articles had a raucous good time calling me a cow. At least that's what Maggie and Mom were always laughing about. They said one even called me a heifer.

I can feel all of my frustration and fury rumbling like an avalanche ready to go. "Well, guess what?" I cry. "It doesn't matter how much you make fun of me or how bad you and all of America make me feel because I don't need the stupid dress anyway because Keith didn't really want to marry me and he couldn't wait for me to wake up so he could tell me! So there!" I huff and puff, furious tears pushing into my eyes.

But I can see that he's looking at me again.

"Jack," I say, with a little more control, "I chased you up this mountain because when I woke up in the hospital, it was clear to me like never before that I have a *life*, a life I almost lost. So I need to get a backbone and do something with this life. Make my life *count*."

When I finally shut up, the woods are quiet. I look at Jack. He looks surprised and confused, and something more, but

I can't place it. He looks me over then, from head to toe. He must see the one thigh-high that's come loose from its garter and fallen around my ankle. The stocking sags there, irrevocably stretched out by my gargantuan thigh.

"What?" I ask, not able to stand him looking at me for one second longer.

"You have good legs."

I tip my head, as might Benji in a similar situation. *Good legs*?

But Jack backpedals so fast I think he leaves skid marks. "Not *good* good," he splutters. "Not sexy good. I just meant, they look strong."

Oh, God, he's actually talking about how thunderous my thighs are. I mean, God forbid he was saying I could possibly look tempting with RoboCop's quadriceps. After all, for my whole life, guys and my mother have commented on my big thighs. Like in high school, when Billy's best friend Sean got his car stuck in the snow in our driveway. Their efforts to push the car out were fruitless, so Sean said, "Let's wait for Lisa to get home. She has big legs." How do I know this if I wasn't even home yet? My mom told me. Then she laughed.

And yes, we got the damn car out.

"Thanks," I say dryly.

He's still looking me up and down, checking out my torn-up half-a-business-suit. At least I had the sense to leave the jacket in the trunk.

"Did you just decide on this plan of yours today?"

I sigh. "I heard you telling someone you were going into the mountains after class, so I seized the opportunity to spring it on you."

"Why didn't you just catch me at USC?"

"Just catch you?" I kind of laugh. "I tried. It took me this long to catch *up*."

Jack nods, as if considering something. “Sorry about your suit,” he finally says.

That’s it? That’s all I’m going to get for my sweltering effort? I suddenly feel very tired. “No worries.” I sigh again. “I have lots at home.”

And I do. All because I didn’t want to feel like a complete fraud on my first day of business school. I mean, I had to walk into MBA classes when I barely even know what the NASDAQ is. So, I decided to wear a chic power suit to look the part of the business maven I purported to be. Donna Karan, black, subtle, sensational. I couldn’t miss.

Actually, I missed by a lot. Nobody else looked so polished. They all dressed anywhere from business casual to downright grunge, and I stuck out like a kangaroo in a Twinkies warehouse. But I held my head high and acted as if they were all *under*dressed. After that, I had to wear a posh suit to every class. It was either that or lose face.

So now, I have a closet full of poseur designer business suits with matching shirts and heels. And everyone thinks I’m weird. But I look so svelte they stay away, almost as if with respectful distance. But I don’t think they really respect me.

Not yet, anyway. Not like they respect Jack Hawkins.

“Well,” Jack says, standing up, “you’re clearly no hiker.”

I blink at him. “What gave it away?”

His gaze remains steady. “But you kept up with me.”

I open my mouth, but nothing comes out. *You kept up with me*.

“Come on,” he says. “You won’t find your way off this mountain without me. But I’ve got more to do, so you better keep keeping up.”

I feel a beam of sunshine blast through me, swear to God. “You’ll let me go with you? And do stuff?” Everything is going to be all right!

"It's better than leaving you here and worrying that a bear'll get you."

"So, there are bears?" I try to keep my voice as unshaky as possible.

"Lisa, we're in the woods. What did you expect?"

* * * * *

I didn't expect this. And I bet he didn't either.

I'm standing at the base of a rock wall—this one really *is* steep—and I've got bleeding hands. I'm holding a shoe that isn't mine. And yes, a pair of pants.

Windbreakery pants.

And I'm getting blood all over them, but I can't help it. My hands don't hurt as much when I clench them into fists. When I clench them into Jack's pants.

I look up at the twelve-foot cliff I just rappelled down. Is that even the right word? Have they come up with a word for what I just did?

Jack's still up there, splayed against the rocks like Spider-Man. Only his superhero costume is a windbreaker, a magic pack around his waist, and boxers. Blue plaid.

I knew climbing down the rocks with him was a bad idea. I knew it. Feeling *that* scared has to mean *something*, right?

But I want to get brave, so I did it. I started my descent just after Jack, and everything seemed to be okay for the first second or so. Then Jack yelled up at me—I think he was telling me to do something with the metal hook thing, but I must have done it wrong. Way wrong. Because in a flash, gravity pulled the rug out, and I was spiraling down fast. I remember seeing my running shoes glance off the rock wall in front of me as I worked to find traction.

See? I actually tried to stop myself and control my descent.

Initially.

But then I just panicked and screamed—a lot—and down I went, the rope sliding through my hands at blistering speed. It really hurt, so I screamed more, and more loudly. I tore at Jack as I slid over him, trying to grab hold of something to slow me down.

That's how I ended up with those windbreakery pants, not to mention his shoe. In my own defense, though, his pants wouldn't have come off if he'd been wearing jeans. And I did slow down enough to land safely on my butt.

I look down at my bleeding hands, then back up to Jack. He's descending the rest of the way, as quietly as a tarantula, one shoe and all. I do not say anything. He does not say anything. The forest is so still I don't even hear branches rustle or varmints chirp. The silence of damp earth and fallen leaves is almost creepy. Jack touches ground, so he's standing next to me, wearing his windbreaker and boxers. One socked foot, one shoed foot.

"Here," I say suddenly, thrusting the crumpled pants at him and dropping the shoe. "At least they're dark green, so the blood stains won't show so badly."

"Thanks." He takes the pants, steps into them.

I'm surprised he can get them on over his one remaining shoe, until I see the reason. A long rip along the outside seam. So, there Jack stands in a pair of pants slit all the way up one leg, making him look like some sort of lame-ass trying to be a harem princess for Halloween.

He picks up his other shoe and slips it on. "Let me see your hands," he says, holding out his hands to take mine.

I place the backs of my hands in his palms, and then slowly unclench the fists. *Owww.*

He makes a noise like an extended *oh* then I notice a deep cleft form between his brows. He pulls his hands away, reaches into his pack, and rips open two more wipes.

"This," he says, and looks right into my eyes, "is going to kill." He lays an unfolded wipe lightly across each of my palms.

I breathe. "It's not so bad."

"Now make a fist with each hand."

I look to him in panic, but I see that he's not kidding. Holding his gaze—I don't dare look down at my hands—I clench both sets of fingers into tight fists, squeezing the medicated wipes. I do not break eye contact with him, but I swallow hard about a million times.

"Okay," he says, gently tapping at my fingers so I'll unclench my fists. He takes away the bloody wipes, then squeezes a mound of hypericum cream into my palm and tells me to rub my hands together. He turns away from me to retrieve his gossamer-thin rope, now red in some places.

"I'm sorry," I say quietly. "About everything."

Jack stops what he's doing to look out into the woods, as if contemplating how exactly to tell his teenage son the facts of life. Not that he has a son. That I know of.

"Lisa, I can't do this. We're done."

He puts the rope back into his pack then strides off. "Let's go," he calls back to me.

I run to get slightly ahead of him, backpedaling so I can face him. "Done?" I say. "For good? That's it? But I can do better. Try harder."

"Lisa." Jack stops so suddenly that I tumble backwards as though someone's pulled a chair out from under me. He stands over me as I sit in a bush, my legs splayed like Bambi's. "Lisa." He looks around, then back at me. "You're totally inexperienced."

I scramble up. "I never said any different!"

"You can't tag along with me," he says with iron-clad decision. "You don't know what you're doing. On top of that, you didn't even listen to me."

"I tried. It all happened so much faster than I expected!"

"Gravity is like that." Deadpan. Calm. He's not changing his mind.

"I'll replace your pants," I say, showing him how contrite I am.

"Fuck the pants! If you'd let go of that rope, you could be dead now. Don't you get it? That's the trouble with beginners. You just don't get it!"

"Then why did you let me try in the first place?"

He doesn't answer.

"Well, Jack?"

"We have to get off this mountain before it gets dark," he says as he pushes past me.

I scramble to get in front of him again.

"Answer me, Jack."

He stops. "I don't have to answer you. Now let's go or you're spending the night. And by the way, there are mountain lions up here, and they hunt after dark."

He takes off.

I chase him, but at least it's downhill this time. "You must have had a reason," I call after him. "You must have thought I was worth it."

He stomps on in stony silence. Well, silence except for the actual stomping. That part makes a lot of noise.

"Jack, you believed in me," I shout. "I know it!" I can feel my case building strength, even as he starts to growl at me.

"Lisa …"

I'm straining to hear over the crunch and snap. "What, Jack? Tell me. I know we can make this work. You had faith in me."

"I felt sorry for you."

I take the direct hit. Right in the throat, apparently, because I can't say a thing. Jack just keeps on going.

"Sorry for me?" I finally rasp. "Listen, Ace, you don't have to feel—"

"No kidding! You're a millionaire! The world is your Goddamned oyster and you're whining about it!"

"I'm *trying* to change my stupid, average life!"

"By chasing a guy you don't know up a mountain and risking your neck?"

"I think our partnering up is a good idea."

"No," he says, "our 'partnering up' is a dangerous idea."

I stop in my tracks. "I thought you were supposed to be brave!"

He stops.

Uh-oh.

He turns.

Um…

He's walking back toward me.

I can't move.

He stops right in front of me. "Maybe I'm brave," he says. "But I'm not stupid. And there's a big difference."

"I just wanted—"

"I *get* what you wanted." His syllables are clipped, his tone vicious. "I get that you think people have been unfair to you, but you know what? The way to fix that isn't by barreling through other people's lives thinking only about yourself. Money doesn't give you the right to act that way, no matter how much you think it does. So, if that's what you mean by getting brave, I am *not* the man you should be talking to."

"But—"

Jack turns, pushes forth like a steam shovel, and leaves

me no choice but to follow.

"I didn't mean to barge into your life," I call after him. "And I'm not exactly barging. This isn't your mountain and I can be here if I want."

He stops and turns to face me. "Right," he agrees. "See ya." In a flash, he's through the brush and gone.

"WAIT!" I charge after him. "I'm sorry! Please!"

And there he is, a few feet ahead of me, waiting, his hand resting against the bark of some tree.

I walk up to him, catching my breath. "I never did anything like this before— just decided, just like that, to actually *do* something. Do you see why I need your help?"

He looks at me. Just looks. "Let's go." He turns away and jogs lightly down the slope.

I feel a hot, pulsing knot of frustration surge up behind my ribcage as I follow him. I know Jack knows where he's going and everything, but it makes me mad that I'm forced to tag along. It's like Keith all over again. Finished with me but stuck with me. Jack dragging me down the mountain, Keith sitting by my bedside all those weeks, feeling guilty because he hadn't dumped me before the coma.

"And I suppose I should be grateful!" I don't even realize I've said this out loud until Jack answers.

"Damn straight," he shouts, loudly enough so I can hear him over our brush stomping.

He doesn't even sound out of breath!

"Well, thank you," I yell, "for being so upfront and quitting on me like a pro."

Wham!

I crash into him so hard I immediately reach up to feel the bone of my throbbing nose. He stopped and turned around so fast I didn't have time to put on the brakes. But he doesn't offer any salve this time. He just looks at me, and I swear he wants to pull my hair.

"I do *not* work for you," he snarls in a low, Clubber-Lang-takin'-on-Rocky kind of voice. "But with ten million dollars, you can hire your own personal outdoor guides and make them take you wherever you want and teach you anything. Then when they see what a liability you are, they'll quit. *Like actual pros*."

He takes off again so fast, and he's wearing such dark clothes, that I run to keep up, genuinely afraid that I might lose him and he might not care. I don't know why I have to be such a bitch to him. After all, he's right. About everything. Why did I ever think someone like him would put up with someone like me?

Finally, I see street lights. More accurately, a parking lot light. Glory be! In a few minutes, I'll be able to get away from Jack. I'm beginning to sense just how embarrassed I'm going to feel when I wake up tomorrow.

As the trees thin, I see the wooden bridge that crosses the stream between the trailhead and the parking lot. And since I'm about to put this all behind me, I take my parting shot. In self-defense, really. "By the way, Mr. Know-It-All, I don't know why you think I got ten million. I got barely half of that." I lick my lips and swallow. "You don't know anything about my money."

Jack doesn't even look at me. "I know you're going to have to use some of it to buy a new car."

"What? Why?" I put my hands on my hips. "What's wrong with Sugar?"

Jack looks toward the parking lot. "She's not here."

I run onto the pavement, seeing nothing but Jack's junky blue pick-up truck.

Sure enough, no red and black Mini. Sugar is gone.

CHAPTER 3

"I'm telling you, I read about it."

"Even if he *can* drive," Jack argues, "Bigfoot did not steal your car."

I sit and sulk in the front seat of Jack's truck. Ha! I knew he was a beastly man. He's killing the environment with his big old diesel monstrosity. This thought comforts me as I sit stiffly, trying to keep the brunt of my mortification from penetrating too deeply into my psyche. But it's almost impossible. On top of losing my chance to become brave and respected, I've lost Sugar as well. The mature-looking Mini that replaced my crushed butter-yellow Bug is gone. First Chaka, now Sugar. Sugar is gone. Gone! Plus my wallet, cell phone, and keys. I left them on Sugar's roof in my haste to chase down Jack. That is my best recollection, anyway. Still, I'm a victim. And so is poor Sugar.

"I'm not making this up," I insist through clenched teeth.

"I know," Jack says in a world-weary voice. "Ron Carlson made it up. It's called 'Bigfoot Stole My Wife,' and it's fiction."

Okay, maybe Bigfoot didn't steal my car. After all, doesn't Bigfoot live in Washington? The outskirts of L.A. flash by, and I sigh. A Bigfoot mystery would have been interesting, though. A nice river of denial leading away from the tortuous tale of how badly I've regressed. Despite all my working out and my new size eight body, I've had it made mercilessly clear to me today that I still have huge thighs. My demure Dolce and Gabbana business suit is toast. My apartment keys and all my identification are in the hands of some reprobate. My plan to get brave has been trashed by yours truly. I've left Jack in no doubt of what a loser I am. And I'm freezing. I'd pull up my other stocking if it hadn't been torn off during the stampede down the mountain.

I could tell Jack I'm cold except I'm sure that heating this mammoth truck would take so much fuel that I'd have a hole in the ozone named after me. Jack probably never gets cold. What a jerk.

"You know," I say, "this truck is a disgrace. You're killing the environment. Not so friendly to those woods you love tromping through so much."

"Number One," he says almost as soon as I close my mouth, "you don't know me or what I'm friendly to. Number Two, you have no idea what I love. Number Three, this truck has been converted to run on vegetable oil, most of which is recycled, and I know that's a pet concern of yours. And finally, I'm not killing anyone—yet."

"Jeez," I say, ignoring his words and choosing instead to react to his bristly harshness, "you don't have to get so mad. What is it with guys and their cars? You'd think I insulted your —"

"Maybe I just think you're going off half-cocked, *again*, without knowing what on earth you're doing or saying. God, you're annoying."

"You don't have to be rude."

"You've got a point," he concedes. "But then, I don't think we have the same definition of 'rude.' Which exit?"

"Take the 405 North, exit Santa Monica, and turn left."

At last! In a matter of minutes, Jack Hawkins will be out

of my life. Except for my seeing him in classes three days a week. Damn. Every time I look at him, I'll remember that we have this one humiliating day between us. And I've got the lion's share of the humiliation. Actually, I don't think Jack has any of it. Sure, he was hanging from a rock in his boxers, but they were nice boxers, and *his* legs don't have a spec of cellulite.

"Turn left here."

He does.

"This is it," I say, pointing as we approach my building.

"Where?"

"Here."

He peers through the windshield and crinkles his forehead. "You live *here*?"

"Yes, *here*."

Jack pulls up to the curb and kills the ignition. Without waiting for me, he gets out of the truck and walks onto the small patch of lawn to get a better look. Dusk has fallen, but the street lights, ground lights, and lights above each apartment door illuminate the place pretty well. I climb out of the truck and he turns on me.

"You live *here*?"

It's Tuesday night in L.A., and since my stretch of street is pretty quiet, Jack's voice can be heard down the block. "Jack, what is your problem?"

"You got a multi-million dollar settlement a few months ago, and you live in a two-story walk up?"

He's staring at me with this funny look on his face that I can't read. But I'm sure he's judging me and once again finding that I don't measure up. Not only do I live off my diabolical corporate money, but now I'm also a greedy miser, hoarding my riches in my little hovel.

"Listen, buster." I step forward, not caring how un-menacing I must look in filthy business suit dregs and running shoes that don't match the rest of the outfit. "I only live here because my landlord tripled my rent when I got home from the hospital."

"So you decided to stay?" His eyes open wider. "Are you and your landlord …?"

"No!" I shout. "Jesus, I'm not actually paying triple! Keith moved out while I was in the hospital, so right there, my share of the rent doubled. And on top of that, I'm going to pay triple? Are you nuts?"

"Am *I* nuts?"

"Don't try to twist this around to make me sound like a barking lunatic."

"You need my help for that, do you? Let's review—"

"Let's not." I cut him off before he can start saying stuff that will make me cry. "It's very simple. Raffi tried to triple my rent. I decided to move. But the price of every house I tried to buy just happened to escalate astronomically as soon as I put in an offer."

"Oh." Jack is quiet for a few seconds. "You need a new realtor."

"I tried three."

He looks at me. "Is that why you're in business school?" he asks. "To learn how to handle your money so people don't take you for a ride? That's not exactly what an MBA is for."

"I have big plans for my money," I tell him. "Important plans."

Jack walks back to the curb and locks his truck. "We better get Raffi to let us in so we can call the police."

And yes, Raffi's been mad at me ever since I refused to pay triple. But he takes one look at Jack and lets us in to my apartment. Whatever.

"This apartment's not very secure." Jack looks around my living room, his brows slammed together. He swipes aside the curtain to check out the sliding glass doors that lead to my matchbox balcony.

"But I've got a broomstick in the tracks," I say, defending my sophisticated home security.

"Anyone who knew what he was doing could pop those doors off in a matter of seconds." He says this as he moves across the living room toward the bedroom.

The bedroom!

Quicker than a snow hare being chased by a cougar, I race to the bedroom door and block Jack from entering. "You can't go in there."

"Why? Is it a mess? You got a man in there? I don't care. I'm just checking out how safe you are."

"It doesn't matter," I argue. "There's nothing in there worth stealing."

"There's your identity, and with a bank account like yours, it's an identity worth protecting."

I still don't move.

Jack looks right into my eyes, and I have to concentrate so I don't flinch. "Lisa, someone out there has your keys and your license. With your address. You're vulnerable, and I'm trying to help."

My breath hitches. I swallow once, then slide out of his way.

He swings the door open. "What the hell?" He turns to look at me. "You're certifiable. Completely nuts." He looks around at my beautiful, wonderful fantasy bedroom. The four poster bed, the snowy white comforter, the mounds of pillows, the billowy curtains, the free standing wardrobe, the ornately carved dressing table with its plush stool. "Why would you care if I came in here?"

"Because I said I wanted to do something important with the money—and I do," I quickly assure him, "but I spent some of it on me." I gesture toward the cornucopia of classy comfort. "Obviously."

Jack looks at the room, then at me, then back at the room. "On this? This is what you squandered your millions on? A bedroom?"

"It's the room I've always dreamed of having, and I really went overboard." I cringe inside, but decide to be brave and confess. "There are four others. Bed sets, I mean." I take a deep breath, saying it all as fast as I can, hoping he doesn't have time to judge me. "Okay. The quilt that reminds me of *Little House on the Prairie*, the orange paisley comforter that reminds me of my bedspread when I was four years old, the tartan plaid down that looks like English Christmas, and the comforter sprigged with wild flowers that makes me think of The Hundred Acre Wood. There. Now you know." I stop to gulp air. "A total of five different bed sets. I couldn't help it. I had all this money, and I just went crazy."

Jack considers me. "It's okay, Lisa." His voice is deadpan. "I don't think you're going to hell over a dust ruffle."

I think about that for a second. "Wait. You *know* what a dust ruffle is?"

But he's not paying attention to me anymore. He's behind my curtains as he checks out the window. Next, he goes into the bathroom to inspect the small window in the shower. After that, he walks into the living room and just looks at me. "You're not safe. You need to get a locksmith here first thing tomorrow morning."

I nod.

"How long have you lived here?"

"Seven years, about."

He looks at me. "Then lots of people know this is your address? It's on file all over the place?"

"I guess."

"You really should move."

"Haven't we been through this?"

"I don't get it," he says. "I know it must be hard, everyone knowing who you are and how much money you got. But you've had the time to do this right, to make it work. Find a decent, safe place. You've been out of the hospital for months, right? What have you been doing with all your time?"

"Well," I begin, hating that he wants me to just explain my life to him. "Classes at USC, for one—"

"Classes started three weeks ago. What about before that?"

"Why do you care?" I shoot back.

"You barged into *my* life, remember?"

"Okay, fine," I snap. "Whatever. I was getting in shape, okay?"

His eyes get wide. "In shape for what?" He makes it sound as though I'm fit for little more than competitive chess.

"Just … in shape. When I got out of the hospital, I was a mess, like a malnourished whale who could barely walk."

"That's better than most whales."

I glare at him, mostly because he accepts so unquestioningly that I was indeed a whale. "Getting in shape and eating right really took a lot of time and concentration." Seriously. No wonder I was never this fit before. I didn't have the energy when I had a job. "Plus," I add, "I had lots of therapy and I had to study for the GMAT."

I guess the part about therapy is what finally shuts him up. His eyes sweep across the living room and settle on the shabby-chic couch. "All right," he says after a minute, rubbing his hands over his face. "I'm going to go down to the truck to get a change of clothes," he says. "Then, I'm taking a shower. I'm spending the night here, on the couch."

Jack Hawkins, spending the night in my apartment? He's

gonna be, like, my bodyguard? Maggie better stay the hell away. She still has my last bodyguard.

"Um," I say. "What about the cops?"

"It won't take me that long," he says. "Call them, and I'll be out of the shower long before they get here." He looks me up and down. "You'll have time to clean up, too."

* * * * *

Did I mention I hate him? Even the cops fell under his spell. They paid more attention to Jack than to me. It makes no sense. I stepped into a totally serious Chanel frock when I got out of the shower, hoping to seem more responsible than my behavior with my wallet and Sugar's keys would indicate. Jack, on the other hand, put on jeans and a white T-shirt. And no shoes. Or socks. Plus he's unshaven. But the cops listened to him while making me feel as though I were a pesky interloper. And I'm the one who was robbed!

I could tell myself it's some sort of sexist guy thing, but I know it's not. It's Jack. After all, I was with Keith for five years, and no one ever paid particular attention to him.

I look at Jack's back as he stands in my doorway watching the police make their way down the outside stairs. I'm so jealous of his comfy clothes that I dart into the bedroom. I return a few minutes later wearing blue cotton pajama pants and a clingy white long-sleeved T-shirt with an equally clingy short-sleeved pink Fanboy and Chum Chum T-shirt over it. And I took off my bra. That's why I'm wearing two T-shirts. They're tight enough to hold me up quite decently.

I sit on the couch to put on my thick white socks and notice that Jack still stands by the door. In fact, he's leaning with his back against it, and he sighs. Not audibly, but I see it. I don't really think of superheroes as guys who sigh, but I guess this is what I've brought him to. I mean, he's Jack Hawkins— part Batman, part George of the Jungle. But right now, he just looks beat. His stubble doesn't make him look roguish so much as it makes him look worn out.

He stares at me. He so doesn't want to be here, I can see it. I can *feel* it, with every pore of my skin. I am an unpleasant duty. Again. Just like Keith and his obligatory coma-watch.

I feel so rotten that my stomach hurts. I need to make this better for both of us. Jack's rucksack sits on the couch next to me, so I pick it up, a brilliant idea blasting through my bummer of a mood. I look up at him. "Do you mind if I go through this?"

"What?" he asks, pushing off the door. "Why?" He strides over to me and takes back his backpack. Despite his tangible exhaustion, he still moves with cougar-like grace.

Damn. How does he do it?

I reach out and yank the pack back. "I want to get your pants," I explain.

"My pants?"

"I want to fix your pants. The ones I ripped off—the ones I ripped. I can fix them and wash them. It's not fair that today cost you a pair of pants."

"I'll survive," he assures me, reaching to take back his bag.

"But they're fixable," I argue, holding the rucksack out of his reach, "so I don't see any reason why—"

"I can fix them myself."

"You know how to sew?" The blurted challenge puts me right up on my Some-Things-Girls-Can-Do-Better high horse, even though it is a totally sexist stereotype that only an idiot would lay claim to. Not to mention I can't sew much more than a button.

"I've been hiking for over twenty years," he answers.

"Hikers need to sew?" My sarcasm serves me well. "For what?"

"Head wounds, mostly." He tries to take back the rucksack, thinking I'm going to be satisfied with leaving myself so miserably beholden to him.

I pull the pack even further away from him. "There's no reason you should do the work when it's my fault. I'll fix your pants."

"No, you won't." He reaches across me and jerks the pack back.

"Jack," I bolt off the couch so we stand face to face. Man, he smells good. It's so unfair. He used my shower and my soap, and *I* never smell this good. "Give them to me."

"I'm not giving you my pants."

Just then, I kind of hear what we're saying to one another, and it gives me a different idea. "Do you want to have sex?"

"What?" He leaps backwards to get away from me. "No! What? No," he says again. "Are you crazy?" He pushes past me to go sit on the couch. But he immediately stands up again. He moves to the center of the living room where he paces like a tiger with ADD. "I can't believe you just said that!"

"Sorry," I say, wearing my petulance like a badge. Jeez. Does he have to act so repulsed? It's not like I'm lusting after him, or anything. I mean, yeah, he's got this incredible warrior kind of magnetism and this way of moving that makes me think …

But never mind! I don't actually *like* him. Come on! He's Jack Hawkins. I will not act like some geeky piccolo player drooling after the captain of the football team. And that's exactly what it would be like if I were actually stupid enough to *want* Jack Hawkins. I mean, sure, I'd do him, but that doesn't mean—

Oh, my God! Does he think I actually *want* him? "It's

just that you're so miserable," I rush to explain.

He looks at me like I've just told him his duck is on fire.

"Seriously, Jack. Your mood is blasting into me like this dark beam of ... of ... like, dirty snow on the side of the road, you know? Yuck. And I can't stand it. I'm so depressed."

He slams his brows together. "That's why you have sex? To get rid of depression?"

I'm thinking this doesn't sound like such a crazy reason when I realize what he's doing. "Oh, no you don't!" I thrust my fists onto my hips so my elbows jut out in a really commanding way. "Where do you get off psychoanalyzing me? You don't even know me!"

"No, I don't," he agrees. "But you said—"

"Forget what I said!" I take a deep breath, let it out. "Just forget everything I said. I was just trying … I was … I … I really ruined your day, and now your night, too. And you have to work tomorrow, but you're stuck here all night. I was just trying to make things better. For both of us. That's all."

His eyes bug out of his head in true Odie-fashion. "By having sex with me?"

He says this like having sex with Lisa Flyte could NEVER improve ANY situation for ANYONE. I want to punch him. Hard. But I don't.

Because I'm scared.

Not of punching him. I'm sure my hand would hurt for only a day or so if I tried. I mean, I'm too much of a chicken to tell him to get the hell out. I don't want to spend the night alone in my apartment when some criminal has my keys along with my license telling him exactly where I live. What could I possibly do to defend myself? I have no weapons or fighting skills. I can't even think under pressure. I've heard that in times of great stress, people revert to doing whatever activities come most naturally to them. But how on earth would watching reruns of *Scarecrow and Mrs. King* help me in a home invasion situation?

I need Jack tonight, but in a strictly utilitarian sense.

"Never mind," I finally say on a sigh, giving up trying to explain myself or salvage my dignity. "I changed my mind. I don't want to have sex with you."

Jack eyes me suspiciously.

"But I want the pants."

Apparently, the threat of my having sex with him worked wonders. He hands the pants over without another word.

* * * * *

I am happy to say I have grown accustomed to spending time in my bed all by myself. Since Keith left, I've redecorated to my heart's delight. My bedroom palace now fills me with a contented warmth that spreads from my toes to the tips of my hair.

Still, it rankles when a rough and ripped adventurer sits awake on my couch in the other room. Makes the beautiful bed seem like such a waste.

Plus, being alone makes it easier to think, and I don't want to think. Reflecting on the day is making me restless. And not because I regret how I acted on the mountain. I'm sure that will come later. But something Jack said keeps pinging around in my mind like a pinball that just won't quit. I've got to get to the bottom—

Sha-clink.

I sit bolt upright on the bed. That's the key in the door! Someone is trying my key in the door! I run out of the bedroom to find Jack standing still, silent and alert, like a crocodile waiting out its prey. Why isn't he taking action? Doesn't he realize this is the perfect time to strike? I run through the hallway-like kitchen to the front door. Out of the corner of my eye, I see Jack lunge to stop me, but the breakfast bar separating the kitchen from the living room blocks him. I get to the front door and wrench it open!

"AAAAHHH!" What am I doing!?!?

A guy wearing black jeans and a dark blue sweat shirt jerks up from where he's bent to the keyhole. We stare at each other for a millisecond, then using my hands on each jamb to brace myself, I do the first thing I think of.

I head butt him.

Smack!

White light! White light! White light! THAT REALLY HURT! I thought it wasn't supposed to hurt the butter! I collapse. As I go down, someone steps on me.

When my vision clears somewhat, I see the criminal guy sprawled unconscious on the cement walkway outside my door. His chin sports a round, red mark about the diameter of a coffee mug.

I guess I missed.

I squint at Jack. He curls one fist into the other palm, rubbing his knuckles. Wow. Did he punch the guy out and save my ass? "Are you hurt?" I ask him.

"What the hell did you think you were doing?"

I wrinkle my forehead and look down at the passed-out guy. "Trying to get him," I say. I look more closely. "His clothes don't match."

* * * * *

The cops listen to Jack. Hell, by now they're probably all canasta partners. Then the cops take the bad guy away. I get back my wallet but Sugar is already history.

Jack spends another ten minutes rubbing a clear goo on my forehead and asking me to count his fingers. Then he starts asking me state capitols.

"Carson Freaking City. Okay? Jack, I'm fine. Really. You can go."

"Okay," he says and gets up.

As he heads for the door, I can scarcely believe it's all over. I pick up his tube of arnica and lope across the living room. "You forgot your goo."

Jack turns to look at me. He looks at my forehead, then back to my eyes. "Just take it, Lisa. You'll need it more than I will."

Then I watch as he walks out the front door and closes it behind him. Just like that, he's gone and I'm by myself. I go back to my bedroom, collapse onto my snowy-white comforter, and fall asleep.

When I wake up, I know I've got to get the hell out of Dodge.

CHAPTER 4

Traffic has been oozing like drain sludge since Greenwich, but still it's too fast for me. I've been almost at Norwalk for forty-five minutes, and every second has been as precious as that last cigarette before they jerk the black hood over your head and take you out back to shoot you. Exit 16 off the I-95 looms ahead of me like the Black Gates of Mordor. It's still at least ten minutes away, but I can feel its dark pull. Why couldn't getting through Stamford have taken longer? Is an hour or two in Friday morning Connecticut traffic too much to ask?

Ten million dollars.

My stomach seizes up. Again. Jack said Burger Barn settled ten million dollars on me. I did some research on the net, and sure enough, ten million is the figure everyone reports. Why had I been so determined NEVER to look up anything about my story once I woke up? Okay, the initial tabloid exposé was so embarrassing it almost put me back into another coma. But I should have been strong enough to get over it. So they called me a cow. And seriously, who cares that my mom told the world that I wet the bed after seeing *C.H.U.D.*?

When I was 11.

Had she done it on purpose? Embarrassed me so much that I would hide away and never realize that Burger Barn gave me ten million dollars, as opposed to the six million I actually got?

Ten million.

Who am I kidding? Who? Didn't I know, all the damn time, that something was wrong? But I was too spineless to do anything about it. To even *say* anything about it.

I'd been so mad the day I found out about the money. Mad because Keith still hadn't been to see me since I'd woken up, mad about that stupid magazine with the horrible picture of me on the cover. Mad, mad, mad!

* * * * *

"I don't think you look like a smock." That was Mom's best defense when I glared at her across my hospital bed, pointing at the cover of *People*. A picture of comatose me—greasy hair, double chin, drool. "You don't look that messy," she insisted.

"Not a smock, Mom. SHHHH-muck. I look like a schmuck!"

"Lisa." Dad was looking down his nose at me, getting ready to Tell Me How It Is. "People will forget about this. Soon, some crazy lady will murder her family and put them in the mulcher." He slid a glance toward my mother, an avid gardener. "Your story will be history. But you get to keep the six million dollars. Just remember that."

"Six million dollars?" It was the first I'd heard of it. "What? Like the Bionic Man?"

Even then, I knew it wasn't right. Steve Austin got hurt in the 1970's, so that figure of six million needed some serious inflation. I began to splutter, making my pulse jump and machines beep. "You mean it's all settled? What about me? Don't I get a say? I'm thirty-four years old. I should have a say. They really messed up. Big time. I could have been killed!"

Dad clearly Didn't Want to Hear It. "You signed the papers. Six million dollars, plus all your medical bills taken care of, plus free health insurance from Burger Barn for life." He said it in his End of Discussion voice.

"What?!" My fury detonated across the room. "This isn't fair! This—hey!"

Mom came to my bedside and actually pressed her hands into my shoulders, pinning me to the bed. Dad covered me with more blankets and tucked them around me so tightly that I couldn't move my legs. A nurse who looked an awful lot like Frau Blücher came in and threatened to give me a shot. Ever-present Rick shook his head dolefully at me as he stood at attention by the door. I felt like the hysterical passenger on *Airplane!*, about to be socked by anyone who wanted a go.

"I could have been killed," I repeated mutinously once the nurse was out of the room.

"That would have been more money," Dad agreed.

"No!" I protested. "I mean, I'm awake now! I can deal with this myself!"

"You were out a long time," he explained. "We had to get things settled." He made it sound as if I had been so thoughtless to be in a coma for so long.

"But six million? They were negligent. Don't they at least go to jail?"

"Lisa. They acted responsibly and rectified matters. They've taken good care of us."

I looked from Dad to Mom and back again. "How much money did they give *you*?"

"And don't forget," Mom said, ignoring my question completely, "you're famous."

I pointed at her with the force of a South American dictator. "That is NOT a good thing."

"You know you love this," she said smugly. "This is

better than when you set up that big stage show in the living room so you could sing 'You Light Up My Life' in front of all the relatives." She giggled. "You didn't even know all the words."

"That was in third grade! I'm thirty-four now!"

She raised her eyebrows and slanted me a look down her nose. "You're still you."

* * * * *

Didn't I know then that my parents had taken some of my money? Deep down, didn't I know? But I had been wallowing in tears of hopeless frustration. How long would it be before everyone in my family stopped judging me according to the stupid things I'd done as a kid? Wasn't there any statute of limitations on growing up?

As I pull to the curb in front of the two-story colonial I grew up in, autumn leaves crunch under the tires of my aquamarine rental. I step out into the stony morning and shiver as the chill manages to line my coat. Sucking in damp air to brace myself, I take a minute. Then another minute. I have to do this. I have to go in there. I want to hear them admit it. I do. So, I lift my chin, straighten my spine, and head down the driveway. Without knocking, I open the back door and walk right in, as if I still belong there.

The kitchen smells like warm caramel. I don't remember it smelling that way when I was growing up. The post-my-daughter's-coma kitchen looks so different from the linoleum-and-paneling way it did back in '89. Now there are dark wooden beams across the ceiling. Wow. I didn't know you could get those installed. Shiny copper pots hang above the sink, flowers and herbs dance all over the wallpaper, and dusky lighting makes the room feel cozy. I notice the curtains are new since Christmas.

The fridge, too. I'm looking at its stainless steel surface littered with pictures of Billy's kids when I hear voices and feet coming down the stairs.

"Get Maggie's—" She stops when she sees me.

"Hi, Mom," I say, and put my hands in my coat pockets.

"Lisa." My mother goes to the sink to take a sip from her cup of tea sitting under the spider plant. She looks at me over her shoulder then takes a kind of gulp. "This is a surprise. I didn't even know you knew Maggie would be here for her birthday."

Damn! I forgot about Maggie's birthday.

"Lisa!" Rick rushes into the kitchen.

He comes at me then stops, as if he was going to hug me but thought better of it. He stands about a foot from me and looks me up and down. "You look different," he says, his sparkling smile as radiant as ever. "Kind of." He sounds as if he thinks I could have tried a little harder. "Is that a big bruise on your forehead?"

"Rick." It feels so surreal. He's still just as lady-killer gorgeous, but he's not wearing his bogus scrubs. Rick the Bodyguard. What a colossal joke. He didn't protect me from the media. Let alone from my own family. Too busy getting it on with Mags. Now it's like he's a different person. The kind who no longer has to work for a living because his girlfriend stole a bunch of money from her comatose sister.

"We're here for Maggie's birthday." He looks around. "She's getting a pedicure."

They're still together. It's hard to process that anyone could put up with Mags for that long. But then again, if what I suspect about the money is true, and it's not just my parents, but Mags too…

I don't want Maggot-Face to have any of my Burger Barn money! She doesn't even like me!!! I decide to count to ten. But I feel stupid by six, so I say, "You're spending her birthday here, in Norwalk?"

Note: If I had a guy who looked like Jude Law, I wouldn't be spending my birthday down the hall from my parents.

"They leave for Paris on Sunday," my mother chimes in.

Of course they do. Regardless, I head back to L.A. tonight, so I have to get my answers today. Mags will complicate things with distracting static, but I've been putting up with that my entire life. I'll cope. The material point is that Mags isn't here now, so I have to strike.

"Mom," I say, "what happened to Burger Barn's ten million dollar settlement?"

Rick freezes like a possum, but Mom hones in on me like a rattlesnake. "Lisa, you don't deserve all that money."

"Mom," I say, "there are lots of things I don't deserve, present company being no exception. I just want to know what happened to it."

"And as soon as you find out, you'll throw a big tantrum and go ranting all over Connecticut until you get what you want."

Just then Dad comes in and sees me. His eyebrows shoot up. "Lisa?"

"Dad, where's all the money? The other four million from Burger Barn?"

Dad darts my mother a look. "That's none of your business," he tells me.

"None of my business?"

The back door flies open and smacks hard against the fridge. "Aaah!" Mags stands there, theatrically backlit by the morning light. "What are *you* doing here?" She marches toward me, sneering like a Scooby-Doo villain. "You're trying to ruin my party. You want everyone to talk about you all night instead of me. Well, think again!" She moves to Rick's side and hooks her arm into his. "You're not invited!"

"Lisa," Mom scolds, "that is so childish."

I roll my eyes. "Thanks, Mom. But I don't care about her party. I'm here to find out what happened to all the money from Burger Barn."

Maggot-Face tosses her hair. "Oh, and I guess you think *you* should have it?"

"Maggie," my mother interjects, "we aren't talking to her about this without a lawyer."

I stiffen. "A lawyer?"

Mags snorts. "It's no big deal, Mom. She can't do anything to us. She signed all the papers."

My inner ears pulse and the floor seems to tilt. I grab onto the edge of the granite counter. "I just came out of a thirteen-week coma and all you cared about was the money." I try to catch my breath. "You made sure I was miserable and humiliated and then you pounced."

My father throws up his hands. "You said you trusted us and you signed. What the hell, Lisa! Six million dollars isn't good enough? You don't do anything with your life, anyway."

I blink at him, trying to get my eyes to stop rattling in their sockets.

"At least *I'm* starting a fashion business," Mags brags. "You're almost forty and you don't even have kids like Billy."

So Billy got a cut, too.

Billy, the guy who didn't even show up to my graduation. High school or college. "Billy didn't have Megan until he was thirty-five," I point out. "And I'm only thirty-four."

"But he was going out with Amy for years already by the time they got married," she hoots triumphantly. "You're not even close to getting married. Your fiancé dumped you the second you woke up. Now you'll never have time to meet some loser, convince him to marry you, and have kids in the next few months."

"I didn't realize having kids was a race." I turn to include my parents in my line of sight. "*Or* criteria for not getting bamboozled by your family."

"Take us to court for the rest of the money if you want." My father shrugs. "But you'll just end up looking like—"

"I DON'T CARE ABOUT THE MONEY!" This gets me a split second of shocked silence, long enough for me to take the floor. "Don't you get it? I almost *died*, and when I didn't, you tricked me!"

"We had to make sure everything was fair." My father speaks in Mandate Tone.

"Well, you screwed up," I say.

"Lisa," he warns.

"Being this mean isn't fair." I storm my way across the kitchen, whip open the screen door, then turn back to them. "And you're wrong about something else, too. I *am* going to do something with my life."

CHAPTER 5

Who am I kidding?

I'm a size eight, thirty-four year-old millionaire with all my own teeth and I can't even think of anything to do with my Saturday night.

And I live in Los Angeles!

Shouldn't I be going to a movie premiere or checking out the latest club or taking part in a fiery protest, or, at the very least, getting laid?

But no.

And I think I'm going to do something important with my money? When I can't even make plans for Saturday night?

But I've *got* to come up with something to do with my life. I no longer have any choice. Jesus. What made me rush across the country just to tell off my parents? I accomplished exactly nothing.

As usual.

I am an expert at doing nothing constructive. On Tuesday, Jack Hawkins noticed it right away, demanding to know what I've been doing with my life since the hospital set me free. Thank God he's not here to witness my pathetic Saturdays.

And what about Sunday?

Tomorrow, Mags is jetting off to Paris with Rick, my parents will probably be lawyering up in case I want my money back, and Jack, I'm sure, will be scaling something huge.

But what will I be doing tomorrow? What *can* I do? The Giants play on Monday night this week. And anyway, watching football is hardly *significant*.

Sorry. Scratch that. Of course it's significant. But still, the game would consume only four hours of my life, tops.

I look again at all the sheets of paper scattered across the table. I've been looking stuff up and making lists about what I can do to make my life count.

But what do I do next? Take action? Me? Now?

I get up from the table and head to the freezer.

An hour later, I'm curled in front of the TV watching Jane and Lizzy leave Netherfield. I pop the last bite of red pepper pizza into my mouth and wonder what to eat next. I get up to look for olives and—

Dong.

I jump about a foot into the air. The doorbell? After midnight on a Saturday?

It's the criminals! They're back!

I pause the DVD but this does nothing to ease my thumping heart. New security door, new double locks on the front door, new reinforced windows and patio doors—nothing to worry about. Right?

But what if whoever is at my door at 12:30 on a Saturday night (!!!!!!) has a gun? Or a hostage he can threaten in order to force me to do stuff, like give him all my money?

I have neither a gun nor a hostage, putting me at a serious disadvantage.

On my way to the door I pick up the fireplace poker. I know it's only a gas fireplace, but the tools make the set up so much cozier. Plus, they are very handy once you know you suck at head butting. I sidle up to the door, too afraid to even peek through the spyhole.

"What do you want?" I yell. Then I brandish the poker above my head.

"Lisa?"

My pounding heart kicks up a notch. It's Jack Hawkins.

"Who is this?" I demand, as I suck in breath through my nose, trying to calm down.

"It's Jack," he says.

I lower the poker and massage my breastbone. "Uh … Jack who?"

"Jack Hawkins. Can I come in?"

"Hold on." I scoot across the living room and put the poker back on its stand. Then I turn off the TV. Then I put my pizza plate in the dishwasher. Then I dash into the bathroom to brush my teeth.

"Lisa?" he calls through the door. "Are you okay?"

I spit. "Hold on!" Once I rinse, I jog lightly back to the front door. By the time I get there, I can hear metallic thumping. Jack sounds like he's trying to kick in my security door. Wow. But I can't be giggly about this. I have to play it cool.

I undo both locks to the front door and jerk it open. "What do you think you're doing to my door?"

Jack gives the door a sharp nod. "Hey, Lisa. Just checking out how secure you are. Good choice."

"Thanks. Is that all you wanted?"

"Can I come in?"

I open the security door and let him in.

"Did I get you out of bed?" he asks.

My hand flies to my hair, which I've been dragging my fingers through all day. "Why would you say that?" I put my hand at my side and stand up taller. "I'm awake."

He looks me up and down. "You're wearing pajamas."

"It's the weekend."

"I know," he says. "Where've you been the past few

days?"

I catch my breath. Jack was checking up on me? Maybe he doesn't think I'm a total loser.

I gulp and narrow my eyes at him. "Were you checking up on me?" My chin tilts up a fraction. "I can take care of myself." I've got to be sophisticated, penguin pajama pants and Zac Efron T-shirt notwithstanding.

"Hope so," Jack says, looking around the apartment. "What are you? Thirty-two? Thirty-four?"

Hey!!!!

"Do you mind if I check things out?" And without waiting for me to answer, he heads to the balcony doors and slides one open. When he closes himself outside, I fight the urge to lock him out there.

"Jack," I demand, when he comes back into the living room. "How do you know I wasn't here the past few days?"

"I stopped by." He heads for the bedroom. My fantasy bedroom. When he doesn't even *like* me.

Not fair.

I follow him as he heads straight for the window. It's as if he doesn't even NOTICE the big, beautiful bed. "Why didn't you just call? I could have saved you a trip."

"Two trips," he corrects. "But I don't have your number. And I'm happy to report that it's unlisted."

But he doesn't ask for my number, or even coyly wait for me to offer it. He just pulls back from the bedroom window and heads for the bathroom.

"So where were you?" he asks, all distracted as he checks out the small window above the tub.

"I had to talk to my parents." That's right. Jack Hawkins is standing in my shower and I'm talking about my parents.

"Did you have to go into hiding to do it? What are they, CIA?"

"They live in Connecticut." I walk out of the bathroom, leaving him standing in an empty shower. I'm waiting for him when he comes back into the living room. "Thanks for the seal of approval, Jack. Really. And for everything else you did. Especially cleaning up my paltry attempt at a head butt and saving me a trip to the DMV to get a new license. But as you can see, I'm good." I walk to the front door and open it.

Jack heads toward me, but pauses at the threshold. My heart stutters, but I just raise my eyebrows and purse my lips.

"Lisa—" Jack's voice is quiet, hesitant.

Shivers snake down my back. "What?" I demand, all Loretta Castorini.

"Can we take a walk?"

I never take my eyes off his. I have to be chill. "Let me get my shoes."

* * * * *

We're two blocks from my house before he finally speaks. "I've been looking for you because I want to discuss a business proposition with you."

I want to say something snarky about the hour and locale being odd ones for discussing business, but my curiosity allows me to curb my sarcasm. If Mr. Anti-Corporate-Money is about to ask me for *my* corporate money, I want to hear it, loud and clear. "Okay." I shrug affably.

"I don't know how much you know about Into the Wild …"

"Your company? Not much." Maybe that was the wrong thing to say. "But I'm a quick learner. But not sloppy. Careful, you know? But efficient." I should go on the offensive. "Why did you start it? When? Do you like the USC classes?"

He stops walking and turns to face me. "Because I

wanted to design things I could really use out in the wild, about five years ago, and yes, very much."

Holy baloney, he's answering my questions. I have to stop to remember what they were.

While I'm thinking, he continues speaking. "My team and I design and sell highly specialized gear for extreme outdoor adventures. But we don't take short cuts. Especially in the manufacturing phase."

"So your profits aren't exactly through the roof," I guess.

"We're surviving. Not thriving."

"Okay." My stomach clenches as I wait for him to fall from grace and ask me for my money.

"I've come up with an idea for a new line," he continues. "An untapped market. It could make all the difference to every one who works for Into the Wild."

I just keep listening, feeling numb.

He takes a deep breath. "More and more people are getting out there these days, trying to be adventurous. I think reality shows have a lot to do with it. And the internet."

"I never watch reality shows."

"Okay."

"But I have a computer."

"Right." He gives his head a little shake. "Okay." He continues. "I want to design a new line of gear for the absolute beginner. Gear that's so easy to use that it'll be helpful to a person who knows nothing about outdoor equipment or safety."

"You want to protect the fledglings," I coo.

"Not just them," he says, practically jumping on my words. "Beginners don't realize how many people they endanger when they don't know what they're doing."

I feel my face and neck grow red-hot, remembering how I ripped off his pants on the mountain.

Jack tucks his hands into the pockets of his jacket and

continues walking. "The people they're with, the people who have to come rescue them. It can be a real mess, and I can design stuff that'll help."

"Cool."

"That's where you come in."

"Me?" I stop, and so does he, but he doesn't turn to face me. He wants me to bankroll a new line he's designing and he can't even look me in the eye to ask me?

"I test all the gear myself," he explains. "Everything, before we'll sell it. Testing is half the design process." Now he turns and zeroes in on me, like he's trying to kill me with his laser eyes or something. "But I'm not an absolute beginner."

A chill ices through me so fast I'm scarcely able to breathe. "And I am."

The tension in his jaw relaxes, almost into a smile. "Yes. And this way, if you come with me to test the gear, you'll get the adventures you want."

Jack Hawkins doesn't want my money. He wants ME. Not sexually or anything—he made *that* clear enough a few days ago—but he wants me, Lisa Flyte.

Me.

Even Keith and I just kind of ended up together after our dates hooked up at a party and ditched us. It's not like he ever *chose* me. Or specifically wanted *me*.

But Jack does. He needs me to test his gear. Me.

"Sounds like a fair trade." I make my voice as even as I can. I'm trying to be calm and professional, when what I want to do is scream and jump like Fran does when Scott tells her he wants to dance with her at the Pan Pacifics. "How would it work?" I ask. "Would I have to go into the Into the Wild offices every day?" I crinkle my brow. "Do you even have offices?"

"No!" he shouts. Then he says, "Yes. We have offices, but you wouldn't have to come in every day. The way I work, I work on a design, and test it as I go. So, I figured I could just call you when I need something tested."

Like I can just sit around all day with nothing better to do than to wait for The Amazing Jack Hawkins to call. "I may not be as available as you think," I say.

"That's okay," he says, pretty much shrugging it off. "I have a company to run, so if you can't test something the second I design it, there are about a million things to keep me busy until you're free."

"How convenient."

"I like to eliminate complication." He says it matter-of-factly, like he's already penciled me in.

"So when do I come in?"

"When I call you. And I'll be picking you up."

"Yeah, but, don't I have to sign a contract or something?" I can actually feel my life getting more important as we talk. "And I'm interested in getting to know the lay of the land. I want to know who and what I'm working for."

And maybe, just maybe, after some adventures, I'll have the courage I need to actually end a conversation with my parents without flouncing out or slamming a door. I peer at him. "Jack?"

Crickets chirp and traffic hums a few streets away.

"Jack?"

"I thought we'd keep things less formal."

I can feel myself blush hotly all over, even though I've got goose bumps from the September night air. "I don't mean I expect a salary or anything."

"It's not that," he quickly assures me. He kind of smiles. "By the way, did you get a new car? What did you name it?"

My Spidey-senses tingle. "What did I *name* it?" Aragorn-With-a-Bungee-Cord wants to know what I've *named* my car? "Jack, what's going on?"

He stares at me hard, as if daring me to look away. "Nobody can know. Especially not anyone at Into the Wild. *Nobody.*"

"About *me*?" I squawk. "Are you so embarrassed that —"

"About the gear."

Nobody can know about the gear? "But Jack," I point out, "isn't designing gear what Into the Wild does? As a company?"

He doesn't say anything.

"Jack. Why don't you just admit that you don't want to be associated with—"

"Lisa, it's not you." His nostrils flare for just a sec. "It's Into the Wild."

"You're ashamed of Into the Wild?"

"I'm not ashamed of anyone." He faces me squarely. "Lisa, I made sure that everyone I hired at Into the Wild is good at some sport or some outdoor activity. I want a staff that's invested in the company. They understand everything we make and sell, and they help me test the designs."

"Sounds good," I offer cautiously.

"It was a sound idea," he agrees, "but then something happened that I didn't expect."

He says it as though it was something world-altering, like Bilbo finding the ring in Gollum's cave. I stay quiet, wondering if he knocked someone up or caught someone embezzling, and what it has to do with me.

"My company became …" He pauses, barely able to say whatever it is.

My mind races. Became *what*? "Jack?"

"Elitist," he finally says.

"Huh?"

"Elitist," he repeats. "A crack team of super-adventuring

snobs."

"Yeah, but—"

"I know they won't go for the idiot gear. Not unless I can prove its viability first."

I stare at him.

"I've had this idea for the new line for a while," he explains, "but no good way to test it. It's a potential gold mine and I want to pounce."

"And that's where I come in?" My voice is as sharp as a Ginsu knife.

"Yes."

"You want to hoodwink your snobbish company?"

"Not hoodwink," he says. "It's just that I didn't realize —"

"That you're just as big a snob?"

He seriously does a double take. "What? I'm not—"

"You called it 'idiot gear,' Jack. To my face. And you want *me* to be your undercover idiot."

He looks so busted that he doesn't even try to spin it. "Everyone's an idiot at something," he finally says.

And his voice is just rational enough, just sympathetic enough, to make me REALLY hate him. "Oh yeah?" I challenge. "What about you? What's something you're an idiot at?"

Even in the shadows cast by the streetlights, I swear I see his eyes darken. Okay, maybe not his eyes, but definitely his expression, like he's sinking back into the dimness of a dark, evil emperor hood. He opens his mouth to answer, looking as resigned as Mr. Darcy trying to confess that he's socially inept. "I … It's just that …"

Holy caramba. He actually has an answer. The wind dies out of my self-righteous sails, making me feel deflated for having brought him down to my level.

"I …" He looks right at me. "I guess I've always had a

knack for avoiding things in life I would be bad at," he explains. "So I'd never have to deal with being an idiot at something."

WHAT? *This* is his big confession? That he's purposely perfect?

"But you want *me* to deal with it? You want me to jump right in blindfolded?"

His lips quirk up. "Having spent one afternoon with you on a mountain," he says, "I have to say, a blindfold couldn't hurt."

I give him a tight-jawed Not Funny look.

"Remember," he reminds me, "going out with me into the wild was your idea in the first place."

"'Going out with you?'" I simper, batting my lashes. "Gee, do I get to wear your ring?"

"Say yes to this deal, and to keeping it secret, and the ring is yours if I can find it."

CHAPTER 6

Doin' it our way! On your mark, get set and go now ...

My heels make this totally sexy *click click click* as I stride in rhythm, making my way across the cold cement of the parking garage floor.

Despite the downpour and the worse-than-usual Friday morning traffic crush, things are going my way. Sure, I'm getting ready to become Jack's undercover idiot, but I will do so responsibly and capably. After all, I'm not really an idiot.

I've lubed myself into my slickest black business suit and sharpened the look with a pair of deadly four-inch heels so that Jack will see that I take my association with his new gear seriously. I may know little about outdoor adventuring, but I am a confident professional woman ready to conquer the world.

I check my cell before dropping it into my chic black bag. 8:40. Perfect. Jack and I have a meeting at nine o'clock, even though he wanted to keep me hidden away like a teenager's copy of *Playboy*. But I wouldn't stand for it. I insisted on this meeting so I could see his company and ask him questions.

It's not practical to be some airhead like Goldie Hawn in *Protocol* who almost gets bamboozled into marrying a sheik because she doesn't know any better and never paid attention. *I* want to know better. You can bet good Burger Barn money that I won't get tricked into marrying anybody.

Jack told his staff we were working on a project together for class. That's my cover, and it makes me feel super-sexy like I'm a spy or something. As I walk into the glass-enclosed foyer in the middle of the garage to call the elevator, I catch a glimpse of myself in a tall pane. I check out the silhouette of my butt and —

Ding.

The elevator doors swoosh open, so I step in and push the button that will take me up to the offices. The elevator starts moving, on its way to the top floor of the converted warehouse that has become the hub of Into the Wild. I am on my way to a braver me.

I look around to see if I can catch my reflec—

"AAAAAAAHHH!"

I clamp my hand over my mouth to keep from screaming again. As I do, all my joints unbuckle, causing me to slump into a duck-and-cover position on the floor of the elevator.

A GLASS elevator.

You have to be kidding me! A glass elevator? In a converted warehouse? WHY?

I huddle against the metal doors, keeping my head down, but I still catch terrifying glimpses from underneath the crook of my arm. Levels of the converted building flash by. I see what look to be loading docks, then storage bays, then work stations …

Ding.

Oh! I jump up but not fast enough. A damp, sandy surfboard knocks into me. "Hey!"

I see wet, dark hair then the edge of a face peer around the board.

"Sorr—"

"Jack?"

"Lisa." Jack and his surfboard crush into the small space

with me. "You're early."

The elevator lurches into motion. I freeze, locking my knees. Only my heart moves, beating at the speed of Secretariat. My eyes stay fixed on Jack.

"Lisa?"

Oh, God. He's going to know I'm terrified. Of an elevator. He's going to fire me! On my first day!

"Lisa?"

I tear my eyes from his face and rake them down his body, careful not to look *anywhere* near the glass walls.

"Why are you all wet? And sandy? Were you surfing? In the rain? Today?"

"Testing is half the design process." He hefts the board as the elevator comes to a stop but looks back at me and smiles. "I'll be ready for our meeting by nine."

Ding.

"You're going to clean up and be ready to meet me in fifteen minutes?"

The doors open. "Watch me."

Jack takes off, striding through an oatmeal-carpeted open office area bathed in recessed light. Leaping out of the elevator, I trip along in his wake. Some workers at their desks turn and stare, but I hold my head high as if I belong right where I am. At the end of the hall, we sweep into a spacious office with pear green walls, but he doesn't even slow down.

"Peg," he says, nodding at the woman with stainless-steel gray hair sitting at the desk. "This is Lisa."

She smiles at me, but before I can say anything, I pull up on a dime as Jack stops at a big black door set into the far wall. The portal to his sacred lair.

Totally acting like I'm not even here, Jack turns back toward Peg. "Why don't you continue the appraisals on the loading docks?" He says it like it's a suggestion, but then again, it's clear it's not.

Peg stands up. "No," she says. "I can't."

"Ah." Jack leans his surfboard against the wall and turns to face her. "Haven't found your iPad yet?" Even I can tell that his voice is too casual to be anything but smug.

"Jack," Peg says soothingly. "Soul Caliber isn't for everyone."

Jack folds his arms and shrugs. "Well, without the iPad, I guess you'll just have to start the appraisals over from scratch."

Peg stands at attention, her nostrils flaring. "Fine," she says. "A rematch."

Jack tilts his head and gives a ghost of a smile. "Filing cabinet under 'I'."

She retrieves the iPad, then leaves.

Still ignoring me, Jack turns back to his office door and puts his eye next to a panel that whirs, lights up, then disengages the lock. A retinal scan? Adventure gear must be some high stakes game. How cool am I? Jack is through the door and I stumble in behind him.

He surges through the office, yanking his wetsuit top over his head. "I'm going to take a quick—"

He stops talking. And walking. He just stands there in the middle of the room in black wetsuit shorts down to mid-thigh and a wetsuit top, half on, half off. This pose exposes an incredible set of abs, his lower back and an amazing pair of hipbones beneath taut skin—I have this total weakness for a guy's hips. But I can't see his head, which is buried somewhere inside the wetsuit shirt. I think he's stuck.

Jack tugs. He yanks. Yup. He's stuck. The thin, rubbery fabric of the wetsuit looks welded to the skin halfway up his back. He's in the dark, and it must smell yucky in there, like the sea at low tide.

He flexes his muscles, trying to break free. "Damn!"

This from inside the shirt. "What good's a wetsuit if you can't get it off when you need to?"

He's asking *me*?

He tries to yank the shirt over his head by pulling at the back of the collar, but gets nowhere. His head stays covered, with his arms kind of stuck stretching forward.

"Hmmm…" I say, making it clear that I'm trying not to laugh, "Is this what Superman's like behind closed doors? Getting all tangled up in his tights?"

"Laugh it up, Lois," he says. "This is a new neoprene blend I've been working on for making the best pockets. Now, I've discovered a flaw. So this is all good."

"Right."

Giving up the fight, he turns toward me. "Help me out here, will you? Just grab the back of the shirt and pull it over my head."

"What? You want me to, uh, *help* you?" I throw the word *help* in there at that last second, just so he doesn't know how freaked out I am that he wants me to *touch* him. To touch him. On the bare skin.

His voice gets quiet but serious. "Lisa, our plan is never going to work if we can't help each other out."

I bite the inside of my cheek. Hard. "What do you want me to do?"

He bends forward. "Just grab the back edge and pull it over my head," he coaches patiently.

I reach out, getting a grip of the dark, thin fabric. I try to ignore the scrape of my fingernails across his skin as if this is no big deal. Really. Touching Jack Hawkins and deliberately taking his clothes off is hardly the scariest thing I've ever done. Really. I mean it.

Holding my breath, I tug, starting to undress him.

And I get chills.

I'm the one touching him, and *I* get chills. Good lord, this is too bizarre. He's totally hot, yes, but in a lust-after-him-from-afar-like-you-lust-after-George-Clooney kind of way. Not in an actual feel-a-rush-of-close-up-tingles kind of way. How dumb can I get? I'm starting to work for the guy today, as his own private idiot.

The dynamics are so wrong.

I flex my fingers, and *Jack shivers*.

OH. MY. GOD.

"Damn, I'm cold," he says. Then in a singsong voice, "I know, I know—that's what I get for running around barefoot in a rain storm."

I stupidly look at his feet. No socks or shoes.

I try to shake myself out of my steamy trance. I'm hot, he's cold. I really AM an idiot.

I give the shirt a sharp yank, and Jack pulls back. The rubbery fabric stretches up across his back, loosening its grip on him. With a wrenching jerk of his shoulders, he breaks free from the suit and stumbles back.

And there we stand. Me, looking like a million bucks, and Jack making me feel seriously overdressed.

I hold his icky shirt by two fingers, keeping it well away from my Gucci threads. I cock one eyebrow. "*Voila*." I hope I sound oh so cool and blasé. That's my intention. Because the truth is, I'm scared down to the tips of my split ends.

Jack is totally lean and defined and squeezed into nothing but a pair of maritime hotpants. I try to remember to breathe. I'm really scared of good-looking people. Isn't everyone? I mean, everyone except the people who are actually gorgeous?

Jack takes his wetsuit top from me. "Thanks."

He heads over to a closet built into oak paneling, pulls out some clothes, and then disappears into a bathroom set in the far corner of the gargantuan office. He shuts the door behind him and in a second I hear the shower start.

I need to sit down.

I push some books, newspapers, and two and a half pairs of socks aside to sit down on a roomy brown plaid couch pushed against the far wall. I slump back, take a few deep breaths, and try to relax.

Jack's lair is part sporting goods store, part rec room, part county clerk's office, part garage workbench. His desk is littered with a computer, a phone, papers, gear-looking things, a bike tire, strips of cloth, and what looks like a chicken alarm clock. And this is the guy who's going to make me stronger than a locomotive?

The bathroom door opens. Jack steps out, wearing an untucked white button down shirt with the cuffs undone and a faded pair of Levi's. His hair is wet and his feet are still bare.

I swallow. He's wearing more clothes than I've seen him in so far today, but seeing him fresh from the shower and in the process of getting dressed is so ... intimate.

"What were you testing this morning?" I try my hardest to sound truly interested in the work. Not the man. Definitely not the man.

Jack breaks his stride and looks up. "I need seriously choppy waves to test the accessibility of pockets in the suit," he says with a complete command I envy. "We're supposed to get rain on and off from now through Halloween, but I have to take advantage of days with no lightning."

I feel like I black out while staying conscious, if that's possible. Did he say *choppy waves*? And … *no lightning*?

Sudden sweat beads my spine. I will myself not to shiver as I picture the reality of what he does on a daily basis. Of what he did this morning while I was blow-drying my hair. I try to breathe, feeling all gummy-like in my limbs and ready to slide off the couch. He was in the turbulent ocean where he could have been drowned by a riptide or electrocuted by an unexpected flash of lightning or eaten by a shark or sucked to the bottom by the tentacles of a giant squid—good God! What have I gotten myself into?

Jack flicks the switch of a coffee maker sitting on the windowsill. "Lisa? You okay?"

"Um, how do you know a certain rainy day won't have lightning?" I make my voice sound all interested and chirpy.

"Generally, if I don't see any."

Maybe I really am an idiot. And I'm making it really obvious. He's going to fire me if I don't shape up.

"Hang on." He goes to the outer office and gets the surfboard, so I race to be helpful and pull the door open wider for him. As Jack and the board brush past me, I feel something move through my hair. A jellyfish!

"Aaaah!" I scream. " Get it off! Get it off! Get it off!"

I hop up and down and shake and shake and shake my hands.

Jack shoves the surfboard aside and steps toward me. "Stand still."

But it's crawling down my collar! "Eew eew eew eew eew!" I hop back and rip off my jacket. "Get it off get it off get it off!"

Jack rips my jacket out of my hands and throws it across the room, saving me from the slime.

"Jesus!" he rasps in a gruff whisper.

"What was it? Is it in my hair?"

"Seaweed," he says, sifting a hand through my hair. "You're clear."

I breathe and blow like I'm having a baby. Thank God. I'm safe.

It's then that I realize I'm standing there in my bra. And

not a chic, sexy black one that matches my skirt, either. Not even a nice silky one with flowers or wide satin straps. I'd like to be wearing a bra like any of those, but I haven't done laundry in a while, what with securing my apartment, going to Connecticut, and becoming an undercover idiot. Plus, I hate chores.

So, today, I'm down to wearing The Beige One from the very back of my underwear drawer. You know—that way un-sexy tannish-nude color that you only ever see as a functional underwear color. Bras that your great aunt can buy in a box come in this color and so do girdles.

I look up at Jack to see if he's noticed, but he's not even looking at me. He's looking right past me.

"Excuse me," someone says behind me.

I whip around toward the door. But with Jack standing so close, the turn is more like a sweetheart move that tucks us closer together. Jack is half dressed—no belt, no shoes, shirt all disheveled. And I'm in my nude-colored bra, with my jacket flung across the couch.

In the doorway, a young man wearing a pencil-thin tie looks like he's smirking.

"I was scared of the seaweed!" I blurt.

He just looks at me and blinks.

"Alan, what is it?" Jack's voice pulses with complete control, and he doesn't move. Like there's nothing irregular at all about this fix. Of course, he's not the one caught wearing mom-colored underwear.

"The team from Sawyer called again," Alan explains with dispatch. "They're insisting on a meeting."

I cannot believe it. They're conducting business right over my head, as if I'm not even here. Like the woman in the ugly bra doesn't matter. Then again, their ignoring me in my un-sexy undies is probably a good thing.

"I'll deal with them later."

"Right." Alan scoots away, leaving us alone.

As Jack pulls back to button his cuffs, he gives me a once over.

"What?" I demand.

"Interesting," Jack muses. "Your first reaction to intense fear is to strip." He nods thoughtfully. "Good to know."

"That's it?" I ask. "That's your reaction, to make a joke? Your whole staff is going to think I'm your booty call. Don't you care?"

He slides me a look, then grabs a duffle off a shelf. "No one is going to think that."

"Why?" I challenge. "Am I so out of your league? Would the idea be just too absurd to anyone who knows you?"

He stops and looks at me. "Lisa, I don't have sex in the office. It's not a rule, exactly, but I just never do. And I don't encourage it among my staff." He starts to fill the duffle with gear from his drawers and shelves. "But if it will make you feel better, I'll tell Peg how crazy hot I think you are."

"You're making fun of me."

"That's because you're whacko." He doesn't even pause what he's doing when he says this.

"So," I say, trying to step back into a more professional mode, "what's up with Sawyer? *The* Sawyer, right? The big sport shoe company?"

Jack zips the duffle shut. "I already told them once to go fuck themselves because I'm not interested in joining up with some nightmare conglomerate of cheap labor and mass marketing. Let's go." He brushes past me on his way to the door.

"Jack," I say. "This deal is never going to work if you get mad at me every time I ask a question or make a suggestion."

"I'm not mad."

"Then why are you so edgy?"

He turns to me, his hand on the doorknob. "Because I

hope to God I'm doing the right thing."

"Why?" I ask. "What are you doing?"

"I'm taking you on your first adventure."

CHAPTER 7

"Yes, Lisa. Naked."

"Naked, naked?" I swallow, then take a deep breath. He can't be serious. "You want my naked skin touching this thing?" I look at the long, black wetsuit in my hands. We drove all the way back to his house up in the hills of Glendale just to get this stupid suit that's not going to fit me, no matter how naked I get.

"It's the best way."

"So there *are* other ways."

Jack sets the duffle on his kitchen table. "Yes," he says, unzipping the bag. "Some people wear a swimsuit underneath, or Under Armour."

"Armor?" It's for the sharks, I know it!

"Under Armour. It's like a spandex body suit."

"Let me do that, then. You must have one lying around here somewhere." I look around Jack's house. Nothing.

Just beyond the big wooden table in the kitchen, the room morphs into a family room. But the kitchen looks like a normal kitchen with a fridge and stove and all, and the family room just looks like a regular family room. Couch, TV, coffee table. No spandex lying around anywhere.

I wander into the living room at the front of the house and hit pay dirt. At least, potential pay dirt. The spacious room, which I think is supposed to be part dining room—the demarcation is unclear because of the mountain bike and the saddle—is messy with gear, junk and working-type stuff just like his office at Into the Wild.

Jack follows me.

"Lisa, do you know the point of a wetsuit?"

I don't answer. As far as I'm concerned, a wetsuit is for wearing if you're on a show like *The Man from Atlantis* or if you work at Sea World.

He gets in front of me, right in my face. "It keeps frigid water away from your skin."

"But you were in shorts this morning!"

"I had to test the suit, and I didn't want to wait until July. Anyway, I'm a little more used to it than you are."

"Then the body armor stuff will keep me a lot warmer than wearing a wetsuit with nothing on underneath."

"Wrong."

In that one word I hear the thumping finality of a guillotine.

"Anything you wear underneath," he explains, facing me squarely, "even a bathing suit or a pair of underwear, allows air between the suit and your skin."

"Letting your skin breathe is good. I saw that James Bond movie where—"

"Air in a wetsuit is bad," he says, cutting me off as he heads back to the kitchen.

I have no choice but to follow him. Back to the kitchen. Back to the duffle of doom. He starts unloading the bag. A small yellow box, flippers.

"It increases the chances that ice cold water can seep in," he continues. "And guess what, Lisa?" He turns to meet my eyes. "It won't seep back out again. You'll just freeze your ass off until you become a medical risk. Then I'll bring you back."

The mean bastard turns his attention back to unloading

the duffle. Is that a bulletproof vest? What the hell kind of adventure is this going to be? Beginners have to deal with bullets? He must be purposely trying to scare me to see if I'll back down.

I look back at the wetsuit I'm holding. It looks so much slimmer than I feel.

"So I just get naked and squeeze in?"

Jack hands me the little yellow box. "This should help."

I look down at it. "It's cornstarch."

He taps his nose. "Full marks for being able to read your native language."

I look at him. I'm guessing he doesn't want me to bake a cake with it. "Thanks?"

"Use it like talcum powder."

I am so totally screwed. "Where do I suit up?"

* * * * *

He put me in a downstairs bathroom. It's cheery with its yellow tile and colorful shower curtain sprigged with open umbrellas. Despite the décor, I'm still depressed. Why did he have to bring me back to his house, anyway? The place is clean and comfortable, making me want to leave for the ocean even less.

Okay, so I couldn't exactly get suited up at the office where the staff could see me, but still. Donna Reed's bathroom is hardly the best place to prepare for diving into shark-infested waters.

Anyway, wasn't it enough of an adventure today when he made me get into that damn glass elevator again?

I look at the suit and suck in my stomach. I don't like this.

* * * * *

I meet Jack back in the kitchen, where he's suited up himself. When he sees me, he looks at me kind of funny but doesn't say anything.

"What?" I ask, wondering if I put it on backwards.

He looks me over. "Nothing."

I look down at myself. Jeez! I forgot to dust off the cornstarchy handprints all over me. Jack now has a veritable map of where I put my hands to press in my bumps and bulges as I stood in front of the mirror.

"I … uh … had a little trouble getting it on … making sure it fit right."

Jack just nods. "Let's fill the pockets."

The pockets are in weird places on the suit—the forearm, the outside of the upper arm, the outside of the thigh.

I especially hate the thigh pockets. When filled, my quads look as monstrously invincible as Godzilla's.

And I don't even know what they're filled with.

The only things I recognized that Jack handed me were power bars and some kind of gun. I hope not the kind with bullets. Unless it's for the sharks.

I don't ask though. I don't want to know.

In a few minutes, we're ready.

"Let's go." Jack opens the kitchen door to the garage.

My stomach lurches. Oh God. OhGodohGodohGodohGod. "I really like your shower curtain!" I shriek. "The one with umbrellas."

"Really?" he asks, big smile. "I have little towels that match."

"Really?"

"No." His smile disappears as he swipes the duffle off the table. "Let's go."

"You know," I say, looking out the glass doors of the kitchen, "this is an awesome view. Do you own that mountain?" I gesture to the steep incline starting about two hundred feet from his back patio.

Jack turns to face me. "No, Lisa. I don't own the mountain. My property ends where the grass stops and the scrub starts."

I scrunch up my nose. "Huh."

"What?"

"Nothing," I say. "I just expected a guy like you to own a ranch or a mountain or a lake or something like that, since you're so into nature and the outdoors and everything."

"I don't have to own it to love it."

"So," I continue, "you just tramp around the globe, conquering nature wherever you find it?"

"I don't conquer it," he tells me. "I try to understand it. At least to the point that it doesn't conquer *me*."

He stands on the other side of the garage door threshold. It's as if he's daring me to cross over.

If I don't do this, I'm a failure.

I step into the garage.

"Lisa? Are you okay?"

"Fine," I answer lickety-split. "This just feels weird. I don't usually wear my clothes so tight."

It takes me three tries to get myself into his truck, and then we're off.

We drive from Glendale down to rainy Santa Monica, heading toward the beach. The ocean gets closer with every block, making the lining of my stomach feel electrified.

I hate this so much. I think about what a lucky girl I was just yesterday before I had to put on a wetsuit and dive into the ocean during a storm.

Jack turns south, instead of heading west toward the

Pacific. He pulls into a parking lot.

"What are we doing at the airport?" Even to my own ears, my voice sounds unnaturally tinny. Please just let him need a map of tides or something.

"We're taking a helicopter," he explains as he parks. Then he gets out of the truck.

I fly out after him, stumbling awkwardly on the pavement. I try to get my panic under control.

"Taking one *where*?"

"About a mile or so out."

"Out over the ocean?" I squeal. "We're jumping in from a *helicopter*? From how high? Is it safe? What if the wind blows me into the propeller?"

"Regular rules of gravity apply," he says, opening the tailgate. "When you jump, you'll head straight down and hit the water. Promise. Here, take this." He shoves the vest thing at me.

"Why do I need a bullet-proof vest?"

"It's a buoyancy compensator," he says. "Put it on."

"So it'll make me float?"

I try to look graceful as I struggle into the thing, but it has lots of straps and buckles like one of those monster backpacks teenagers take to Europe.

"Or submerge," he says. "It does both."

"Submerge? How far? I've never done deep sea diving. Will I get the bends?"

"Today," he says, slamming the tailgate, "we're just going to float."

Jack adjusts my straps and gets the vest ready, and I have to say, it looks pretty complicated. "Couldn't I just wear a life vest or something simple?"

"This covers more of your body," he explains. "I want to test the accessibility of the pockets and a BCD is the greatest hindrance to the ease of use."

Oh.

Carrying our flippers, we walk through the rain toward a chopper. Holy fuck. It's *tiny*. Like a metal chestnut with an angry wasp stuck to one end. And it HAS NO DOORS.

"Jack." I stop on the tarmac and put my hand on his arm. "Should we really be taking a chopper? I mean, how many rookie divers are going to be dropped down from a helicopter?"

"Very few, probably." He shrugs. "Most would be dropped off by a boat, but this is faster and much more manageable."

"So, what happens? The pilot drops us off then picks us up later?"

"Pretty much."

"How much later? What if he can't find us?"

"The pilot is a she, and she'll find us. I've got a transmitter on me."

Once I'm seated in the helicopter, I notice the pilot's graying hair curls up at the ends and her rosy cheeks dimple when she smiles. Honestly, she looks more like a country grandma than a sadistic harbinger of death. As the blades begin to pump, I wonder whether Jack hired her on purpose to relax me. As if. A helicopter with doors would have been better.

We begin to move.

Our Father, who art in heaven...

No. Not heaven. It's way too close to the sky.

Strapped in, headphones in place, microphone I can use to communicate with Jack right near my mouth, I shut my eyes tight and stiffen my entire body. I hang on to the edge of my seat with the grip of a snapping turtle.

Don't look. Don't look. Don't look.

My stomach dips and rolls anyway. Oh, God.

Don't think. Don't think. Don't think.

Tears squeeze out from under my closed eyelids. Then I

feel Jack's hand on my arm.

Bam!

Just like that, my eyes pop open. I jerk up straight, sitting high in my seat. I can't let Jack think I'm a coward.

I can't *be* a coward. Not anymore.

This is my chance to change, to prove myself worthy to live my life. I look at open sky through the windshield in front of me and tell my brain to just stop working.

The tears continue to fall, but I keep my eyes wide open and focused straight ahead. The pilot doesn't seem concerned about flying so high up with no doors, and neither does Jack, so that gives my sanity something to hold on to.

I think Jack is trying to talk to me quietly through the headphones, but I don't care. The ocean stretches out before and below me, so I'm concentrating on feeling courageous.

"Jesus," I hear him say more loudly. "I knew this was a big mistake."

"Oh, God!" I scream. "We're crashing!"

"We are NOT crashing."

"We're not?"

"Damn! I *knew* you were all wrong for this."

"All wrong? No, I'm not!" I stiffen my spine, making myself as tall as I can. "This is my first time in a hel—"

"It's not the helicopter," Jack says. "It's you. You're just —never mind."

"What?! Tell me! I can do this! I AM doing this!"

"I better just take you home."

"No!"

"Yes. You said this was what you wanted, but you clearly don't want to be here."

"Yes I do! I can do this and I will."

"Okay." In a flash, he rips off his headphones and mine, snaps open his seatbelt and mine, and pulls me against him as he stands.

"Hey!"

Jack turns me around and wraps his arms just under my ribcage. I figure out what he's doing just as the helicopter banks sharply.

Out we go, tumbling backwards through space.

"AAAAAAAAHHHH!"

We fall and fall and fall and fall and fall and—

Shoom!

We hit the water and IT'S COLD IT'S COLD IT'S COLD!

We're under water and I'm confused but then we surface.

He lets me go.

I flop around, slapping at the water like a Labrador puppy.

Jack unhooks a pair of flippers from a Batman-like utility belt and slips them on. He unhooks a second pair.

Grabbing my feet one at a time, he fits a flipper snugly onto each foot. I'm bobbing up and down, batted around by the choppy waves. I'm in the middle of the ocean. I can't get my bearings or hear anything but the chopper and the churning water.

Jack swims right up to my face. "Are you okay?"

My heart is beating so fast. I can't catch my breath. Shouting is impossible. I give him a thumbs up instead.

"Answer me!" He raises both hands out of the water, palms facing me, pulsing toward me gently.

Calm down. Calm down. Calm down.

"I'm good!" I finally shout, and Jack beams.

I think it's a real smile.

The first one I've ever seen from Jack.

Oh God! I must be dying! I must have landed wrong!

But then Jack signals up to the chopper and it flies away.

He probably wouldn't have done that if I were dying.

He takes my hand and pulls me along. We start swimming side by side like Tom Hanks and Daryl Hannah at the end of *Splash.* Waves keep whapping me in the face, but this doesn't really slow us down. I'm surprised at how much the flippers propel me. But not enough to outswim a shark.

I saw that movie where the couple gets left in the middle of the ocean. Just like I am now. Sharks come and eat them. Eat them! What the *hell* kind of movie ending is that?

We stop swimming and float, facing each other. I try try try not to think of my legs dangling in the water beneath me.

"What now?" I've always been a loud shouter, and every time I yell over to Jack a few feet away, I feel better.

"Get me the flare gun out of your left shoulder pocket!"

I dig at my shoulder frantically. "Oh, my God! Are we in trouble!?"

"We're just testing the pockets!"

Oh. Right. That's why I'm here.

And that's how it goes. He has me swim around and dunk under, then asks me to get something out of a pocket.

The pockets are harder to get at in the water than I thought they would be, and more than one power bar or piece of equipment floats to the bottom, however far down that is. The ones I successfully retrieve he then makes me put back. And I keep having to rest. Just being in the choppy water is taking its toll.

Finally the helicopter flies back into sight and my already frozen bones double-freeze up all over again. The dread reaches all the way into the muscles of my jaw.

The chopper has a ladder dangling from it.

A LADDER.

My stomach sinks to the unfathomable bottom of the sea. I'm pretty sure I'm going to faint. I didn't think about how we'd get back into the chopper. But a ladder?

I'm scared to climb up or down ladders when they're leaning against something, let alone dangling.

The flimsy thing is swaying all over the place. How am I supposed to climb that? And when I reach the top, how will I let go of the ladder to haul myself in?

Before the chopper gets too close, Jack swims right up to me and shouts in my ear. "I'll go first. Once I start climbing, grab the ladder to anchor it. Once I'm up, we'll haul you in. All you'll have to do is hang on."

"Okay!" I shout, and then get a choking mouthful of water.

While I'm trying to catch my breath, Jack grabs my feet, takes my flippers, and hooks them to his belt with his. Then he's climbing up the ladder like a monkey. I grab the ladder and hang on.

This is the worst worst worst part.

I'm almost safe, but a shark or squid could still get me. I'm in the ocean, the middle of the ocean, all by myself.

Why can't Jack climb faster? I thought he was supposed to be good at this kind of stuff. I get my feet into the ladder rungs and climb up so I'm just above the dangerous water.

I look around. Grey turbulent sky, grey turbulent sea. It's amazing. And beautiful. And sublime. At this one moment, it poses no danger to me, and I think I love it.

But I want to be the person who loves it even *with* the danger. That's why I'm here.

Because moments like this, moments suspended above the danger, almost never happen in life.

I feel the ladder start to pull me up. Jack is safely inside the chopper a million miles above me.

I let go of the ladder.

As I Nestea plunge back into the ocean, it's just about

the greatest feeling I've *ever* made happen in my life.

I give a whoop of joy and dive back under, face first, butt in the air. When my vest brings me right back up, I look up to the chopper to give Jack a thumbs up so he doesn't think I'm in trouble.

This is my moment.

I swim and splash and kick. Then I get calm and still. I look around as the waves beat at me. Life is good.

* * * * *

But it's too bad life isn't quite as good as it is in made-for-TV movies. If it were, my Helicopter-Ocean Adventure would have cured my wimpiness forever and made me a brave person.

But it didn't.

If it had, I wouldn't be back in the hospital.

CHAPTER 8

"Do you want to tell me what happened?"

No, Jack Hawkins, I do not want to tell you what happened. You were *there*, you moron. "Why don't *you* tell me what happened instead," I suggest. "How long have I been here?"

"A few hours. You had an anxiety attack at the airport, passed out, hit your head. Not hard. But, with your recent medical history, I wasn't taking any chances."

Oh, my God.

"This happened at the airport? You mean the helicopter and the ocean and the shark—it was all a dream? I have to do it again?"

"It happened at the airport when we got *back*," he assures me. "The helicopter ride and the ocean were real, all right. I'm not too sure about the shark."

"I *felt* it," I insist. "It rubbed against my foot. I swear. You had my flippers, remember? My feet were bare, and I *felt* it. That's why I jumped back onto the ladder so fast."

"It was probably seaweed."

"It was *moving.*"

"Seaweed moves in the water."

"It was cold and slimy like a fish," I say. "A *great fish.*"

The great fish moved silently through the night water ...

"Seaweed is cold and slimy," Jack says.

"And it was *scratchy*," I add. "I've watched *Shark Week*. I know shark skin is scratchy."

"If you rub it one way," he concedes. "You rub it the other way, it's smooth like … like a wet pair of galoshes. But if you rub it the wrong way, it's not just scratchy. It'll make you bleed."

I stare at him, clenching my teeth.

"Your foot's not bleeding," he says quietly.

I can feel angry tears burn behind my eyes. Could I really have been terrorized by seaweed AGAIN? In the middle of my Nestea plunge? I look away from Jack, down at my hospital gown. Still naked underneath. "Did they have to cut the wetsuit off me?"

Dear God, don't let him make me do it again in a different suit.

"No," he says. "It's right over there." He points to the thing lying like a selkie's skin on one of those mauve hospital chairs. "They took it off you when they examined you."

"How am I going to get home? I'm not squeezing into that thing again. Do you have any cash on you? Can you buy me a pair of scrubs or something?"

"I brought in some stuff from the truck." He indicates a pile of clothes folded on the stand next to the bed.

"You'll have to take me back to your house to get my suit," I say. "It's one of my favorites."

"Not tonight," he says, dismissing my need for Gucci power gear. "I'm driving you straight home. Tomorrow I can take you back to Into the Wild to get your car."

I jut out my jaw. "But my suit."

"You still have my pants. I'll keep the suit for as long as I damn well please."

* * * * *

Almost two hours later, he drives me home. And the ride is bizarre. Jack talks non-stop. And even weirder, he demands answers of me. Constantly.

"I don't *know* which Hardy Boy dated Nancy Drew!" I tell him for the third time.

I swear he's giving me a monster headache. Why does he even care? He thought Linda Carter played Nancy Drew on the TV show, for Pete's sake.

"It doesn't matter, anyway," I say. "In the books, her favorite date is Ned Nickerson. And in the old books—the *real* ones—she would never fool around on him."

"What's your middle name?"

Just like that, he changes the subject, like he has a chamber loaded with questions. "Don't have one."

"Did you ever want one?"

Good lord. We've driven barely three miles and already I've heard him say more than I've heard him say since I've met him.

"Oh, my God." I turn to look at him. "I have a concussion, don't I? And you don't want me to fall asleep. That's why you're talking to me."

"Just a precaution."

"Great."

We sit in silence for a few minutes, staring at the sluggish traffic, then he asks, "Who was your favorite character on *The A-Team*?"

"Why does this truck smell like Chinese food?" I demand instead. "I'm starving. Are there some egg rolls under the seat?"

"It's the vegetable oil I use for fuel. I get it from a tempura place near my house."

I suck in another delicious lungful. "Can you stop at Star Wok on the way home? Or McDonald's? Or Burger King? Or a pizza place?"

"I called in an order to Jerry's Deli when you were getting dressed. We'll pick it up on the way to your place."

"Good." The mention of Jerry's Deli makes my mouth actually water, and the promise of such delight to come puts me in an awesome mood, despite my throbbing head. I touch my brow and wince.

I can't believe I got another forehead bruise, just as my head-butt bruise was almost gone. Luckily, though, when I passed out at the airport and landed on my face, I hit a parking curb with my forehead, thus saving my nose and teeth from getting broken. Plus, I didn't die, which is really good. Now I have this really hot guy to drive me home.

And it's weird, but it makes me feel all superior—to whom I have no idea—to have such a completely non-sexual relationship with such a sex god. As though I'm above it all or something. True, our platonic association has more to do with his finding me repulsive, but I so don't care. It's been months since my release from the hospital, and I finally have *someone* in my life.

"Mad Dog," I sigh, sinking back into the seat, engulfed in a cloud of contentment.

"What?" he asks, nudging into a different lane.

"My favorite A-Team character, by far, is Mad Dog Murdoch. And by the way …" I take a deep breath. "Thanks. For taking me to the hospital and now this. You're a pretty cool guy."

"I'm glad you think so," he says, pulling onto the exit ramp. "Because I'm spending the night."

* * * * *

He's in my pajamas, no less. Lucky for him I buy men's pajamas, just so I'm extra comfy. Now he's just as snug as can be, showered and cozy, wearing a pair of dark plaid pajama pants and a T-shirt.

Not that he has any intention of sleeping, though.

Hardly.

He won't let me sleep either. And since it's already been established that the whole sex thing is a non-issue, he's stuck playing *Lord of the Rings* Trivial Pursuit with me. It's the fourth board game we've played so far tonight. Serves him right. Though, I must say, for someone who didn't seem too excited to play, he's doing awfully well.

At ten to midnight, he wins the game.

"Bastard."

"Wow," he says, stretching his legs along my shabby-chic couch and nearly pushing me off. "A chicken and a sore loser. You didn't get picked for too many teams when you were a kid, did you?"

"Hey," I warn, cleaning up the game pieces.

"Just calling a spade a spade."

"Right. Like you're a defender of truth. No way you only saw the movies once."

"I have. But I've read the books more than that."

I slump back on the couch, giving Jack a dirty look. His shins are pressing against my back, making my slouch a very uncomfortable one. I just keep glaring at him. "I can't believe I forgot. You never do things you suck at."

He bends his knees, pulling his legs out from behind me. "I never said 'never.'"

I shift so my back rests against the arm of the couch, making it so we're facing each other from our opposite ends. "So once upon a time you sucked at something?"

"'Course," he answers. "I wasn't born doing everything right or knowing what I was good at."

"So what did you do so badly?"

He doesn't answer.

"C'mon. I've humiliated myself lots in front of you."

"Yeah, well, I've chosen a different path." He sits up and folds the board into the box. "I've learned what things in life I want to avoid, and what things I want to pursue." He puts the top back on the game box and looks at me with a blow-off kind of shrug.

"What's that supposed to mean? That I haven't learned anything because I still manage to end up looking like a fool sometimes?"

He folds his hands, his elbows on his knees, and looks at me. "I don't know, Lisa. You tell me."

What a smug little cretin. "Maybe I just think some things are worth risking, even if I'm not sure and not perfect."

He blinks at me, reminding me of Morris the Cat. "Maybe I won't tell you about my life because it has nothing to do with our deal."

And we're not friends.

He doesn't say it, but I can hear it echo in the silence.

Then, like the slap of a tide that you can't beat to shore, the disillusionment and mortification wash over me. I realize that until this second, I was thinking that we had some kind of connection beyond the deal. Not a boy-girl connection. Not even friends, really. But still, a bond. Like the bond that develops between Nicholas Cage and Shirley MacLaine in *Guarding Tess*. Not exactly friends, but not exactly anything else, either. Like a Mulder-Scully rapport.

But no. I was wrong.

"Of course you don't have to tell me anything," I decide to concede with a smile. "I entered into this arrangement free and clear. Your exposing yourself to me to make me feel better was never part of the deal."

"No, it wasn't."

Jeez, I already agreed with him. You'd think he'd just shut up and leave me alone. "In any case," I say with matter-of-fact clarity, "no one should ever be hounded into turning themselves inside out. Everyone should get to keep to themselves whatever they want. Except criminals." I look right into his eyes. "I'm sorry."

Jack looks at the floor, then back at me. "Look, Lisa," he finally says, taking hold of my foot. "I know it's been rough. What the media did to you …"

"It hasn't been rough," I say, then do a bark of laughter-type throat noise. "I got six million dollars. Everyone should have it so rough."

"That doesn't replace what the media stole from you, or what you lost." Jack's voice is too soft and too nice, especially considering what he really thinks of me.

I remember the things people said about me in the magazines. Some of those people were supposed to love me, but they humiliated me anyway. I can't help but wonder if Jack read the articles. If he remembers.

Binge ... barely fit into a size fourteen ... bull-sized her meal ... almost choked on the cheeseburger in her mouth .... was so happy when Keith finally proposed this Christmas ... Always had low self-esteem, poor thing, ever since she wet the bed at a friend's house in fifth grade after watching C.H.U.D. ... An incredible girlfriend, I don't care what size she is ... She was always jealous of my being skinnier, which is sad between sisters. She could be a decent size, too, if she just stopped eating ... I heard this loud creak. I thought she'd farted ... When you eat like that, how can you expect to float down the aisle on a cloud? ... The combination of big body size and low self-esteem is a tragedy of a modern, over-eating America ... She kept trying to compare herself to Marilyn Monroe ...

I'd been in a coma, unable to comment, unable to defend myself. Unable to explain how scary *C.H.U.D.* was or how I wasn't *always* comparing myself to Marilyn Monroe. And I don't do it anymore now that I'm no longer blonde. It's just that she was a size 12 like I was, or at least that's what she tells Clark Gable in *The Misfits*.

"Jack," I pull my knees in toward my chest, snatching my foot back. "I don't want to get personal, either. Can we stop talking now?"

He doesn't answer. Good.

But his silence is so condescending.

"Why are you so sure I need therapy," I demand, "but you don't?"

"Why am I here?" he asks instead of answering me. "You were in the hospital today, but I'm the only one with you. You didn't call anyone. Don't you think that's a little weird?"

"I thought this was all supposed to be a big secret!" Damn, talking that loudly really makes my head hurt.

"From the staff at Into the Wild," he reminds me.

"If you didn't want to drive me home or stay the night, then you shouldn't have done it. I never asked you for any of this."

"I'm responsible, Lisa. Do you think I'm just going to walk away and not take care of you?"

Take care of me?

"You were testing *my* gear when this happened," he goes on. "The truth is, I should have been better prepared for something like this. I will be next time."

Oh. It's all just business and gear and liability for his guinea pig.

"Why do you care who I do or don't call, anyway?" I

ask. "Psychoanalyzing me wasn't part of the deal, either."

He shrugs. "I thought maybe you were bugging me about my secrets because you really just wanted to talk about yours."

"Secrets?" I squawk. "Like I have any left!"

He just looks at me.

"Is it so hard to believe," I ask, "that I was asking about *you* because I actually want to know about *you*?"

He looks at me as if it *is* hard to believe, but I'm so tired that his skepticism sits just fine with me.

"It's midnight," I say, stretching out. "Can I go to sleep?" I shut my eyes.

"I'm going to wake you every hour."

"Whatever."

CHAPTER 9

Armory Street in the heart of Los Angeles makes me squint from the glare of the September sun bouncing off faded concrete. There are no trees, except for a line of impossibly tall palms lining the side of the road. The park across the street and down the hill hogs all the nearby shade with its few clusters of scraggly sycamores. I get out of my new blue hybrid, beeping it locked. I have to keep Dalton safe. Sugar lasted only a few months before I sacrificed her on the altar of stupidity. I pat Dalton's roof, silently promising to be more vigilant.

My hand still on Dalton, I look up at what appears to be a six story white apartment building. I scan the parking lot and minimal lawn before I see the sign flanking the back door of the ground floor. HEYA: Helping Everyone Young Achieve.

Deep breath.

This is the place. I've arrived.

I look down at myself. Jeans, ironed green button-down worn open over a crisp white T. Casual, but clean. Confident, but down to earth. Boy, did my wardrobe raise some eyebrows in class today. Some people looked at me quizzically, as if wondering who I was, and then their eyes would grow huge as they figured it out. Jack even paused in stride to give me a once-over on his way past my seat. Whatever. Like I have time to play dress up. I have something much more important to do today.

I take in another big gulp of air and straighten the cuffs of my shirt. Was green the right choice? I'm pretty sure it doesn't have any gang affiliations. Plus it sets off the fading purple and yellow forehead bruise, which I'm hoping will make me look tough enough to work in the 'hood. My stomach roils. Man. What good is six million dollars if you still feel all the icky old feelings? Seriously, nervousness at a job interview? Millionaire-status should at least take care of *that.*

I grit my teeth, try to feel six million dollars strong, and approach the building where HEYA has its headquarters. Well, not headquarters, really, since there are no other quarters. Just the one rec center, and they need me. Not my money, not my fame. They need *me*, Lisa Flyte. I just keep telling myself that as I walk in.

But other voices in my head are louder. My father declaring that I don't do anything with my life. Keith telling me he can do better. Maggot-Face braying that nobody cares about me now that I'm awake. Mom's bedside condemnation is loudest of all. *You're still you.*

But I am going to change. I am. Starting now. I close my eyes and pray that nobody here saw the 10-page color spread in the February issue of *People*.

"Help you?" a voice asks.

My eyes fly open in time to see a young man taking a seat behind the reception desk in the bright lobby. His jeans and T-shirt give me confidence about my own wardrobe, but the Capri pants and jewelry on the young woman standing near the desk freak me out. I stare and swallow like Anna Paquin winning her Oscar. "I'm…I'm Lisa Flyte."

They stare back at me, then burst out laughing.

"Oh, my God," the woman says. "You're never going to believe this!"

"I *told* you," the young man says to her.

When the young woman catches her breath, she manages to speak. "I thought you were gonna be that Lisa Flyte person from the magazine! The one whose car got crushed by Burger Barn?" More laughter. "I'm sorry. I guess it's a more common name than I thought."

She doesn't recognize me with my size eight body. I'm even a size six when I wear Gap jeans. And my short brown hair with coppery highlights looks nothing like the Vanna White look I was sporting last winter. Plus I'm awake and not drooling.

"Well," I offer, "there were two Engelbert Humperdincks." They both stare at me, obviously never having heard of either. Come *on.* The second Engelbert guest-starred on *The Love Boat* and kissed Julie! "And there're two actresses named Vanessa Williams," I add.

Their eyes light up.

"Right," the young man says, nodding.

"I'm Guadalupe," the young woman says. "Lupe. We spoke on the phone. And this is Julius."

I smile and nod at both of them.

Guadalupe smiles back. "Let's go back to Mr. Bennett's office."

I follow in her wake, even more nervous than I was a minute ago. Did I just lie to the prospective employers for whom I want to work so badly? I think I did. I know I did.

Not technically, of course. I never said, "I am not the Lisa Flyte who was crushed by Burger Barn."

But still. It was enough of a lie that when it's discovered, and of course it will be discovered because I am a terrible liar, I will leave HEYA covered in inky ignominy.

But I can't leave. I love HEYA already. Its cinderblock walls painted in primary colors pulse with vibrant goodness. They really do. I can feel my bones absorbing it.

Surrounding me on these walls is incredible artwork—

paintings, photographs, and collages made by students of all ages, according to the nifty little placards under each one. Everyone gets his or her very own placard! No one's ever given me my very own placard.

Off to each side of me as we wind through the corridors are rooms where I can see and hear kids playing ping pong, goofing off, studying with older volunteers, or reading.

I know I'm in a place where things matter. Where people matter.

We arrive at a small office maybe ten by ten. A large, balding man in a white shirt and yellow tie sits behind a desk. He looks both doleful and sardonic with a long mustache that curves down to his jowls.

Guadalupe looks to him, then back to me. "Mr. Bennett, Lisa Flyte. Lisa Flyte, Mr. Bennett."

Introductions complete, she ducks her head as she scurries to lean against the window sill with two young men, both of whom wear jeans. When she notices the looks they all pin her with, she just smiles and shrugs.

Mr. Bennett stands, extending his hand to me. "Ms. Flyte, I'm Mr. Bennett. Lupe, I mean Guadalupe, you've met. She's in charge of Academic Programs. Edgar…" the young Alpha male with his eyebrows slammed together nods. "… oversees Recreational Programs. And Jimmy is in charge of our Outreach Programs."

"Hey." The last guy sends me a disarming smile.

I smile back, but bite my bottom lip. Both young men are compact and ruthlessly in shape. I suck in my stomach. Mr. Bennett motions to a chair, and I take a seat. When I do, my eyes fall to the magazine on his desk.

A tattered copy of February's issue of *People.* I cannot help but stare. I think my mouth drops open. I mean, it's so unfair. I wish like crazy that I had embarrassing pictures of

Guadalupe, Edgar, Jimmy, and Mr. Bennett to even out the playing field.

"I apologize," Mr. Bennett says, glancing down at the magazine. "Guadalupe got us all thinking that you might be THE Lisa Flyte, come here to save us all." He chuckles, the regret echoing through.

They just wanted my money.

"I am." I lift my chin and feel Wolverine-like adamantium squaring my shoulders. "Here to save you, that is."

I feel a sense of moxie whip through me like a minty arctic wind. "I know you're in financial trouble, and an influx of a couple million dollars is NOT what you need."

They stop *heh-hehing*.

I think I've offended them, so I plow on, before anyone can yell at me. "I've read your history. You got a swarm of celebrity donations three years ago when your dot com backer went belly up, and now you're in trouble again. You need to generate, maintain, and manage a working budget. I can help. I've been working in financial offices for over a decade, so I know a thing or two about how to manage money." Okay, so I had only one management position in my early twenties, and I hated it. Since then, I've learned from watching those above me screw up. But the HEYA folks don't need to be bothered with such sordid details. That's why I worded my résumé so carefully. "Plus, I'm currently earning my MBA at USC."

"Yeah, but do you know what it takes to run a center like this?" demands Edgar.

"I know what it takes to survive."

Oh, my God. Did I just whip back the perfect response? Suddenly I think of Jack and wonder if his courage has rubbed off on me just a tiny bit.

Mr. Bennett's raised eyebrows tell me he's somewhat impressed with my gusto. Or maybe he just thinks I'm nuts.

"I've read the résumé you faxed over this morning, Ms. Flyte, and I can see you have financial experience. But did Guadalupe explain on the phone that we can't pay anywhere near what you used to get? This job is only fifteen hours a week, at twelve dollars an hour."

I blink. I'm about to lose my dream job because I made too much money at my middle-of-the-road jobs that had me living paycheck to paycheck as I tried to make rent in West Los Angeles? I'm not here to save them with a check so they're writing me off?

"This isn't about the paycheck," I say vehemently, fabricating as I go. "I've saved and invested enough over the years to pay for school and rent, so all I really need is enough for food and gas and insurance and stuff like that."

"Ms. Flyte," Mr. Bennett begins. "Your enthusiasm *is* impressive…"

"It's for real," I insist, trying to stave off the rejection I can feel brewing.

"Is it?" Edgar takes a step forward. "Or is this just some business school project? Do you even understand that this is our *life*?"

I grab the magazine off the desk and hold it up in front of me. "This is *my* life."

They all stare.

"I'm Lisa Flyte. *The* Lisa Flyte. This is me."

They all exchange Let's-Call-the-Psych-Ward looks. But if I have to bring out the big guns to get this job, I will. I will NOT be brushed aside any longer.

"I know it doesn't look like me," I say. "But I lost a lot of weight when I was in the coma, and when I got out of the hospital, I cut my hair and dyed it back to its natural color."

"Uh ..." But Mr. Bennett doesn't seem to know where to go from there.

"Please," I say. "Please hear me out."

"Hear out your story?" This is Jimmy, sounding all eager, as if he's in for a good sci-fi adventure. "Shoot. We're listening."

I quickly take out my wallet. "I can prove it's me." I find a picture and hand it to Mr. Bennett. "This is me and my parents at my high school graduation. My parents' pictures are in the magazine. So is my sister's." I hand around the second picture. "This is me about to dump freezing cold water all over Mags as she lays out in the sun." I *love* this picture. I wish I had ones of her just after I doused her, but my friend Sandy who was taking the pics was laughing so hard that the rest of the shots came out blurry. "Compare them," I insist. "You'll see."

Mr. Bennett, Guadalupe, Edgar and Jimmy all gather into a huddle, holding my pictures up to the ones in the magazine. Then they lift their heads to look at me as though I've sprouted wings and a hood ornament.

Thank goodness. They look convinced, which means I won't have to show them the final picture.

"What's that picture there?" Edgar notices I'm holding something behind my back.

"It's nothing," I say with a chipper look of innocence.

"What are you hiding?"

"I'm not hiding anything." I thrust my hand forward, giving them the picture. "Here. It's of me and Keith."

Guadalupe looks at the picture then at me. "Your fiancé! But then ..."

"I know, I know," I say, cutting off any accusations about how I'm STILL not wearing an engagement ring. "He dumped me, okay?"

"When you had all that money?"

Thank you, Edgar. "Turns out the money didn't matter to him," I explain. "He just wanted out. Said he could do better."

Edgar sputters. “Than ten million dollars?”

I take a very deep breath. “Better than me, apparently. The whole time I was in the coma,” I say, willing my eyes not to fill up, “the media made such a big deal of our love story. It made him wonder what true love like that would really be like.” Good God, why am I telling them this? I need to shut up, before they start wondering what makes me so repulsive.

Guadalupe shakes her head woefully. “He probably had someone else.”

And a cut of the ten mil.

“Is he the one who gave you that bruise?” Jimmy is looking at my forehead.

“No!” I shout. “I mean, Keith isn’t like that. I had to head butt a car thief.”

They all look at me, mouths open, foreheads crinkled.

“Look,” I say. “I almost died in February. It took me a while to get back on my feet, but now that I am, I know I want to do something good and important with this life of mine. I want to help save HEYA.”

“But not with all your money?” Lupe seems skeptical.

“With *your* money.”

“We don’t *have* any,” she tells me.

I smile. “You will. I promise. And you’ll know what to do with it. What do you say?”

CHAPTER 10

"I got the job!"

I let out a screech of triumph, giving Dalton's steering wheel another hug. "They hired me. *Me.* They hired *me.*"

Tie a yellow ribbon 'round the old oak tree...

I jab the button on my cell phone that silences the ring. As much as I love that song, my ring tone embarrasses me, even though I picked it and I'm the only one in the car.

It's Jack. He's the only one with the number. Jesus. He wants me to test something, and that means he's invented something. While I was blabbing my most embarrassing secrets in order to land a job, Jack INVENTED something.

I slump back in my seat and answer my cell.

"Jack?"

"Lisa." Crisp, commanding.

No *Hello*.

No How are you?

No I haven't been able to stop thinking about you.

"What?" I can be gracious, too.

"Can you test something today?"

Oh, no. What if I end up in the hospital again? "Uh, this afternoon?"

"Can you do it?"

Great. It's probably something terrifying.

"Lisa?"

"Yes," I say, sitting up. "I'll do it. What do you want me to wear?"

"Whatever. We'll be staying in the office. There are some things I'm working on here that I need your help with."

"At the office?" I groan, relieved and put out at the same time. "You mean, like, filing? I signed up for harrowing adventures, not some nine-to-five bull."

"Hey," he says, almost laughing at my petulance, "you just had a head injury three days ago. How're you doing by the way?"

"Fine," I say, slapping into my words and ignoring his actual attempt to be nice. "Now that I get to sleep in my own bed."

"Where else was I supposed to sleep?" he demands. "You were on the couch."

It's true. I fell asleep on the couch Friday night and would not budge. So, Jack slept in my bed, in my big beautiful bed, without me. HE SLEPT IN MY BED WITHOUT ME. Wrapped in the flower-sprigged comforter and leafy sheets that remind me of The Hundred Acre Wood.

Bastard!

After he got up, I went into the bedroom to discover that the covers were still warm from his body. STILL WARM FROM HIS BODY.

"Can you come?" He gets right back to the business at hand, as though sleeping in my bed, in my pajamas, didn't affect him *at all.*

"I can be there in about an hour. Or so." I have nothing to do right now, and I'm about fifteen minutes from Into the Wild, but I'm not just going to *say* that.

"Fine. So around three?"

Just like that. The guy's life is so chock full of

meaningful activities that waiting to see me is no big deal. He doesn't even care that I'm making him wait.

"Probably," I tell him. "But I might get stuck here at HEYA. If I need to be late, I'll call." I don't start until tomorrow, but he doesn't need that kind of detail.

Pause. "Got it."

Great. He doesn't even take the HEYA bait so I can let him know that I'm becoming more significant by the second.

"See you later." I disconnect quickly, so at least I'm the one to hang up first.

* * * * *

At three-ten, I arrive at Into the Wild. I actually drove home to West L.A. and back to downtown an hour later just so Jack doesn't think I'm at his beck and call. I had lunch, watched CNN, and changed clothes.

Like I'm going to risk messing up my favorite shirt with buttons. Now I'm wearing jeans and my long-sleeved black T-shirt that says "I"— then there's a big red heart, then —"Orlando." It's a typical tourist shirt that refers to the city in Florida, but Keith's sister got it for me shortly after we watched *Fellowship of the Ring* for the fourth time.

This time when I pull into the garage at Into the Wild, Jack is waiting for me by the elevator so we can ride up together.

"Haven't you ever read *Pride and Prejudice*?" I ask as we whir up through the levels of terror. I'm concentrating so hard on staring at Jack that my temples throb. "You said no one would think we're involved. But all this special attention you're giving me is going to make people think I'm your special lady friend—not the opposite."

"No worries," he says as we step out of the elevator at the top floor. "Everyone can see that your heart belongs to

Orlando, not to me."

Jack is better at this than Keith was. Deflecting conversation, I mean. Keith would use much more clunky humor and make stupid jokes when he didn't want to answer me or talk about whatever I wanted to talk about. Jack has a much dryer wit.

All the same, if he doesn't want to concede a point, he won't. But he should. Didn't he tell me Into the Wild is employee owned? His staff of co-owners isn't going to like him sneaking the Woman in Nothing but a Bra into his office all the time.

When we get to the top floor, I can feel the stares as we step off the elevator. I sense everyone's eyes stabbing into me like a thousand tiny pins as we make our way back to the lair. When Jack finally lets us both in and closes the door behind us, I gulp in air like Wesley and Buttercup just emerging from the Lightning Sand.

"Will you get over yourself?" Jack heads across the room toward one of the cabinets hidden in the oak paneling. "This isn't a spy movie and nobody thinks you're Mata Hari."

"Seriously, Jack. What exactly did you tell them about me?"

"That you're in my class at USC and we're working on a project together." He tosses items on his desk as he fishes them out of the cabinet. "Oh yeah. And that you're clueless. Come here."

"You did not!" I work my way across the messy room, stepping over rope, a muddy pair of hiking boots and what looks like a punching bag. I reach the edge of his desk. "You didn't, did you?"

"Maybe I did."

He walks up to me, stops, then puts his hands on my face. My lips part in surprise. I'm confused and embarrassed about being confused, all at once. He's touching my face and ...

my lips ... and ... he puts his thumbs in my mouth?

"Yeah," he says, letting me go. "I think this'll work."

What just happened?

He crosses to the gigantic windowsill behind his desk, where I notice a hot plate sitting next to the coffee maker. He flicks on the coils, grabs a small beat up pot from his desk and heads to a water cooler in the corner of the room.

"What are you doing?" I press my fingers to my lips. A warm buzz like the kind from a refrigerator hums all through my face and mouth where Jack touched me.

He goes back to the windowsill, puts the pot now filled with water on the hot plate and turns to me. "What were you doing at HEYA?"

No preamble or pleasantries. This makes me wonder whether Jack lacks social skills or simply chooses not to use them with me.

"I work there," I toss back.

"As what?"

He asks this as though he's sure I'm nothing more than a mascot who wears a big rubber head. "I cook the books," I tell him.

Pause. "Since when?" No inflection to indicate whether he is surprised, pleased, disgusted, ambivalent, or concerned.

"What is this? An interrogation?"

"Since Connecticut?" he asks.

Just like that, he asks me about Connecticut. Like he knows *anything* about me. "What do you know about Connecticut?"

"It was just a question."

"Connecticut is no longer part of the equation."

"What equation?"

"*My* equation." I growl this with such fierceness I can feel the foam bubble up at the back of my teeth.

"So, is it a job or volunteer?"

I look down to the hot plate and the pot of water.

"What are we doing?" I ask, gesturing toward all the stuff he's gathered. "Shouldn't I be doing something?"

"We're waiting for the water to boil," he explains. "Is it a job or volunteer?"

I notice the way Jack's throat ripples underneath the tanned skin of his neck when he talks, so I decide not to be affronted by his questioning.

"A job."

"You're a multimillionaire drawing a salary from a ghetto rec center?"

He delivers this question with the unmistakable sting of judgment.

Jerk.

"I'm going to do something important with my millions. Something big. And HEYA needs a plan, not another infusion of cash."

"So you work at HEYA to hone your financial skills?"

"Are you seriously giving me a hard time for working there?" I huff out a snort. "Of course you are. You just want to accuse me of Machiavellian motives about everything and be done with it."

"I—"

"Well! Let me just set you straight, buddy. I saw this job posted on the net and I went in and got it because I wanted to do something to help, something good. So just you watch, Jack. I'm going to save the center and then all of you will have to shut up and give me a standing ovation."

"Lisa—"

"The water's boiling. What do we do now?"

Jack doesn't answer right away.

"I'm here to do a job," I remind him. "Remember?

Talking about ourselves isn't part of the deal."

Jack looks at me for a few seconds. "I'm making you a mouth guard," he finally says.

I raise my eyebrows, considering. Really, though, I'm trying to get back to focusing on gear-testing. "Why?" I ask. "What are you going to do to me that I need a mouth guard?"

"Nothing." He shrugs. "Nothing today, anyway. But I think it makes good beginner gear."

"But you can't invent a mouth guard," I argue. "Mouth guards already exist."

"I'm thinking of a different kind. I've got a few ideas to make it less intrusive. I don't know quite how, exactly, which is why I need you, to try some things out."

Jack takes a hunk of clear, Jell-O-like plastic off his desk and drops it into the pot. "Once that softens up, you'll mold it to your mouth. Then, I'll make some adjustments as we go."

Before I can say anything, like *Mold it to my mouth*? *That hunk of hard lard*? He's back at the water cooler, filling a pail. He puts the full pail on his desk then turns to me.

"Ready?" he asks.

"Ready for what?" I ask back.

He picks up tongs from his desk. "I'm going to take this out of the water and put it in your mouth. Then—"

"What?!"

"Then you bite down hard, sucking out all the water you can. After a few seconds, take it out and put it into this bucket of water so the mold can solidify."

I just look at him standing there, holding the tongs.

"Ready?" He's all no-nonsense.

Holy icky-thing-in-my-mouth, Batman! Did I actually agree to this? "How is this supposed to make me braver?"

"It won't," he concedes. "It's meant to protect you while you're finding your courage. Now open wide."

I open my mouth.

Jack fishes the plastic out of the boiling water, shakes off the excess water, and—

AAAG!

It's hot!

It tastes like plastic!

AND he shoves it in so far it hits the back of my throat and I feel myself gag!

"Bite down," he instructs.

"Nnnnn!"

"Bite down!"

I bite down hard into the hot, soft plastic, giving myself a mutant ice cream headache.

"Suck out as much water as you can," he orders.

It tastes disgusting, but I do it because the intense sucking eases my impulse to wretch.

"Okay," Jack says after about a century. "Good. Now take it out and put it in—"

I spit it into the bucket. "Ack!" I swipe my sleeve across my mouth. "Yuck! Jeez! Arg!"

Jack just watches as I stand there panting and salivating. When I look up at him, he says, "Ready?"

"For what?"

"We have to do another one."

"No!" I cry. "I did everything you said!"

"I know. But we'll need more than one to work on, so we may as well mold them all at once."

"Are you serious?"

"Are you scared?"

I pin him with such a stern stare he looks away. It was a low blow and he knows it. "It *tastes* awful," I explain, enunciating viciously.

"I'm going to do one, too, this time," he offers.

"You better, Goddamnit."

* * * * *

"Awwckg." I swallow again, and then clench the mouth guard between my teeth.

Jack keeps saying he's "adjusting" it every time he takes it out of my mouth, cleans it off, and starts working on it. But when he sticks it back in my mouth, it never feels any different.

Well, hardly any different.

"I on't ink iss is oing ooh wook," I try to tell him through the mouth guard.

"We're getting there."

"I ant eben alk!"

The stupid mouth guard is molded all along the inside of my teeth and along the roof of my mouth, curving around the bottom edges of my teeth, anchored in at my back molars.

"I think if I shave a little off the roof plate and the back ..."

I take it out and drop it in the bucket. "Can we just take a break from the mouth guard for a sec? I need a Coke or something to get rid of this plastic taste."

He goes to a small fridge concealed in the oak paneling. In one smooth motion, he takes out a bottle of Coke and tosses it to me. I watch it sail across the room, keeping my eye on the prize until I catch it.

Whap. Right into my hand. Wow. I can't believe I actually caught it, in front of Jack and everything.

"I feel like Mean Joe Green," I say, letting the soda settle before I open it.

Jack takes a Dasani for himself. "The kid *hands* him the Coke," he says, correcting me. "Mean Joe Green never catches the Coke."

"Oh," I say, "Right."

"Wait a second," Jack says, before I can get the bottle to my lips. "Aren't you supposed to throw me your shirt now?"

I spare him a jaded glance then chug the Coke.

"Hey, *you're* the one who said you felt like Mean Joe Green," he points out.

I thump the bottle down on his desk. "You seriously want my shirt?"

"You said—"

Ffft.

My shirt hits him right in the face. I was so quick to whip it off and fling it at him that he wasn't even ready for it. Ha!

I don't think he thought I'd do it.

He takes the shirt off his head, looks at it, shrugs.

"Okay," he says, barely glancing at me in my blue-green sports bra. "Let's work on the helmet." He tosses my shirt onto the couch.

"Helmet?" I pick up the Coke and chug and chug and chug. What else am I supposed to do? I can hardly ask for my shirt back after having pitched it at him so brazenly.

By the time I come up for air, Jack is next to me, fitting this contraption onto my head. "Jack," I say. "No. This won't work. Head gear is never cool, and a beginning adventurer is never going to want to start if they have to look like a total dork."

He stands back from me. "You don't look like a *total* dork."

I think he's noticing how busty my sports bra makes me look. I gaze up at him. "What's wrong?" I inquire innocently.

"Nothing. It's just that you were much more skittish last time you were prancing around my office in your bra."

"I *wasn't* prancing." I move my hands as if to straighten

the stupid helmet. Jack gets closer to me to adjust some of the straps on the helmet. "I was *skittish* because of the seaweed," I say. "And I didn't like that bra. *This* bra makes my eyes look fantastic."

"You are so weird." His T-shirt-clad arms brush my naked shoulders as he works. "And your eyes are brown." He says this as though I deserve to be held back in kindergarten until I learn my colors.

"They have flecks of greeney-blue."

Jack gets a strand of my hair caught in one of the buckley straps.

"Ow."

"Sorry." He loosens the buckle thing. "My plan," he tells me, "is to make the rubber straps thin enough that you can wear a knit cap over it."

"Big deal. Head gear is never cool, Jack. Never. Honestly, what do you think whenever you see someone wearing a Bluetooth? Those things look dumb strapped to a person's head."

"True. But they make money and lots of people wear them."

"Sell-out."

"Go look in the mirror," he suggests, sidestepping my unassailable rejoinder. "You look kind of cute."

"Right." In order to prove just how wrong he is, I march off to the bathroom mirror.

Hm. It almost looks like a swim cap made of soft tan straps, with wisps of my hair poking out all over the place. My eyes look huge and surprised. And damn near algae-colored thanks to my bra. Okay. I guess I look cute in a cartoonish kind of way, like a Teletubby or one of those aliens who comes down to visit Bert and Ernie. I'm trying to get the quirks and kinks out of my hair when Jack appears in the mirror behind me.

"Here," he says. "Try this. I shaved off some of the roof plate."

He reaches around to slip the mouth guard into my mouth, once again brushing my bare shoulder with the cotton of his long-sleeved T. But this time, I'm practically enclosed in his pseudo-embrace.

"How does it feel?" he asks.

Awesome.

"Uh feews…" He is standing so close behind me I can feel his heat on my mostly bare back. I want to press my fingers onto the skin where he touched me, even if it was through his T-shirt, but I'm afraid that if I move, he'll move. "Beh-orh. A wih-oo beh-ohr."

He puts his left hand on my left shoulder, then, looking at my mouth in the mirror, reaches around with his right hand. With his thumb and index finger, he adjusts the mouth guard while it's in my mouth.

We look at each other in the mirror.

He's still touching me.

But I'm wearing the stupid helmet and mouth guard. Fantastic eyes or not, I look like the Bride of Frankenstein's mentally handicapped younger sister. I lower my eyes.

Jack brushes a finger along my chin, trying, I think, to make me look back up.

Whap whap.

We both jump. Someone is knocking on the office door.

Jack rushes out without a word. A second later, something soft hits me on the arm. "Get your shirt on," he calls to me from his office.

But I have to turn the shirt right-side-out first. Then, when I'm putting it on, it gets stuck on one of the straps of the helmet. When I finally untangle it and get myself dressed like a big girl, it's too late to take off and stash the secret idiot gear.

And closing the bathroom door is out of the question. But at least I'm not completely obvious to someone in the office because of the angle of the open bathroom door. I'll just have to stay still and quiet.

Through the bathroom mirror, I see a woman who must have pushed her way past Jack. She sweeps into the office as though she owns the room, but not the grunge. She looks to be about forty-five, fit to command an Armada, and positively lovely in a thousand dollar business suit set off with a choker of pearls.

"Jack," she says, hitting her mark in the center of the office. She turns to him on cue. "I thought you could take me for cocktails and an early dinner."

"I'm in the middle of something."

I can't see Jack, but I'm curious. His voice is level, but not as impenetrable as it is with me. There's something not exactly softer about his voice, but ... resigned. That's it. He sounds resigned. To what, I have no idea.

"Your riff raff told me you were working on some project," the woman says, looking around the office without taking anything in. "But you can make time for me."

"If you want to eat with me," Jack says, shutting the office door, "you could come over when I invite you."

She looks to where he must be standing. "Our weekends are very busy, Jack." She gives a tinkly little laugh. "I think our schedules are a little harder to work around. Real business keeps us busy. Not that you would understand, running a rinky dink pipe dream in an old warehouse."

Sllhuuh.

No! My hand flies to my lips, but it's too late. Without really meaning to, I sucked in a slurpy sounding gasp of indignation, totally giving myself away.

"What?" The woman turns around, spotting me watching

her through the mirror.

It's not my fault! I couldn't help it! Just an involuntary reaction of my throat!

"Lisa," Jack says, striding into view. "Come out and meet my mother."

I whip around to face the woman. His *mother*? My eyes dart back and forth between them. What the hell? Was she eight years old when she had him? And how on earth did *Jack* come from someone like *her*?

With that poised confection of a diva just staring at me, I have no choice. I walk into the office. No time to take off the helmet. Or to remove the mouth guard. How could I spit it out right in front of Attila the Perfectly Coiffed Queen?

"Hel-lo," I enunciate very carefully around the mouth guard.

She gets this confused look on her face.

"Mom, this is Lisa. Lisa, this is my mother, Edna Hawkins."

She flashes me a bright, sweet smile, gently shaking my hand. "Hello, Lisa." She talks back to me kind of slowly, and I wonder if she's making fun of me.

I look to Jack, but he's harder to read than *Ulysses*. I feel familiar family friction and I know I have to get out of here. Plus, she might be checking out the helmet and getting ready to mock Jack's design. Bitch.

"Jack," I say clearly as I can. "I haff to go back to the center."

"Right," Jack moves so fast I can tell he wants me gone just as badly. He plucks a blue and green knit cap off his desk and fits it on my head over the helmet. His solicitude in helping me get ready to leave makes me feel like a toddler getting dressed to play in the snow.

"Thank you," I say, then turn to leave.

"Isn't someone going to drive her?" Edna asks.

I turn around. Drive me? Do I look twelve in this get-up?

"Don't worry," Jack says, then looks at me. "See ya, Lisa."

I wave and head out, not looking up or opening my mouth the whole way to the elevator. It's not until I'm out of the parking garage and on Flower Street that I spit out the mouth guard. Pulling to the curb, I wrap it carefully in a Starbucks napkin sitting on my passenger seat. Next, I yank off the cap, making my hair fly with static. I try to pank it down, then I reach back to unhook the straps to take off the helmet.

Stuck.

Great.

* * * * *

I look up from the jeans and shirt I've chosen for my first work day at HEYA tomorrow. Someone is banging on the security door. Finally. That better be Jack to get this damn helmet off my head.

"It's about time." This is my greeting as I fling open the security door.

"You're still wearing it?"

Jack is very observant.

"I couldn't get it off." I pull on it to show him.

He steps into my apartment, then puts his hands in my hair.

HIS HANDS IN MY HAIR.

"How hard did you try to get it off?"

I'm so lost, though, in the tingly sensation of his hands on my head that it takes me a minute to register the question, then another second to register the annoyance in his tone.

"Dude," I swat his hands away from my head. "I didn't

want to break the prototype."

"Uh, thanks," he says, turning to close the front door. "Let's go by one of the lamps so I can see enough to get it off."

"I think we've found a design flaw." I move into the softly lit living room toward one of the big, Victorian-looking floor lamps that remind me of foggy old London.

"Any way to make these things brighter?" Jack asks, joining me in an arc of warm light. He finds the switch, brightens the room. "Turn around."

When I do, Jack starts to undo the straps running across my head. As his fingers work through my hair, I realize I'm in imminent danger of once again getting all hot and bothered over a guy who thinks of me as a test dummy and finds me about as attractive as a department store mannequin.

"How was lunch with your mom? Or dinner, or whatever?" I ask these questions quickly, just to forestall any lust on my part.

"Same old, same old," he says. "She gave me a check for two thousand dollars."

"What?!" I twist around to look at him. "Ow!"

"Hold still and your hair won't get yanked out."

"Two thousand bucks?" I squawk. "Did you take it?"

"Sure. Been takin' it for years. Easier that way."

"What do you do with it? Put it into Into the Wild?"

"I told you before, Into the Wild doesn't operate on corporate money."

"But you do, it seems."

Silence.

Jack takes off the helmet then moves around to face me. "Her checks go into a scholarship fund."

"Oh, really? What scholarship? For whom?" I have to be this bitchy to hide my terror that Jack has kids somewhere. Kids he never sees.

He stares at me, and then decides to answer. “Boys of a friend of mine who I used to climb with. He died a few years ago. There was lots of life insurance, but no college funds set up. The kids were just babies, and I guess he thought he had plenty of time. He was the kind of guy who would have set something up eventually.”

“Oh.” I twist my hands together. “Was he killed in a climbing accident?” I’m scared that Jack was there and saw the whole thing.

He shakes his head once. “9/11. Where’s the mouth guard?”

I stare at him with my mouth gaping open.

“Lisa?”

“Uh ...” I start massaging my head. “I’m really sorry. Does your mom know what you do with the money?”

“Doubt it.” He examines the helmet. “She sees it as her way of getting me my rightful inheritance so I never have to embarrass her with public penury.” He looks at me. “She hates my truck.”

“Maybe," I say, "the checks are her way of saying ‘I love you.’”

He dents his forehead. “There are more obvious ways.”

“Such as?”

“Just say it.” He looks at me with a steadiness I can’t look away from. “‘I love you.’” He doesn’t even blink. “It’s not that hard. She’s my *mother*.”

“Right,” I say. “‘I love you.’” I don’t dare look away. “Easy-peasy.” I shake my head. “How many times have *you* said it, Jack? As an adult, I mean? Since you were ... say ... twenty-three?” I have to figure college doesn’t count for a guy.

His jaw tightens.

I cock my head just a fraction.

“Look,” he snarls, “don’t you get it? She’s my *mom*.”

I back off, slowly nodding. But I cannot let it go. Not completely. Not when he looks like he looks. "You guys obviously don't speak the same language. Giving you a check could be hers."

"You suck as a shrink."

"I'm not trying to analyze you."

"Then what, Miss Know-It-All? Just being nosy?" He waits a second for me to answer.

But I don't say anything.

"Right." He turns to leave.

"Jesus, Jack. I'm just trying to wipe that look off your face before it makes me cry."

He snaps around. "What look?"

"I have parents, too," I say quietly. "I know what it's like, that's all."

Jack nods, looks down at the helmet. "Thanks for taking such good care of this. The mouth guard?"

I go to the table by the door and hand him the Starbucks napkin bundle.

"Thanks." He closes his hand around it. "Good-night." Then he leaves.

This time I let him go.

CHAPTER 11

"So, how 'bout a movie Friday night?"

"No!" I let my feet fall from my desk as I twist into a more upright position. "Definitely not."

Doleful, hurt, puppy dog eyes stare into mine. "Why not? Why do you always have to be such an ice queen and turn me down?"

"'Why not'?" I echo. "'Why not?' Since when do I have to give a reason for *not* wanting to spend time you? It's my time and I said 'no.'"

"But I'm a good guy. I have a good job, and I'm nice to my mother, and I'd be so good to you."

"I agree with all that," I say. "But the answer is still 'no.'"

"Why?"

"Because you just don't rev my motor."

"Aaaah!" Guadalupe cries, covering her mouth with her hand. "I could never say that!"

I lean back, feeling oddly exhausted after our bout of role-playing. "You want him to get off your back, don't you?" I demand.

Guadalupe and I sit facing one another. This, of course, means we're touching knees. My office is very small, little more than a corner nook. I'm pretty sure it used to be a closet.

"Lupe," I insist, "don't you?"

I'm hoping our little skit will help her believe she can shake her unwanted suitor. My pretending to be her and her pretending to be the guy who won't stop bugging her was the best idea I could come up with to show her how she could control her own love life.

And I had to come up with *something*. I mean, she actually came to me, seeking my romantic advice.

Mine.

Even though I got dumped the minute I woke up from a coma. So that just goes to show you how people will listen to anything you say if you're on the cover of a magazine. It doesn't even matter that I was comatose and drooling on said cover.

But she really did want my help so I gave it a whack. I imagine all sorts of things about how relationships between men and women should work, but I never really get a chance to put any of my ideas into practice in my own life.

Well, maybe I get the chance, but I've never actually taken such a chance, or shown any kind of logical, powerful confidence in a relationship. I mostly just kind of let relationships happen to me.

Like Peter Halloway in twelfth grade. I never meant to go to homecoming with him. But I let him down so easy he thought I meant 'yes.' So, we went.

"I want him off my back," she agrees, "buuut–"

"But what?"

"But I used to be crushin' on him all the time, okay?" Lupe puffs out a gust of air. "When I was in high school, okay?" She crosses her arms and juts out her bottom lip. "He was four years older, and I was crazy about him."

My eyebrows shoot up and my eyes open wide.

"That was a long time ago," she insists. "But he won't believe that he doesn't rev my motor since all I used to want was for him to jump start me, if you know what I mean."

"Did he ever?"

"No," she pouts. "Eric would have killed him if he ever touched me."

I nod. "Brothers can be such jackasses."

"No kidding! Now he's all like, 'Lupe, why don't you give Jorge a chance. Stop playing so hard to get. We both remember how much you like him.'"

"But you're not a kid anymore!" I protest. "You've got to set these guys straight."

She smiles and nods back. "Yeah. I'm not stupid little Lupe anymore."

"Yeah!"

"And maybe if I can find the *cojones* to get rid of Jorge, then I'll be brave enough to go after Jimmy."

"Jimmy?" I lean so close to her that our foreheads are almost touching. "You like Jimmy? I thought you liked Edgar."

She sighs. "I do. But Edgar's gay."

"He is?" I cannot process this fast enough. "But—but—but—he scowls all the time!"

"That's because he likes Jimmy, too."

"Is Jimmy gay?"

"No. That's why Edgar scowls all the time."

I lean back in my chair. "Got it. But won't it be weird if you two—"

"Lisa! Lisa! Lisa! Lisa!"

Gabriel comes tearing into the office, tears streaming down his little face behind his big glasses.

Someone's made my favorite kid cry!

"They're taking Pacquito!" he screams. "They're beating him and they put him in a cage!"

I'm out of my chair in a To-the-Batmobile flash. I don't even pause to ask questions. "Come on!"

Gabriel takes the lead and we charge through the HEYA parking lot and across the street to an abandoned apartment building. "Pacquito!" Gabriel yells.

Two men lift a cage holding the tan mongrel into an Animal Control van. I march up to them, feeling six million dollars brave. "What's going on here?"

The men ignore me.

Gabriel hangs onto the bars of Pacquito's cage as they try to push it into the van. One man lifts an arm to swipe him away.

"Don't you touch him!" I get right up into their faces. "Or I'll have the cops on your ass so fast for child abuse—"

"Then will you get him out of here?"

"Pacquito!" Gabriel wails. The dog has inched forward in the cage to lick Gabriel's teary glasses through the bars.

I struggle to bite off my words. "Then tell me what you're doing."

He thrusts a piece of paper at me. "Look, lady. The new owner called us and told us to get all the strays out. That's what we're doing."

"But look at them!"

Pacquito has a nasty gash down his front right leg, and two skeletal greyhounds sit on top of one another in a bigger cage on the sidewalk. I can't even look at the two huge dogs in the van, drooling through their leather muzzles. "They need medical attention!"

"Are you gonna give it to them?"

"Someone has to!"

"Fine." The man jerks his head toward his partner and they take Pacquito's cage out of the van. The man then takes out a clipboard. "All of them?" he asks. "Even the cats?"

I look at the cages of cats, seven of them. Some of them look a little worse for wear, and two of them look pregnant. "All of them." A burst of righteous power shoots through me.

He hands me the clipboard with a document to sign. Something about helping stray or unwanted animals marked for termination, so I sign it.

"So you'll make sure they get to a vet?" I ask.

They take out the cages of muzzled dogs and then close the van's big back double doors, leaving all twelve caged animals on the sidewalk.

"No, lady. You will." He tears off a pink carbon copy of the document I just signed. "You just claimed in writing that you're taking responsibility for all these animals."

My mouth drops open. I did *what*?

"You saved Pacquito! You saved Pacquito!"

I look down at Gabriel. He opens Pacquito's cage door and crawls in with him, hugging the dog like Diane Keaton hugs Warren Beatty outside the train in *Reds*.

"That's right," I say, shoving my hands onto my hips with unmistakable authority. I take a deep breath and look at all the animals. "I'm going to need a truck."

* * * * *

I wake up to the sound of water dripping. It's *rat-tat-tatting* at a pretty rapid rate. I blink. It's the shower. *My* shower. The shower I now *own*.

As it turns out, I needed way more than a truck for the twelve animals. Nothing less than a house with a yard would do. Jack Hawkins would say that this is what I get for going off half-cocked. But what choice did I have?

Raffi wasn't too happy with the number and species of my new roommates. Honestly, I don't blame him. I'm still getting used to it myself.

Twelve abandoned animals.

I needed a house.

Quick.

And I did my best. I did.

I decided I didn't need any damn realtor to suck me dry, so I bought the house myself. Eight-hundred thousand dollars for a three-bedroom bungalow that smells like beer.

I stare up at the water-damaged ceiling as my heart tries to claw its way out of my chest.

Breathe in. Breathe out.

My six million that I was trying to be so careful with is now diminished by a full sixth. Sure, the house was only eight hundred thousand, but tack on everything else so far, and I'm out a million. Or, I will be as soon as I tie up all the loose ends on this place.

I know. I can still do lots of good with five million. But I'm scared. Maybe I'll let another million slip away, then another.

I look around at the marked up walls of the tiny bedroom. Truth is, I'd be a lot happier if I'd gotten a little less of a dump for almost a million. A stucco ranch with no central air in the Valley. Eighteen hundred square feet, a detached garage and a dead yard.

At least there are a few trees. And a fence around the big dirt backyard. Sagging, rusted chain link. It's ugly, but good enough to hold back Aaron, Christian, Pacquito, Fred and Ginger, and that's the material point.

I wince, thinking about the vet bill. Twelve spays and neuters, and two of the cats were extra because they were pregnant. Plus the patch up jobs and de-worming. And de-flea-ing. Then the shots, the tests, the teeth cleanings. But then again, I don't regret it. I want to do good with the money, right?

I take a fortifying breath and get out of bed. I go to the kitchen to put on coffee and feed the rascals. This really isn't so bad. My own kitchen, my own coffee, my own safe haven for me and my impromptu family of ragtag misfits.

Okay, so it will take some time and effort to find the home underneath all the grime of this house. But what else can I expect?

This place was rented to frat boys for years before I bought it. And okay, maybe I was totally screwed by a greedy owner capitalizing on the combination of my desperation and the vicious real estate market.

But why bemoan the purchase? Can't be undone. No place to go but forward.

And despite the pervasive beer smell, there is hope for my hovel. The army of maids I had sanitize the place the day before yesterday actually did a pretty good job making the house recognizable as a place that one might live.

Anyway, the best thing of all about my new pad is that nobody knows I'm here. I didn't tell *anybody*.

The day after my Jack debacle when all my ID was stolen, I got myself a P.O. Box so no one could figure out where I lived. So really, my dumpy house is my own private castle.

By seven a.m., I'm out in the front yard, digging up all the naked Barbie dolls that have been buried waist deep. All five dogs run around in the fenced-off backyard, but as long as they can see me, they behave. And honestly, I think the stench of beer is making them a little drowsy.

The cats are in the house doing God knows what. I haven't seen any of them since I let them out of their cages yesterday morning. But I know they're eating because their food disappears when I'm not around.

"Well, hello there, pretty lady." A sweet, scratchy voice from behind me has me turning around on my knees.

Just then, the dogs start barking up a storm. A little late as guard dogs, but they make up for their tardiness with volume.

An older lady with a platinum blonde perm shakes a rose-painted nail at me. "Are you the new tenant?"

I stand, dusting off my hands along the thighs of my jeans. "Owner actually. I'm Lisa."

"Ohh!" She claps her hands together. "Even better! This neighborhood has put up with those college boys long enough." She thrusts out both hands. "I'm Dolly Blue."

We shake, and Dolly encloses my dirty hand in both of hers. I take a good long look up the street. Pristine houses complemented by manicured lawns. Every last one.

I twist around to look at my house. Peeling pool-blue paint reveals the pink stucco underneath. The dead grass makes the yard look like a hayfield harvested by one-legged zombies.

"Those guys must have been aggravating," I say, feeling guilty. I mean, my house is bringing down the whole street. I'm a Neighbor now. I have responsibilities. "I guess I've got a lot of work to do."

"Are you all alone?" Dolly looks around. "A pretty girl like you?"

I look toward the now quiet back yard. Aaron and Christian prance and wag their tails in Dolly's honor. Apparently, the other dogs have gone to hide. Yup, great guard dogs. "I've got the dogs to keep me company."

"Oh!" Dolly swats at me, grinning at my 'joke.' "Well," she says, giving my arm a squeeze, "I'll let you get back to work now. Nice to meet you!" And she toddles off down the street to the peach stucco house with sea green trim. Two magnificent birds of paradise stand like sentinels on either side of her front stoop. I turn around to look at the Barbie torsos decorating my dead grass. I guess they're *someone's* version of paradise.

I'm just putting the last few dolls into the trashcan when I hear, "Hey there!" from off to my right side.

I look up and there he is.

I mean, WOW.

It's Neighbor Guy. He's walking across his lushly emerald lawn toward my demented scruff of tumbleweed. He's smiling from beneath his ball cap. The dogs are kicking up a hell of a fuss, so he walks right up to the edge of the fence and talks to each of them, calling them good boys, even Ginger, until they quiet down.

He turns to me, and I swear, he's too awesome to be real.

And by that I don't mean that he's impossibly amazing or anything. But he's just cute enough and wholesome enough to make one believe that life can be as simple as finding a good man. Furthermore, he's right next-door. Not that he's the boy next door.

Better.

He's The Man Next Door.

He walks toward me. Looks to be maybe late thirties or early forties. Brown hair. Nice smile. Goes-to-the-gym-every-morning-but-doesn't-take-steroids-or-do-coke kind of body. Grass-stained sneakers, navy blue athletic shorts, white T-shirt.

Mmmmmmm.

"Hi," he says, stretching out his hand. "I'm Casey."

Hint of a down-home Southern twang in his salutation. Dear, sweet Lord.

"Lisa," I say, dropping a Barbie so I can shake. His gaze follows the doll as she plops back onto the ground, but then it re-focuses on my face. He likes me better than Barbie!

"You just moved in?" Hands on hips. Uses his chin to gesture at the house.

"Yeah." Smile, laugh. Feel like a dork.

"See you're working on the front yard." He surveys the lawn full of Barbie holes.

I nod. "Looks pretty bad."

"You just need to water it." Casey crouches down and pulls at some of the dead straw-stuff. He looks up at me. "This is grass, not sod. The seeds are here. Water it, and it'll come back. We should be getting some more rain in the next few weeks, and that'll do wonders. Add a little seed to those holes, and the grass will come in just fine."

"Okay." I nod enthusiastically, relishing this strange new role as Neighbor Lady. Who knows? I might even be Cute or Sexy Neighbor Lady. I go to dust off my butt with my hands, feeling proud of my workout regimen. But my hand ... my hand ...

Oh, God. I think I've sat in dog poo.

My hand is stuck in the dog poo on the ass of my jeans. In front of The Man Next Door!

I don't move. I can't. If I take my hand off my butt, I'll have a stinky hand of dog poo. So, I simply stand, hand resting nonchalantly on my butt.

"Wow," I say. "I should make a list. I need some grass seed. What else?"

Casey looks around. "This yard doesn't have a sprinkler system, so you'll need a hose. I just installed a sprinkler system last summer, so I've still got the kind of sprinklers you attach to a hose, but I'm not using them." He looks over his shoulder toward his place.

"They're sitting somewhere in my garage. One should cover the front, another the back. You can have 'em," he offers. "They're just collecting dust."

He's handy and nice. Soooo nice. He must be flirting. Maybe he's noticed my butt, but not the dog poo, and admires all those squats and crunches I've done.

"Great," I say brightly. "I'll get myself a hose. Then, I'll be all set." I wonder if we're talking in *double entendres*, so I think I blush.

Casey puts his arms out like Jesus with the fishes and loaves. "We can get you all set right now." A corn-fed smile breaks across his face like the sun rising over a Carolina pasture. "There's a great hardware store not far from here on Colfax. I'll lend you hoses until you can pick some up, and I'll go get some grass seed from Manny."

"No, don't." Keeping my hand planted awkwardly on my caboose, I kind of chase him as he heads across the street. I don't know who Manny is, but I fear a *ménage à trois* based on gardening favors is in the works. I don't know, maybe that's how things work in the suburbs. Best be careful since I'm clueless.

Casey turns at the curb and looks at me.

"Uh, never mind," I say, not wanting to lose the heart of The Man Next Door. "If Manny's got the seed, well ..." I laugh. "Thanks. That would be wonderful." I keep *huh-huhing* until he heads across the street. Then I turn around with a confident air, as though I always walk with my hand on my ass.

By the time I change my jeans, Casey and an in-shape man with curling, graying hair are in my front yard with a box of grass seed and a bag of topsoil.

"This is Manny," Casey introduces as I walk up to the pair, offering a bottle of water to each. "He and his wife Robin live in that blue house." He points to a house across the street that blooms in the middle of an elaborate garden of succulents.

Man, he must hate me already on account of my house.

"Lisa," I say and we shake. "Thank you, very much. What can I do?"

"Come with me," Casey says. "We'll go get the hose and sprinklers."

I want to bounce on my toes and shake my hands like a *Flashdance* maniac. He's taking me into his garage. *Nice*. We walk across my lawn, up his driveway, and into his open garage.

We work our way through the dim interior. This is it.

I'm sure he won't make a move or anything, not with the entire street watching, but we're going to have some sort of awkward or flirty moment.

I'm sure this impending moment will let us both know we want to get to know each other better. This could be my future, and all for just under a million bucks.

"Hi there."

I spin around to face a petite blonde with big blue eyes and an even bigger smile. "You must be Lisa. I'm Jessica." She pumps my hand enthusiastically.

"Hey, hon," Casey says.

Hon? Did The Man Next Door and Future Father of My Children just call her *hon*?

And did she call me Lisa? What? Did Dolly Blue run home to phone everyone to tell them the frat boys were gone?

"Have you seen the old sprinklers from last year?" he asks her.

"On the shelf above the lawn mower." She looks back at me. "A new neighbor. And not a teenage horndog or somebody's grandma. I'm *so* glad you're here."

I want to kill her. She's got Casey and a size 2 butt and a size 6 rack.

That's probably the only reason he likes her, that small butt and those big boobs, and the blonde hair and the innocent blue eyes. Casey's such an asshole. I bet he'd dump her if she got fat. Suddenly, I'm on her side.

"Glad to be here!" I chirp with gusto. I want to tell her I'll be there for her whenever Casey tells her to go easy on the Baskin Robbins.

"Listen, I'm done grading papers, so I'll be over in a jiffy to help." She practically skips back into the house.

"What does she do?" I ask, taking the hose from Casey.

"Teaches third grade."

Jeez. A sweetly gorgeous elementary school teacher. For real? I bet she sings in the church choir and calls her Mama every morning.

"Grading papers for third graders?" I ask. All I remember about third grade is recess and my crush on Chad Guazo.

"Haiku poems and short multiplication."

Oh, God. He knows what her kids are learning. He must really love her.

"Hm." I try to invest the syllable with interest as we get back to my yard.

* * * * *

It's eleven-thirty as I lock Aaron and Christian in the garage and put the other three dogs in the house to sniff out cranky cats.

Casey moves the hose and sprinklers to the back yard. Dolly washes the windows in front. Manny and Robin trim back the few bushes and trees.

Dom and Jeffrey, another couple from up the street, work on the roof. They straighten tiles, clean the gutters, and put all the underwear they find in one big pile.

Ethel, a faded, down-to-earth old woman from across the street—and yes, her name is really Ethel—does something with a small gardening tool near the front porch.

Jessica scrubs my woefully chipped stucco. Mia helps her.

Mia's parents dragged her over here two hours ago then waved as they left for their son Dylan's football game. I asked Mia whether she wanted to go too, whether all her friends would be there, but she claimed she wanted to stay here.

All these people are jumping in to spruce up the house

that has been bringing down their property values for years. Except for Mia, who was sent as proxy for her parents.

Nobody's even asked me my last name or where I've moved from or anything. They don't care about me. I don't *count*. All they care about is my house.

Part of me wants to kick them all off my property. Every one of them. I sigh as I kneel on the driveway to start washing off lewd phrases and explicit pictures. I begin to scrub and my stomach growls.

Of course! I want food, and I bet I'm not the only one. Why didn't I think of that before? Food always works.

Twenty minutes later, I return from the supermarket with all the supplies I need to win these people over. I will transform their calculated kindness into true camaraderie.

I spread an assortment of quilted moving blankets across the lawn, then start laying out the picnic. All sorts of cold-cuts, spreads, breads, condiments, drinks, and snacks abound. I even got Jessica to bring two lawn chairs from her house for Dolly and Ethel.

"Come and get it!" I beam at them all and beckon, and they flock to me like pigeons.

Dolly, however, balks at the lawn chair. "I'm not a rickety old relic," she announces. "I can have a picnic as easily as the next person!" With that, she plops down on the blanket.

Ethel, it seems, is not to be outdone by the flashier old lady. She says, "Same goes for me. I still do all my own gardening, so I think I'm capable of sitting on a lawn." She eases herself down more gingerly.

Once everyone is settled, Manny looks around pointedly. "Any Diet 7-Up?"

Seriously, Manny? Who buys Diet 7-Up? "Um, don't think so," I say. "How 'bout ..."

"It's okay," Robin interrupts. "I'll run across and get

him one."

"Get me two," he shouts as she crosses the street.

"So," Jessica says, leaning toward me with a sparkle in her eye, "what made you buy this place and save us all? I can't tell you how happy we all are." She bites into her dainty turkey sandwich, probably being careful not to get too hippy for Casey.

"I needed a place," I tell her, "and dreaded looking. I spotted this one below any realtor's radar, so I jumped."

"Far be it from that cheapskate Turner to use a realtor," Dolly chips in. "Of course it was 'For Sale by Owner.' He wasn't going to give anyone a piece of the profits."

"Except," Casey corrects, "all the workmen he's ripped off over the years who had liens on the property."

"He sounds awful," I chime in.

"Well, I bet he bilked you good."

"Manny!" Robin returns with his sodas. "What's the matter with you? How can you be so rude?"

"I'll be right back," Jessica says, putting down her soda and getting up. "Bathroom," she explains.

But her attempt to distract conversation away from the subject of money and how much I squandered does not work for longer than the time it takes her to get to her own front door.

"How much did you pay?" Manny asks.

Dom shoots him a look. "I'm sure you didn't get bilked." He puts a reassuring hand on my arm and looks to Jeffrey for back-up.

But I have to give Jeffrey credit. He can't lie, even to side with his true love. "It doesn't matter," he says. "We're thrilled to have you. And we're going to paint this place tomorrow, after we take you to get the colors of your choice. Once we all put in a little more elbow grease, you're going to love it here."

I look around at all of them, and decide they're not so

calculating after all. "I already do."

"I'm surprised you didn't buy a bigger place." This from Ethel, who hasn't addressed me directly all morning. Not even when she showed up with her three-pronged gardening tool.

"Because of all the dogs?" I ask. "We'll all fit here, just fine. We just need some time to settle."

"I mean because of all your money."

Everyone stops eating and looks at me.

"Money?" Dom asks.

Ethel speaks up again. "You *are* Lisa Flyte, aren't you?"

Great. Ethel must be one of those women who religiously reads tabloids, committing every article to memory in case aliens ever try any funny stuff with her.

"I am," I say quietly. "But I didn't get nearly the amount the papers have been reporting."

"You're rich?" Mia squawks, her eyes getting huge. "And you live in *this* neighborhood? You could live anywhere! In Beverly Hills or Bel Air! You could live next to famous people, like Justin Bieber or Johnny Depp!"

"Doesn't Johnny Depp live in France?" I ask. Please, please let everyone start talking about Johnny Depp now.

But everyone just stares at me. Not one of them joins in to talk about Johnny Depp.

I feel a hand on my arm. I look around to see Dom looking into my eyes, his concern as palpable as warm, fluffy nougat. "How do you feel, honey? Are you all better from the accident?"

The instant lump in my throat is so huge I cannot answer. No one has EVER asked me that before. I open my mouth, try to speak, but I can't.

Instead, I start crying.

"Dom!" Jeffrey turns to him and whacks him with the back of his hand. "Look what you've done!"

"No," I snuffle. "That's the nicest thing—" I choke up with embarrassing, racking sobs. "My parents," I try to explain, "and my sister ... and my stupid brother ... and Rick ... they were all mean to me, all tricking me. Then Jack ... on the mountain ..." I peter off and try to smile, but they all seem to have stood up and backed away.

Except Dolly, who sits regally munching a cracker, and Ethel, who eats a roll of ham like she hasn't got a care in the world. Casey has a particularly clueless look on his face as Jessica, just back from the bathroom, looks at him curiously. Mia stares at me open-mouthed. Only Dom doesn't desert me.

He puts an arm around me and squeezes. "It's been rough, hasn't it?"

I look at him and nod. "But I'm done screwing up. I really am. I'm gonna be such a great neighbor, just you—"

Manny's strangled cry cuts me off. "What the hell!" he bellows. "I've got beer all over my ass!"

* * * * *

Eleven o'clock on Sunday night, and I'm taking a shower. It's the first chance I've had all day! I lean my head back into the spray and laugh. My weekends have *definitely* improved. My life is getting more constructively busy by the minute. Which is amazing, really, especially after the beer-ass incident yesterday morning.

How could I have been so stupid? I prepared a picnic on a freshly watered lawn that had been doused by nothing but beer for years. So, all my neighbors had butts wet with cheap beer.

On the upside, though, they all stuck around after that, convinced more than ever that I needed help. And I'm pretty sure that Mia had a downright good time. After all, none of the adults treated her like a second-class kid. Instead, she was one of the crew. She did a hell of a job on my driveway. I hadn't been able to get all the markings off the pavement, so she set about with some paint, turning the random marks and partial obscenities into flowers and leaves and butterflies. Now the driveway looks like a psychedelic flying carpet from the seventies. It's awesome.

"An atypical driveway, to be sure," I said, coming up behind her, "but a gorgeous one."

She turned and beamed at me. "You think so?"

"You've got a talent for making things pretty," I noted. "Cool. Maybe you can help me work on the interior of my place in the next couple weeks."

"Really?" she asked.

I'm not sure if I meant it for real when I first said it, but as soon as she bit on the offer, I figured, why the heck not? Going with a high school girl as an interior designer is a definite step up for me. After all, my current décor was decided by a bunch of drunken frat boys.

My shower curtain, for instance. As I lather up, I look around at the glossy bevy of mostly-naked women posing lewdly and throwing suggestive looks my way. The curtain came with the house.

I used to have this beautiful sepia shower curtain dusted with tea roses that reminded me of romantic photos from the 1920's. But the dogs tore it apart first thing.

And I didn't have time to get a new shower curtain due to the cataclysmic pace of my life in recent days. So, now I've got tacky babes in Day-Glo colors undressing for me. It's like a porno version of *South Pacific*.

I squeeze shampoo into my hair and start singing. The dogs start barking, as if to tune me out, so I sing louder. I can sing as loudly as I want. After all, this is *my* house.

Duh-nuh-nuh-nuun. Duh-nuh-nuh-nuun.

My body jerks at the sudden, unrecognizable sound

buzzing through to the bathroom. "Ahhh!" I slip. I gyrate. I scream again. I grab onto the shower curtain. I catch myself from falling. I settle, standing kind of tilted, one shoulder resting against the shower wall.

Leaning there with the curtain as my anchor, heart racing, I realize that the weird, robotic sound is my doorbell. A digitalized recording of Beethoven's Fifth. Who would invent such a demented doorbell?

I try to pull myself into a straightened standing position so I can quickly rinse myself.

I hear a loud crash, a whine, a yelp.

Oh, no! Someone's hurt. I jump out of the tub, right into the shower curtain, my weight yanking it down. More yelping, hissing and growling.

"Stop it!" I bolt out of the bathroom, visions of Pacquito ripping into one of the cats blasting through my mind in vivid red.

"Stop it! Stop it! Stop it!" I run into the hall, shower curtain stuck to my wet skin. "Stop it! Stop it! Stop it!" I jump over a knocked-down table as I head past the front door toward the living room. Fred and Ginger jump around barking, watching Pacquito wrestle one of the cats.

"Pacquito!"

Pacquito jerks his head wildly, trying to get one of the tabby cats off his face. He succeeds in sending her flying across the room, and I see that it's Blanche. She lands safely on the floor, but then springs back onto his face.

I dive into the fray. "Pacquito! Blanche! Pacquito! Blanche!"

Aaron and Christian are going nuts in the backyard. Someone at the door is pounding and calling my name over and over. I just scream and scream. Blood smears off Pacquito and Blanche and onto me, but I don't know who the blood belongs to! I yank Blanche off Pacquito, but she twists in my arms and springs onto my head.

"Aaaah!"

Pacquito jumps on me trying to get at her, shredding the shower curtain plastered to my body. Blanche jumps off me, racing to slide under the couch. Pacquito goes after her, but he's not quick enough to catch her. When he slams his muzzle into the bottom of the couch, I know she's safe. She left no trail of blood, but Pacquito leaves a crimson smear on the couch. The blood belongs to him. His muzzle is dotted with claw pricks but at least his eyes seem fine.

He forgets Blanche and rushes to the door to bark at it. "Will you shut up!" I shout at the door, "I'm fine!"

"Open this door!"

"Just hold on!" I adjust the shreds of the curtain as I work my way to the door.

I'm gonna punch him. His ringing, pounding, and shouting have already cost me another shower curtain, not to mention a hall table and a near-heart attack.

"Excuse me!" I shout at the dogs who are rioting in front of the door. "I said ''Scuze me!'" They still don't listen. So, I start to shove my way through, grabbing scruffs and tails when I can. I really need to look into collars.

Fred, at least, backs away from the door, runs in a few circles, then leaps onto the couch and continues his barking from there. I make it to the door, but before I can look through the peep hole, Pacquito jumps on me, paws on my back, causing my forehead to thunk against the door. "Ow!"

Just then, the door gets kicked in, sending me flying back. I land hard, with my bare wet butt smacking the floor. I'd be laid out flat if my head hadn't come to rest against the shredded padding at the bottom of the couch.

"Lisa? Jesus, are you okay?"

I look up.
"God damn it, Jack. This is all your fault."

CHAPTER 12

When I was a pre-teen dreamer, I had this soft-focus fantasy of someday finding a hero who would come to my rescue, protect me, and take care of me, no matter what. It took a long time, but I finally found him.

His name is Fred.

Fred leaps from his position on the couch and lands on my chest.

"Uh!" I say, but not on purpose—the air just comes jutting out of my body.

Then, as Ginger and Pacquito wriggle up to greet Jack, my hero Fred stands strong to defend me. He digs his paws into me as he barks and growls at my intruder.

"Lisa?" Jack steps toward me. He squares off against Fred, ignoring the other two dogs snuffling and writhing in a Mags-like play for attention.

"Jack," I say, lifting one hand to stop him, like Diana Ross trying to stop him in the name of love. I use the other hand to stroke Fred and calm him down. The dog slides his feet off my body and stands straddling me.

I manage to get myself into a sitting position, so I take Fred in my arms, shushing him and crooning to him. I lift my eyes toward Jack. "It's okay. They're just not used to visitors."

Not that you could tell from Pacquito and Ginger,

who're practically taking Jack's coat and offering him prosciutto wrapped melon balls. Mr. Talks-to-the-Animals seems to notice them then, the wraith of a greyhound and the mutt in a cast.

He looks up with a bewildered expression befitting a man who just woke up on a different planet with a different haircut. His eyes drift over what he can see of my house, with its overturned table, torn curtains, lewd graffiti on the walls, and ripped living room furniture with the stuffing everywhere.

No sense cleaning it up until the pets've done their worst. Right?

Jack just stares down at me, moving his head and opening his mouth a few times like he's going to say something. I'm thinking he doesn't know where to begin in pronouncing judgment on my current situation—abode, attire, home furnishings, domestic companions. You name it, I'm sure I don't measure up.

"You're bleeding," he finally says, crouching down in front of me. Fred sniffs at him, and then licks his face.

"It's not my blood," I say with a certain degree of truculence. The dogs already like Jack better than they like me. And I'm the one who upended my life for them!

"Listen," he says, looking me up and down. At least, looking at what he can see of me through the three wriggling dogs.

"Why don't you ... finish showering, and I'll clean up this guy's face?"

He looks at Pacquito's muzzle and says to him, "What do you think of that, Big Guy?"

Jack is already male bonding with MY dog.

"Fine." I get up carefully, trying to keep what's left of the shredded plastic between my body and Jack's eyes. "There are paper towels in the kitchen next to the sink."

"Nice shower curtain."

"Screw you." I turn and make my way back toward the bathroom.

"I can see your butt," Jack calls after me.

I can hear the smirk in his voice. Man, he's awfully fresh, seeing as how he's caused so much trouble. I whip the strips of plastic off my skin and let the mangled curtain drop to the floor.

"If you run real fast and get in front of me," I offer, "you can see the whole shebang."

Just then I realize he *will* see the whole shebang, in profile, when I turn into the hallway. Ah, who cares? He's in *my* house after all, *uninvited*. I can walk around naked and soapy if I want.

* * * * *

After my curtainless shower, I make my way to my bedroom and close myself inside. Taking a deep breath allows me to absorb the ambiance of the tiny room. I let the essence of my perfect sanctuary work its magic. I've made the bed with the homey quilt that reminds me of *Little House*. Curtains hung, wardrobe in place, dressing table set up. It's pretty crowded, this tiny room of mine. Nevertheless, its quiet warmth seeps into my bones like elixir from the gods.

More than anything, I want to collapse across my bed. But I know I'll fall asleep if I do. So instead, I dry my hair and get dressed in pajama pants and two T-shirts.

When I walk into the kitchen, Jack is sitting in the middle of the linoleum floor, surrounded by the boxes I haven't unpacked yet. He's petting Pacquito and Ginger, who sit in worshipful abeyance.

"Why are you here?" I ask.

He looks up, but I do not give him a chance to answer.

"And how did you find me?"

"Yesterday, I went by your place," he explains, "but Raffi told me you bought a house on Wednesday and moved. Just like that. So I went on the net to look for houses in L.A. County that just sold, then I drove around to each one, looking for your car."

"You've been looking for me since yesterday?"

"You didn't answer your cell."

"Pacquito ate it. I have to get a new one."

"You couldn't have gotten in touch with me and told me that?"

"I've been busy. And you said you had a billion things to keep you busy if I couldn't test right away."

Jack looks down at Pacquito's silky ears and strokes them. The mutt's eyes close, and he begins to hum a soft doggie grunt.

"Jack," I say. "I need an animal wrangler. Do you want to move in with me? You can have the biggest bedroom. It has its own bathroom."

He looks up at me. "You'd let the help sleep in the master bedroom?"

"*I'm* the master," I say, "and I'm not in that room, so it's *not* the master bedroom."

"Why *aren't* you in there?" he asks, suspicion darkening his brow. "What's wrong with it? Haunted?"

"No. I don't think. Nothing's wrong with it. But I don't want the animals in my bedroom, and since they need as much square footage as possible, I took the smallest room."

"So your animals could get most of the house," he says, getting clarification.

"Duh," I say. "That's why I bought it."

He looks back down at Pacquito. "I bet Raffi wasn't too thrilled when you came home one day with ..." He looks around, noting the two dogs out back, as well as Dorothy and Sophia, sitting on the counter, "... seven animals."

I open the fridge and grab myself a Coke, the only beverage in there. So far, I've moved in only the essentials.

"Twelve," I correct. "There are still five cats you haven't met. But I didn't bring them all home at once. Some stayed at the vet longer than others."

I look toward Jack, who's looking at me now. I nod toward the line of red cans in a way of offering. He nods back, so I toss him one.

"But, I managed to barter myself enough time to find a place and move out."

"Enough time?" He takes a pull from his Coke. "I last saw you–what? A week ago?"

Actually, not counting sightings of each other in class, it's been more than a week since he came to get the helmet, and I tried talking to him about his mother. "Do you want to meet the dogs out back?" I ask.

"The Rottweiler and the Mastiff?" He looks toward the kitchen door. "We introduced ourselves while you were in the shower."

"Jack, why are you even here when I'm in the shower? What's so important that you had to kick my door in?"

"I kicked your door in because I heard you screaming."

"Oh. That was nice of you." I rub the bump he gave me on my forehead when he kicked the door right into me.

"Can you test Thursday, all day?"

"All day?"

Jack extricates himself from the dogs and stands up. "Can you do it?"

I swallow. "Yes."

He walks to the front door. "I'll pick you up at 6 a.m."

I let out a wail. "In the morning?"

Jack doesn't even turn his head as he lopes down the porch steps. "Just be ready."

* * * * *

"Do you know what you have to do?"

I turn to look at Jack, but don't say anything. I just breathe. In and out. In and out. But for how much longer?

"Lisa?"

"I pull the Goddamned parachute cord when the altimeter reads 4,000 feet."

That's right. He's making me jump out of a plane. Bad enough that he made me get *on* the plane in the first place. Now he's making me jump out.

JUMP OUT!

Of a PLANE. That's FLYING!

"Or?"

"When you tell me to."

"Then?"

"Jack!" My bark is sharp enough to make the pilot glance back. "You made me get up at no-o'clock in the morning just so I could listen to EIGHT HOURS of instruction. I passed all the stupid tests. Now just let me jump in peace."

"Answer my questions, or you're not jumping anywhere."

"Is that supposed to be a threat?"

Jack pulls in a deep breath. I see his nostrils flare when he does it. He looks at me then, and even through his goggles, his stare makes my skin go cold.

"What do you do next?"

"Steer myself. With the toggle. Follow you. When I see the big X, head towards it. As I get closer to the big X, I use the cords to help steer."

"Remember, you have the reserve chute."

"I know. I know. It's going to be fine. So, just leave me alone."

Jack reaches out and grabs me by the lapels of my jumpsuit. "No, Lisa," he says sternly. "It's not going to be fine." But then his face breaks into a smile. "It's going to be *awesome*."

Some guy called Mattie gets out of his seat next to the pilot and steps into the back of the plane. "Ready?" he bellows.

I suck in my breath as he rolls open the door to the sky. At least Jack promised to take care of the animals if anything happens to me.

Jack takes my hand.

"Let's go," I say, trying to pretend none of it is real.

He leads me to the gaping door of the plane. We wedge ourselves into the opening. He lets go of my hand. "One, two—"

"Three!" I shout.

Together, we jump.

"AAAAAAAAAAHHH—"

The air catches me. The falling sensation disappears. I'm floating. Flying. Flying! Flying! FLYING!

My body stretches out. I spread my arms wide.

"Wooooooooh-aaaaaah!"

Jack has spiraled away from me. He mimics looking at his wrist. I look at my altimeter. 8,000 feet. I give Jack a thumbs up. Our eyes catch for a sec, and we smile.

"Wooooooooh-aaaaaaah!" I scream again, looking at the world all around me.

ALL AROUND ME! All around me. All around me.

I check the altimeter again, and release the chute.

I spin far away from Jack, the air jerking me up. I look across the sky. His chute opens.

I grasp onto the toggle, twist around to float in Jack's wake, take it all in. All of it. All of it. EVERYTHING.

The ground below comes into focus as more than a beige-on-beige patchwork quilt. I see the big white X. I've drifted out of Jack's wake, but I can see the X. That's all that matters.

Suddenly, the ground is coming up fast. Faster and faster.

"Jaaaack!" I twist around and see him off to my left, but he doesn't seem at all concerned that I'm barreling toward earth with the velocity of a meteor.

Jack is landing. He's landing. He's touching dow—

"Hwaah-" My feet touch earth. I run to keep up with myself and fall right on my face into the dirt.

I'm on the ground. The ground. I did it.

Rolling over, I press my back against every scrap of earth my body can cover. I take off my helmet, so even my scalp can press into the glorious ground. I fling off my goggles to better see the amazing sky which is now safely above me.

Arms flung wide, I curl my fingers into the grass, gripping on with all my might. I'm down. I'm safe. My body is held together in one wonderful, miraculous piece!

I DID IT.

"Lisa?" I can hear Jack call from some short distance.

But I'm too psyched about breathing in and out, in and out. Oh, the wonder of it!

"Lisa? Lisa!"

He runs to me, and stops just before trampling my invincible body. "Lisa?"

I look up at him and notice he's flung off his goggles and helmet too, leaving his hair messed. And he looks so concerned. About me. Damn, that Jack is a sexy guy.

He throws himself onto his knees right next to me, leans over me. "Lisa?!" He puts his hands near my face as if he wants to grab my jaw and shake it, but he doesn't touch me.

It occurs to me that maybe he thinks I've broken my back. Or my neck.

"Lisa, are you okay? Answer me!"

"I'm wonderful!" I shout on a geyser of laughter erupting from my way-alive body.

Jack exhales, smiles, relaxes.

I grab him. With both hands, I take fistfuls of the front of his suit. I yank him down onto me and kiss the daylights out of him.

Man, it feels good! I'm just so alive that I want to suck every drop of life out of him. He gets on top of me, mauling me right back. Next thing I know, he's peeled my suit, leggings, and panties down to my ankles and—

Now he's—

WOW! We get enough clothes off to slam into each other so hard my pelvic bone throbs. Wow wow wow! I just want more and more and harder and harder and faster and faster and FASTER. Yes, yes, yes, YES!!!!

CHAPTER 13

When I can breathe again, I try to move, but Jack's body on top of me keeps me down. I shift around beneath him. I even say, "C'mon," trying to get him off me. Seriously, I want to get up and run a marathon or ski down a mountain or go out for a Hail Mary on fourth and long. I'm THAT pumped. "Fuckin' A, man, get off me."

Using his arms, he levers his torso off me and looks at me. "You curse a lot."

"So?" I say, trying to get up for real this time, but he's still pinning my thighs, immobilizing my strongest asset.

"It's lazy to curse all the time. Can't you think of anything smarter to say? And a better way to say it?"

"Hey," I retort. "I was on the speech and debate team in college. I even took first place in my very first competition."

"So, I'm right. It *is* just laziness." He pulls himself off me.

"I guess it *is* lazy," I concede, pulling up my panties and leggings. "But I like to spend my energy on *other* things."

Jack zips himself up. "I thought you didn't want to be average anymore."

My head whips up as I'm fumbling with the jumpsuit around my ankles. I just alluded to what we—and he said—

"*Average*?" I choke out.

"Anyone can curse."

Average? AVERAGE?

We just HAD SEX and he called me *average*. I'm going to ... going to ... die, I think. But not in front of him. "That's what makes this country great," I note as I straighten up, zipping myself back together again. "Anyone can curse however much they want. Fuckin' liberty."

Jack turns away from me. Without another word, he goes over to gather his parachute.

I bend down to gather up mine. "Why do you even care about my freaking language?"

"It's just another thing about you that annoys the hell out of me."

"Dude, you came to me with the offer, even *after* you knew I annoyed you, so suck it up." I walk toward him, feeling buffered by the mess of parachute in my arms. "What were we testing today, anyway?"

"A camera in my helmet. A lot of consumers complain that helmet cameras wobble, so we've been working on stabilizing—"

"You fuckhead! That's not beginner gear! You made me jump just so you could laugh at me! You are SUCH A DICK!"

"And *you're* a bitch." He folds his parachute with flag-like precision. "But I guess you think that's okay now that you have all that money."

"What? How am I a bitch?"

"For one, you just called me a fuckhead. And a dick. All for giving you what you wanted."

"Giving me what I wanted?"

"You *said* you wanted to do scary stuff!"

Good God, he's already completely forgotten that we just had sex. Really average, forgettable sex.

Jack comes at me and tries to take my chute from me,

but I yank it back.

"What the fuck?" he demands, trying to take the parachute off me.

I shove the whole mess at him. "Why do you have to be so mean?"

He doesn't answer as he untangles the carnation and magenta mass of material.

I tighten my jaw. "You are such—"

"Who paid your hospital bills?" he asks, cutting me off.

This question throws me, so I answer it. "They did. Burger Barn."

"*Other* than the however many millions of dollars they settled on you?"

I refuse to feel shame or embarrassment over my settlement. "Yes." I barely open my mouth to grind out the word.

"What else did they give you? Pay your living expenses while you were in the coma? Your parents'? Keith's?"

"Yes!" I shout. "Their restaurant fell on my car! With me in it! Don't you get it?"

"What I get is that they paid for their mistake, long before they even made the settlement."

"Mistake? Is that what you call it?"

"That's what it *was*. What do your millions have to do with what happened?"

I grab one end of the parachute to help him straighten it out. I'll be damned if I'm going to let this jerk take care of me. "How is this even your business?" I ask. "And anyway, does it really matter who has the evil money, me or them?"

He just looks at me a few seconds. "I think it does."

"Why?"

He walks toward me, then takes the ends of the chute I'm holding.

"Why did they even have that much money lying around

to give you?" Jack demands. "Why don't they use their billions to pay their workers a decent wage? There's so much money in the world and it's in all the wrong places. In the hands of the wrong people."

"But my hands are good hands." I actually look down at my splayed palms. "I'm going to do something good with that money. Something that counts."

"That's why you're working at HEYA?"

"It's a start."

"I don't suppose you're doing that because you feel guilty for having the money in the first place?"

"No."

He picks up both chutes, barely acknowledging me.

"Don't you get it?" I demand. "You've talked to me. You've seen how I live, heard how I used to live. How can you not understand that I'm trying to fix my life?"

He still says nothing, acknowledges nothing.

"Jack—"

"Here comes the jeep."

I look toward the horizon and see a yellow range rover. I turn back to Jack but he looks so flinty, like anything I say will just spark right off him and ricochet back to burn me in the eye. I can tell he doesn't think my piddly life is worthy of so much money.

"Besides," I blurt, "what's wrong with doing things out of guilt?"

He looks up at me. "I can't believe you just asked me that."

"I'm serious."

He turns around and walks toward the approaching truck, as if he's going to meet it half way. "I *know*."

I talk to his back. "I mean it. What's wrong with trying to do good things because you feel guilty? If you've messed up, and you can never fix what you screwed up in the first place, why not do good things and live a better life because you're sorry and you don't want to mess up again?"

He turns to me, his stare boring into me like that earbug in *Wrath of Khan*. "Money can't fix things like that. It can cause pain, but it can't take it away like a goddamn Swiffer."

"A. Money can fix a lot of things. B. How do you know what a Swiffer is?"

"I own a house," he says. "And I clean it when it gets dirty."

My forehead bunches up. "You don't have a maid? I thought everyone in L.A.—"

"I'm only one guy and I can clean up after myself," he says. "And guess what else? I do my own laundry."

I know I should try to come up with some witty retort, but I'm so befuddled at the thought of Jack measuring out fabric softener that I honestly can't speak.

* * * * *

When Jack drops me back at my place less than an hour later, I'm starving. I figure he must be, too. "How 'bout something to eat?" I can tell he's going to say No. Maybe No Way. "I've got some fried chicken that Dolly brought over last night."

Jack opens his mouth as if he's about to diss me. Then he looks at me. "Wait. I thought you were a vegetarian."

"I'm *trying*," I tell him. "But it's fried chicken, made by a woman who grew up in Alabama. And besides, she gave it to me as a present, and I don't want to be rude."

Jack juts his jaw, thinking. "Genuine Southern Fried Chicken?" He says it with such reverence.

"Mmm-hmm."

"Fair enough. I'm in."

We both race out of the truck then charge through the front door. But on the way to the kitchen, I stop. The answering machine is blinking at me.

Weird.

Very few people have my number. Pretty much just Jack. And Jack is right here.

Jack sees me walk cautiously up to the machine. "It's a pretty new, untested invention," he says, "but I'm almost positive it won't bite you."

I just stare down at the blinking light. "You're here," I say, trying to explain my confusion. "No one else has my number. I mean, I put it on the paperwork at HEYA, but ..."

Jack comes up to me. "Do you think they've found you?" There's such concern in his voice, concern that the big, bad media might be out to take embarrassing pictures of me again, that I feel like a wimp.

I tear my eyes from the hypnotic light and look at him. "I doubt anyone's even looking," I say on a laugh. "I guess I've just gotten used to my little cocoon."

"Lisa, you just jumped out of a plane. You can push the button."

"Of course I can," I chirp back quickly. "It's probably just Lupe." I keep smiling at him and nodding, until I realize I actually have to push the damn thing.

So I put my finger on the button, close my eyes, and press.

Beeeeep.

"Hi," Manny's voice greets. Wasn't that nice of him to agree to do this for me? "Leave a message. *Ruff ruff! Arf*!" I like that I was even able to get Aaron and Christian to harmonize at the end of the greeting. It makes the message really say, "I'm a tough guy with big dogs, so back off!"

The message begins. "Cripes, Lisa."

Good God, it's Maggot-Face. Her voice is in my house. Yuck.

"Are you trying to sound like Tattoo from *Fantasy Island*? Because I can tell it's you. That's really lame. Anyway, after Paris, Rick and I got married in Italy, so I just wanted to let you know. We're registered at Pottery Barn, Brookstone and Nordstrom, plus you can find a list of our favorite boutiques at maggieandrickinsomuchlove.com. Bye." *Beeeep.*

When the message ends, my breathing pumps so hard it makes this echoey, raspy sound. I'm pretty sure there's also fire coming out of my ears.

"Your sister, I take it?"

"I HATE KEITH!"

"Lisa." Jack's voice is quiet, so I ignore him.

Huff, heeee, huff, heeee.

"Lisa," he says again.

Huff, huff, huff, huff—

"Lisa?"

I turn to look at him, so mad that I don't even care that tears gush down my face.

Jack lifts his hands and allows them to hover, one above each of my shoulders for a few seconds, before he sighs, and lowers them so he's touching me. "You know, Lisa, marriage isn't all it's cracked up to be."

I fling his hands from my shoulders. "I know that! Is that what you think? That I'm mad at Keith because he didn't marry me? Well, seeing that he didn't even love me I'd say it's a pretty good thing that he didn't marry me!"

"Lisa ..."

"That *bastard* is giving out my phone number!"

Jack snaps out of shoulder-to-lean-on mode. "What?"

I stride across the living room, kicking empty moving

boxes. “When I first moved in, I called Keith.” I turn back to Jack. “It was stupid, I know. I was lonely and depressed and I had a box of his stuff. What a lame excuse! Like what? He’s going to want his Deep Blue Something CD back? I wasn’t even thinking about caller ID. Then *he* called *me* a few days later to tell me to trash the stuff. That's when I realized he had my number.”

“Maybe he won’t—”

“Don’t you get it?” I throw myself down on the couch and look up at him. “My family called Keith, and he gave them my number. None of them were supposed to have it. This is my castle. My island. My Helena.” I sit panting.

“Helena?” Jack echoes.

“The island. Napoléon?”

“You mean *Saint* Helena?”

“I don’t care. Whatever. I don’t want my family here. They’re talking behind my back to work their way in.”

Jack sits next to me as I slump against the back of the couch.

“They don’t even like me,” I say, “but they won’t leave me alone. Why can’t they just leave me alone?”

“Because you’re the runt.”

“Excuse me?”

“Everyone has a role in a family.” His hand moves toward my head, lingers, then musses my hair like I’m a kid. “Regardless of who you become or how you grow, your family sees you in your role. You’re the runt, the one everyone else gangs up on. That’s not going to change just because you’ve become a millionaire.” He pauses. “And made them all millionaires, too.”

I turn my head to look at him. “You know about that?”

“I figured it out.”

“They were so intent on getting that money,” I say. A

shaky sob rattles out of me, catching me off guard. "Just hours after I woke up."

I see a muscle in Jack's jaw jump, but he doesn't say anything. He doesn't want to hear my pathetic story and I don't want to tell it.

"It doesn't matter," I say. "It's just that, I don't want them in my life anymore."

"They're your family. It won't be so easy to shake them off."

"So?" I challenge. "I don't HAVE to include them in my life if I don't want to."

"So, tell them that. Confront them. Make them understand exactly where you stand."

I bolt up from the couch and turn to stand over him. "Confront them? Am I hearing right? *You're* giving me advice about how to handle my family? Are you *kidding* me? You with the mother made of snots and snails?"

Jack stands to face me. "Lisa, you're the one who wants me to make you braver."

"I'm not scared of my family!"

"Right." He doesn't raise his voice or even blink. "Everyone's scared of their family."

I close my mouth. Really? Is that true? Everyone? Even Mags? And Mom? And Jack?

"Well," I finally say, "that's not the kind of courage I'm after. Not from you anyway." I flounce away from him into the kitchen.

"Yes, it is."

The stony resolution of his voice stops me in my tracks. I hear him walking up behind me. "It's all the same, Lisa. The courage it takes to jump out of a plane isn't so different from the courage it takes to tell your family who you really are."

I turn to him. "How profound, Jack. Really. I'm touched

by your sensitivity. But there's a difference between physical courage and emotional courage."

"Not really," he says, standing there with each hand on opposite sides of the doorjamb into the kitchen.

So here I stand, practically enveloped in Jack's wingspan. Suddenly, I remember we had sex a little over an hour ago. But that's just so impossible.

Oh, God.

I can't look at him. I can't. If I do, he'll know I'm thinking about it, and he won't ever want to see me again for any reason. Then I'll never get brave. I just have to forget it and box it into a separate part of my brain like guys do.

"One may be easier than the other," Jack is saying, "but it all has to do with your mind, Lisa. With flipping that switch in your brain that turns off the fear. Whether it's fear of bungee jumping or of asking someone to the prom, it's all a matter of flipping the switch."

"You're the expert, Braveheart." Shrugging him off, I walk across the scarred linoleum, open the fridge, and scan the contents. "Can we just shut up now and eat? Or did you change your mind about the Southern Fried Chicken?" I take the platter out of the fridge.

"I haven't changed my mind about anything."

"'Course not," I say, slamming the fridge door. "That'd be too much like being wrong."

Jack just laughs, heading toward the refrigerator as I move toward the counter. "I'm gonna grab a Coke, you freak. Want one?"

"Yes, please," I mutter, biting into a drumstick.

* * * * *

Ten past midnight and I cannot get to sleep.

I keep replaying the day in my head. Mostly, I keep replaying the part after the sex.

AFTER THE SEX. I had *sex* with Jack. With Jack.

But I don't think about the sex. Or I try not to, anyway. Because he called me *average* just after. Average. So I cannot think about it much without all of my skin burning with humiliation.

I fast-forward to the part of my day when we arrived at my house and we talked and ate. Talked and ate. As if the sex never happened. Ever.

I know why *I* ignored the fact that we'd had sex. *I* was in shock after his calling me *average*. Seriously. My body and mind simply refused to acknowledge the possibly life-ending trauma. I'm just like that woman in the first chapter of *Jaws* who thinks she's simply scraped her leg on some coral. Her body and mind will not let her process that a shark has just bitten off her leg. Until she reaches down to feel the scratch on her leg, *but her leg's no longer there*. Every time I think about the sex and how Jack called me average, I feel like I'm reaching down to discover my leg is missing.

I pull the English Christmas comforter over my head. Today, Jack acted as if nothing happened between us because for him, nothing did. Okay, he came. Big deal. He probably gives himself more satisfying orgasms in the shower. Because I'm sure the hand of Jack Hawkins is anything but *average*.

How could he have sex with me then call me average? Was I really the only one who felt such a rockin' climax? I guess I was. Damn. This isn't the first time I was the only one feeling anything. Take my entire relationship with Keith.

Maybe the sex this afternoon wasn't so hot. Maybe I thought it was so good simply because I was jazzed by my bizarre bravado. I mean, I've had sex with boyfriends before, but until today, I'd never attacked a gorgeous guy on a barren stretch of field. I've never even had a one-night stand.

It must have really freaked him out, how disappointing I was. After it was over, he must have been telling himself "Don't say anything. Don't say anything. For God's sake, don't say anything about how boring she was." But then that one thing he was trying so hard not to say just popped out. *I thought you didn't want to be average anymore*.

I curl into a tight ball and suck on the corner of my comforter.

That was why he was fighting with me about such stupid stuff. My cursing and my money and everything. He was desperately trying to cover up his huge faux pas of telling me I was average right after we had sex.

Well, at least it didn't change anything. The sex I mean. The deal is still on. It must be. Jack was Jack from the orgasm on. Still acting all superior and complaining about me. For him, the ill-advised romp was just some let down he's already forgotten. I hope.

Oh yeah, Lisa Flyte. I knew her once. Lousy lay.

I cringe but can't compress myself into a tighter ball.

Oh, no! Charlie horse Charlie horse Charlie horse CHARLIE HORSE! "No, no, no, no!" I snap into a sitting position and rub my calf muscle hard, trying to forestall the intense pain.

But it doesn't work.

"Oooooowww! Ow! Ow! Ow!" I collapse back onto the bed as the severe muscle cramp finally relaxes. Jack! Calling me average then giving me a Charlie horse.

Jesus. Why do I even care? So what if he thought I was average? He still had an orgasm, and it only took a few minutes, if that. Where does he get off being disappointed?

Why am I even thinking about Jack? He's so not even worth it. After all, what happened with Jack today hardly counts as sex at all. We didn't exactly "have sex." I mean, we didn't touch enough to call it that. We fucked. Plain and simple. No relationship hassle, no wondering if I can trust anything he says, no wondering if he loves me, no wondering if he's after my five million bucks. Just a quick wham-bam-thank-you-ma'am, and I can handle that. Over and done. Good. Fine. He'll never be a guy I bring into my beautiful bed. For just so many reasons.

Number One: He doesn't like me.

Number Two: He comes from money, which is like coming from a different planet as far as I'm concerned.

Number Three: He hates the fact that I got money from Burger Barn.

Number Four: He thinks he knows so much more than I do about people and how they work when really he's just as clueless as the rest of us and it's very annoying that he does not realize this.

Number Five: He's probably a huge bed hog who flings his entire body across the mattress, barely leaving anyone else a corner.

Number Six: What if I started caring about him? His life is way too scary and I would worry all the time and get wrinkles.

Number Seven: Our last names are too ridiculous. Hawkins. Flyte. Hawk in Flight. No way.

Number Eight: He's probably NOT a New York Giants fan.

Number Nine: Jack doesn't get me. At all. I want to do something important and something helpful.

I roll over in my big, beautiful bed. I punch my pillow. Nothing between Jack and me has changed. Nothing.

I get out of bed and open the door. By the time I re-cross the room and snuggle back under the covers, Pacquito and four cats have joined me.

CHAPTER 14

"Come on."

"Come on what?" I toss back, my pulse picking up. I tighten my grip on the receiver, hoping my voice sounds casual. Nonchalant, even.

"What do you say we do something for real. Go out to dinner with me."

"That definitely wasn't part of our deal," I remind him, keeping my voice light and airy. But my heart is hammering right through my ribcage. I bite my lip to force myself to get under control. "I can't do anything to jeopardize this."

"Don't tell me you're not interested."

"Wouldn't dream of it," I assure him. "But I'm more interested in saving HEYA, so I'm making a choice."

"Well, when this deal finally goes through ..."

"I'll have you to thank," I tell him.

When Crispin hangs up, I shove my hands into my hair, cradling my head. I didn't mean that last comment to be flirty. I really didn't. But I don't entirely mind if he took it that way. Am I being a tease? Am I using my feminine wiles to save HEYA? I shake my hand-held head, trying to forget about Crispin Joyner and what he thinks I might do.

"What the hell?" Edgar barks.

By the time I look up, he's closed himself into my office

with me.

"Time is ticking away," he harsh-whispers at me. "And you haven't saved HEYA yet. Stop relaxing."

"No, I—"

"Did you mess up the plan?" he demands.

I can't stop the smile threatening to split me apart. "I got my first investor today!"

The harsh Alpha male line running down the middle of Edgar's forehead falls away as he steps back. "Really?"

"Really!"

"Who?" he asks.

"Crispin Joyner," I answer. "He owns Got Game. One store here and one in Lincoln—"

"I know who he is," Edgar interrupts. Then he smiles. Edgar actually SMILES at me. "Score, Lisa! *Everybody* knows who he is. Ever since he was at USC. Did you invite him to the Spaghetti Supper?"

I cannot suppress the smug grin. In fact, I don't even try. "I even got him to *advertise it* in his stores!"

Edgar gives me a high five. "Man, Lisa! Do you know what this means?"

My buoyancy deflates into a weak smile.

"What's the problem?"

"I'm pretty sure he thinks it means I'm going to sleep with him."

"Are you?"

I consider. "Dunno." I look up at Edgar. "I told him that after the deal goes through, I'd have him to thank. Do you think he expects me to show up at his house in a cheerleading outfit or something?"

Edgar shrugs. "Save HEYA, then put out if you have to."

"Uh, really? I can just do that?"

Edgar laughs. Snickers, actually.

"It's not funny," I tell him.

"Lisa," he explains, "people with money like other people with money. Get used to it."

Edgar opens the door to my office, sees Jimmy down the corridor, and takes off in that direction. He tries to look all bad-ass and aloof at the same time. And pulls it off.

What does he mean, *people with money like other people with money*? Crispin Joyner likes me because I'm so sassy and quirky and savvy in emails and over the phone. And Jack has money but he doesn't like me at all. He thinks I'm *average*.

* * * * *

My alarm rings, so I push the snooze again. Another night of not getting to sleep until four because my mind would not stop replaying how *average* I am. Damn, I need more sleep. I can't move anything but my snooze-button arm. I really can't. I have four cats and two dogs on me. Plus it's really early.

Duh nuh nuh nuh.

The doorbell! I look at the clock. Past seven? How did that happen? I only pushed the snooze button ... oh, hell.

Bolting up, I yank myself into the jammies tossed to the bottom of the bed. Then I careen toward the front door. "Sorry!" I'm yelling as I swing it open through the dogs.

But Mia just stands there laughing. "It's okay," she says, coming in and noticing me in my pjs. "You overslept. Big deal."

"But it's so inconsiderate," I counter. "You got up early on a weekend."

"Yeah, but it's easy for me. I'm a lot younger."

* * * * *

Twenty minutes later, we stand in the living room. All the cats are in the garage with my furniture, except for Wash, who I couldn't find. He better have the sense to say hidden.

Mia surveys the scene: bare house, plastic on the floor. “Perfect,” she says. “I always thought your house was kind of crappy, and I guess it is, but it makes it a lot easier to paint with no trim or molding or anything.”

“What was left of it I pried off before the guys came this week to install the new windows. Anyway,” I chide, “you’re my decorator, so it better not be crappy when we’re done.”

She turns to look at me, her eyes gleaming. “It’s going to look so fantastic with the fake wood trim we got.”

“It’s not fake. It’s maple ... or something that grew.”

“But it wasn’t built into the house,” she argues. “I know it’s real wood, but we’re adding it on.”

“So? Do you think the old molding was born here? Someone had to add it on at some point.”

Mia crinkles her forehead. “Hm. I never thought about it like that. I guess you’re right.” She sweeps her gaze across the room. “Yeah, it’s going to be beautiful.”

“Better be.”

“Well,” she says, turning to me, all bright and eager, “let’s get started.”

“Wait.”

“Why?” she asks, flicking at the wheel of a paint roller.

I whip a dust cloth off my little black CD player. “Ta-da! We’ve got tunes.”

“Nooo,” Mia groans. “You’re going to make me listen to eighties music.”

“And seventies and nineties and even some current stuff,” I assure her, pushing PLAY.

As the opening drumming of “Burning Down the

House" throbs through the floorboards, Mia can't help but get her groove on. Neither can I.

* * * * *

Two CDs later, Mia and I brush the finishing strokes of sage green onto the living room walls as we bop our butts to Bonnie Raitt. Caterwauling to the heavens, Mia turns to me to harmonize, I'm pretty sure. "*A little mystery to figure out* ..." Suddenly, her eyes grow huge. "Aaaah!"

Something brushes my shoulder. "Aaaaah!"

"Lisa!"

I spin around. The sight of Jack right there makes me jump and scream again. He reaches out as if to put a hand on me to calm me down.

"Whaa-!" Jack jumps back as Mia attacks him with her roller.

"Mia!" I laugh. "Mia, it's okay!" I stumble to the CD player and click it off. "Jack," I pant, "This is Mia. Mia, this is Jack."

Mia, who holds Jack at bay with her goopy paint roller, turns to me. "*This* is Jack?" She looks back at him, then back at me. "The old guy from your MBA class?"

"I never said he was old," I deny. But really, I might have given her that impression. I mean, I didn't want her to think I had a crush on the guy.

"Man." Jack looks down at the gobs of green paint slashed across his T-shirt and arms.

"Serves you right for not knocking." I walk over to my Dasani and take a swig.

"I *did* knock," he says. "And I called your cell. Three times."

I crinkle my brows. "Why?"

Jack goes into the kitchen and comes back with his own Dasani. “We’re working on a project together. Do you want to fail?”

“Fail *what*?” I bark back.

Jack just looks at me.

Oh. I get it. He’s slipping right into our cover story. Wow. He doesn’t even sound like he’s lying. “*I* never fail anything,” I toss back at him. “Anyway, I’m busy today. Mia and I are painting the house.”

Jack looks around the room, frowning at all the passionate daubs of green. “Hm.”

“Shut up,” I say.

“Yeah,” Mia says. “It’s going to look *awesome*.”

We both turn to look at her. She sounds so ... right.

“Cool,” Jack says. “Will it take all day? Can we test some theories later on?”

Theories. Hmm. I look at him. He’s looking at me.

Sex sex sex, that’s all I think.

I wonder suddenly if he realizes this. Oh, God. I feel a hot blush surge into my cheeks, so I drop my brush on the plastic-covered floor so I can bend down to pick it up.

“Damn.” The brush landed on my shoe.

“Do you have time later?” Jack asks again.

“No,” I say. “Mia and I are going to whip this house into shape today.”

Jack nods. “Okay.” He lifts his eyebrows. “Since I'm here,” he looks down at his smeared shirt, “and dressed for painting, can I help?”

I look at Mia. We're having a barrel full of girl-fun, but we're not idiots.

“Big bedroom?” she suggests, shrugging.

“Big bedroom,” I say to Jack. “Paint, rollers, and brushes are already in there. Hunter green.”

"Will do," he says, and heads down the hall. "By the way," he calls back, "I like the Ramones."

"What are 'Ramones?'" Mia asks.

I sift through my CD's and choose one. "The best band ever."

"Ah." Mia sounds smug, like one who finally gets the joke and isn't impressed.

"What?" I ask.

"Jack," she says, looking like the cat that ate the parrot. "The *old* guy from your class."

"What about him?"

She looks toward the hall, then back at me, giving me a knowing smile. "He knew exactly which room was the big bedroom."

* * * * *

I try to sit up, but I'm too exhausted. I just keep staring at the living room ceiling, wondering what I've been wondering all day. *Why is Jack here*? Does he think we're having an affair? Are we? I have no idea. Sure, he thinks I'm average, but some guys'll have sex with anything, I guess. But it's one matter to stop by hoping for a quick bonk, and entirely another to spend the day painting. Who on *earth* would want to have sex *that* badly? And let's face it, Jack Hawkins could have sex with just about anybody he wanted. So, why is he here? Is my house so pathetic that he felt he just *had* to help? Does he feel *responsible* for me?

"Well," Mia says, "I'm outta here."

"Where ya goin'?" I ask, rousing myself to pay attention.

"Dinner with the folks," she yawns.

"Dinner?" I squawk, sitting up. "We just polished off

two pizzas!"

"You and Jack ate most of 'em," she points out.

"Did not," Jack mutters, from across the room where he's stretched out on the floor.

I get up and walk her to the front door.

Jack gets up and follows us. "Nice meeting you," he tells Mia.

"Right back atcha. See ya both." She turns and jogs down the steps.

Jack and I stand in my doorway and watch her cross the street. The night air smells like rain, feels like fall back home.

"I'm going, too," Jack says, sliding across the threshold. He stands facing me in the dim glow of the front porch light. "Can you test tomorrow?"

"Um, yeah."

"Be at my house at seven."

Wait. Jack's leaving? Without telling me what he was doing here all day?

When he gets to the bottom of the steps, he turns back to look at me. "Wear a bathing suit," he says. "And a T-shirt," he adds. "The tighter the better."

"Why?"

He stands with one foot on the bottom step, one hand on the porch railing. "We're going hiking, with waterfalls. Canyoneering. I've designed a special wetsuit for it. The T-shirt is for when you get hot hiking and want to peel off the top of the suit. The bathing suit is just basically underwear, to help prevent chafing or whatever."

"But..."

"Don't worry. Getting cold isn't really a concern like it is in the ocean. You'll dry off quickly with all the hiking. See you tomorrow."

Chafing? Did he actually say *chafing*? On my bikini

parts? I'm still trying to process this when I hear his truck door shut. I look up and he's already pulling away from the curb.

Chafing? We are clearly not having an affair.

* * * * *

"Lisa! Are you even listening to me?"

Swaapft!

"Jack." I swat away the branch he let zing back into my face. "I know what I'm doing. If I didn't, why did you ever let me off that stupid practice rock in the first place?"

"This last waterfall is different. The highest one you've jumped down so far was only about twenty feet."

Only? "What about the one I had to slide down?" I counter. "That rock chute or whatever was way longer than twenty feet."

"True," Jack says, "but not much higher. And you weren't on the rope."

"But you'll make sure I don't fall with that bagel thing, right? So what do I have to worry about?" I push past him and head up the trail like I have better things to do.

"Lisa—" Jack runs ahead of me and turns to face me. "I just want you to be ready, that's all. And it's a belay, not a bagel, dumbass." This time he's the one who pushes ahead, leaving me in his wake.

As I watch him stalk off, my eyes gravitate to his butt.

"Hey!" I can't believe I didn't notice it before. "Your butt's not padded! You're not even wearing a wetsuit. You get running pants!"

Jack doesn't even turn around. "My butt's not padded because I'm not a beginner and I don't need padding on my butt."

"What? Your butt's, like, invincible?"

He ignores me. "And I'm not wearing a wetsuit because I hardly ever wear a wetsuit canyoneering. I don't mind getting wet or hiking while my pants dry. Most beginners don't want their clothes to get wet, no matter how quickly the wicking dries."

"Why can't I wear wicking?" Notice how I say this as if I know what 'wicking' is.

"I just told you," Jack says. "You're testing *beginner* gear."

"No *beginner* is going to want a padded butt, I can tell you that right now. You told me corporate retreats go canyoneering. Well, there's no way Judy in accounting is going to want Harold in sales to see her with a form-fitting padded butt."

Jack stops and turns to face me. "I'll keep that in mind. How does your butt feel?"

"How does my butt feel?" I echo.

"Lisa, does it *hurt*? Any bruises or scrapes?"

"Oh." I put my hands on my caboose and pat myself down. "I think I'm okay. It feels, you know, *average*."

"Okay." Jack nods and turns. After a few steps, he stops to anchor a rope on a tree.

"Okay, what?"

"We're here, at the last fall." He uses his shoulder to point to the top of the falls. "Put on your belt."

I realize that I hear the roar of the falls, and have been hearing it for the past few minutes. I give my mind and body silent kudos for being so good at denial up until now.

I turn to look out over the falls and I see ...

I see ...

I see ...

Nothing.

NOTHING.

This can't be real. At every other fall today, when I looked over, I could see, well, the bottom. I rush toward the edge of the fall, stopping about five feet from NOTHING. The ground just ends. I get down on my hands and knees and crawl closer toward the edge. I still can't see anything below. "HOW HIGH IS THIS WATERFALL?"

"Lisa." Jack walks slowly toward me, sounding all compassionate.

"Don't come near me!" I shout. "You'll make me fall! Stay!"

"I'll stay," he says, stopping.

I crawl a little further until I'm almost at the edge, and I still can't see the bottom of the fall.

"Jack." I'm suddenly panting, "What's going on? It's like the end of the world."

"The fall is concave," he says. "The rock juts inward right when you go over the edge, so for the first ten feet or so, you won't have any foothold."

"You mean I'll just be hanging there? In space? With water pouring down on me?"

"Yes."

"With nothing to secure me but that little rope?"

"And the belay. I'll be able to slow you down and stop you if you lose control and fall."

"How far?"

"How far what?" Jack acts like he just joined the damn conversation.

"How far can I fall?"

"You're not going to fall."

"HOW HIGH IS THE FALL?"

Silence.

Silence.

Silence.

"Jack!"

"One hundred and ten feet."

One hundred and ten feet. Oh. With just a little rope? And no foothold? Just lowering myself, all my weight, supported by just that little rope? I can't even climb a ladder because I'm so afraid of supporting my own weight. In *G.I. Jane*, Viggo Mortensen leaves Demi Moore and her whole crew stranded in the middle of the ocean because even she couldn't support her own body weight enough to pull herself out of the water. And she was totally MUSCULAR.

"Lisa?"

"Yeah?"

"Are you okay?"

"Um," I say, "how do we get back to the car if, ah, I don't jump down this waterfall?"

"We hike back out the way we hiked in."

"How do we get back up all those waterfalls I already jumped down?"

"We climb."

"I don't know how to climb."

"I'd teach you."

"But it's almost dark."

"We'd camp out, tackle the hike back tomorrow."

"But it's cold. And it's gonna rain. And my pets."

"Your animals will survive for a night," he tells me.

But how does he know?

"And I've got two compact Gore-Tex sleeping bags in my pack," he adds.

I scrunch around like an inchworm to look up at him. "So you prepared for this?"

"I try to prepare for everything."

"But you prepared for my chickening out."

"It's a big waterfall."

I stand up. “Big fall, my ass. You’re not going to let anything happen to me, are you?”

“No.”

“Then let’s go,” I say, ripping off my pack to get my gear. It’s when I’m rummaging around that I notice I’m shaking.

“You’ll need to put everything in the dry pack,” Jack says quietly.

“I know!”

Other than that, he lets me vibrate as I get ready. And why shouldn’t he? I mean, this is SCARY. I’ll be controlling the descent of my own body weight one hundred and ten feet above the bottom.

Finally, I’m set. I shake out my limbs. We step into the water at the top of the falls. The rope is taut, keeping me from going over. I put my hand on the hook at my waist so I can control my descent. I back toward the edge. I back up. I back up. I stop.

Jack, who stands in the water facing me, doesn’t say anything.

“Jack,” I say. “Maybe you should go first. I can belay you.”

“I can self-belay,” he says calmly. “One more step and you’re over the edge.”

Over the edge.

“Come on,” he coaxes. “One more step.”

I try to laugh. “This isn’t exactly the moon landing, you know.”

Jack looks straight into my eyes. “Lisa, I know it’s scary. The first step into nothingness is terrifying. It’s okay. I’m not going to let anything happen to you.”

I’m not going to let anything happen to you.

For a second, I can breathe. I think I want to marry Jack, and just stay lost in those safe blue eyes forever.

"Let's face it," he laughs when I still don't move, "if I let anything happen to you, your parents'd probably sue me for everything I'm worth. They'd destroy Into the Wild, and probably even go after Hawkins United."

"My PARENTS? How could you bring them up at a time like this?"

"Lisa," Jack says, spearing me with a look. "Your parents don't think you can do this. In fact, they would laugh their hea—"

I jump. Without a word, I go backwards over the cliff.

As I leap into nothing, I swing into the rushing water, but no matter how I kick out in front of me, there's nothing there to brace myself on. Nothing, nothing, nothing! NOTHING! AND I'M JUST, I'M JUST, JUST, JUST—

I'm just swinging back and forth, gasping for breath as the cold water pelts me. I look down at my waist. Every few seconds as I swing out of the rush of water, I see the hook at my waist. When I jumped back, I must have automatically locked in that hook, stopping my descent after a few feet.

Oh, my God. I'm swinging like a big, fat, padded pendulum. Nothing holding me but the skinny rope. Nothing under me but—

NO.

Above me. Above me. I'll think about *above* me. I'll even look above me.

I look up, and through the gush of water in my face, every few seconds I think I see Jack a few feet above me, giving me a thumbs up.

"All right!" I think he shouts and laughs. "Way to go, Lisa!"

That makes me laugh. Then I let out a whoop of joy. I did it! I went over the edge! I finger the hook at my waist, then release the catch."Wooooo-hoooooooooooo!"

I go down and down and down, splashing in and out of the fall as I go go go.

"Wooooooo!"

I pull up, and just look all around. The mountains unfold before me, spreading out green-grey in the mist. I feel like an intruder in a secret primeval forest. It's so raw and vital, this cold forest, hidden away from everyone except the most intrepid. Into the wild. Maybe I understand, a little bit, what makes Jack do what he does.

I'm about half way down to the pool at the bottom, and I know I've done something amazing. From here on down, my descent will be nothing short of paradise. But I cannot give this up yet. I dangle, my mouth open and my heart hurting with all the beauty.

After what seems like an eternity, I slowly lower myself into the bath at the bottom. I signal up to Jack that it's his turn, then I get out of the way so he doesn't land on me.

My stomach seizes up when I watch Jack go over the falls, but he's okay. As he starts to rappel his way down, my heart jumps into my throat. I know he's Jack Hawkins, and all, but he's up so high. On that skinny rope.

I can't watch, so I swim around the pool until Jack is closer to the bottom. I hope he doesn't take as long as I did gaping at all the nature. I mean, Jack sees stuff like this all the time.

Finally, Jack is lowering himself into the pool and I can breathe. But I don't go near him, feeling suddenly ridiculous for having been so worried. I hover in the shallows near the wall of rock as Jack unhooks himself.

Jack swims toward me and raises a brow. "Well?" I think I see him say, but it's hard to hear at the bottom of a waterfall.

I can't keep my face from breaking into the hugest smile

ever. "I really did it!" I shout above the splash of water. "Just like you."

Jack gets his feet under him as the water becomes shallower. "Yeah," he says, still heading toward me. "You did."

"Yeah," I say. "Thank—"

But Jack doesn't hold up as he gets closer. I take a step back. "Ja—"

He sweeps into me with a kiss that takes hold of my entire body. The instant he's on me, I kiss him back. He's cold and wet and so feral I want more. More and more of Jack Jack Jack.

He unzips my wetsuit, peeling it off as he goes down on his knees. Before I know it, his face is at my—

And he's taking off my—

And his mouth is on my— "Jack!" I dig my fingers into his shoulders, wishing I could—

He stands up, pushing down his—

Oh, YES! I *love* this part.

CHAPTER 15

What am I supposed to do?

The doorbell rings again. I can't just get off the ladder and abandon the trim. The wooden strip has only one nail holding it so far, and if I let go now, it'll shift and scratch the new paint.

The doorbell rings a third time. I don't have to answer my door if I don't want to.

Finally, all the ringing and barking stops. But I hear something else. A muffled voice. "She has to be in here somewhere." Heels tapping across the floor. "Lisa!" she calls. "It's Dolly." And she's got someone with her.

I focus on the trim.

"Oh," Dolly says from the doorway. "Here you are."

I don't look over my shoulder to where she stands. "Hey, Dolly." I bang in another nail.

"Lisa!"

The grating voice hits me like a shot, jerking me nearly off the ladder.

"Lisa, what are you *doing*?" she brays.

I right myself and turn to see Mags standing with her hands jammed onto her hips. Mags. Mags is in my house. Mags is in my house.

I take a few short, measured breaths. "Dolly?" I say,

turning from Mags.

"I saw this pretty young thing on the porch," Dolly explains. "I knew you must be in here working, and when she told me she was your sister! Well, I have to get to brunch now. Love ya!" Blowing me a kiss, she scoots off, leaving Mags in my house.

"Jesus, Lisa, how long have you lived here? And you still don't have any furniture?"

* * * * *

A little while later, I slide a freshly brewed cup of coffee across the counter to Mags. I'm unclear about how much time has passed since Dolly left because I cannot recall how I got from the bedroom to the kitchen with Mags in tow. All I remember is seeing the world through a dotty, darkening haze as I muttered, "Redrum, redrum, redrum" over and over.

I take a seat on a kitchen stool and with a gesture, invite Mags to sit on the other one. These stools are the only pieces of furniture I've brought back in the house since painting, for the sole purpose of providing me and Mia with somewhere to sit when we stop working long enough to eat.

I feel like a traitor letting Mags sit there.

She cups her hands around her mug and looks around. "All those millions and this is where you live? In a crappy house in the Valley?" She sighs and shakes her head.

I sit there looking at her, wondering what to do. Should I simply play it cool until she leaves? After all, she can't possibly stay for long in such a déclassé house that doesn't even have the gumption to be retro. Or should I grab her by the collar and physically throw her out?

Suddenly, I wish Jack had given me at least one bouncer adventure. Jack. I would so rather be parachuting into tar pits with him than sitting here with Mags. But I haven't heard from him for days. It's as if he needs serious detox time after the sex under the waterfall.

"How did you find this house?" I am woefully unable to keep the edge out of my voice.

"Like it was hard," she snorts. "Please, Lisa. You're old news. You don't have to hide from the media anymore, because nobody is looking."

"You obviously are."

"That's different. I'm your *sister*."

"Whatever *that* means."

"It means," she drones, "that I'm not after a story." She yips out a little bark of laughter. "Ha! There *is* no story anymore. Not since you woke up."

"Then what are you after?" *You already have your cut of the ten million bucks.*

She curves her lips into a sweet smile as she crinkles her eyes a la Alicia Silverstone. "I'm here to help you."

Uh-oh. Mags is pretending she's a Nice Person.

"It's about your wedding present," she says, nudging at me with the conversation, trying to get me to pick it up. Seriously, she's like a dog trying to get me to play fetch, but not at all as lovable.

"You got me a wedding present?" I chirp. "Thanks. I didn't even get married."

Mags takes a deep breath, then bats her lashes. Method faker, that Mags. "Look," she coos, opening her purse and spreading some internet printouts on the counter. "These are my registry pages and I came over to help you pick out some nice gifts for me. The things I really want from what's left on the lists."

"I already got you something."

I know I told Jack I wanted to sever ties with my family

completely, but sentimentality or compassion or nostalgia or something got hold of me and shook me until I turned stupid. "It's up here." I climb onto the counter and reach into one of the highest cupboards.

I actually wrapped the thing and stored it for safekeeping. I didn't pack it into the garage with everything else because I was so pleased with it that I didn't want to risk damaging it.

"Here," I say, handing Maggie a box about the size of a See's Candy Sampler. "Happy, uh, wedding."

She slides off the wrapping without reading the card. I wrote, "To Maggie from Lisa."

"A picture," she says, staring down at it.

"Remember how we used to play Bride when Mom would take down all the curtains to wash?"

"I remember." She stares at the framed snapshot of four year-old Magnolia and nine year-old Lisa swathed in the gauzy sheer panels taken from the dining room windows. "My actual wedding dress looked nothing like this," she says dully.

"Hmmm."

"Is that why you got this?" she demands. "To make me feel guilty for getting married in Italy without you?"

"What?" I squawk. "I didn't *get* it. I made it. I made it to ... to ..." I can feel hot tears throb behind my eyes. "To remember that ... we used to get along. We used to ... things used to be different. I thought it would be something nice to remember."

She puts the picture back in its box and slams the lid on. "Lisa, this is just like you. You *have* to be different. You *have* to be weird. You can't get something from the registry because it's what everyone else is doing."

"What are you talking about? I thought this picture—"

"You're just so weird, Lisa." She pronounces this with disgust. "Skipping through life, not giving a damn what anyone else thinks."

"*So*?"

"Don't *we* matter at all? Your *family*? You're always making us wonder what insane, embarrassing thing you'll do next. Your goofy clothes and dumb hair. Sawing away at that stupid viola and driving us all crazy. Who ever even heard of a *viola*? God!"

"Mags—"

"You got to be this total joke between me and Mom. For your birthdays and Christmas, we would buy the ugliest, weirdest clothes for you we could find, just to see if you'd wear them. And you always did! You didn't care! Do you know how embarrassing it was growing up with Napoleon Dynamite for my sister?"

"Napoleon Dynamite didn't even *exist* when we were kids!" I scream at her. "I can't believe you bought me those stupid clothes on purpose! Mags, I wore them because they were *gifts*. The one time I returned that purple mini skirt with the fringe, Mom *cried*."

Mags gives a giddy laugh. "That's right," she says, remembering. "She was *good*."

"I can't believe it!" I cry. "My whole life, you've conspired to make me look ridiculous. And you did it *again*. When I was in a coma!" My heart slams into my breastbone. "With that awful story. You made me look terrible on the cover on purpose."

"That cover made you famous."

"For being pathetic. *Why*? Why did you all do that to me? Were you that afraid your plan to swindle me might not work?"

Mags storms dramatically across the kitchen, as if shocked, wounded. Then she spins. "Lisa, we deserve that money. You were out of it. We were the ones who were awake, who had to deal with everything. We're the ones who *suffered*."

"You couldn't have discussed this with me?"

"You mean you wanted us all to come crawling and *ask* you for the money. Money that was rightfully *ours*."

"If it was so rightful, Burger Barn would have given it to you in the first place. Or the courts would have. Or I would have. You didn't have to swindle me. My own family."

"What do you want, Lisa? The money? Will that make you happy?" Mags gestures at the empty room. "You have no clue what to do with the money you have."

I snuffle for a few seconds. "I w-w-want ... I w-want ..."

"You don't know *what* you want," Mags says. "But I'll tell you what you need. You need to find a man."

I blink. "A man?"

"You're the older sister," she sneers, "and you're still alone." She looks around the kitchen. "It breaks my heart to see that you've given up."

"Given up *what*?"

"Lisa, look at your life. You bought a house. You're fixing it up, furnishing it, I hope." She looks at me with puppy dog eyes. "All when you're not married."

I stare at her, wondering what planet she comes from.

She shakes her head. "You can't expect me to believe that you're happy living alone in some dumpy house in the Valley." Her voice hisses with such desperate insistence you'd think she was doing a crack intervention. "It's like telling the world that you've accepted that you're going to be alone forever." She shakes her head again. "You need to find someone. I know it didn't work out with Keith, but you can find someone if you *try*. Then maybe you can stop blaming your family for every little thing."

"Like stealing four million dollars from me?"

"Lisa ..."

"Mags," I say, "take your picture, and get out of my house. Now."

"Lisa ..."

"NOW."

Mags crosses her arms and lifts her chin. She's not budging until she's good and ready.

Great.

I can jump out of planes and swim with sharks, but I cannot get my own bitch-face sister out of my kitchen.

All the air gushes out of me and my shoulders slump. I'm not Jack or Edgar or Mr. Bennett or even Ethel. The force of my personality is not enough to expel my sister.

"All right, Mags," I finally say. "You want to stay in my kitchen? Fine."

I walk back to the bedroom to resume work on the wood trim. I'm juiced with bitter anger and my eyes tear up, but I get to work and hammer away.

I could've told Mags there was no way that "finding a man" would ever be on my list of Things To Do. But what would be the point? The woman takes umbrage at the existence of the viola, and I'm supposed to talk to her as if she's capable of processing a rational thought?

We don't live in the same worlds. But at least I don't go barging into her world just to belittle everything I see and hear.

Mean Mags! Mean Mags! Mean Mags!

I just get done hammering in another nail when I hear the front door slam shut. Mags is gone. I feel like someone finally cut the current to the electrodes spiked into my gut.

Mags is gone. I bet she didn't even take the picture.

My cell phone rings. "Hello?" I say it like a generic question, all casual-like, even though I know it's Jack.

He pauses then says, "Are you okay?"

Oh, God. A one word greeting and he can tell I'm about

to cry. I don't answer him for a sec, not trusting my voice.

"Lisa?"

Swallow. "What's up?" Too desperately chipper. Damn.

Another pause. "Can you test tomorrow?"

"What time?"

"Ten."

"Ok-kay." Damn! My voice *cracked.*

"Lisa, what's wrong?"

"Nothing. I'm definitely okay."

But then I start crying. I don't say anything more because I really don't want to sob into the phone *Mags was mean to me*!

Jack told me to take a stand with my family, but here I am, dissolving into a pathetic dishrag. I have to get a grip.

"Thanks for calling Jack. I'm really glad you called." But I tumble back into crying by the word "called."

"Lisa ..."

"Gotta go," I say quickly. "See ya tomorrow."

I hang up and snuffle my way back to the kitchen to find some ice cream.

* * * * *

Can't test today. Sorry.

From: Jack

9:27 am

I blink at my phone.

Jack texted me. He TEXTED me.

He's NEVER texted me before. Are we BFF's now, and nobody told me? As if.

He's canceling on me, and he doesn't have the balls to tell me himself. I punch in his speed dial. No answer.

I punch it in again. No answer.

Damn! This is because of that STUPID phone call. Why did I have to cry? And then *thank* him for calling? He must so think I was crying from sheer relief that he finally called me after our last bout of sex. He thinks I was crying over *him*. I knew I should have called him back to explain. I *knew* it!

Still no answer!

* * * * *

Ten hours since the text. Still no answer.

I know he went testing without me.

WITHOUT ME.

He must have. Jack wouldn't just do nothing all day. And even if he didn't test without me, which I'm sure he did, he still just plain cancelled on me. Where does he get off treating me this way?

I look out the kitchen window to watch the encroaching night get darker. He's bound to be back by now, fiddling with his gear.

I grab my keys and bolt out the door. Fifteen minutes later, I turn onto Jack's street. The pick-up is in the drive. I park and slam myself out of Dalton.

I'm so mad I feel righteous anger throb through my thighs with every step I take. I'm so glad I'm wearing my black booty shoes with the scrap of heel. They sound much more impressive than sneakers or Sketchers would. But Jack's driveway is far too short and my satisfying *clickety*-strides end way too soon.

I ring the doorbell and wait. Where the hell was he all day? And how dare he force me into the role of a shrew, demanding to know where he was?

How DARE he. If he wants to end our deal, he can TELL ME TO MY FACE.

The door swings open.

"Jack."

He hasn't even turned on a porch or foyer light, but I can see him from the glow of streetlights. Just one look at him tells me I have to switch gears.

Fast.

Jack is hurt. His face alone is so bruised and scraped he looks like he's spent the day using his head to play the washboard in a hillbilly jug band.

"What are you doing here?" He looks grumpy and I don't blame him.

I decide in the space of a mini-second that I will NOT be girly. I push past him and walk right into his house, without insulting him with a coo or "poor baby" of any kind.

"Lisa—"

"Jack," I say, turning to face him, cutting short his growl. "I'm here, and I'm staying." I give him a confident smile as I push up my sleeves.

"I don't want you here."

I look at the careful way he's moving and the ice pack he's holding in one cut up hand, and then I notice his scraped arm. I'm betting one whole side of his body took quite a beating. I swallow down my worry. I cannot be wimpy. Not with Jack.

"Maybe not," I say in brisk agreement. "But I'm going to pamper you anyway." With a wink, I turn on my way-cool heel and head toward the kitchen.

"What? Ow!" He says the two words almost on top of one another as he makes too sudden a move to follow me.

I have to do it. What choice is there? Jack is hurt, so I *have* to be nice to him first if I want answers. I cannot be a bitch. Not yet.

"Just lay down on the couch over there or whatever makes you most comfortable." I call over my shoulder, "I'll get started in here."

Jack follows me to the kitchen in a slow but clearly pissed-off gait that has me biting back a laugh. He just looks so un-him, trying to chase me down like he's any sort of threat.

When he steps into the fullness of the kitchen light, I get a good look at him in his faded navy sweats, a ratty T-shirt, and clean white socks. He's got just-out-of-the-shower wet hair and a soapy smell. I swear I'm about to tackle him while he's defenseless.

But I've got to concentrate. "I've never really done the pampering thing before," I explain as I wash my hands at the sink. "Keith never got sick or hurt or anything." I dry my hands on a paper towel then walk up to Jack. "I'll help you get settled. Just tell me where."

Jack sucks in a deep breath, probably to yell at me, then winces. "I don't need to be pampered, and—I hope you're listening this time—I don't want you here."

A nasty shock zaps through me.

What if there's already someone here? Like a woman? A tall, built, in-shape woman with thighs of iron who can climb mountains in a porno nurse's uniform? I'm ready to apologize and run for the door when instead I hear myself ask to use the bathroom.

"What?" Jack squawks. "No. Get out."

"I gotta go." I dart around him and head past the stairs toward the back hallway.

"Where do you think you're going?"

"Looking for a bathroom," I explain with mounting impatience, pretending like I've never been in his bathroom before and have no idea exactly where it is.

I start opening doors, any door behind which a sexpot might be stashed. Not in the laundry room where I find a dusty pile of shredded motorcycle leathers on the floor. Not in a small downstairs office. I get to the garage but can't find the light switch. I step down and hit a button I find on the wall. The whirring noise startles me as the garage door scrolls up.

"What the hell are you doing?"

"I told you," I call back, lowering the door and flicking another switch.

The empty garage bursts into fluorescent light as Jack yells at me again. "The bathroom is right here, you lunatic! You walked right past it!"

No woman in the garage. I rush to the bathroom—no woman, not even in the tub. Jack stands right in the doorway, blocking my path with his sheer malevolence.

"What's the matter?" I ask innocently. I try to slide past him but he grabs my shirt.

"Listen, Lisa. Ow!"

I poked him the ribs to make good my escape.

"Jesus!" Jack slumps against the wall. "I thought you said you were going to pamper me! You SUCK at pampering!"

I race up the stairs. Three bedrooms. I head toward the one at the end of the hall, sure to be the master since it's over the garage and must be the biggest. But nobody's in there or in the master bathroom. I get out quick, not wanting to be suspected of scoping out Jack's bedroom. Way too embarrassing to be the chick who commits to memory the color of his comforter (white with grayish-blue seer-suckery stripes) and the number of throw rugs in his bathroom (two.)

I check the other two bedrooms lickety split but what I find is ... um ... weird.

Regardless, nobody seems to be lurking. Unless said woman, or man, I suppose, is hiding in a closet or under a bed.

But why hide from me?

I walk slowly back down the stairs toward Jack who waits, looking up at me.

"You are a whacked-out freak." His unassailable pronouncement.

"Just wanted to make sure nobody else was here and I wasn't interrupting anything."

"You could've asked."

"*You* could've lied."

He huffs out a breath. "Satisfied?"

I look at him. "Puzzled."

He chucks the melted ice pack at me then heads toward the couch. "Too damn bad."

Deciding to ignore his surly temper, I walk into the kitchen to re-freeze the pack and make us something to eat. Luckily, the kitchen opens onto the family room in a very homey kind of way so I can keep an eye on Jack as I cook.

"Can I get you anything?" I call as I open every cupboard in the kitchen.

"Lisa, you're not welcome." He's super-serious, or trying to be.

"That hurts, Jack. But I'm going to push past the pain, as I'm sure you might instruct me to do in other circumstances."

"Why are you even here?"

"I came to rip you a new one because you cancelled on me."

Jack stretches out on the couch and closes his eyes. "Lisa, the Blackhawk brothers finished making some bike gear we've been working on." He sinks more deeply into the cushions. "What I'd usually do is I'd test it right away. So, I had to test it today, or else the staff might've suspected something."

I set my palms on the counter and stare at him. "That better be the truth," I say. "I will not put up with you just unilaterally deciding to end our deal without so much as a rational conversation."

"You mean rational like this one?"

I start slamming items I choose for dinner onto the counter. "*I'm* not ending the deal," I point out. "We're in this together, whether you like it or not."

He scowls at me. "So ... what? We're in this thing for life? I can never get out?"

I close the freezer with a *thwack*. "Of course you can. But you could talk to me when you're having misgivings. Give me a goddamn heads-up before the decision is made. I'm just so sick of others making these decisions and—wham! My life is changed forever and there's not a damn thing I can do about it. Now, can I get you anything, or what?"

He just looks at me for a few seconds. "Scotch," he says. "Top shelf, over the toaster."

I take down the Glendronach and a glass. "How much?"

"The bottle should just about do it."

* * * * *

Forty minutes later, I'm nestling myself into the big comfy chair next to the sofa, ready to tuck into the supper I've whipped together.

Jack is looking at his plate. "You cut up all my food."

"I know," I mumble around a mouthful of the best steak ever. I know, I know. I'm trying to be a vegetarian, but sometimes, I just jump right off the wagon.

He's still looking at his plate as though his food has been cooked in a language he doesn't understand. "Why?" he asks.

"Just eat, G.I. Joe. I promise I won't tell anyone that I cut your meat for you."

Jack still looks like I swiped his favorite lunch box, but he takes a cautious bite.

"Do you have kids?" I ask when his mouth is full.

He swallows. "No." He scoops another forkful into his

mouth.

I'm part impressed and part peeved that he was so ready for my question. Jesus. Now I can't think of anything else to say.

But I still want to know why there are two kids' bedrooms upstairs.

As I mull this over, Jack cleans his plate with the efficiency of an anteater. I put down my own plate, stand, and take his empty plate. In less than a minute, I return it to him, loaded with second helpings of everything.

"You made seconds?"

I nod.

"My niece and nephew," he says. "My brother's kids."

"Are you their foster dad, or something?"

"They stay with me whenever he and his wife are both away." He takes a few bites. "Which is at least once a month. They travel a lot for business. And they usually manage to include weekends away."

"But the rooms, they look lived in. Not just rooms they stay in, but *their* rooms. Posters on the walls and stuff."

"I want them to be at home. Not feel like they're in the way."

"Are they rich?"

"Yup."

We eat in silence for a few seconds. "So, if the kids didn't spend time with you, they'd be stuck with a nanny?"

Jack shrugs. "One of 'em. They've got two."

"Hmm. So, do they get to be totally wild when they're here?"

"They run with scissors and everything."

I take a swig of Coke. "Where do they live?"

"Laguna Nigel."

I put down the bottle. "Orange County? So, on weekdays, you drive them to school? Glendale to Orange

County?"

Jack swallows a mouthful. "Nuh-uh. We either hang glide or take the horses."

"Hmm," I say again, this time with an undertone of a snide Hanna-Barbera villain, "be as funny as you want, but I've got your number."

"I hope it's pi. I love pie."

"You like kids," I accuse with triumph.

Jack sets down his plate, then stretches along the wide, long couch. "I'd like some after-dinner coffee, Jeeves."

I get up and make my way back to the kitchen. "Have any brandy?"

"As a matter of fact, I do."

Later, after polishing off two cups of spiked coffee and a bowl of vanilla bean ice cream mixed together with Rice Krispies and Nestlé's Quik (which he claims is for the kids), a very comfy-looking and contented Jack sinks back into the couch and closes his eyes. I'm still working on my ice cream, since I like it best when it gets all melted and soupy.

"So, you wiped out on the bike?" I ask.

"Happens."

"And the gear?"

"Pretty good. Have a few ideas."

"'Course you do," I say. "Far be it from you to let a little spill get in the way of action action action."

"May as well not waste the day."

"That's why I stayed."

Jack opens his eyes and looks at me. "Why? Because of the gear?"

"You never give yourself a break," I explain. "So I thought I'd stick around and do the honors."

"This mean you're going to do the dishes, too?"

I nod and smile. "When do you see the kids again?"

"They were supposed to be here all Halloween weekend, but Ted and Suzy decided to stay in town. There's some big costume party at the club, and they want to be sure to be seen. And they're bringing the kids with them."

"Mmmm," I say, savoring my ice cream. "You sound bitter. You never sound bitter. You've got something to say about Ted and Suzy?"

Jack sighs. "No." He sounds like a pouty kid who's being asked if he's going to play ball so close to the house ever again. "Not really. It's just ... Nevermind."

"Okay. What do you and the rugrats do together?"

"Cameron and Isabelle. They've usually got their own things to get done. Homework. Then we just hang out."

"Running with scissors?"

"Running with scissors," he confirms.

"Do you wish you had your own kids?"

Jack doesn't answer, but he picks up his empty coffee mug and pours a few fingers of Scotch into it.

I take a sip of my un-spiked coffee.

"It's what I suck at."

What?

I breathe carefully, afraid I'm going to pull a penny out of my pocket and ruin everything. "What, exactly," I ask lightly, "do you suck at?"

He takes a swig of Scotch. "Forging relationships. You know, the kind that matter."

That's it? He-Man's big secret is that he's commitment-phobic?

"You suck at relationships," I say, trying not to judge or fix, trying to remember anything I can from Mars and Venus. "Well ..."

"No," he says, "not relationships. *Forging* relationships."

"I'm confused."

"Some people fall into relationships or are born into them, and I'm pretty okay with those kind. No better or worse than your average schmuck, I guess."

He pauses.

"Okay," I say.

"But when I actually set out to forge a relationship ... to make it happen because I want it in my life ... well, that's what I suck at."

"You're sure about this?"

"Jesus!" He shoots to a standing position, then deciding he has nowhere to go, sits back down. "Just look at Into the Wild. I tried to build this totally non-corporate company. I decided I would go employee-owned, and that we'd all be working toward the same goal. But look what's happening. They think they're better than other people, not just other companies or other gear. They don't want to expand into anything that's too 'normal.' I got it all wrong."

"But Into the Wild's a business, Jack." I try to sound off-hand, as if what he's told me is no big deal. "Relationships with people are different."

"Who do you think makes up the business? Nobody?" He starts laughing. Then he says something, I think.

"'Loose all over again?'" I echo, just for clarification, sure now that he's three sheets to the wind.

"Loose," he agrees, "and Edgar and Griselda."

"Oh," I say, cluing in, "Luz."

"Ruiz. Well, Montez. Luz Montez and Edgar and Griselda Ruiz. Luz is their daughter."

"Oh, no," I say, "this already sounds tragic."

He stops laughing and looks over with raised eyebrows that almost serve as shrug. "Nobody dies," he offers, then his eyes become bleak. "Until later."

He switches positions on the couch then, stretching out on his stomach, with his head closer to me than it was before. I want to hear whatever he's about to tell me. I really, really do.

But I'm afraid.

If Jack realizes when he sobers up what he revealed to me while he was drunk, he may never want to see me or talk to me again. And he might even blame me for getting him drunk and prying the dirt from his stingy heart. I could play the odds, though, and hope he never remembers. Then I'll just have to keep the secret to myself.

Right.

"Jack," I say, leaning toward him, "I think it's time you went to bed now."

"No, Lisa. I want to tell you this. I know, like, everything about you. You can stand to hear this one thing about me."

I get out of my chair. "No, I can't, Jack. I don't want to hear anything after all that Scotch and brandy."

He grabs my hand, but I can't let him do this. If he speaks, I know he'll hate me in the morning. And for the rest of my life.

So I lean down and kiss him. Long and slow, more sensuously than we ever kiss in the wild. This is bound to freak him out and get him back to his senses.

But before I know it, instead of throwing me off him, he's kissing me back. His hands are ON me and oh, God. Jack's going to take me to bed when he's drunk.

"Jack!" I yell, pushing myself away from him, "Stop this!" I scramble to my feet.

He looks up at me from the couch, eyes hazy with confusion. "You kissed me."

"That was *supposed* to repulse you so you'd storm off."

"What?" He clambers into sitting position. "Storm off

where? This is *my* house." He bolts off the couch and across the room, away from me. In front of the fireplace he turns around, absolute disgust etched onto his face. "Get out."

"That's not fair!" I cry. "Where do you get off, making me the bad guy in this scenario? I was trying to be nice, you jerk! I just didn't want you to tell me anything you'd regret!"

"Get. Out."

As I open my mouth to defend myself, I realize that this is exactly what I want. No way he's going to tell me anything *now*. But I cannot shut up. I must defend myself against his really unfair fury.

"Jack!" I'm breathing so hard I have to gulp in air to get my next words out. "Stop being so mean to me and listen."

"*Me* listen?" Jack puts his hand on the mantelpiece, and it flashes through my mind that he does this because all the kissing and shouting has hurt his ribs. "Why don't *you* listen for a change? You know," he scoffs, "the fact that you always just blunder on through without thinking, totally unaware of how you're affecting us around you, doesn't excuse you. Not one bit. I'm so sick of all this aggressive stupidity. Now get out."

I don't budge, adamant that I won't be scared by all his mumbo-jumbo designed to make me feel inadequate and in-the-wrong. "How am I stupid?" I demand.

Jack looks at me with cold, hard fury. "I try to tell you how I suck at forging relationships and you respond by trying to trick me with sex games. See anything wrong with that picture?"

My voice is so soft I can hardly hear it. "I just didn't want you telling any secrets while you were drunk."

But even as I say it, I realize that what he just said doesn't sound drunk at all. In fact, it makes a scary sort of sense.

"I'm not drunk."

I can't move.

"But if you really thought I was," he asks, "why didn't

you just leave? Why this stupid test I was set up to fail?"

He stares at me, but I have no answer. I'm still trying to process what I've done.

"Let me guess," he says. "You didn't think of just leaving. Because you didn't *think*. Like always. Now get out. It's easy, Lisa. Just turn around and walk out. No thinking required. Just go."

I'm absolutely numb. The undeniable truth of everything he's saying is icing through me like Novocain.

"To hell with it," he finally says. "I'm going to bed." He flicks off the family room light on his way to the stairs, then climbs up while I stand there in the dark.

I hear his bedroom door shut at the top of the stairs. *Shut*. Not slam, but shut. Even his rejection of me is completely without passion.

So. Here I stand, no one to watch me if I should flounce out. No one to say the last word to. No one to even close and lock the door behind me.

I slink out of his house, stepping into the black, starless night. It's so dark and quiet. Back there, in the house, Jack kissed me back. Jack was going to take me to bed.

And Jack isn't drunk.

CHAPTER 16

"There's the lady of the hour!"

I turn so quickly toward the kitchen door that I slip on the wet floor and barely catch myself on the edge of the sink.

"Crispin ..." I turn toward him with my feet firmly under me. Damn, that man is gorgeous. Like Phillip Michael Thomas with a dash of Rick Fox.

"Lisa?" He does a double take to get a good look at me.

I'm soaked from head to toe and covered with spaghetti sauce. "How are you liking our little shindig?" I ask. "Meeting lots of awesome people? Like these two?" I smile as Michael and Antawne come through to get another stack of clean dishes.

"Everyone is great," Crispin agrees. "I'm glad I came." His eyes flick across my messy body. "Too bad you got stuck doing clean up." He steps closer, but not that close. "I was thinking that after the dinner we could go ..."

"I'm going to take a shower then right to bed," I say, then laugh. "That's where I'm going. I've been annihilated by an annual spaghetti carnival."

Crispin nods, "Yeah," he says, his mouth turning down. "I hear that. But I would have thought you'd be out mixing with the people all day, being such a mover and shaker here at HEYA."

"A good leader steps in where she's needed," I point out.

Even though I totally volunteered to do clean up weeks ago because I hate schmoozing.

"Well, I was thinking about taking off soon."

"Crispin," I say, walking up to him—and he BACKS UP. "Thank you so much for coming, and for advertising this in your stores. You mean a lot to this project and to this community."

"You're welcome," he says. "Good-night."

I'm pretty sure he couldn't get out of the kitchen fast enough. Good thing. I'm a very busy and important person.

Jack doesn't think so, but so what? I turn back to the sink and resume washing dishes.

Big deal that he doesn't even acknowledge me in class anymore. I don't acknowledge him, either. And of course I haven't tried to call. Why would I? We have no reason to contact one another except to arrange testing jaunts. And I sure haven't invented anything.

I jump when the kitchen door slams open behind me. But this time, I don't skid around all Bambi-like.

"Thanks, guys," I call over my shoulder to Michael and Antawne, back for another batch of warm, clean, sanitized plates. "The clean ones are over there." I gesture with a shrug of my right shoulder.

"LISA!"

I spin around to see Mr. Bennett standing in the doorway. He does not look happy. Not that he ever does. But this look is worse.

"*What* is going on in here?"

"Uh …" My eyes dart around the kitchen. Suds all over almost every surface, suds all over me, water dripping off the counters, clean and dirty dishes everywhere. Looks pretty bad to someone who doesn't understand the way I clean up, which is pretty messy until the very end.

"LISA?"

"Mr. Bennett," I jump at his booming voice just a little. "I've got this plan."

"What are you doing to our kitchen?"

I stand up straight and lift my chin. "There has not been one single glitch for the past three hours with getting hot, clean, sanitized plates out there. I know what I'm doing."

"You're a mess."

"I'm not done yet." I make the pronouncement as I step carefully across the kitchen. I sweep my arms like a *The Price Is Right* model, indicating stacks of dishes. "This is part of a system, so don't knock it."

"A system?"

"Aw, don't take that tone, Mr. Bennett. I'm in here to do a job," I say more briskly, "and I'm doing it. I volunteered to do kitchen duty by myself so all you guys could mingle and show everyone why HEYA is worth investing in. So, go help save the center and let me take care of the kitchen."

His face remains impassive. "Just get this mess cleaned up." With a shake of his head, he finally leaves the kitchen.

I look around at my soapy domain and smile.

"Let's hear about this system."

My entire body goes rigid as if I've just been stunned with a taser.

I take a few deep breaths, then turn around slowly, livid with myself for reacting like such a teenager to the sound of his voice. He's standing in the other kitchen doorway, the one that leads to the back hallway.

"Jack." I keep my voice even.

I don't know what else to say or how to say it. I'm not sure how I feel. But I'm pretty sure I'm blushing.

I'm so ridiculously glad he's here. And this makes me want to smash every plate in the kitchen.

"Let's see," he says, walking into the kitchen, surveying the scene. The first time he acknowledges that I exist in over a week, but he looks around the kitchen instead of at me.

"Wash, put in the rack, rinse everything with scalding hot water from the hose on the sink." He looks at the counters, considering. "How are you going to dry up all the excess water at the end of the night?"

Mr. Smug thinks I haven't thought it through. "Dishtowels under the sink," I say. Clipped, terse. "I'll bring them home to launder tonight, return them tomorrow. Plus I have some moving blankets in my car for the floor."

Still looking at the counters, Jack nods. "Good plan."

"I know."

Then he starts ... he starts ... helping. Just like that. Without even asking, he picks up a dirty plate from a stack by the sink, scrapes what's on it into a big plastic bin designated just for food scraps, then puts the plate in the sudsy sink.

"Why are you here?" I demand.

"I saw The Spaghetti Supper ad in the *Times*."

"I mean here, in the kitchen, right now. How is it that you showed up just when Mr. Bennett did?" I look out the small barred window toward the parking lot. "What are they saying about me out there?"

"I saw Pacquito running around out there," he says, clearly not answering me.

I decide to humor him for just a sec. "Gabriel, a kid who comes to the center a lot, loves Pacquito. I bring him in whenever I can so they can be together."

"Gabriel is the kid with crooked glasses?"

"Yup."

Jack nods. Doesn't say anything else.

Ha! His attempt to derail the conversation led nowhere.

"So," I say. "What are they saying about me out there?"

"Nothing much. Michael and Antawne…."

"Those two ratted me out? After I made them a paper towel path so they wouldn't slip on the floor?"

"They didn't rat you out. Mr. Bennett just thought he'd check to see how things were coming along."

"It was bad enough for you to follow him."

I'm listening to the angry blood of betrayal marching through my ears when I hear something else. Jack squeaks.

Squeaks?

Then his shoulders jerk a few times.

Then he breaks into hoarse, choking peals of laughter. "Really, Lisa," he manages to say, "I was just curious." He looks at me, then starts laughing even harder. He turns from the sink to lean his butt against it as spasms of laughter rack his body.

He finally chokes down the guffaws. "Michael and Antawne said you were 'one whack bitch,' and I had to come check it out for myself. And you do look pretty funny."

"I've got dishes to clean," I snap, hip checking him as I position myself in front of the sink. I grab the sink hose to rinse the dishes. But instead of turning the water to hot, I turn it to cold.

Then I aim, hit the trigger, and blast Jack right in the face.

"Hey!" He grabs my wrist, forcing the jet of water to hit him squarely in the chest. He wrenches the hose from me and drops it. The second he releases me, I have the good sense to back away.

Jack looks down at the wet spot smack in the middle of his chest, where the faded T-shirt is now soaked to midnight blue. "You are going to be so sorry that you did that."

"What are you going to do to me?" I challenge. "Get me wet?"

He comes at me with a menacing gait. I can almost hear

the distant whistle signifying an Old West duel.

"You've got me there," he says. "You definitely can't get much more soaked." He reaches up to the shelf just above us and picks up a big canister labeled FLOUR.

"Jack, no." I try to look serious.

"I think I remember from kindergarten that when you mix flour and water, you can make paste."

"Jack, no," I say again. "That belongs to HEYA. They must use it for baking cookies or brownies or something. You'd be stealing from HEYA, Jack."

"I'll pay 'em back."

I run for it. In about a step he catches me.

"Aaahh!"

With one arm clamped securely around my neck and shoulders, he dumps the flour over my head.

But it's not flour. The can was labeled wrong. It's sugar.

SUGAR.

Sugar stuck all over my soaking wet body. "Iiiiiiick!"

He lets me go. As I stumble away from him, he launches the rest at me.

"No!"

"Relax," Jack says, standing back to get a look at his handy work. "You look …" he flashes me a cocky grin, "sweet."

I glare at him.

But his stare doesn't flinch as he moves in on me. "Let's see how you taste."

Just like that, he scoops me up against him, then sinks his teeth into my neck for a bite. Oh, God. His fingers dig into my hips, work their way under the soaked waistband of my shorts to my wet skin.

I grab his T-shirt with both hands, but suddenly I remember Michael and Antawne with their ever-present cell phones. Video-taking cell phones. In a flash, I imagine shots of my getting nailed in the HEYA kitchen posted all over the Internet.

"We can't," I say, trying to back away. "Not here."

Jack's off me in a second and pulling me along behind him as he dodges through the kitchen door into the back hallway. In the darkened corridor, he presses me up against the painted cinderblock wall and kisses me.

Wow. He's never kissed me like—

"C'mon." He grabs my hand, runs down the hall, and pulls me into the small office Jimmy and Edgar share. He shuts the door, then asks, "Which desk is Edgar's?"

"You know Edgar?"

"Just met him. Which one?"

"This one."

After a few seconds of ransacking, he finds a box of condoms.

"Wow," I say, just before I jump him.

* * * * *

I'm back in the kitchen, trying to hose off all the sugar from the kitchen floor, the counters, my skin, my hair, my clothes. Jack is cleaning up the sugar trail we left all the way to Edgar's office.

By the time Jack comes back into the kitchen, I'm back to my dish-cleaning frenzy. Without saying a word, Jack steps in next to me.

And here we are. Not like a companionable couple cleaning up the supper dishes or anything. More like the girls from *The Facts of Life* when they're first assigned to KP duty together under Mrs. Garrett. Resigned, but still willing to engage in shenanigans.

It's so weird. We just had sex, but I'm pretty sure we're

still not getting along.

"I meant every word I said last Saturday," he says quietly, out of the palest of blues.

Jesus. He *is* still mad at me. Damn.

He better not list all my copious faults. AGAIN.

"But," he continues, "I didn't acknowledge that at least you were trying to do something decent. As messed up as your plan was, you were thinking of me." He hands me a plate to put in the rack. "Thank you."

I swallow. Jack used sex as an icebreaker. He walked in here, knowing he had something all girly to say, something almost like an apology, so he seduced me to make it easier.

The first time we have sex indoors, plus all that fantastic kissing on the mouth? He just needed to get himself ready to say something quasi-nice to me.

Bastard. He doesn't need an icebreaker when he's telling me what an annoying bitch he thinks I am.

"Okay," I say. "You're welcome."

What else *can* I say? I mean, if this is how the guy operates, I'll just have to cope. If I have to put up with hot sex every time Jack wants to have a nice conversation with me, I'm okay with that. I didn't even have to try to entice him or anything. I look like a refugee from a flooded Peeps factory, but still I got this totally rocketing orgasm. All for the small price of having to listen to the guy when it's all over.

Score.

We stand there in silence for a few minutes doing dishes. I begin to wonder how much conversation the sex is good for. I know I'm pressing my luck, but I can't seem to bludgeon my curiosity into submission.

"Jack," I say, "I don't get it. Not really." Am I really going to say this? Am I really? "Why do you bother with me at all? You have a pretty comprehensive list of everything about me that bothers you. It doesn't make sense."

Jack lets go of the plate he's holding. It sinks below the suds, and after a few seconds, he flicks the soapy bubbles off his hands. He turns to me. "You presented me with a unique opportunity."

"Are you talking about the gear?" I probe. "Because there are lots of absolute beginners out there. Just throw a rock."

"But they're not like you." He dries his hands on a towel that's too wet to do the job. "I knew you'd have the guts to do what needed to be done. With you, I wouldn't have to spend all our time together coaxing you into jumping, or swimming, or climbing, or whatever."

"How could you possibly know that?"

"That first day on the mountain, for one."

"And for another?" That's me. I just keep pushing and shoving.

He doesn't answer.

"How did you know I'd work out?"

I *really* want to know. I mean, he's saying I'm The One. Not in a romantic or life-partner kind of way, but The One for this project. And I've never been anyone's The One before, not for anything. It's never before been the case that someone's particularly needed me, Lisa Flyte. Finally, I'm the star of the show. You bet I want to know all about it.

"Lots of reasons," he says.

Really? Lots?

"The way you tried to head-butt that guy in your apartment," he says. "Even the way you write."

"Write?" I echo. "Write what? I haven't written anything since a haiku in tenth grade. It was supposed to be a sonnet."

"Anything you write," he explains. "The way you write stuff on a page, with a pencil."

"Huh?"

"I noticed it in class on the first day." He leans back against the counter. "You walked in so cool, looking like Jean Harlow or something. Like nothing could get to you. You sat off by yourself, but I watched you."

He smiles and raises his eyebrows for a sec. "You have a way of calling attention to yourself. Anyway, I noticed your writing. You pressed really hard with the pencil or pen or whatever you were using. You couldn't even use the back of the paper. It was all dented from your writing."

"You noticed that I wasted paper?" I ask. "I recycle, you know."

He smiles again. "I remember. No, I'm not saying you waste paper. But you do. I've seen you."

"Hey!"

"I knew there had to be some serious intensity under the surface."

"Intensity? Me?"

"I can work with that," he says.

"But Jack," I counter, "you're the most easy-going guy I think I've ever met. You could work with anyone."

"Doesn't mean I want to," he says, tossing aside the wet towel. "I don't want to work with my parents. I never wanted to be a part of Hawkins United."

I think of how he feels about all the Burger Barn money. "I get that."

"My family never made any sense to me." He hands me another plate.

I take it, even though it's still dirty.

"Or at least, not like ..." He sort of laughs. "When I was a kid, Edgar and Griselda worked for us. She was the housekeeper and he was the general handyman."

A chill seizes my body. Don't mess this up. Don't mess this up.

"It's weird," he goes on, "but at some point, it hit me. My parents were never around and I was always wondering if I would see them at supper or over the weekend. But Edgar and Griselda were always there. When I was about ten, maybe, I realized that they were the perfect parents. Always there, in my house, taking care of me."

"They lived with you?"

"In the second biggest guest house."

I swallow, feeling suddenly slovenly. I keep forgetting what kind of economic bracket this guy comes from.

"They were always nice to me," he says, "so I started fantasizing about how they could be my real family."

I nod, wanting to ask where Luz fits into this fantasy. But I don't say a word.

"So, I tried to really impress them, show them what a good kid I could be. I started making sure my room was always clean. I put my own dishes in the dishwasher, and I'd sneak into the kitchen and unload it as soon as it stopped running. And I started doing my own laundry. Late at night, after Griselda and Edgar went home."

"You were left in the house by yourself at night?"

"I always had a nanny to stay with me over night. But they pretty much ignored me as long as I wasn't making noise. I figured out pretty young that if I didn't cause trouble, they would leave me alone."

"But I thought you wanted a family," I say. "Why did you want them to ignore you?"

"They weren't like Edgar and Griselda. They were mostly college kids who came and went. I could always tell they didn't give a flying fuck."

"Did Griselda notice what you were doing?"

He furrows his brow.

"Probably, and I bet she even knew why," he says.

"Then one day, in the summer, I was at a Dodgers game with E.J." Jack looks at me. "My best friend. Anyway, I hadn't cleaned my room that day because it was Wednesday, Griselda's day off. I'd get to it later. But I ended up sleeping over E.J.'s that night and forgot all about it. Until about five in the morning."

He turns to me smiling and shaking his head. "I woke up in a cold sweat, remembering my room. I left E.J.'s right then." He looks heavenward, as though he can't believe what he did once upon a time. "So there I was, running across Orange County, trying to get home in time to clean my room before Griselda saw it."

"Did you make it?"

He closes his eyes and shakes his head.

"She saw?" I ask tentatively.

He opens his eyes. "Worse. Much worse."

I dare to say it. "Luz?"

He nods. "I was going into fifth grade that fall, and she was going to be a sophomore in high school. I was so in love with her. Luz." He looks all happy and dreamy one second, but then it's gone. "She was in a totally different world." He sounds very matter-of-fact. "But I adored her."

"She saw your room?"

"She was helping Griselda clean it!" He turns back to rinsing. "It was worse than the in-school-with-no-pants nightmare."

"So, did you take off your pants?"

He pauses. "Not right then." He shakes his head. "I must have scared the hell out of them, showing up like that, sweaty and furious at six a.m. I yelled at them to get out. I told them I wasn't lazy and sloppy like my parents, and I could clean up after myself."

"It must have been awful."

"Yeah. But it was the beginning. Edgar and Griselda…

we became a lot closer after that. Then, when I was twelve, Luz went to college. I think they were pretty lonely. From then on, I was practically living with them."

"Sleeping in Luz's room?"

"That part was awesome."

Wham!

The kitchen doors fly open. Lupe, Edgar, Jimmy, Michael, and Antawne come marching through, bearing sauce-crusted vats, greasy garlic bread trays, depleted salad bowls. I want to shoot every one of them.

"Careful," I warn. "Stay on the paper towel trail . The floor is pretty slippery."

"Oooh, girl," Lupe says taking in the mess. Then she sees Jack.

"See?" Antawne says this to the brigade, nodding to the messy kitchen. "I told you."

Then he notices Jack. "Man, Jack. How'd you get stuck helping her?"

Jack?

Antawne knows *Jack*?

"Owed her a favor."

"What'd she do? Give you a kidney?" This from Edgar. I blush, thinking of his desk.

"Hey, man," Jimmy says, greeting Jack with big, dreamy eyes.

Poor Lupe. I'm pretty sure she was dead wrong about Jimmy. And poor Edgar! He looks ready to kill Jack when he notices Jimmy practically batting his lashes.

"Wait a second," I say, then turn to Jack. "You know everyone?"

"Met 'em today."

"And you guys are already best friends?" I feel so betrayed. Not sure why, but I do.

"He said you guys were friends from USC," Lupe fills in.

Okay. That's okay. As long as they like him because of me.

The next second, Pacquito comes charging through the door. All dog energy, ears, and tail, he skids on all the water, careening right into the army of dirty dish bearers.

"Aaaaaaahhhh!"

"What the fu—!"

"Jeez!"

"Nooo!"

Crashing, screaming, clattering.

Gabriel comes running in, just as all the pots, bowls, trays, and vats clang across the floor. "Pacquito!" he calls, flinging himself at the dog.

Pacquito actually pauses in licking all the food from off the floor to slobber all over Gabriel's face.

"Jesus!" Edgar gets up off the floor, covered with what looks like French dressing. "Lisa! Take your damn dog."

"It's okay," Jimmy says. "It's not that bad."

"This place is a mess!" Edgar fumes as he glares at Jack.

"I'll stay and help clean up," Jimmy offers sweetly.

"No!" This from me, Jack and Edgar, all at once.

"It's cool," Jack says. "You guys've all had a hard day. Lisa and I'll take care of this."

The tired volunteers drift out, one by one, to tidy the parking lot. "Gabriel," I say, once Pacquito has licked clean all the pots and trays and bowls, "why don't you take Pacquito outside to play while we finish cleaning up in here?"

A few seconds later, Jack and I are once again alone. We stand looking at the mess on the floor.

"How many moving blankets do you have in your car?" he asks.

"Four."

"That's enough to dry the entire floor." He looks at me, one eyebrow raised. "Shall we?"

For the next twenty minutes, we wash everything on the floor, right where it is. Then I hold each item aloft, Jack rinses it, and I set it on the counter to dry. A few minutes later, we're both soaked, but every surface in the kitchen is squeaky clean. Flooded and dripping, but shiny and clean.

"Let's go get the blankets," Jacks says.

On the way to the car, Jack picks up the story. Yes! I didn't push or cajole, and now I'm being rewarded with the rest of the story.

"When I'd been out of college about a year," Jack says, "I went home one weekend to visit Griselda and Edgar."

He'd jumped ahead about ten years in his story, but I could keep up.

"But I ran into Luz, instead."

Oh.

"She was married by this time, but not so happily. Or so I believed." He huffs out a huge breath. "I thought it was the greatest romance. I was going to save her from her unhappy marriage and everything would work out. Me and her and Edgar and Griselda. We would all live happily ever after."

"You had an affair with her?"

We stop at my car.

"Yeah," he says. "But to me, it was a desperate, unstoppable love."

His sarcasm laced with bitterness makes my throat feel hot and huge. "What happened?"

"After a few months, and one incredible summer, we got caught."

"Oh."

"Luz had a choice, right then. She could throw herself on

the mercy of her parents and husband, blame everything on me, or ..."

He turns away, rests his elbows on the roof of my car and looks up at the sky.

"I actually thought she would choose me. I really did."

"I'm so sorry," I rasp. I clear my throat. "So, so sorry."

"Edgar and Griselda quit that day. Thirty-two years and they quit without even a second thought. They were so damn *disgusted* with me. Luz said I'd seduced her, that she was afraid for her parents' jobs if she didn't sleep with me. God!" He slams a fist into Dalton's roof and I wince. He hits Dalton again. Hard.

"Did you ever see them again? Edgar and Griselda, I mean?"

"Four years later," he says. "Edgar's funeral. Luz called my parents and they told me. That's the end."

We stand there quietly, not even looking at one another. I lean my butt against the door but don't say anything because there's nothing to say. I don't even ask why he never went after them, tried to explain.

How could he? For Edgar and Griselda to believe him, they would have to accept that their daughter had willfully and joyfully jumped into bed with a man who was not her husband. Jack would never ask them to do that. Never.

I bet he's spent a chunk of the past fourteen years hoping Luz would find it in her heart or soul to tell Griselda the truth. But I guess she never has. And anyway, it's too late for Edgar. Too late for Jack.

Bitch.

Jack turns to lean against Dalton like I am. He squints at the golden glint of the setting sun, looking at nothing in particular. As I watch him, I can feel it steal over me, like the solution to a Brother Cadfael mystery. Suddenly, I just know, probably because it's so obvious, that Jack wants to be alone.

Jack looks across the street toward the HEYA parking lot, as everyone begins to drift away for the night. "Party is totally over," he says. "I guess we better—"

"No," I say. "It's okay. You've been an amazing help. But I've got it from here."

Jack nods, still not looking at me. "I'm over here," he says, kind of shrugging down the street to his egg roll truck.

"'Night."

"'Night."

CHAPTER 17

I'm in the garage shoving dishtowels into the washer, still fantasizing about meeting Luz and destroying her. The phone rings in the house. I run to grab it, in case it's Jack.

"Wait, wait, wait," I say, trying to make sense of the voice on the other end. "Who are you? Where did you get my number?"

"Keith," yells the guy on the other end of the phone. I can tell he's trying to hear me and be heard over background bar noise.

Great. Keith is freely giving my number to drunken guys on slow Sunday nights as if I'm a last ditch party trick.

"He said I was good at what?" I shout, trying to be helpful.

"Trivia! It's free drinks if we win and the next round starts in twenty minutes."

"A big trivia competition on a Sunday night? This late?"

"That's the only way to keep anyone in here on Sunday after the games are over. C'mon. Be a sport and come down, will ya? Keith said you're the guru of trivia."

It's true. I am.

It's the one thing I'm really good at.

Funny, isn't it? The one thing at which I excel is defined as, "That which is unimportant; insignificant minutiae."

Still, I do kick ass at it. And I need to stop thinking about Jack. I really do.

"Where are you?" I ask, as I look around for my shoes.

* * * * *

The first round is almost over, and I have to say, I'm disappointed. Three guys and I sit at a bar table. We watch the TV monitor in front of us as it flashes questions, then we race against four other tables to be the quickest to enter the right answer. Either A, B, C, or D.

That's right. It's multiple choice. How lame is that?

It's hardly a challenge at all when they're options. I can't believe I sacrificed a night of *Mystery*! for this. At least the guy to my right is cute.

"Pacers and trotters." I speak softly enough so the other tables can't steal our answer.

"What?" This from Charles, who insists on being the one who punches in the answers. Even though he doesn't know a single one. Ignoring him, I reach over and punch in C.

"Hey!" He hovers protectively over the console.

The monitors flash with confetti graphics. We win Round One.

Charles, of course, takes all the credit. As he pumps his fists into the air, I feel a hand slide along the back of my neck.

"So," the cute guy says, giving me tingles down my spine, "how did you know pacers and trotters? You a big gambler with your millions?"

Why did I ever agree to meet a bunch of Keith's friends? Why?

I give him a hint of a smile. "What's your name again?"

"Josh."

"Well, Josh. One of the Black Stallion books," I answer.

"I forget which one. But for some reason, Alec ends up spending time at harness racing stables. That must be where I picked it up."

"Ooo-kay," he says, then smiles. "You're cute."

"So are you," I chirp back matter-of-factly, noting to myself that he can't handle talking about horse books. "I'm going to get a drink. Wanna come?"

Pressed shoulder to shoulder at the bar, waiting for our drinks–me for my Coke and he for his Rolling Rock–I sneak a glance at his profile. He reminds me of Aaron Eckhart.

"Keith was right about you," he says with a slow, sexy smile. "You *are* good at trivia."

My Coke arrives in one of those long glass bottles. With an almost orgasmic sigh, I take a long pull.

Josh holds his Rolling Rock, just staring at me. He leans in close, even though the bar is pretty tame and I can hear him just fine. "Makes me wonder if he was right about all the other stuff he said."

I shrug. "Maybe," I say, refusing to let him bait me.

Josh straightens up, giving me this totally hot look where he crinkles his eyes. "He said the sex was great."

I just met him and he's talking to me about my sex life? Like he has any right? But then he takes a drink, giving me a good look at his Adam's apple.

I have this thing for a guy's Adam's apple. When it comes to turn-ons, for me, it's a guy's hips, then Adam's apple, then haircuts. And hands. Definitely hands.

He lowers his bottle. "Never boring. He said you always came at the same time."

It takes all of my control not to react. Fucking Keith! Like the world doesn't already know enough about me?

Now Keith is telling people about my orgasms? For sure that means he also told them all the awful, embarrassing stuff, too.

At least Josh has the sense not to trot out everything he knows. Smart move, since it's pretty clear he wants to get busy with me.

"You call that great sex?" I ask.

"Yeah," he laughs. "What do you call it?"

"Sex that's not boring? I call that the bare minimum for what I expect out of a date." I take a drink. "Is a lot of the sex you have boring?"

"What?" He bobbles the bottle that was on the way to his mouth, spilling some. "No. I didn't mean that. I wasn't saying that. I just meant, you guys came at the same time."

"When do your sex partners come?" I ask. "Or don't they?"

"What? Of course they do. I just—"

"Round Two is starting." After making this important pronouncement, I head back to the table, Josh following in my wake.

I get back to our table, slide into my seat, and pull the answer console in front of me.

"Hey!" Charles is not happy.

"I work the controls from now on." I state it, simple as that. "I've had enough of this bogus team spirit. Either you want me to win for you, or you don't. What'll it be?"

They back off.

For the next ten minutes, they mostly leave me alone.

Good.

It makes me sick to think of how I showed up tonight just so I could distract myself by trying to impress three guys I don't even know with my awesome trivia prowess.

Did I think that would mean they liked me? And that Jack is no big deal in my grand scheme of things? Jack uses me to test his gear, which I agreed to.

Now these guys are using me, but to win free drinks. Something else I agreed to.

When I punch in the answer to the last question, I stand up to leave. Josh looks up.

"Aren't you going to wait to see us win?"

I shrug into my barn jacket with the frayed corduroy collar, shaking my head. "I've got laundry to do."

I'm almost at my car half way down the block when Josh comes running after me. I slow down, letting him jog up to me.

"Laundry?" he asks. "Seriously? I can guarantee that sex with me is better than that."

I need to stop thinking about Jack.

I give him a coy, assessing smile. "Really?"

"Really." He reaches out, takes me by my frayed lapels, and pulls me into a kiss.

* * * * *

Driving home, I try really hard to concentrate on the road, not on my stupid life. What have I done? Why did I do it? I can scarcely breathe every time I contemplate convincing answers. But I need to know. Am I fool? Or not?

I should have gone home with Josh.

Okay, maybe not.

Josh seems like the type to sell the story to the tabloids. But is that really the reason I didn't get down and dirty with him?

By the time I get back to my house, I'm so confused I top off the litter boxes with dry cat food and give Ginger's vitamins to Christian.

I have to get a grip. It's just that, I feel like I don't know what's going on in my own life. I think I might be doing everything wrong. I mean, look at Keith and me. I thought we really hit it off when we met. Then I thought we fell in love and built a forever kind of relationship. I even thought we were getting married. But I was wrong.

Sometimes I wonder what was really happening for those five years.

* * * * *

I hunker down into the couch and pay attention as the commercial ends. This is the best movie Clint Eastwood ever made.

Duh nuh nuh nuh.

"Come in," I yell.

I'm not missing this part for Jack. I don't care if he is helping me Advantage all the pets today.

The front door opens.

"Hey," Jack says, practically making love to my dogs. "You ready?"

"Not yet," I say.

Jack moves further into the room. "You're watching TV? I have to wait for this? Lisa, I called you. You said you'd be ready."

"The fleas will still be here in five minutes," I tell him. "Just chill. I had no idea *this* was on. I was flipping to CNN or WNC or one of the news channels and just found it."

"Lisa ..."

"Please? They're almost to the best line *ever*."

Jack's spots TiVo sitting right next to the TV. "Just record it."

"Haven't hooked up the dish yet. Now just be quiet. Please. We're almost there."

Jack stands, jaw set. "Lisa ..."

"Shhhh! Here it comes."

On screen, the Russian spy says to Clint, "*Gant, can you fly that plane? Really fly it?*"

"Yeah," Clint says, "I can fly it. I'm the best there is."

Wow. *I'm the best there is*. I hug my knees and rock back and forth a little. I think I even make a squeaky/hissy sound, like that of air escaping from an inner tube.

"I remember that," Jack says, staring at the TV.

"You've seen this?"

"No," he says, crinkling his brows. "At least I don't recognize any of this. I think I remember that line from an ad, from when I was a kid." He pauses a second. "*Firefox*, right?"

"Yup," I say, feeling vindicated.

"I remember." He says it this time with a ghost of a smile. "But back then, I thought they were saying, 'Clint, can you fly that plane.' Anyhow, move your ass."

I try to gut him with a glare. "*Don't* talk about my ass. Ever."

Jack just looks at me. He doesn't know that my post-hospital fitness regime has begun to decline. But I know it. I know it every time I look at my butt or try to squeeze it into my treacherous clothes.

"Well," I insist, "if a bald guy was sensitive about losing his hair, you wouldn't say to him, 'C'mon, move your head.' Unless you really wanted him to move his head, like if it was in the way or something."

Jack looks at me for another few seconds then opens his mouth. "Look, as long as I'm here helping with the fleas, why don't I just install your dish for you? It won't take long."

"Oh, no, you don't."

Jack looks at me. "What? Why not? I installed mine. It's not hard."

"I know," I tell him. "That's why I'm going to do it

myself."

"Have you ever done it before?"

"No," I say. "When I bought it, it came with free installation. So, the TiVo guy, or the Direct TV guy, I forget which, did it. But I know how to read an instruction manual, so I'll be fine. But thank you for offering."

"Lisa, it'll be faster if—"

"You men are all the same!" I bolt up from the couch and throw down the remote.

Silence. Then Jack says, "You mean we all offer to help? Because that's all I'm doing. I'm just offering to help. I can do something for you in twenty minutes when it'll probably take you all day."

"So what if it takes me all day? Then I'll know how to do it. And this is not just some 'offer to help.' I've got your number, Hawkins, so back off."

He actually laughs at this. "You are so insane."

"No, I'm not," I say. "Guys do this all the time. I've seen it. I've lived through it. You offer to help. Again and again. So we women get used to it. Then we start expecting that you'll do anything for us that's just the least bit challenging. Fix the air conditioner. Change the light bulb. Plunge the toilet. Go up to the roof to get the tennis ball out of the gutter. Pretty soon, the resentment builds. Then, you start complaining how we're nags. And lazy. And we can't do anything for ourselves. Then you leave us and we're clueless. It's all a trap. An awful, vicious trap. So, no, thank you."

Jack doesn't say anything for a minute. "You don't seem like the type to play tennis," he finally decides.

"I don't," I say. "But I might be throwing a tennis ball for Aaron or Christian to go after."

"And you'd throw it on the roof?"

"Not on purpose, but I have really bad aim. Major

tendency to overthrow." I turn to him. "And don't think I don't see that you're changing the subject because you know I'm right."

"Fine, I won't help you."

"I know you won't," I say. "Because I said 'No,' to your offer of help." I huff out a breath. "But, thank you."

"So, why am I here again?"

"Shut up."

* * * * *

Ninety minutes and four peanut butter and jelly sandwiches later, we're almost done with the lot of them.

"Who's left?" Jack asks from the bathroom doorway.

"Dorothy and Jayne," I say, peering into the mirror over the sink.

I suck in my breath as I press the cotton ball soaked with hydrogen peroxide to the scratches on my neck. Damn damn damn.

I swear my droopy dough-boy chin is coming back. I blasted it to hell once I got out of the hospital and got in shape. But now, thanks to Jack, with whom I pig-out on a regular basis, I'm gaining my weight back. And the sex between us never lasts long enough to burn comparable calories. This is not fair.

Jack doesn't move from the bathroom doorway to go look for the cats or anything helpful like that. "Lisa, they're both boys. You didn't change their names yet?"

"No," I state, "and I'm not going to. Besides, Jayne *is* a boy's name." I dab at my neck. "At least, he's named after a guy named Jayne. And Dorothy from the *Golden Girls* could totally pass for a man."

"But—"

"*Jack*." I bite into the one syllable. "Not every guy needs a testosterone-injected name in order to feel his manhood."

"Hey! I didn't pick my name."

"Noooo," I concede, "but you've certainly lived up to it. I mean, seriously. What were the chances you'd end up becoming a pot-bellied actuary with a name like Jack Hawkins?"

"You're bitching about my *name*? Seriously? What bug crawled up your ass?"

Now the big bully is actually *trying* to piss me off. He *knows* I'm sensitive about my ass!

I put the hydrogen peroxide away and shut the medicine cabinet door. "You are such a *guy*," I accuse, pushing past him on my way back to the kitchen.

"Lisa!" he yells, following me. "What the hell?" He laughs, like I have no reason to be upset. "I come over here to help you and you lay into me about my name and ... and ... what? That I'm a *guy*? I could have sworn you knew all along."

I turn, launching into him. "You eat whatever you want!"

Jack stops in the kitchen doorway. "Don't most grown-ups?"

"Not women," I fume. "We can't. *We* gain weight when we eat. *You* never gain weight. I bet you've never counted a calorie in your life."

Jack just looks at me like a gym teacher would who warned me not to play so rough with the boys. "With your talent for losing millions at a time," he says, "I wouldn't be so cavalier about betting when you don't have a clue what you're talking about. As usual."

I set the last two tubes of flea medicine on the kitchen counter. "Let me guess. You were stuck on top of some mountain with a herd of Yetis and you had one power bar between you to last through a blizzard and doling out the calories correctly was a matter of survival." I blow my hair out of my eyes. "That's *not* what I'm talking about."

Jack picks up Dorothy from where he sleeps on one of the kitchen chairs. "What *are* you talking about?" But he says it in this soft, *coochy-coochy-coo* kind of voice as he scratches Dorothy between the ears. Jack is SUCH a sap.

"You're making me fat." There. I said it.

"You're not fat." He says this in a high-pitched falsetto, and I can tell he's pretending to be Dorothy talking. "Have you seen Sophia?" he continues in Dorothy's voice. "Now, she's got a big gut."

"I'm fatt*er* than I was when I got in shape after the hospital. Every time I'm with you, we eat. You're my enabler."

He shifts Dorothy to one arm and opens the fridge with the other. "I did not buy all this stuff," he says, peering in. "In fact, I didn't buy any of it. And I doubt elves fill your fridge at night. So ..." He shuts the door and shrugs. "Time to face the awful truth, Lisa. You like to eat."

"Shut up!"

"It's not a sin. Some even argue that it's necessary to sustain life."

I reach out to take Dorothy from him, but of course the little traitor doesn't want to budge. So I have to pry his claws out of Jack's shirt, one by one. "You don't get it," I tell him. I tell Jack, not Dorothy, though I'm sure Dorothy is equally clueless.

"Yes, I do," he counters. "To look like Tyra Banks, all you can ever eat is water and broccoli. But you want more. But then you can't look like Tyra Banks."

He delivers Dorothy to me. "Just decide which you'd rather be: happy or skinny."

"Why does it have to be a choice?"

"Because that's how life is, Lisa. It's all about choices. Do you want to have friends, or work your ass off so you can get rich? Do you stay to close the deal, or do you go home to your kid's birthday party? When you love your best friend's girl, do you give up the friend or the girl? Do you rescue twelve animals, or do you lead a carefree life that allows you to go on vacation?"

"But—"

"You just have to shut out the world and decide what *you* want."

"But the world is still out there. It's always out there."

"Make your own world, Lisa. Stop worrying about everyone else."

"I *am* making my own world. But I want to show everyone. I want everyone to see that … I …"

"Stop thinking about how everyone is looking at you."

"What about how you're looking at me?" As soon as I hear myself say it, I wish I'd kept my mouth shut. And God. The way he's looking at me right now. Like I've taken everything too seriously.

"What do you mean?" His tone is deadly calm.

"Jack." I decide to use my best rational voice. I've got to sound like I'm so NOT serious about him AT ALL.

"I understand what you're saying about forgetting what others think. But what they think affects me in ways I never imagined. So just forgetting is hard. You know?"

"The best stuff usually is."

"Shut up! You're totally stealing that from *A League of Their Own*."

"Lisa, I can speak for myself. I don't have to quote some stupid movie."

"It's *not* a stupid movie."

"What are you doing?" He sounds disappointed in me, as if I brought him slippers when he asked for the paper. "You want to fight about a movie? Why? So we get off topic and onto a subject where you can kick my ass? Will that make you feel better?"

I set Dorothy on the kitchen table, lean over him, and use my thumbs to part his fur. I wait until Jack squeezes the medicine onto the cat's neck.

"You're an asshole."

Jack empties the tube, then pushes Dorothy's fur back together. "Good boy," he says, kissing him on the head just before I release him. I release Dorothy, not Jack.

Jack turns to me. "What the hell is that supposed to mean? I'm an asshole for—"

"Don't you dare call me out for wanting to talk about things I'm smart about. Not when you've spent your life specifically avoiding things you suck at."

Jack occupies himself wrapping the empty tube of flea medicine in tin foil. Apparently, this keeps Mr. I-Can-Snowboard-Down-Everest-While-Checking-Emails-on-My-Blackberry so busy that he can neither look at me nor respond to me.

"So you see," I say nonchalantly, "I'm not the only one who likes to focus on the things I'm good at."

Jack tosses the foil-wrapped tube in the garbage.

"Jayne's the last one? He's sleeping in the living room window."

"That's it?" I ask. "I've made a valid point so now the conversation's over?" I try to catch his eye as he concentrates on poking open the next tube of flea medicine.

He meets my stare. "If I'm such a jerk, why do you care what I think of you?"

A direct question. I don't want to answer it, but I asked for it. And I am supposed to be getting braver. "I want you to respect me, Jack."

Silence.

"You've taught me a lot," I continue, "and, since you're my coach, in a lot of ways–"

He looks away. I've lost him with my bullshit.

I take a deep breath. "I want you to respect me because I respect you."

He comes back to meet my eyes.

"I want it to be mutual between us," I say. "I like you and, well, I think you're a cool guy. And I want you to like me back. That way, we'd be friends."

He blinks a few times. "You want to be friends with me?"

"Yeah," I say, never quite having thought of it this way before. But I can work with it. "Like Holmes and Watson, you know? Holmes is obviously better at a lot of stuff, but Watson brings his own dynamic. Or Poirot and Hastings, more like. Poirot often uses, and definitely appreciates, how Hastings can be an idiot about a lot of things."

Jack's eyebrows move closer together, making me think he's considering what I've said.

"No," he says.

"What?" I squawk. "'No?' 'No' what?"

"No, I don't want to be friends."

"B-but," I sputter. "Why not?"

"Because we fuck."

Just like that, he turns everything inside out. I mean, he just *says* it, right here, in my kitchen. While we're medicating cats! He makes it like it's real or something. But it can't be.

My scalp gets really cold, making me feel like I'm in the wrong place. "Well, yeah," I say, my ever-present rhetorical skills to the rescue. "That doesn't mean we can't be friends."

"That's what women always say."

"How would you know?" I zing back. "You've surveyed all women, have you? I must have been absent that day because I don't remember getting the questionnaire."

"Lisa, just like you and your TiVo, I know how to avoid

a trap."

"Then why did you tell me about Luz and her parents? Why tell me if you don't consider me someone with friend-potential?"

He looks around, huffs out a puff of air. "I told you because I wanted to tell someone. Not so much because I needed someone to listen. Make sense?"

I try to swallow. "So far."

"You're someone I know, but you're not ... well, you're not someone in my life. I needed to tell someone who wouldn't know too much about me and try to analyze the whole thing. After fifteen years, I just wanted to exorcise the ghosts. That's all. And here you are, and as it turns out, I know a lot of bizarre things about you. So you were safe. To tell."

"Like a secret box to put stuff in then bury."

"Kind of."

I stare at him. He's telling me right to my face that he's using me like he'd use an old shoebox. He's saying it as if it's okay to do that.

He doesn't say anything else. Nothing to make anything any better.

It's clear that he doesn't care about me. Not as a person.

Certainly not in a boy-girl way. Not even, apparently, in a mammal-to-mammal way.

And it's not something dramatic I can rail at him about. He just doesn't care.

"Uh, thanks for answering me," I finally say. A few weeks ago, I charged into his house demanding honesty. And he just gave me honesty. In spades.

He honestly doesn't care.

But I honestly do.

CHAPTER 18

I look out the window at the steady drizzle. Cold, wet water getting all over *everything*. I put down the hairdryer and wonder why I even bothered. Why warm up my scalp before I heartlessly expose my whole head to the nasty bite of late October rain?

Why am I still agreeing to let Jack use me like this? Sure, we had a deal. And supposedly I'm getting bravery lessons out of all this.

But that's all talk. Meaningless words, words, words. I'm pretty sure I've fallen for the guy. And he doesn't give a damn about me. I should have ended the deal two weeks ago. But no. Then I wouldn't see him anymore.

I'm so pathetic.

I take in a shaky breath. Tonight on the mountain, I am going to seduce Jack. If I have to spend the night in a damn tent, I want that guy plastered all over me until dawn. It's not like I expect affection or anything from the encounter. But I know these testing jaunts won't last forever. So, for as long as Jack's in my life, I want to get as much of him as possible.

Feeling like a sex warrior, I surge to the closet and fling it open. What should I wear to seduce Jack on a dark, cold, muddy mountain?

When he called me yesterday to set this up, he told me to

dress for hiking. But can I do that and get away with sexy undies? Or is my unadorned naked body enough to entice him to spend the night with me? I run to the mirror to check myself out.

Hearing an engine cough to a stop outside, I run to the window to peek past the curtain.

Jack gets out of his vegetable oil truck, and suddenly I know why so many country songs are written about men and their trucks. Jack just looks so damn hot.

I really hope he wants me as much as I want him. But would anyone write a song about *my* getting out of truck?

I hear him ring at the front door, but I'm naked and in the middle of something important. I open the window and holler around the corner for him to come in. In a few seconds, I hear his voice above the excited-to-see-their-favorite-person dog noise in the living room.

"You almost ready?" he calls.

"Hold on."

I dash back to the mirror to mercilessly evaluate my assets.

First, my abs. Somewhat defined, but not as tight as they were before I chased Jack up the mountain. I eat way too much when I'm with him. But maybe he likes softer curves.

Next, my neck. I've been obsessed with how my neck looks ever since I saw *Emma*. I stretch my chin up as high as it goes.

Okay, so I'm no Gwyneth. Then again, Jack's no Jeremy.

Next, my boobs. Damn. When I was a size fourteen, they had some definite va-va-va-voom to them. Now, they look like two small Fuji apples.

I take another look at my entire body. Trim, but not lethally so. Butt okay, bosom nothing to write home about.

Overall, I look—I look—Oh, my God.

Average.

I look *average*. That's how the police would describe me if I were a suspect being hunted by the law. Average build, average height, brown hair, brown eyes. They probably wouldn't even mention the greeney-blue flecks.

All this time, all this work, just to become *average*?

I can scarcely breathe. I'm going to hyperventilate. Then faint. And hit my head.

It's not fair. Before the accident, I was at the interesting edge of the bell curve. I hefted more weight than the average L.A. chick, but I carried it off. I had it goin' on.

How could I have forgotten that I used to rationalize my big butt and bulky thighs by consoling myself that I had the boobs to match? And I don't care what evil Madison at *June Brides* had to say. Damn her stupid boob pads.

I was a happenin' chick. I liked my boobs.

They weren't exactly Weezy Jefferson boobs, but they were mine and I loved them.

And so did Keith. A LOT.

And now they're gone, exercised into oblivion.

I hear sharp, rapid knocking at the door. "Lisa?"

It's Jack. And I've got no rack!

"What's wrong?" he shouts. "Are you okay?"

I can hear the dogs snuffling at the door, but I know they don't give a damn about my emotional breakdown. They're just flanking Jack. I throw myself across the bed and press my face into my pillow.

Through the door, "Lisa?"

I roll myself into my comforter like a burrito. I'm in my thirties and hopelessly average.

Do people like me ever suddenly get UN-average? The six million dollars isn't helping. What are my chances? My whole body tenses when I feel hands on my shoulders.

"Lisa?"

Not through the door this time.

I jerk around to face Jack, who's leaning over me. I scurry to sitting position, but since I'm wrapped in the comforter, I inch up like a grub.

"What are you doing in here?" My anger at my averageness funnels into my voice.

Jack steps back. "Trying to get in the truck and leave. What the hell's going on?" He looks me up and down. "And are you naked?"

He says it like my being naked is just a bad idea on principle.

"I can be naked if I want to be naked." Jack looks confused, but I don't relent. "And guess what, Spider-Man?" I'm really on a roll now. "You don't have to have rock hard abs or a supermodel butt to earn the right to be naked. Anyone can be naked if they want to be."

"O-kay," he says slowly. "But why are you naked *now*?"

I can hardly tell the guy that I was scoping out my assets to gauge my chances of seducing him, especially as my current situation is drastically damaging said chances. "I wanted to get back in bed," I say, just a tad haughty. "And I never wear clothes to bed."

"This is insane," he says, clearly losing patience. "You're naked more than, like, any other woman I've known, and it's not even a good thing. There's got to be some damn calamity."

"That's not always my fault!" I shout. "And it always happens in *my* house. I didn't invite you here the night I was in the shower. And I sure didn't invite you into my room."

He pins me with a look. "Since *when* do we need invitations to barge into each other's lives?"

He's got a point, but I've still got some ire left in me.

"Not the same thing, bucko. That day I chased you up the mountain I might have been a little pushy, but it's not your mountain."

"Speaking of," he says, looking down again at my comforter cocoon, "are we going to do this, or what? Are you changing your mind?"

"Of course not," I say, scooching my way toward the edge of the bed so I can stand. "Why do you think I was buried in bed?"

Jack pauses a sec, looks down. Then he meets my eyes. "You're that scared?"

"No!"

His head jerks back. "Then what?"

"It's just that I'm going to miss all my guys." I look at the beastly traitors where they hunker at Jack's feet. "We've never really been apart since I rescued them."

Jack ruffles Pacquito's ears. "Do you trust Mia to take care of them?"

"Of course." I look down at Ginger. You'd think at least *she* could muster a show of female solidarity.

"Then what's the problem?"

I want to whack Jack but my arms are wrapped up tight. "There is no *problem*. I'm just taking a minute to *feel* how much I'm going to miss them. Is this such an alien concept to you?"

I see a muscle in his jaw flicker. "I'll wait outside." He walks out with the dogs, closing the door behind them.

I stand up and toss the comforter back on the bed. Why do I want Jack, anyway? The guy has issues.

* * * * *

I lean against the tile counter and breathe. My muscles are so tense I feel like a plank of driftwood .Wet, stiff, adrift.

What a weekend.

And it's only Saturday night.

I glance toward Jack's spic and span shower. I want to thaw out. I do. But I get reminded of how cold I am every time I move and my icy clothes touch me. I need to get myself into that shower, but I don't want to inch my way over.

Jesus. Did I actually think I had a chance of seducing Jack tonight? I'd be lucky to bed a horny goat looking like this.

I pivot on one foot, scarcely moving a muscle. I look directly into the mirror, which is enough to crush all my ridiculous illusions.

My hair sticks to my head in dull, muddy spikes. The grime on my face makes my eyeballs look really white. I don't even look cute in Jack's big jacket.

Nope. I look like I pulled a bulky, misshapen grocery sack over my scrubby pin-head.

I turn away in disgust, making my rickety way to the shower. I just turn on the water when someone, I'm assuming Jack, knocks on the door.

"Come in," I say. "I'm not naked or causing trouble."

He walks in wearing a navy bathrobe and without looking at me, sets a pile of clothes on the counter. "Pajama pants, T-shirt, boxers, socks, and a sweatshirt. After you thaw out in the shower, these should keep you pretty warm."

"You own pajama pants?"

He looks at me. "I've spent as much as four days in a row in a harness, scaling a cliff. So you better believe that when I get the chance to kick back, I'm not going to be wearing any buckles, snaps, Gore-Tex, or spandex."

I nod with my eyes downcast, trying to look ashamed for making fun of his owning jammie pants.

"I put the other clothes in the washer, so, before you get in the shower, just throw the rest of what you're wearing outside the door and I'll add it to what's already in there."

Great. I'd planned to nail the bejesus out of him this weekend, but instead, he's washing my dirty undies.

"And take it slow in the shower," he advises. "You need to thaw out, so give yourself time to do that."

I nod again. "Thanks."

He pulls back to leave.

"Wait," I say.

"Yeah?"

"You're taking a shower, too. Right?"

"Yeah, upstairs. Why?"

"Well, I mean, do you think we should both take separate showers at the same time?"

He looks at me and opens his mouth, but he doesn't say anything. He just stands there, looking curious but unsure. Like how Pacquito looks when I whistle the theme to *Sanford and Son*.

"I mean ..."

Jack closes his mouth.

"I'll wait," I say. "I could just soak my feet or something. You can go first."

Jack's eyebrows inch upward. "Go first?"

"The washer's running. Plus two showers? There won't be enough water. Especially not enough hot water."

He shakes his head and I could swear in my numb state he looks a little pissed off. "Lisa, your house was built in what? 1927? And the plumbing's never really been updated. But in these modern houses built in the nineties? There's plenty of water. Hot *and* cold."

"Oh."

"I can even run the dryer and the dishwasher at the same time without losing power."

"Are you making fun of my house?"

"Yes," he says. "Now get in the shower."

After the door snaps shut behind him, I hold my breath, peel off the clothes, and throw them outside the bathroom door. When I step under the shower spray, I screech at the pain of thawing out. But when the scalding sensations subside, I can't stop wailing.

How the hell could this happen? How could I have messed up so badly? It was just a creek. A creek! We were minutes away from setting up camp for the night and I had been gamely impressive all day. Jack was about to be mine for a whole night.

That damn, damn creek!

* * * * *

"It's wider than the Mississippi." My stomach dropped to my ankles.

"The rainwater's made it higher than usual." Jack stopped along the bank at a place where he found a few rocks dotting their way across. "Just remember what I told you about crossing. Keep your momentum going forward."

I swallowed, needing Moses to part the waters for me.

"You can do this Lisa. It looks nasty right now, but it's just a creek."

"And Jaws was just a shark."

Jeez! Why did I have to think of sharks when I was about to step into the water? Okay, okay. I can do this. Think of another movie. Think of another movie. *Climb every mountain/ Ford every stream/ Fol—*

"I'll go first," Jack said, "in case there are any trouble spots." He chucked a finger under my chin. "Look on the bright side. You're already pretty wet."

I gave a shaky laugh. The roaring in my ears drowned

out the roaring of the water. “You think I’m pretty?” My voice sounded very far away, and I wondered if Jack could even hear it.

He laughed. “See you on the other bank.” And just like that, he glided across the water like Eric Heiden.

“It’s all good,” he called across the crashing water. “Just remember, don’t stop to balance on each rock. Keep your momentum going forward.”

Momentum. Momentum. Momentum.

The creek looked strong. Jack said I could do it. But the creek looked so powerful. I felt sick.

“Ready?” Jack called.

Oh God. I tried to remember that I’d leapt out of a plane and rappelled off a cliff.

“Go!”

I jumped off the bank into the raging torrent. I skipped from the first rock to the second, but just as I took off for the third, I saw the rushing water swell. It was coming right at me!

I rushed toward the third rock, panic upsetting my balance.

My foot glanced off the rock as the water grabbed me by the ankles and yanked me into the torrent.

Water hit me all over. I couldn't hear or breathe. I bobbed to the top. Jack was already twenty yards away. I tried to raise an arm so he could see me. The current jerked at my pack, pulled me back under. I choked, spit, spun.

I tried to find the surface. I felt ground under me so I pushed off, trying to kick to the top. My pack was caught on something! It held me down! I tried to wrestle my arms out, but my jacket had twisted itself all around the straps. Uuuuh! I couldn't breathe!

I ripped the jacket off my shoulders, pushed to the surface.

"AAAAH!"

But the water sucked me back into its vortex, mashing my hips against rocks. The velocity of the raging water flipped me over and around. I felt a pointy rock jutting up and I grabbed on. Freezing water pelted me, pelted me, pelted me. But I didn't let go.

"Lisa!"

Suddenly, Jack was there, in the water with me. His arm wrapped around my waist like an iron vise. "Let go!"

But I was too scared to move, afraid we'd both be washed away. Jack pulled, I held. He poked me in the ribs. In an automatic reflex, I jerked back and Jack hauled me into the current. In a few seconds I felt grit and pebbles scrape the backs of my thighs. Jack was dragging me onto shore. He heaved my body well away from the water, then collapsed beside me.

"Oh ... my ... God. Oh ... my ... God. Oh ... my ... God." I turned my head to look at him. I breathed and breathed and breathed. "How?" I panted. "How did you get me out of there?"

Jack takes a deep breath. "I walked."

"What?" Pant, pant, pant. "Like, on water?"

He turned his head toward me then. "The creek's maybe four feet in the deepest places."

"But all the rain."

"It's usually about a foot deep here."

This made no sense. I was bested by water no deeper than what's in an assemble-yourself backyard pool? "How long was I in?"

"About fifteen seconds, before I got to you."

Fifteen seconds? No way. He had to have meant minutes. Had to.

I opened my mouth to ask him, but my teeth started chattering so hard I was sure my jaw would shatter.

Jack stood up. He walked up the bank about ten yards,

retrieved his pack, and came back. He dropped the pack, began stripping off his wet clothes.

Was he serious? He was getting naked after all that?

Once his clothes were off, the removal of which took about three seconds, he bent to the pack, fished out dry clothes. Then he started putting them on. Boxers, jeans, shirt. No socks, though. Mr. Survival Packer forgot socks.

He yanked me to my feet then, and started peeling the clothes off my shivering body. "Sun's almost down. It's supposed to drop to forty tonight. It'll take a little over an hour, but if we race down the mountain, we should make it before you really start freezing. We'll have to go fast. You'll have to keep up, Lisa."

"But t-testing. Y-you st-st-still have your g-gear."

"Too risky. You have to get warm."

Once he had me naked, he grabbed his shirt off the ground where it was lying under his jacket. They were both mostly dry, so he must have ripped them off before he jumped–walked–in for me. He started running the shirt over me roughly, drying me off.

"Ow!"

"That's good that you can feel it."

Then he grabbed silk long johns out of his pack and helped me into them. Next, he put me into his jacket. Then socks. He did bring socks, after all. Huh. He put each of my feet into a cushy pair of clean, dry socks as thick as slippers. Then he took a pair of shoes out of his pack. They looked like a cross between swim shoes and baseball cleats.

"Put these on."

As I did, he gathered up all our wet clothes, rung them out, put them in his waterproof pack. He got the gear onto his back, then pulled a flashlight out of somewhere and flicked it on.

"I c-can c-carry something," I offered.

"Just keep up."

He grabbed my hand and we were off. My feet slid around, but the shoes stayed on. Branches and thorns snagged at Jack's coat, but we kept going. Soon, my blood heated up and I moved faster. Jack, feeling my strength returning, picked up the pace. We drove ourselves down the mountain, through brambles, under brush, over logs, across puddles, into mud. It's like Jack was hopping me through Frogger at warp speed. We cut a direct course down the same mountain we'd spent the day winding our way up.

When we finally got back to the truck, Jack opened my door, hustled me in, scooted around to his side, got in, and blasted the heat.

My body hummed and throbbed. I huffed and puffed.

Jack spared a second to look at me before peeling out. "Are you okay?"

The world came back into focus. "I lost the pack," I said, tears rolling down my face. "I panicked in the creek. I thought I was drowning. I thought I was being swept away. And it was just a creek, hardly even waist high." I sniffed and swiped at my cheeks. "You had no idea I would freak out like that. My spaz attack was off the charts. It ruined everything."

Jack punched the gas, speeding us up. "Lisa, I don't care about the pack. You DID almost drown. You got scared, and you went under. I should have been ready."

I sniffled some more.

"Tomorrow," he said, sounding quiet and very serious, "when you wake up, when this has had some time to sink in, think about forgiving me."

"Jack, I was in the water less than twenty seconds. You said so yourself. You saved me." I pulled back to look at him. The heat from the car started seeping through the damp clothes I was wearing. I didn't forgive him because there was nothing to forgive. But I knew what he wanted to hear. "I forgive you."

"You don't get it," he snapped back. "I took you up there. I should have been taking care of you. Better care. I know you're a beginner. I know how scared you get." He sighed. "I forget, Lisa. Sometimes, when I'm with you, I forget. Today on the mountain, you were hell on wheels, taking everything I dished out. I kept making it harder and harder, and you just kept going. I didn't even care that you ripped your favorite jeans. Those were your Bruce Springsteen jeans, weren't they? But you kept right on going."

"You know about my Bruce Springsteen jeans?"

"You told me about them once. I figured this had to be them, when you started crying when you ripped a hole in the knee. But why'd you wear them to go camping in the rain?"

I didn't answer. I wasn't going to tell him my ass had gotten too big for all my size eights and I had to wear the jeans I'd retired after seeing The Boss when I was a husky teen. "Nice try, Jack," I said, sniffling. "But I messed up. This is my fault. I'm supposed to be getting braver. I've jumped down a hundred-foot waterfall, but I almost killed myself crossing a creek. And you want me to believe it's your fault because you forgot I was Lisa Flyte? You expect me to believe I tricked you into thinking I was Indiana Jones with a manicure?"

"That's not what I mean," he said, not even busting me about the pathetic state of my nails. "Sometimes ..." he said, "I forget how different our attitudes are, how you're not going to react to something the same way I would. I forget that what's instinct to me makes no sense to you. Sometimes it feels like we're on the same wavelength, you know? But we're not. We're not even on the same planet. Do you get it?" he asked. "I stop thinking about how different we really are, and that's what causes all the trouble. It's just plain dangerous."

* * * * *

The hot water blasts me in the face but the tears keep coming. I'm such a mess. Such a fool. I was going to try to get closer to Jack, to spend an entire night with him. For what? To prove to myself that he wants me in his life, despite what he says?

We're not even on the same planet.

I sob harder, making wracking, choking sounds like Claire Danes makes at the end of *Romeo and Juliet*.

Swish.

The curtain slides back, and Jack steps into the shower behind me.

I sniff and look away. Oh, God. Could he *hear* me? I'm *louder* than the shower? Is he in here because he feels sorry for me?

Without trying to get me to look at him, he picks up the shampoo bottle and squeezes a dollop onto my head. Then he puts those big hands of his in my hair and starts lathering up.

We're not even on the same planet.

He slides his sudsy hands down my neck, massaging as he goes. My shoulders. My back.

Maybe he didn't hear me crying. Maybe he has no idea I'm having a meltdown in his shower. Maybe he just wants to have sex.

He slides his arms around my waist, tucking me close into his body. "You're all right, Lisa," he says quietly into my ear. "You're all right. It's okay. It's going to be okay."

I start to cry again, and he just holds me as the water pelts down on us.

CHAPTER 19

When I get into my cubicle of an office at HEYA Tuesday after class at USC, the phone is ringing.

"Yeah?"

"Hello to you, too," he chuckles. "So, are we a go?"

Crispin. His voice sounds so up-beat and happy, as if everyone loves him.

"Next week," I boom, trying to make my voice sound as if I'm smiling. "The investor from Rankin gets back from Detroit next Wednesday, then we all sign on Thursday."

"Awesome. Want to grab dinner to celebrate?"

"Very slick," I say, "sliding it in there oh so casually like that. But no. We'll talk *business* next week."

"Sounds good."

He sounds so un-fazed by my rejection that I almost reconsider. Maybe we could skip dinner and just have sex. In a bed.

"Bye." I hang up quickly, before I destroy the plan to save HEYA with my desperation.

The phone rings again. "What?!"

"I'm working on something. Can you test Saturday, late afternoon into the evening?"

"Jack?"

"To quote you, 'Duh.'"

"But you just saw me in class," I splutter. "And you didn't say a word to me."

"You didn't say a word to me either."

"But I didn't have anything to say."

Which is such a big lie. I *really* wanted to tell him he's a terrible person for not even calling me since he dropped me home Saturday night. And for dropping me home in the first place! Mia was there to babysit the pets all night. We could have curled up safe and warm together and slept in his bed.

But what's the point of regretting what *didn't* happen, when Jack won't even acknowledge what *did*. He's never said a word about the shower. I mean, we were *naked*, and he was *nice* to me. It wasn't just a quick, post-adventure bonk.

I feel myself blush hotly.

"Neither did I," Jack says, making me blush harder. "Now I do. Can you test?"

Back to business. "Don't know," I answer. "I'll let you know in class tomorrow."

* * * * *

In the corner of my beautiful bedroom, as the sun streams through the filmy curtains, I look into the mirror, turning this way and that. Yup. It's the same from every angle. I'm practically busting out of my Ann Taylor. I reach back to feel my big butt. Damn. I tighten my tummy and stand up as straight as I can, trying to streamline my figure. Who am I kidding? I can't remember to stand like this all day.

Forty minutes later, I *clip clip clip* on my heels to the classroom to see if Jack is around yet. Nope. I turn away from the door and almost slam right into him.

"Whoa," he says. He looks me up and down. "I thought you had HEYA today."

"I—I do," I stutter. "I have a meeting with Fidelity at two, to discuss our situation. HEYA's situation. And I have a request or two. They need to be on board for my plan to work."

"Well," he says, still looking me up and down, "just ask them for what you want, nice and slow, and I think you'll get it."

I stupidly look down at the suit I'm spilling out of, then back up at Jack. "I can test on Saturday. Where should I meet you? What should I wear?"

"A dress," he says. "A nice one. And I'll pick you up at your house at five-thirty."

"Excuse me?"

"We're going to a party. But not a kegger. More like a ball."

I just stare.

"With dancing," he says, almost in a whisper.

I step back. "You're crazy."

"And you're scared of dancing in public."

"That's none of your business!" Students are starting to filter past us, so I do that harsh whisper thing.

He lowers his voice as well. "Did you, or did you not, come to me asking me to make you braver?"

"Physical bravery, Jack!"

"Dancing *is* physical."

Damn it.

"Just where exactly is it that you think you're going to take me?" I demand.

"Friends of my parents are putting on this big shindig. They bug me to go to this stuff a few times a year, and when something pretty innocuous comes up, I accept."

"So you need a date," I accuse. "And what? You think you'll just humiliate me in the process and kill two birds with one stupid party?"

"Nobody ever *needs* a date, Lisa. It *is* possible to go to a party alone."

"Oh, I get it. You go to stuff by yourself just to hook up, don't you?"

"Are you even listening to yourself? First you accuse me of needing a date, now I'm a player preying on unattached partygoers. You make no sense, Lisa. None. I'm taking you to this party because you're afraid of dancing."

"I never said so."

"Every time you hear music you start to twitch to it, but you stop as soon as you think someone might be watching."

"*Twitch*?"

"If you don't go we'll both know it's because you're scared."

"Scared, my ass! Maybe I just don't like being hoodwinked into going to some ritzy party."

"That's no reason not to go."

"Yes, it is."

Jack nods. "So you won't do it?"

Holy hell. Does he look *relieved*?

"I'll see you on Saturday."

CHAPTER 20

Underwear.

I need to get some serious underwear.

Why did I wait so long to try on this stupid dress? I'm not as in shape as I was when I bought it. Jack was right all along. This is what I get for splurging with my evil corporate millions.

Once I got out of the hospital, I realized I had enough money to buy clothes I loved but would never wear. Dreamy, fabulous clothes. Long black satin gloves, boots that look like Witchiepoo's legs, a downy soft feather boa, a mocha cowboy hat with a rhinestone band, and a shimmery white evening gown that slides along my curves as would sun-sparkled rain.

Make that SLID along my curves.

Past tense. Before my country-lane curves expanded into interstate highways. Now the gown sticks and clings. This is what I get for post-adventure pigging out. What am I going to do? I can't snap my fingers and conjure up a perfect dress. I can't even buy one. I'm on a budget now, with the house and all the pet food and everything.

I look at the clock by my bed. 2 p.m.

I have less than three and a half hours to find something to wear, so I'm down to relying on underwear. I'll need to get something like a girdle so I can squeeze myself into the dress. I know such contraptions exist. I saw that *Emergency*! episode where John and Roy had to cut a woman out of the girdle that was suffocating her. Plus, a few months ago, bridal-shop bitches all over the Southland were all but throwing body-sucking underwear at me.

But are those things even still called girdles?

Three hours later I squeeze into my brand new Flexees one piece. It's like this strapless bathing suit that compresses me so tightly I would get the bends if I ever tried to swim in it.

Plus I'd drown. You know, not being able to breathe and all.

Next, I barely manage to get myself into a brand new pair of stockings. I should have put them on before the Flexees, when I could still bend and stretch, but it's too late now.

No way am I taking off the Flexees and then re-squeezing myself in. I have neither the endurance nor the will power.

After the thigh highs are in place, I wedge myself into hellish biker shorts-ish underwear meant to shape my thighs into sleek gazelle-like limbs. My entire body hurts when I try to move or think.

Finally, I slip the dress over my head.

It glides over me! It doesn't get stuck on my bumpy curves. I look in the mirror at the smooth line of my S-like figure. I'm sleek with cleavage.

The doorbell rings, so I run-limp-gasp to the door. Thank God I put the dogs outside. If they got in my way now, I would tumble to the floor and wouldn't be able to get up, just like snow-suited Randy. My underwear doesn't allow for things like bending or calling for help. If I trip, I'm so dead.

Thoughts of death by underwear evaporate as I realize that Jack is on my porch. Remembering that I'll have to dance soon scares me so much I don't even *want* to breathe. As I open the door to let him in, I peek into the mirror over the mail table to check myself out one last time.

Wham!

I slam the door in Jack's face and turn fully to the mirror. Oh, my God! The top of my underwear is sticking out! The dress is too low cut! Movement of any kind causes my sleek-a-fying underwear to show!

"Lisa?" It's Jack, through the door.

"Come in." I scamper and wheeze my way back to my room. I hear him come through the front door just before I slam the door to my room.

Oh God Oh God Oh God! What the hell?

I want to scream and cry but I know I'll never get enough oxygen to do that. Not to mention, Jack is outside, and I'm not about to be a woman who makes him wait a year while I get ready.

Swiping the straps off my shoulders, I let the dress fall to the floor. I struggle out of my underwear, noticing the red dents in my flesh. I toss the Flexees into my enameled trashcan painted with flowers and leaves. I step once again into the biker-shorts contraption, trying to salvage what I can. On goes the dress.

No good. Wearing just the bottoms of my flesh-compressing unmentionables doesn't work. It leaves a big groove in the middle of my figure where the underwear ends and I burst out.

I lift my skirt, pulling off the biker-like underwear which quickly joins the Flexees. I go to my dresser, find a pair of panties, step into them. I look in the mirror to see myself billowing out of the white, shimmery dress. I'm the fat caterpillar about to burst out of a frothy cocoon. And tonight I was supposed to be a butterfly.

I go to my closet and rummage around, desperately looking for an answer. And there it is, wrapped around the printer that doesn't work anymore.

The white feather boa.

I take it out of the closet and drape it around me. The plump snake of feathers distracts attention from the dress plastered onto my flesh. Hardly perfect, but on the up side, I can breathe.

I sweep out of my bedroom and head straight for the front door, ignoring Jack. But he snags the boa as I breeze past him.

"Hold on."

Drat. My plan was to keep moving so that he couldn't get a good look at my figure.

"Can I at least look at you?" He pulls me toward him by the boa.

I turn around.

Jack's scrutiny is merciless. "That's, uh, some dress."

I notice he doesn't exactly compliment me. He knows the fit is awful.

"Shouldn't we get going?" I play all innocent, so he'll feel really low when he tells me that my dress and I just don't measure up.

He rips his eyes off the offending dress to look at my face. "Yeah, I guess. Look ..." He stops talking.

"What?"

"It's just that I think you should take off the dress."

"I knew it!" I stomp my foot as I flounce my boa. "You *said* a nice dress! And now you want me to change?"

"No," he says slowly. "I want you to take. Off. The. Dress." He looks at me, his gaze steady and hot.

Oh.

We're not even on the same planet.

"Listen," I say, backing away. "If you want to have sex with me, you can wait until after my death-defying dancing.

Because honestly, I just can't get in the mood without that intense hit of adrenaline."

"Oh, no?" And then he's on me, hands in my hair, kissing me. A long, slow, wet kiss.

But I'm not about to let it last three days. "Unh-uh," I say as I break away from him. I open the front door and walk out first, trying to ignore the tingles all over my body. "Close the door behind you," I toss over my shoulder.

But before I can even take two steps, he's right behind me, hands on my arms, lips on my neck. "I'm not playing games," he whispers, then bites my ear.

I turn, putting my hands on his shoulders to keep enough of my own space. "I'm not either, Jack." My voice is level enough to show him that I mean it. "Jack, you can't kiss me like this then expect to have sex with me like it doesn't even count."

His lips part in surprise, just a little bit, and he looks at me. He doesn't say anything.

At all.

Turning away from him, I look toward the street. "What's with the car?" A long black Mercedes sits at the curb. "Does it run on vegetable oil?"

"It's not a diesel." He hooks my arm to lead me down the path. "I was thinking of you. Thought you might not want your dress ..." he reaches out to tweak my boa "... or your feathers, to smell like egg rolls."

I slide him a glance. "Sure you weren't thinking about yourself?" Jack looks incredibly lithe in a dark suit, white shirt, no tie. And no tie means I can see his neck and his throat. I look away. "No tie, I see." I say this like it's an accusation, like he's bringing me down.

"Stepping out for a night once a year to see my parents is one thing. Wearing a tie for them is entirely another."

He opens the passenger side back door of the car for me.

"Huh?" I say, peering into the car. "A driver? *You* got a driver?"

"Renting a luxury car at the last minute on Saturday didn't leave me with a lot of options." Jack shuts me in then walks around to the other door to join me in the back seat.

"Hi," I say, scooching up to address the driver. He looks like he's in his early twenties, and he's not wearing a uniform.

"Hey," he says, turning his head slightly to acknowledge me.

"This is Chick," Jack introduces.

"Lisa," I say.

"Hi, Lisa."

"Hi, Chick."

I sit back into the comfy seat. "Nice."

"I figure I'll ease you into my parents' world," Jack says, "one toe at a time."

"So a party with them is like getting into a really hot bath?"

"More like a really cold pool."

I inch forward again to talk to Chick. "How come you're not wearing a uniform, like in the movies?"

"Mr. Hawkins requested I didn't."

"Mr. Hawkins? What does Jack's dad have to do with anything? Wait. You mean Jack?"

"I mean Jack."

I look back to Jack.

He shrugs. "I can take only so much. A uniform was pushing it."

"You look good," I tell Chick, then flop back into the seat.

"Thanks," he says. "You, too."

I beam. "Thanks." I look at Jack. "So, off to the OC?"

"The Ritz Carlton Laguna."

"Sounds very bling bling. What's all this for?"

"Darcy and Simon Kitzmiller just had a baby about four months ago. Fourth of July, I think."

"So there're going to be kids there? And, like, balloons and stuff? What was it? A boy or a girl?"

"No idea. And no, no kids and probably no balloons. This party has more to do with Darcy showing off her red-hot after-baby figure. It's not really about the baby at all."

"You know Darcy?"

"Not really."

"You nailed her in high school, didn't you?"

"I nailed everybody."

"Even Simon?"

"And his mom."

"Right." I move my butt so I'm not sitting on my boa. "Jack, why are you going to this? A baby party for a bunch of people you barely know?"

"Much less dangerous than a wedding or any kind of luncheon my mother can devise."

I turn to him. "Why go at all? Why dip into your parents' world if you don't want to? It's like going swimming when you're not even hot."

A deep ridge appears between his brows. "You're saying I'm not hot?"

I catch Chick glancing into the rearview mirror.

"What do you think, Chick?" I ask on a laugh. "Is Jack hot?"

He smiles and shakes his head. "Whatever you say, ma'am."

I look back at Jack. "So, Jack? Why?"

"You know what it's like, Lisa. Living in a different world from your parents."

"Yeah. But I don't visit."

"But I do," he says. "I decided a long time ago that I couldn't blame them for not knowing me and my life and who I am as long as I stayed on my side of the line. So, every once in a while, I visit them in their world. I don't accept every invitation, but I accept some."

"How 'bout them? Do they come visit you on your planet?"

"Not so much."

He says it all casual, like it's no big deal.

"But wait," I say, as if I know his life better than he does, "your mom was at Into the Wild. That's where I met her."

"She stops by the office once or twice a year to tell me to take her to lunch."

"That's something."

"It is."

Hm. I cannot think of what to say to that. "Do they ever come to your house?" I ask instead.

"No."

"Never?"

"Not once."

But you still try.

I am so amazed by his fortitude in the face of parental disapproval that I cannot muster the will to speak. It occurs to me in the silence that I'm about to dance through his family drama. Well, better his family drama than mine, I suppose.

At least I like what I'm wearing now that I've got the boa.

* * * * *

"Whoooaaa," I breathe, a giddy warmth wafting through me as we stand in the doorway. The Ball Room. An actual ballroom. Miss Flyte, in the ballroom, with Jack.

Gauzy fabric drapes the walls, crystal sparkles on every table, and a small orchestra softly plays songs so classic that I feel like I've slipped into an Ernst Lubitsch movie. Could life be any sweeter?

"Shall we?" Jack offers his arm.

I take it and smile up at him. A deep breath, then we get set to glide into the gala. Suddenly, my muscles lock. I refuse to move.

"Oh. My. God."

All the women in the ballroom wear slick, short, snappy cocktail-casual clothes. Black. Some glitter. Denim. Tight pants. Little skirts. Even the older members of the crowd try to look hip and pull it off with chic panache.

I look like a prom queen thrust into the dark glare of The Viper Room. What I wouldn't do for a bucket of blood right about now. "You did this on purpose!" I hiss.

"What? Lisa, what's wrong? What are you talking about?"

He has the *nerve* to sound concerned. After what he's done. "What I'm wearing!"

He looks me up and down. "Huh?"

I growl.

"What?"

"Look at everyone else!" I screech in a strangled whisper. I feel myself turn to stone, except for the angry tears pushing from behind my eyes. "How could you do this to me?"

Jack takes me by the shoulders. "Do *what*?"

"I don't look like everyone else!"

Jack looks around. "Why would you want to look like everyone else?"

"Because!" Is the man dense? "Wearing the wrong thing is worse than wearing no pants!"

"I did tell you to take off the dress."

A tear leaks down my face.

Jack moves to me then, cupping my face in his hands, wiping away my tear with his thumb. I feel his fingers run along the back of my skull and settle on my neck. He looks right into my eyes. "Lisa, I want you to walk right in there and pull this off."

He is just so intense. *So intense*. And blue. His eyes are really blue. I close my own eyes, but I still see the blue through my lids. Oh, God. I'm wearing the wrong thing, but the cutest guy in the whole world still believes in me.

It's better than a John Hughes movie. At this moment, *my* life is *better* than a John Hughes movie. I open my eyes and look right at Jack. "I'll do it."

We turn to face the ballroom, but before Jack can even take my hand, I'm off.

I can hear Simple Minds playing a triumphant soundtrack in my head as I sashay into the room, flicking my boa off one shoulder. I surge through the milling people like a supermodel on her runway. As the band plays "Fly Me to the Moon" at background volume, I can see people turning to stare, so I smile with cool amusement.

I strut right onto the empty dance floor, and I—

I've got nowhere to go! I'm going to run out of room soon. Then what do I do? Hit the wall then stride back like a swimmer doing laps? Where's the bar? I can dock at the bar, toss back my hair, and order a Scotch. But like a quarterback who just can't deviate from the play to find the open man, I can see nowhere but straight ahead of me. End of dance floor. Wall beyond. But there's a door to the right. Kitchen, maybe? I could offer to help. That's it. I'll detour to the kitchen.

But before I can tuck my boa around me like an apron, Jack is in front of me, at the edge of the dance floor. In one fluid movement, he sweeps me into his arms, and before I know it, we glide out onto the middle of the parquet floor, floating along to the ambient strains of the band.

Jack looks down at me with a hint of a smile, as if we're simply tripping the light fantastic and he didn't just save my ass.

... what life is like on Jupiter and Mars ...

He dips me. Everyone is watching. He swings me up with confident flair.

"You're pretty good at this," he says, pulling me close.

"I think you make me look good." I twirl into his embrace. "And anyway, this kind of dancing isn't scary. It's fast dancing, alone on the floor, that freaks me out."

"You weren't doing so bad on your own." He spins me away from him but doesn't let go of my hand. "That was a hell of an entrance you made." He folds me back in to him.

"How'd you get to the other side of the dance floor so fast?"

"It was like running through a roomful of statues," he murmurs in my ear. "Everyone was looking at you." He swings me out then pulls me into him as the song ends. Next, he kisses me on the forehead.

I step back but we're still holding hands. "Thanks for the dance," I say looking up at him.

"Drink?"

"I'm jonesing for a Coke. Let's go."

We walk toward the bar, where it's surrounded by potted palms and flanked by a fountain shaped like a champagne glass. I'm so fascinated by the fountain I almost plow right over Jack's mother. She's standing with a balding man who must be Jack's father.

"Hello, dear," she says to me, standing back to look at me in all my snow-blinding impropriety.

I steel myself for her imminent cattiness.

"Don't you look charming," she says instead. Her smile

sparkles as much as her black and copper top. “Frank,” she says to the man peering at me over his glasses. “Isn’t she sweet?”

“Oh, yes, yes,” he says, falling in line. “I’m Jack’s father,” he says to me. “His, uh, dad. Daddy, really.”

Daddy?

I look over at Jack and he’s staring at his parents as if they’ve started speaking Klingon.

Edna looks heavenward, then looks back at Jack. “Wasn’t it nice of you to bring your little friend. What center did you say she was from again?”

“Center?” I echo.

“Yes, dear,” she says, looking tenderly at me, still all smiles and charm. “Where you and Jack met.”

I look at him.

“Are you talking about HEYA?” he asks.

“HEYA,” she says. “That’s it! They do good work, don’t they? Look at you,” she says, turning back to me and pinching my cheek.

Pinching my cheek!

“You are just so precious,” she says.

I look wildly back at Jack. But his eyes are bugging out as much as mine are. He’s doing the George-Bailey-has-just-realized-he-doesn’t-exist look.

Shock. Utter stupefaction.

Terror, even.

“Mom?” He sounds like he’s checking to see if she’s dead or merely asleep.

She turns to him, her dark hair swinging as she takes a sip of her cocktail. “Is it okay that she’s not wearing her helmet?”

In stereo, Jack and I say, “Helmet?”

Edna laughs with such airy delight it has to be fake. “Relax, Jack. You need a drink, but just a small one so you can get your little friend home safely. Frank, go get him some Scotch. And something for his little friend, but probably nothing with alcohol or caffeine in it." She adds the last part in a loud whisper that I can totally hear.

When Frank takes off, Jack takes my hand. "Lisa, you remember this is my mom, Edna. Mom, this is Lisa. You can stop calling her my little friend."

"Yes," I say, shaking her hand, feeling very confused. "Uh, Lisa."

"Li-sa!" she says in a sing-song voice. "I remember. What a pretty name! And how do you spell that?" I swear she sounds like she's talking to a toddler who just learned how to poop in the right places.

"Mom," Jack interrupts, "I think I'll take Lisa around and introduce her to some people, I guess."

Edna turns back to me. "Now, Lisa, there's nothing to be afraid of."

She's positively cooing. Where's the Edna from the office? The one who made the final call-back for *What Ever Happened to Baby Jane?*

"We're all very nice people," she continues, taking my hand. "Just say hello and shake hands and everyone will like you."

"Thanks, Mom." Jack pulls me away right quick, leading me off into the crowd.

"How much has she had to drink?" I whisper.

"I don't know." He says his words so evenly I know he must be concerned.

"Does she drink a lot?"

"No." He looks around. "Maybe it's her weight loss medication or something. But that wouldn't explain my Dad. Maybe it's some New Age thing." He stops talking, cocks his head for a few seconds, and then starts laughing.

"New Age what?" I pull on his sleeve, wanting to be let in on the secret.

"Or maybe it's just their idea of a joke."

I still don't get it, and Jack sees as much from my blank expression.

"I survive my relationship with my parents because I don't take them seriously. Maybe they've decided not to take me so seriously. Man," he says, looking their way. "This could be fun."

I'm struck dumb. Parents can be *fun*? Parents who criticize, blame, demand? *They* could be *fun*?

Maybe it could happen somewhere over the rainbow where everything black and white turns to color. Maybe. And if so, and Jack's found it, that makes him Dorothy, the one person special enough to figure out how to get there.

As I realize how black and white my own world is, Jack reconsiders.

"Or," he muses, "it's possible they don't approve of you so they're acting like freaks to scare you off."

"Scare me? Me? Why me?"

"I never bring someone to these things. Never. Now that I have, they must think we're serious. That is, of course, unacceptable to them. You're not from any crowd of which they approve. So, they're trying to scare you away."

Must think we're serious. But are we?

Jack didn't exactly say. Are we? ARE WE?

But before Jack can suspect how desperately I want to know, I bark out a laugh. "Well, their plan would never work. I mean, you're way scarier, and I'm here, aren't I?"

Jack smiles at me. "You are," he says, pulling me closer. "Let's dance."

Heaven. I'm in heaven…

I waft like a feather toward the dance floor with Jack,

but just as we're about to step out together, dancing cheek to cheek, Frank comes rushing up to us. "Here, Jack." He pushes a glass with about two fingers of Scotch in it at Jack.

"Thanks." Jack's brows slam together as he tosses it back.

Then Frank stoops to get eye level with me. "And here you go, little missy." Big, scary smile. "It's a Shirley Temple."

"Uh, thanks," I say, taking the drink.

"Now, don't you spill that all over your pretty dress," he warns.

"Dad?" Jack takes him by the arm.

He pats Jack on the shoulder. "Right. Well. Well." He turns and leaves us, heading back toward Edna.

I set my drink on the nearest passing tray. "Yuck." I look up at Jack. "I mean, it was really nice of him, but, well, yuck."

"Yeah. Shall we?"

I take his hand, and onto the dance floor we go. As each song ends, my pulse throbs in time with terror.

Please don't let them play a fast song. Please don't let them play a fast song.

So far they haven't. And maybe I'm safe for the night. I mean, it's an orchestra. The rowdiest they've gotten is, "I'm Beginning to See the Light."

When the musicians take a break, Jack gets me a sparkling water and leads me to a table. "Hang on," he says, and before I know it, he's gone. I start nibbling at the salad in front of me. I look at the couple across the table. They're both wearing chic black and their teeth are blinding. They smile when I look their way.

"Hi," I say. "I'm Lisa."

"We saw you dancing," the woman says. "You're very good."

"Thank you," I say. "That's very nice of you."

"It's wonderful for you to get out like this," the man says. "Not many ...uh ... not many have this kind of chance."

As the lady elbows him, I just stare. Is he seriously saying that I should be honored to rub elbows with the Orange County elite? Maybe I was right and they're not so nice after all.

"That's a beautiful dress you have on," the woman jumps in to say.

But before I can answer, Jack is back, sliding into the chair next to me. "Are you ready?"

"For what?"

"You're on."

"On what?"

But just then I hear it, the throbbing beat of Jimmy Eats World. I swing my head around. A DJ at a table in the corner is taking over for the orchestra on break.

"Jack ..."

"Go on," he says, smiling. "The DJ's playing it just for you."

"By myself? Fast dancing? Right after I ate?"

"You can do it." His quiet voice belies the intensity of those damn eyes. Tonight, Jack isn't challenging, goading, or demanding. He just believes in me.

You can pull this off.

I smile, grab my boa, and take off for the dance floor.

I get to the center just as the lyrics kick in.

Hey, don't count yourself out yet ...

At first, I just kind of vibrate, trying to feel the rhythm in my heart, like they do in *Strictly Ballroom*. But before I can get a bead on the beat, my leg starts this kind of thumping, making my toe tap. Adrenaline shoots through me, and as the chorus kicks in, I close my eyes and start hopping around.

But it makes me dizzy, so I open my eyes just in time to see myself careening off the dance floor into a potted palm. I grab at the branches to stop my momentum, hop back to the dance floor, and keep right on bouncing my butt all around.

I kick out my feet and flick my boa. At one point, I think I'm channeling Molly Ringwald from *The Breakfast Club*.

I wave my arms in the air, then drop them to swish my feathers like a mermaid tail. I am one with the song. I am skipping, I am spinning. The world is a blur and I am on fire.

No one joins me on the dance floor but I don't care. I am music. I am rhythm.

When the song ends, I stop with a flair, then let the feathers settle. I stand there breathing hard for a split second, like Troy Bolton at the end of "Breakin' Free." Then everyone erupts into applause. There are even a few whistles and shouts of "Lisa!"

My face splits into a huge, unstoppable smile. I did it!

I search for Jack, but his chair at the table is empty. A split second later, he sweeps me into his arms as another song begins.

Jack spins me around and hugs me tight. "You did it, Lisa! You really did."

Jack smells really good. And feels really, really awesome. Wow. I never get this close to him. Even with all the sex we've had, we don't touch all that much. Except that one time in the shower. But that was naked and wet and very different. I sink into him until he finally lets me go.

"How did I look?" I ask.

"Like you were having the time of your life."

I swear I want to kiss him, right here in front of his parents and everyone.

The DJ's voice booms across the music. "Let's hear it for Little Lisa!"

My head whips toward the bandstand. *Little Lisa*?

"Jack," I ask, "was your last date to one of these things

fat, or really tall, maybe?"

"No," he laughs, pulling me into the dance. "I guess it's just that you're so damn cute."

We dance into the next song, and as we do, people keep floating by telling me how much they love my dancing and my dress and my boa. One lady even calls it a 'feather poof.'

After the next song, I go back to the table while Jack brings the DJ a drink, to thank him for playing a song just for me. While I try to be discreet about sucking down my sparkling water, the woman at my table glitters at me. "What an incredible dance," she says with a sigh.

"Yes," the man joins in. "You really are amazing."

Amazing? Jeez. Did Jack tell them about my fear of dancing? I can feel myself blush. "Thanks," I murmur, looking over toward Jack, wondering if he betrayed me to perfect strangers. Sure, he looks so innocent, smiling with the DJ, but—

Suddenly, from across the room, Jack looks angry. And he grabs the DJ by the collar! Jack's arm knocks into the mike, and his voice reverberates through the room, through my head, through my skin.

"—THINK SHE'S MENTALLY IMPAIRED?"

She's mentally impaired.

Oh, God.

Is she okay without her helmet? ... Li-sa! How do you spell that? ... I'm his daddy ... feather poof ... What's the name of the center where you met? ... little missy ... Little Lisa ...

"It's okay, folks," the DJ says into the mike. "We all know about the acci–"

Jack rips the mike out of his hand and flings it toward the bar.

I feel icy sick all over.

"Don't worry, dear," the woman at my table begins.

I whip my head toward her. "That's why you're being so

nice and said I was a good dancer. You think I'm …"

But I can't say it. I can't. My night of crowning glory has been ruined by something far worse than a bucket of pig's blood.

Everyone is quiet now. I look across the room at Jack.

Jack.

He thought his parents were getting fun. But really, they just thought I'm some brain damaged charity case of Jack's. Oh, God. And Jack actually thought his parents might be *trying*.

"Jack," I say across the silent room. "Let's go."

He walks to me, takes my hand, and we head toward the door.

When applause breaks out across the room, we start to run.

CHAPTER 21

Jack and I don't say a word, not the entire way up the freeway toward home.

I'm frozen through. Solid, numb.

Once again, my life has spiraled into uncontrollable humiliation. But this time, I'm awake. And this time, I've sucked Jack into it.

As I watch the lights on the side of the freeway flash by, I wonder how I could have been so blindsided. I've been trying hard to pay attention to my life.

That damn helmet. It all started that afternoon in Jack's office, when his mother saw me wearing that *damn helmet*. And the mouth guard. I hadn't wanted to take it out in front of her. She was so elegant and posh that I couldn't just take out the slobbery thing then shake her hand. And all my politeness did was make her think I have some sort of speech impediment.

The ridiculously inappropriate dress tonight with the saloon-whore boa iced my cake. Jack's "little friend," the fashion-challenged half-wit.

When Chick pulls the car up in front of my house, he has the sense to keep quiet. I want to thank him or something, but I can't. I don't even look at Jack or tell either one of them goodnight.

I get out and slam the car door. I walk up onto my porch,

let myself in, and close the door behind me.

After stumbling into the living room, I lean my butt against the back of the couch and look around. All the cats are hiding. All the dogs are out back. I hear the car drive away. I'm alone with my stupid feather boa.

The front door opens and Jack walks into my house. He looks at me. "It's my fault," he says. "I never told my mother why you looked and sounded so weird that day in my office. I don't trust anyone in my family when it comes to Into the Wild. No way was I telling her about our project. So she must have thought you were … special."

Special?

I open my mouth to say something cutting, but instead, I start laughing. And sobbing. I'm choking on the absurdity of it all so hard that I fall over the back of the couch.

"Aah!"

"*Reow*!"

I land right on the inconspicuous Blanche, making us both spring up from the cushions. Blanche darts under the couch, bringing the boa with her. But half of the fat feather snake still trails out from under the couch. I just stand there and watch as the limp boa slowly disappears inch by inch as it's pulled under the couch. Jack moves closer, also compelled to watch the boa's fate.

Once it is gone, we look at each other.

"I never get to see stuff like that at my house," he says.

I wipe away a tear. "It's a fitting end to the night, I'd say."

He moves around the couch, getting closer to me. "None of it matters. You were unstoppable tonight."

I put my hand out, against his chest, to keep him from coming any closer. He takes my hand and keeps coming.

"Jack," I say, using two hands, both of which he folds in

his.

"The car is gone," he says, trapping me with a look that's hot and steady. "I want to stay."

"STAY?" I push him away then fly across the room, putting as much distance between us as my living room allows. "Stay?" I turn on him. "All night? Are you NUTS?"

"Lisa." He takes a step closer.

"Don't come near me!"

"Lisa, I'm sorry. For everything."

"I KNOW. That's why you're not allowed to touch me!"

"It's not like that." He stops and just looks at me. "I mean, I'm sorry, but that's not why I want to stay."

"Oh no?" Now I sound all bitchy-bitter, and I'm in my element. "You and your mom manage to orchestrate my hyperbolic humiliation. You did it. You saw it. You were part of it. And now I'm going to let you into my bed for a pity fuck? Are you KIDDING?"

He just stares at me, looking all mad. "Pity you? Jesus, Lisa! You have six million dollars. Why the *hell* should anyone *pity* you?" His voice is solid black granite. "Your life isn't so bad, Lisa."

"I know!" I blink at him. I take in a breath. "Come on," I say, walking past him toward the front door. "I'm taking you home."

"I don't want to go."

I turn around. "And I don't want to believe that you want to stay out of pity, but I do. So suck it up and let's go."

"Lisa. It doesn't matter. What they think of us."

"But it does matter," I cry. "It must. When you showed up here tonight, you just wanted me out of my dress. Now you want to make me breakfast? Please. Something had to happen between then and now to make you want to be with me." I turn back to the door.

"It did," he says, but not in an intense arguing voice. He's quieter. "You talked to Chick."

I stop with my hand on the door. "Chick?"

"You sat up in the seat, and just started talking to him. Nobody does that, Lisa. Nobody *I* know, anyway."

I turn around to face him. "Chick? The driver? You've got to be kidding."

He takes a step closer.

If I back away, I'll hit the door, making myself cornered.

"Lisa," he says, stopping a few inches away. "Don't do this. Please."

"Don't do what? Drive you home?"

He doesn't say anything.

"You're going," I say, snatching my car keys off the hall table.

He doesn't move. "We come up with so many reasons for not being together."

"*We*?" The word rips through every other feeling raging around inside me. "All the reasons *we* come up with?"

"Yes."

"You mean *you* have reasons," I say, making sure he is clear on this. "You thought about us and *decided* against me."

His voice is quiet. "Yes."

I stand up much taller. "But tonight I finally passed muster when I talked to Chick. Lucky me."

"Give me a break, Lisa. We're nothing alike. Nothing. And you can be so clueless and selfish. It took me a while, but I got here."

"Bravo," I say. "Like you're Mr. Perfect."

"I never said I was."

"I have a list!" I cry. "That's right," I continue, unable to stop. "I have a list! Of all the reasons we can never be together. But it didn't matter. I still wanted you." I take in a shuddering breath, and he moves closer.

"Really?" His hands are on me, in my hair. "So we both had our reasons."

He kisses me then, but lightly enough that in a few seconds I have enough wits left to defend myself. I push him away using all my might. "But mine didn't matter. Not compared to how I felt when I was with you."

"Felt?" Jack looks at me, swipes a knuckle across the corner of his lower lip. He's breathing hard, looking like a prizefighter ready to come in for the kill. "You still feel it. And you're still running away."

I open my mouth but only a squeak comes out.

"And then there's how you always fight with me after we have sex," he says.

"Me? You're twisting everything! *You* always run away! And *you* always fight with *me* after we have sex!"

"I know." He exhales. "I know," he says much more quietly. "I am so messed up."

"Yeah," I say. "You are."

"But I want to be your boyfriend. For real, Lisa. You and me."

He looks at me, and I look back.

I step to him just as he moves into me. The kiss is real. Me and a guy who really likes me.

He stops kissing me but our foreheads still touch. "Lisa," he says.

"Jack."

He grabs my hand and we take off across the living room. In a few seconds, we both tumble onto my big, beautiful bed.

CHAPTER 22

I open my eyes to find myself looking into Rose's tuxedo face. She's sitting on my chest, staring at me. "Hey, Rosie." I lever myself up onto my elbows and see Dorothy, Mal, Pacquito and Ginger all curled up on the bed, staring at me.

And then there's Jack, lying next to me, out for the count.

Wow.

Jack.

I'M IN BED WITH JACK.

I'm so excited I want to call someone right away, but Jack is the only one I can think of to call, and he's sleeping. Plus, he already knows about us.

So, instead of calling someone, I curl onto my side, dislodging the three cats, to watch Jack sleep. But he doesn't do that thing lovers do in books and movies and wake up just because I'm watching him. Nope. His breathing is deep and regular. I don't think he's waking up anytime soon.

I look down to the bottom of the bed where Pacquito and Ginger rest their chins on Jack's legs. I wrinkle my forehead. Jack must've gotten up at some point to let the animals in. What a nice thing to do. Maybe this means that he meant what he said last night.

Maybe he really does want to be my boyfriend. But how

much does he care about me? So far, enough to think of the animals in the middle of the night. But does this mean he's going to be a couple with me? Will we do stuff together? Will we do everything together?

I watch him sleeping, and I just cannot picture it.

Then again, I can.

Am I crazy? Will Jack actually kiss me in public? I don't mean he'll take me to the mall and start making out with me by the pretzel stand. But when I show up at Into the Wild, will he say hello and give me a quick kiss on the lips? Will he sit by me in class? Will he introduce me to people as his girlfriend, or will I still be his secret? Will we eat dinner together a lot? Sleep together almost every night?

I sigh, snuggling deeper into the blankets. It's not that I need to have all the answers or a plan. But it might be nice to know what's going to happen when Jack wakes up.

Half an hour later, I'm still waiting, still wondering. I look at the clock. Ten a.m. on a Sunday.

The Giants play the early game against the Eagles.

Sliding out of bed, I set off for the laundry room. In the dryer I find my favorite pair of boxers and the threadbare *Ah-ha* T-shirt I've had since ninth grade.

Fifteen minutes later I'm curled on the couch with a cup of coffee and Fred.

Kick-off. Downed in the end zone. Touchback. Boooring.

"Lisa!?" Jack comes crashing into the room, making me yelp and slop my coffee onto Fred. Jack stops short when he sees me on the couch. His hair stands out in all directions and his eyes look all panicky.

And oh, yeah. He's naked.

"Lisa," he says on this huge sigh. "I thought you left."

Putting down my wet, sticky mug, I struggle out from

under Fred, who doesn't seem to mind at all that I spilled coffee on him.

I stand up to face Jack. "Uh ... it's my house."

He looks around. "I know." He looks at the TV, which has the Giants at first and ten. He looks at me, then back to the TV, then back to me. "You're watching the early game?"

"Eagles at Giants."

Jack scrunches his eyebrows together. "You have NFL Sunday Ticket?"

Oh, God. He's mad that I got out of bed to watch football after our night of crazy passion. I'm going to lose Jack because of the New York Giants.

"It isn't like that," I insist. "It's not like I abandoned you for Eli. When I woke up, I *tried* doing the romantic thing. I watched you sleep for a while, but you didn't wake up and it was ten o'clock."

Jack starts laughing. Then he looks at me and laughs harder.

"What?"

He pulls me into a hug, the really good kind where he molds me against his body and runs his hands down my back. Then he lifts his head from my neck and takes a deep breath.

"Jesus, Lisa." He takes my face in his hands and kisses me so tenderly my toes curl against the hardwood floor. He smiles against my lips. "You even made coffee."

* * * * *

Once the Giants kneel on the ball for the win, Jack stretches out. He's all behind me and under me, so I stretch out, too. "I'm starving," he says, moving my hair with his fingers and kissing me on the neck.

I shift into a sitting position. "I'm not sure what else I

have. We already finished all the bagels and eggs, and you polished off the jar of olives. Maybe I have a stick of butter you can eat."

"I can do one better." He sits up, biting me on my naked shoulder. "My fridge is stocked with cold cuts."

"Really?" He might have pastrami.

Man, I SUCK as a vegetarian.

"We can be there in ten minutes."

"Okay." I leap up from the couch and then stop on a dime. "Wait. We can just order food."

"I know." Jack walks to the hall where he finds his pants halfway underneath Pacquito. "But I have these fantasies about having sex with you all over my house. All over the property, really."

"Hmmm," I say, considering. "Do you have Sunday Ticket?"

"Get dressed, smartass."

* * * * *

The cool sheets glide across my thighs as I bend my knees. Jack feels warm where he's pressed against my hip. "So, this is your bedroom." I look around.

"Like it?"

"Definitely my favorite," I snuggle down into the covers. "This might sound boring, but being in bed with you rocks. I mean, the foyer and the kitchen were fun, and the couch was mighty convenient at half time." I smile like the little girl who's found the most Easter eggs. "But this is heavenly. And sinful. Perfect, really."

"So ..." He glides a hand up my leg. "You like my bed. And it only has one comforter."

"But it's a *cool* comforter," I look at the white downy

comforter with grayish-blue seersucker stripes. "It reminds me of an old fashioned summer suit. Makes me think of Country Time lemonade or *The Great Gatsby*."

Jack leans up on his elbow and looks into my face, a small crinkle between his brows and half a smile curving into his face.

"What?" I ask quietly.

"It's just that you ..."

I smile. "I what?"

"Everything in your life reminds you of something else," he says. "Every comforter you own reminds you of something, your floor lamps remind you of London, your wardrobe reminds–"

"So?" I say, cutting him off before he figures out that having so many animals reminds me of Ally Sheedy in *Short Circuit*. "I like things that make me happy."

"But it's all stuff from your past," he says. "Or from make-believe. It all reminds you of something *else*."

I touch the hair falling over his forehead. "You don't," I say. "You don't remind me of anyone or anything. You're totally alien."

"What a thing to say when I'm naked."

"Seriously," I say. "You live on a planet where there's no fear. It's like living on a planet where there's no laughing or no cookies. I can't imagine it."

"Lisa, I'm pretty sure everyone gets scared."

"But you don't get scared of normal things."

"I guess not," he says, considering. "You scare the hell out of me, and you're anything but normal."

I feel my heart stutter, then race, but I pretend Jack hasn't said anything HUGE. After all, I'm not stupid enough to hang my hat on anything a guy says in bed. So, I laugh instead. "What a thing to say when *I'm* naked."

“So you are.” He moves to cover me. “So you are.”

CHAPTER 23

It's seven o'clock when Lupe sticks her head into my office. "You still here?"

"Yeah." I lean back in my chair. "Lots to do. We sign on Thursday." I look away, as if I need to find some sheet of paper on my desk. But really I just don't want her to see my deep blush as I think about Jack *again*. Make that still. I can't stop. "What keeps you here so late?" I ask.

"SAT class just got done. I'm leaving in a minute. You gonna hang out a little longer?"

"A little."

Lupe goes back to her office to get her stuff, and when she leaves, I'm left all alone.

I pick up the phone, deciding to try Jack on his cell. I'm starving, but I don't want to miss out on eating with him if he wants to grab dinner.

Am I being a freak?

Chances are good.

No answer. No Jack since we pried ourselves apart at five this morning. Now, I'm suffering serious withdrawal.

That's it. I'm going across the street for a really fatty pastrami sandwich and a Coke. After that, I'm heading home.

Forty minutes later, I drive through the rich blue night dotted with winks of lights. I turn onto my street and just stop myself from slamming on the brakes.

Holy Lights Camera Action!

Some survival instinct prevents me from making a spectacle of myself and keeps my foot on the gas, allowing me to cruise casually down the street.

The media is in front of my house. No emergency vehicles, just media.

THE MEDIA.

Mikes, cables, people, commotion. The dogs bark up a racket.

I bite my lip and swallow. I need a place to hide. I look up to Dolly's house, but it's two houses beyond mine. Too risky. Dom and Jeff live even further up the street. That leaves Ethel. I turn into her drive, pulling all the way to the back. I dash out into the night chill and scamper to her back door, getting there just as she opens it. Without saying a word, I slip inside.

"Sorry, Ethel." I close the back door so hard that it's peach and white checked curtain jumps. "Something's going on at my house and I have no idea what. I just need a sec to collect myself."

"Well, I was wondering what all that kerfuffle was." She seems put out, but then looks at me from under wrinkled lids. "You don't know either?"

I shake my head, trying to hold back the panic.

Ethel thrusts her hands on to her hips. "You need to get out of here."

"I know," I cry, grabbing the door handle. "I'm sorry."

"No," she interrupts, crossing the kitchen to a pegboard by the fridge. "I mean out of the neighborhood. At least for tonight." She brings me a set of keys. "You can take the Lincoln. It's in the garage and fully gassed. I just had it out on Friday."

I stare at her.

"And I've got a pageboy wig around here somewhere."

* * * * *

Ethel is very organized. It took us only about five minutes to find the wig in the extra bedroom, sitting on a mannequin head next to a pile of *McCall's* magazines from the seventies. But then it took us another ten minutes to dust off, de-cobweb, and style the thing.

Now, with my frosted bob bouncing around my collar, I navigate the buoyant Lincoln through impossibly narrow streets toward the heart of Echo Park. Right now I need a home base, and anywhere near Jack is out of the question.

I just can't shake the feeling that this media kamikaze has something to do with *him*. Ridiculous, I know, that anyone might be spying on me and care about my sex life.

But the only amazing thing that has upended my life in the past 48 hours is my sleeping with Jack. And now cameras are hounding me.

So, I head to Lupe's apartment. I've never actually been to her place, but I've seen her address on her paychecks.

Jeez. Maybe going to someone's house because you've printed their paychecks is illegal.

Like I care. This is an emergency. I just hope she's home. I didn't dare call her. Can't people spy on what you're saying on a cell phone pretty easily?

I pull to the curb across from Echo Park itself, and park. I dart across the street and race up a set of steep stairs. At the top, I find myself on a small, idyllic lawn with big *Fantasy Island*-looking plants all around. The greenery camouflages the aging stucco and ill-fitting screens of a one-story apartment building. A few lights by various front doors help me find Lupe's place.

I knock quietly. "Lupe," I whisper when she opens the

door, "I'm in trouble. I need help."

She sweeps me in with a hug and closes the door. She makes *shh shh* noises as she strokes my hair. "How long have you been pregnant?"

* * * * *

After I've explained to Lupe that I'm not pregnant but hounded by the media, she gives me a shot of vodka then sits down to boot up her laptop. "Where are your parents?" I ask before drinking. "And your brother?"

"Parents are bowling and Eric's out."

"Okay," I say, and toss back the vodka, nearly choking myself.

Lupe slaps me on the back, then returns her attention to the laptop. "Maybe it's not that bad," she says as she types. "But we'll Google you and find out what's going on."

I'm still reacting to the vodka when Lupe suddenly slams shut her laptop.

"What?" I ask, snapping to attention. "What's wrong?"

Lupe doesn't look at me. "It's bad," she whispers. "It's really bad."

"The center?" I cry. "Did the bank foreclose on HEYA behind my back? But we're so close!"

Lupe looks at me. "HEYA? No, it's nothing about HEYA." She looks away and shakes her head. "You don't deserve this."

"What? What don't I deserve?" My voice gets high and tight. "Is it Jack? Did something happen to him? Tell me. Please. Oh, God. Did he fall off a cliff or something? Oh, God."

"No, no, no," Lupe says, putting her hands on my shoulders to steady me. "It's about you."

Jack is okay. It's about me. Jack is okay. "Come on,

Lupe, show me."

She doesn't move.

"Please, Lupe. Just show me. Please."

Lupe turns back to her laptop, opens it, presses a few keys, then turns the screen toward me.

And there I am.

Me in my tight white dress dancing and flapping my boa around as I teeter and strut across the dance floor of the Ritz Carlton Laguna. The music sounds tinny and distorted, adding to the sensation that I'm trying way too hard.

Streaming video of my dance for the whole world to see. And replay over and over.

My stomach turns inside out and my mouth tastes funny. I can't breathe and I cannot look. Not for a second longer. My eyes drift to the right side of the screen where a news byte accompanies the video.

LISA FLYTE NOT RECOVERED FROM BURGER BARN BRAIN DAMAGE?

I read down the screen, trying to gulp air in high-pitched gasps. I recognize the website. It gets tidbits of information then sets them afire with queries and innuendo. And now it's sunk its teeth into me with bloodthirsty euphoria.

Am I trying to get even richer as a celebrity? Is this a ploy to get the world on my side with this pathetic demonstration? Do I even know what I'm doing? Would a mentally balanced person wear that dress and boa? Is anyone taking care of me? Watching over me? Other than *millionaire rebel Jack Hawkins*?

"No." Every muscle in my body clenches up so tight I can't even exhale. "No no no. Not Jack. Please not Jack."

I bolt out of the chair and head to the door. "I've got to see him."

"Have you read this?" Lupe meets me at the door,

pressing her palm against it. "Maybe seeing him right now isn't such a good idea."

"I don't care what they're saying," I say. "It's all untrue. I have to go see him."

"But right now he might not want to be seen with a ..." She stops herself.

"Lupe! I'm not really brain damaged! I'm just me!"

"But—"

I am so outta there that my pageboy tumbles off as I skitter down the steep steps toward the street. I manage to shove the wig back on just before I peel out.

Jack doesn't answer his cell. I decide to drive to Into the Wild. It's late, but Jack might have been trapped there by all the media. And it's practically on the way to his house anyway. I tear through the streets of old Los Angeles as quickly as the wave-like motion of the Lincoln will allow.

But I get careful as I approach downtown. Into the Wild is likely mobbed by reporters, so I rely on the pageboy and sheer dumb luck to get me access to Jack.

And the dumb luck pays off.

I'm at a stop sign looking two blocks down toward the media hubbub clustered around the parking garage door to Into the Wild. The metal gate opens and Jack's truck emerges.

Maybe he'll stop and tell them all to go to hell. Or at least tell them I'm not brain-damaged.

But he doesn't even slow down. He's not giving them the time of day. I can smell the bio-diesel truck from here even as it turns away from me to move in the opposite direction.

Unbelievably, the huddled camera people are unprepared to give chase. As they scurry to their vehicles, Jack and I are handed the few seconds we need to navigate the deserted one-way streets of after-hours downtown L.A. I turn right. In less than a minute, I find myself face to face with Jack's truck at a green light on a one-way street. I'm the one going the wrong way, but I totally planned it that way.

Finally. Jack.

We just stare through our windshields at one another.

Jack.

I mouth the word, my heart sobbing in relief to see him.

His face is unreadable in the greenish glow of the traffic light.

I reach up, pull off the pageboy.

Jack.

Now he knows it's me, and we're in this together.

Jack and me.

He turns left away from me and drives down toward USC. I follow.

My cell rings. Jack. I answer. "Jack!"

"Stop following me. Go home." Then nothing.

My foot slides off the gas and I look at my phone. Call ended.

Call ended?

Jack must have a plan. And he's being cagey about using his cell.

I turn around, heading for the 101 and home. Jack and I are like spies, or super-heroes, on a mission. When I pull onto my street, it looks as though some newscaster is giving a live report. I look at my cell again. 11:05.

Wow. I'm breaking news and I'm not even home.

I slip into Ethel's drive and she opens the back door for me.

"I remembered about the dogs and all the cats and realized you'd be back." She shoos me into her kitchen. "We have a plan. Dom and Jeff are standing by. Casey and Jessica are ready too."

"A plan to do what?"

"To get you past the crowd of vultures, of course."

A few minutes later, Dom storms out of his house like a drunken parade marshal. "All right!" He teeters toward the lights and cameras. "Enough is enough! You've been here all night, and you made your stupid report! Now get out!"

Jeff makes a good show of trying to restrain him, and when Casey and Jessica join the fray, everyone is captivated by the brewing domestic violence. On foot, I skulk across the street, sneak along the drive, and vault the fence into the back yard. Aaron and Christian flank me all the way to the back door. I hear how hoarse they are from barking all night, and I want to KILL someone. I run into the kitchen to refill both their water bowls. Then I make my way through the house closing curtains as I go before I flick on the lights.

I hear the buzz outside as I light up my house. Ha! You stupid gossip hounds. Outsmarted by the mentally impaired.

The phone rings.

Jack!

"Hello?"

"You got in all right?" Ethel.

"Yeah. Thanks, Ethel. And Dom and Jeff, and Casey and Jessica, too. I ..."

"Well, it's been a hard day. Goodnight, Lisa."

I hang up. No Jack.

I look at my cell.

No messages.

I check the machine on the counter between the kitchen and dining room.

A message! The red light blinks out one message. I hit the play button.

"*Lisa.*"

Mom?

"You're brain damaged and you never told us? We have

to find out with everyone else? Is this your idea of revenge? Making us look ridiculous? If you're planning to get back the money just because you're brain damaged, well, we didn't even know about it. See how far you get!"

I throw the machine against my beautifully papered wall as hard as I can.

One by one, I find all the animals, petting, calming and soothing as I go. Then, I feed them all. Then, I scoop the litter boxes. Then, I do dishes, vacuum, and take a shower.

Still. No. Jack.

I try his cell.

Nothing.

I sweep the floors, dust, make the bed.

Still nothing.

I sit down on my couch and let it hit me like a tidal wave. Jack has abandoned me.

CHAPTER 24

I scrub my skin pink in the shower then I make sure my hair is nicely dried and fluffed. I get dressed and brush my teeth. I peek through the living room sheers. Two days of my hiding, and still they lurk, those vampires waiting for the most embarrassing photo op. But they're not going to get one. Not this time.

As I have for the past thirty hours, I get some food from the kitchen and settle in front of the TV to watch season after season of DVDs. No TV news, no radio, no net. I don't want to know.

The doorbell rings. The dogs bark and scuffle. I stay right where I am but crank up the volume to drown out the dogs. In a second, I'll call the cops to get whoever it is off my porch. But not until the end of the episode. This is the one where David speaks in Dr. Seuss rhyme to the maître d'.

The doorbell rings again. The dogs are still barking, so I turn the TV up even louder.

"Lisa!" A muffled voice through the door. "It's me, Mia!" My head whips around toward the door. I get up, approach it slowly, and press my eye to the peephole. It is indeed Mia.

But I cannot let her in. I can't.

"Lisa!"

Then I hear the swarm descending on her, shouting

questions at her. Those hyenas are attacking Mia! I yank open the door and she slips in. I slam the door and there we stand, facing one another.

But what can I say to her? In the past few days, I've completely ignored her for her own good. Now I've let her into my house, which can lead only to her destruction.

Mia looks over at the TV. "Is that Bruce Willis?" She walks toward the screen. "What movie is this?"

"It's *Moonlighting*. A TV show."

"Bruce Willis was in a TV show?"

"Made him famous," I say.

"Really?"

"Yup. Won an Emmy."

"Really?"

"Yeah."

We stand there.

"Uh ..." I look at the TV. "The guy from *Breaking Away* is in this episode."

"What's *Breaking Away*?" she asks.

"Movie from the seventies."

"Oh."

"About bikes."

"Oh." She nods. "Cool."

I pick up the remote and turn off the TV. "Mia, you should go. Everyone thinks I'm brain-damaged, and anyone who knows you've been hanging out with me will think the worst. Whatever that is."

Mia laughs, as if in relief. "It's okay."

"Mia, I'm sorry for shutting you out." I step closer to her and take her hands. "It breaks my heart every time I don't answer the phone or respond to your emails. I know you must hate me for dissing you, but I don't want to hurt you."

She shrugs. "You never would. Don't take the blame for

what the butt-head media is doing."

"Mia, it's not so simple."

She laughs. "Lisa, chill. We're cool."

"We're cool?" I can barely process what she's saying. I feel cold and weird and inept. "I don't want us to be cool! I'm poison, Mia. Every life I touch right now—"

"Is better off," she says. "I am, for sure. And I don't want to lose you over this. And I don't want you to be alone. I know it probably doesn't matter anymore, a kid from across the street when all this other stuff is happening, but—"

"Mia," I say, "Of course you matter! I'm doing this for you. You have no idea what it feels like when they get a hold of you. It hurts. The humiliation is so extreme, and you just want to die all the time."

"You survived it once. I can be a survivor, too."

"This is not a club I want you to join," I tell her. "Your parents will say I ruined your life, and they'll be right."

Mia throws her arms around me, hugging me fiercely. "You didn't ruin my life." She pulls away, a huge, sparkly smile on her face. "What do I want more than anything in the world?"

"Huh?"

The light in her eyes positively twinkles. "What do I want more than anything in the world?"

"Uh ... a boyfriend?"

"Yes!" she squeals. "And I got one!"

"What? When? How?"

"I don't even know! His name is Rob Yeager, and I've known him forever, and he was just so nice to me when everyone else started making fun of me a few days ago and saying the meanest things. So see? You can't protect me because kids in school already know I'm your friend and no WAY the media could be worse than them. Anyway, as it turns out, Rob's liked me since, like, seventh grade. He's one of the smart kids, kind of skinny, and quiet. I never really thought of him that way before." She blushes then, from the collar of her shirt to the roots of her hair. "But you know," she says quickly, "he reminds me of Jack."

"Jack?"

"Yeah. Rob just ... he just does his own thing, you know? He's, like, totally oblivious to what anyone else does. He's cool, but for real, not fake cool. Like Jack. Jack's not fake cool, either. He just does his own thing."

I look at Mia. I don't say anything. What can I say? *Mia, Jack is a fraud. Mia, Jack is off doing his own thing when I just want him to call me. Mia, he's not as oblivious as you think.*

"Oh, God," Mia says, looking at me. "Oh, God. It's Jack. He's the reason you look so sad." Mia pulls me over to the couch and sits me down with her. "What did he do, Lisa?"

She looks around. "He was at the Ritz Carlton with you. He's in this thing, too. Where is he?"

I allow myself to go so still I feel numb. Then my quiet voice drifts along. "I haven't seen him or talked to him since Monday night."

"What did he say?"

Stop following me. Go home.

I blink at her. "Aren't you supposed to be in school?"

"I can miss first period. So, wait. What about after the party?"

"Have you had breakfast?" I ask, getting up and moving to the kitchen.

"No," she says, running ahead of me to open the fridge. "After the party?"

"We, uh, spent the rest of the weekend together." I pull the coffee pot toward me. "I don't know if I should tell you that, but—" My voice is small and high. I'm making it all sound so lame. And what the hell am I doing—telling a teenager about my sex life?

"Then the story breaks and he drops you?"

I don't say anything.

"What is his problem?!" Mia slams the refrigerator door. "I mean, I knew he wasn't talking to reporters, but—"

"He's not?"

Mia stops pacing and turns to me. "Lisa, aren't you following your own story?"

"No." My voice is calm and quiet, like a cold morning with a hush of snow on the ground. "And it's not my story."

"I know, I know. I mean, I know you're not mentally impaired. But you have to admit, one part of the story is true."

"What do you mean?"

Mia giggles. "You're a terrible dancer. We both are."

She walks over to the DVD player, pops out *Moonlighting*. She yanks a CD out of her bag and puts it in the DVD player. As My Chemical Romance pulses through the room, she turns to look at me, her face glowing with an eager smile. I can't help it.

We dance and dance and dance.

* * * * *

After Mia heads out to make second period, I go to my room, where I grab jeans and a long-sleeved T-shirt.

I have to get to work.

I'm not naïve enough to think that the media storm will have no effect on the consortium plan. But I must save HEYA, even if it means bowing out. I don't matter, but the community investment must go forward. The meeting to sign the agreement is set for tomorrow, and I'm not about to let that be affected by rumor and wildly inaccurate conjecture. I've met with every one of the investors. They *know* I'm not mentally impaired. One of them wants to date me, for Pete's sake.

Ten minutes later, after some Rambo-esque moves through the backyards and across the streets of my neighborhood, I back the Lincoln out of Ethel's driveway, waving good-bye to Dalton. I wish I could drive my own car. I could use a friend right about now. But at least all is calm and silent inside the pristine Lincoln. And nobody can link me to this old lady car.

I'm heading down Alvarado toward HEYA when someone honks at me. Okay, maybe I *am* driving too slowly, but I'm not about to sideswipe Ethel's boat into a row of parked cars just to accommodate some speed demon who's late for work.

Hooonk!

Jeez.

Honk! *Honk*!

Now I'm getting scared. Nobody can possibly know it's me in the car. But creating a scene on such a major road is no way to stay inconspicuous. My eyes dart to the curb, looking for a place to dock until traffic can pass me.

Honk, honk.

More sedate this time. I look in the rear view mirror.

Jack.

He's in his truck right behind me, waving his arm across the front of his body. I put on my blinker and pull off onto the nearest side street. I drive along a block dotted with small houses and dirt yards with chain link fencing until I find a spot long enough for both of us to pull over.

As soon as I slam the car into park, I jump out and race over to Jack. I am going to KILL him.

He's barely stepped down from the truck when I throw my arms around him.

"Jack!" But Jack doesn't hug me back.

I pull back, feeling frozen and sick.

Jack puts his hands on my shoulders and sets me further away from him. “Lisa.” His voice is just as unyielding as his stiff, un-hugging body.

I stand back, my arms hanging at my sides. This can't be happening. I will not lose Jack over this. “Jack,” I say, “just tell me what’s wrong and I will fix it.”

“What’s WRONG?” He slams the door of his truck then punches it.

I jump. “I know what’s wrong, but why are you being so mean? It’s not my fault. This all happened because—”

“It happened because we were fucking all weekend while everyone one else was busy putting together a story about you!”

“And you’re blaming *me*?”

“I’m blaming *us*.”

“Will you stop yelling at me? *I’m* the victim. Everyone thinks I’m retarded.”

“No, Lisa,” Jack says. “That was two days ago. Aren’t you even keeping up with your own story?”

“It’s not *my* story.”

“Lisa, they know we were at the hospital.”

“Huh?”

“That first day when we did the helicopter and the ocean.”

“So?”

“So now everyone thinks I bashed you on the head so I can get your millions.”

“*What*?”

But he doesn’t say anything else. I wonder if he even can. I mean, he looks really upset.

Jack Hawkins looks *bothered*.

“Wait,” I say, “what do you mean, ‘everyone?’ Why do you care what they think? You didn’t bash me on the head. And

I've never given you a dime."

"*I* know that."

"REALLY?" Now I'm shouting. "Because you're not acting like it! Jesus, Jack! Where were you yesterday and the past two nights? You never even called!"

"Lisa, this is serious!"

"Jack, this is life! Deal with it!"

He blasts me with his stare. "This is *life*? No, Lisa, this is not *life*. This is some trumped-up nightmare."

"Jack. You've scaled mountains with no ropes, for Christ's sake. This isn't that bad." I huff and puff, trying to believe what I'm hearing from this man. "Have you really made it this far in life without having any idea what it feels like for people to laugh at you and say bad things about you?"

"Jesus, Lisa, don't even try to say you get it. We're not talking about wearing the wrong sneakers to school or everybody seeing a picture of me that makes me look fat!"

The silence echoes like the aftermath of a sonic boom. Could he *possibly* make me sound more pathetic?

My voice gets quiet, but it's enforced with the knowledge that Jack Hawkins totally SUCKS as a human being and definitely as a boyfriend. "We're talking about everyone having the wrong idea about you, and you don't like it."

"We're talking about everyone being wrong about me and being appalled and disgusted. And believe me, I know *exactly* how that feels."

"I get it," I say. "I'm just another glaring example of how your forged relationships are nothing but disaster."

Jack just looks at me, wide-eyed and unblinking. "Can you deny it?"

"I didn't do anything mean to you," I grind out. "I'm not like your parents or Luz or her parents. *I* didn't hurt you."

"This isn't about you hurting me. It's about what I did to

you."

This stops me cold. "To *me*?"

"I get close to people and ruin their lives."

"Are you saying that you abandoned me for *my* sake?"

Jack slams his fist into his truck door again. "Griselda and Edgar? I killed their dreams and ruined their lives. And I wasn't even trying."

"A few days ago you wanted to be my boyfriend, and *now* you're trying to convince me it's too risky? And I don't even get a say?"

"This isn't about whether I want to be your boyfriend or not!"

"No, I guess not." I lean my butt against the car, watch the traffic on Alvarado. "Just like how for your parents it was never about spending time with a whiny kid. Or for Luz it wasn't about changing her life for the guy in her bed."

"Shut up."

"Fine." I push off the car and get all up in his face. "I don't even want you anymore. There are PLENTY of people out there who think I don't matter, so what the hell do I need you for?"

I storm my way back to my car.

"It's all about you, as usual."

I turn around. "Not this time. This time, I wanted it to be all about *us*. What a stupid, ridiculous fantasy."

I yank open my door but Jack slams it shut, almost jerking my arm out with the reversal of such vicious momentum. "Can you just stop thinking about yourself for a second and look at the big picture? Almost half my employees walked out yesterday. God knows what they're planning to do with their shares. All because they think I've seduced you, bashed you on the head, and now I'm after your money. The papers are talking about bringing me up on charges, for God's sake. My company is slipping away, the world thinks I'm Claus von Bulow, and you want to talk about our *relationship*?"

"That's where it all started, Jack. With us. And we could survive this, if you gave us the chance."

"Are you even listening to me? I'm losing Into the Wild, and I'm about to be indicted!"

"Will you get a grip!" I shout back. "I'm not mentally impaired, Jack! Remember? There is NOTHING to indict you for. It's all just what everyone thinks. Which I guess counts now when it's about you and Into the Wild. Now, all of a sudden, what people think matters."

"I can't talk to you."

He stomps back to his truck.

"You WON'T talk to me. All you do is yell. Or ignore me. And I never did ANYTHING to hurt you!"

But he's back in his truck, pulling away from me.

Jack Fucking Hawkins. The hero with issues. I could see it way back in the beginning. I could. That first day I chased him up the mountain, I knew he was just a guy. But still I blundered forward. As if *Romeo and Juliet* might end differently this time. Every time, I hope it will end differently.

* * * * *

The cops are there when I get to HEYA, guarding the place from the TV and magazine worms burrowing in and out between cars and vans near the gated entrance to the parking lot. It takes me a sec before I remember I've already thought of this. Since the meltdown with Jack, though, I can't think of anything except what an unbelievably unfair cretin he's morphed into. He sucks. He sucks. He sucks.

I circle the Lincoln around the block, park it near the front of the tall white apartment building that sits on top of

HEYA. There is only one cop near the door, and no reporters that I can see. I hop out of the car with no stealth at all, lope up the sidewalk to the entrance, flash the cop my HEYA ID, and waltz into the apartment building.

I take the elevator to the basement and find a small window on the far side of the murky storage space. I wedge myself out. I'm covered in spider webs, but I emerge on the other side of the building, *inside the HEYA grounds*. I've bypassed the media completely. I brush off my jeans then walk across to the front door of HEYA. No one is at the reception counter. Weird, but I don't stop to care as I high-tail it to my office. I pick up the phone. In five seconds, Crispin Joyner picks up.

"Crispin, it's Lisa Flyte." I'm cool, collected, and professional. Terrified. Will Crispin listen? Will he be confused? Worried? Demanding explanations?

"Well, well, well." He sounds like Heat Miser taunting Jingle and Jangle.

"Crispin."

"Not even a minute after the segment, Lisa. Classic. Really, I'm impressed with the sheer balls."

Segment? Like, on a TV show? About *me*? "Crispin, I don't care what people are saying about me. It's all just—"

"So you called to officially deny all of it?" Downright glacial.

Stay calm. "Yes, Crispin." I keep my voice smooth and sure. "You've *met* me. You know I'm not mentally impaired. And I've never given a cent to Jack Hawkins. This can all be cleared up soon."

But then it hits me.

Jack is the only one who can clear it up. Only Jack can explain about the helmet and the mouth guard, the need for secrecy, the party in Orange County. It would help, too, if Edna confessed her part in the misunderstanding.

I am so dead. I grip the phone and press it hard into my temple.

"Oh, really?" Sarcastic, unyielding. "Well, just answer one question. Were you fucking him the whole time?"

Crispin's demand poleaxes me. "*What?*"

His voice turns vicious. "This innocent act doesn't fly, Lisa. After what Stewart said, I can't believe you think you can still get away with it."

"Stewart?" I echo. Who the hell is Stewart?

"You were giving it to Hawkins the whole time you were flirting with me!"

"You asked *me* out. And I said 'No.'"

"Just stop with the lies. I know I was the first investor you got. Everyone else came on board after me. Now, let me be the first to jump ship. And believe me, in half an hour, I'll have every other investor following me."

"What? No! Why would you do that? Please, just—"

"I'm doing this to shut you down once and for all. It's a disgrace just to be talking to you. You're a menace."

The line goes dead in my hand. I can barely breathe as I swivel my chair to the computer screen and strike a few keys frantically. It's already on the net. Streaming video of Alan Stewart on *L.A. in the Morning* with Nikki Novy. Alan Stewart. The guy with the pencil thin tie who caught me in Jack's office just after the seaweed scare.

"It was obvious from the first she was his lover. I walked in on them half-dressed, wrapped up in each other's arms. Lisa was in just a bra and skirt."

While Nikki Novy gets clarification on each point, ace reporter that she is, I try to breathe. Okay. So what? People think I'm sleeping with Jack. Is that so bad? Surely the other HEYA investors I've got lined up won't hold it against me.

"Isn't it evident?"

Alan's cocky smarm makes me shiver.

Nikki peers intently at him. "Tell, us Alan. What is going on?"

"It seems clear to me that the two of them are trying to scam Hawkins United. This is all a play for the sympathy of Edna Hawkins. Bad boy Jack and his little mentally impaired friend. They'll lube up Edna Hawkins by getting the money to save HEYA, and Jack will use the nobility of it all to ease his way back into the Hawkins clan without losing face."

Nikki's face, big and earnest. "So this is all just one big con?"

"A multi-million dollar con."

No!

I push back from the computer. I can go no more than a few inches. How can this happen? How can a TV show just let that dickhead go on and say whatever he feels like saying?

My God. As Jack and I were going at it this weekend, Alan was prepping to damn us. And to damn HEYA. And people like Crispin believe him—hook, line, and club on the head.

Suddenly, I feel hot, molten steel surge through me. He's not going to get me. He's not! Damn all the Alan Stewarts and Crispin Joyners of the world. I'm going to—

"What are you doing here?"

I look up. Mr. Bennett stands in the door to my office, security guards hovering behind him. Lupe, Jimmy, and Edgar cluster in as well. "I'm here to save HEYA." I don't know where I found the strength to speak, but I did.

"Save HEYA? You and Jack Hawkins have destroyed any chance we might have had. *Any* chance, Lisa."

"Jack Hawkins has nothing to do with HEYA," I say through my stiff jaw. "Nothing. Neither does his mother." I pick up the big green binder on my desk. "Here's my plan to save

HEYA, right here. We're going to sign everything tomorrow. Hawkins United isn't a part of it. At all. They're not even an L.A. company."

Edgar steps forward and takes the binder out of my hands. He holds it like it's a baby or a puppy. "I know, Lisa. But it's over." He touches my hair. "All anyone has is your word that this is the real plan. The media could claim the investors pledged a tenth of what you have in here, and Hawkins United was to be the silent partner all along. Only the investors could contradict a story like that, but not one of them will affiliate themselves with HEYA in any way. Not now."

Fear shoots through me, and I lick my lips before I speak. "Edgar? Why are you being so nice to me?"

"Because you have to go," he says. "I know how hard you tried. But you have to go."

I open my mouth. But what can I say?

"And you better sneak out of here the same way you snuck in." Mr. Bennett rumbles with the quiet menace of approaching thunder. "No one can know you're here. Especially not today. Not this morning."

"But none of it is true," I finally manage. "I didn't do anything."

"It doesn't matter." His voice is final, mournful. "I, personally, don't believe for one second that you managed to seduce Jack Hawkins into doing whatever it is they think you've done. But everyone else believes it, and that's what matters."

* * * * *

I pull into my driveway, not even caring about avoiding the cameras. I've *destroyed* HEYA.

Me and my stupid media curse. I look into the rear view mirror and see them all at the end of the driveway, filming me, waiting to pounce, gearing up to fabricate the next destructive story.

Fuck them.

Before I can stop to reconsider, I reach up and whip off my shirt. Next, I slide the front seat back as far as it will go, unbutton my jeans and shimmy out of them, taking off my undies, shoes and socks in the process. Finally, my bra. I bundle all of the clothes onto the front passenger seat, then I get out of the car. Naked to the world, I walk to my front door and let myself in.

CHAPTER 25

I shut the front door and lean my bare butt against the gouged wood. “Yow-ha!” Damn, that’s cold. And my feet are freezing, too. I push off the door. “No!”

But the dogs jump on me anyway, oblivious to the fact that I’m naked.

“Ow! Down! Ow!” I run to the bedroom where they all ignore me in favor of leaping onto the bed. I let out a pent up burst of laughter. What did I just do?

I flop onto the bed, into a mass of squirming dogs.

If in times of great stress, one reverts to one’s most basic, essential self, what does this say about me?

Last winter, when I couldn’t find a wedding dress, I chose to pig out. Then, when the restaurant fell on me, I went into a coma. Now, when I lose Jack and HEYA, I strip.

As far as progress goes, this isn’t so bad.

I hop off the bed and put on some clothes. I’ve got a lot to do.

* * * * *

Wow. Less than two hours. That was easier than I thought. I switch off the computer and head to the shower.

Twenty minutes later, I’m ready. I stride out of the house

in my most classic sandstone Dolce and Gabbana, holding my head high as if I'm leading an Armada.

I ignore the shouts and flashes as I head to the Lincoln. I return it to Ruth's house, then get into Dalton and take off. I drive straight to the WNC building on the corner of La Brea and Wilshire. I know the World News Channel won't send me away or pretend they don't know me.

After passing through the metal detector and security check just inside the front door, I step into the World News headquarters. The lobby is quiet, pristine, somber. A crescent shaped reception desk is ensconced in the back of the cavernous space. A bank of TV monitors flashes behind it, each one showing a different news story. Three security guards man the desk.

"Hello," I say, stepping up to one of them. "My name is Lisa Flyte. I want to be on *Garry Minor On Call* tonight."

The guard cocks an eyebrow and I think he reaches toward his gun. "Uh, ma'am—"

"I know what you're thinking." I keep my voice quiet and even. "Why would Garry Minor be interested in me? Well, because every night he does a show featuring the hottest stories in the news, and whether I like it or not, my story is hot."

The guard doesn't even blink. "Ma'am—"

"Look," I say, pointing to a monitor running video of my naked walk into the house. My body is pixilated at the private places, making me look fat. "That's me."

He turns to look. Then he looks back at me, eyes now fixated on my boobs.

"I just want to tell my story."

A guard a few feet down the desk puts down a phone and looks up at me. "Ms. Flyte," he says. "Wait here. Someone from *Garry Minor* will be right down for you."

I swallow. This is really happening. Jesus. I turn to the

guard. "Thank you." Stepping back from the desk to wait, I glance at the door opening onto Wilshire Boulevard.

"Lisa Flyte!"

I turn around. Oh. My. God. It's Garry Minor himself, striding right at me from the elevator. He wears a lavender shirt, a dark blue tie, and pants, I guess. He must be wearing pants, right? But all I can focus on is his larger than life face bearing down on me.

He reaches out both arms and pumps my hand in both of his. "Come upstairs. We have a lot to talk about." As the elevator doors close us in, he looks at me. He up and down checks me out. "Nice suit," he says, grinning.

"Thanks." I bet he got to see the unpixilated version.

When we get off the elevator, he hustles me into a wide conference room where three other people wait for us. Suddenly, everyone's talking at once, shooting questions at me.

"Hold on." I put up my hands to show that even though I am loud, I am also calm and rational. "Can I *please* talk?"

Garry stands back, nods.

"I need to go on your show to try to save HEYA. Helping Everyone Young Achieve. It's a ghetto rec center I work for and it's being shut down. I had this plan to save it, but this week, all the negative publicity ruined it. I didn't do anything wrong. Not fraud, not conning, not sex for money. But HEYA is the one to suffer. So I need to set the record straight."

The four of them stare intently at me.

"*Quid pro quo*, Lisa," Garry finally says to me. "I'll let you talk about your HEYA plans, but you have to answer some of my questions. About the dance, Jack Hawkins, Stewart's accusations."

"Deal!" I grab his hand and shake it before he can rescind the offer.

* * * * *

It's been almost two hours, and not much has happened since my initial debriefing by Garry Minor. Since then, I've just been sitting in this room, thinking about my upcoming public flogging. But it will save HEYA.

Jennifer with the headset and acne scars rushes in. "Come on."

"Where?"

"To the set."

"Already?"

"There's not much time for hair and make-up. Let's go."

* * * * *

"Hello, Mrs. Flyte."

"Good evening, Garry." My mother smiles, though she seems confused by the whole talking-to-a-monitor thing. "Hello."

My parents.

I've been snookered by Garry Minor into confronting my parents on national television. He must have set it up while he kept me in that stupid conference room for hours. What else does he have in store for me?

I sit up straighter. After all, I was the one who walked into the fiery pit of hell.

"Well," Garry says to the giant screen of my parents, "there's a lot to talk about, so let's get right to it."

The pixilated video of my getting out of the car plays to Adam Ant's "Strip." I *love* that song.

Back to Garry, addressing my parents. "Impressions?"

"That's Lisa," my mother sighs, doing her Put-Upon Mother Act to a T. "Always looking for attention. But this is a little much." She and my father nod in unison.

"So that's it?" Garry asks. "Just a stunt? Do you think she could be under the spell of Jack Hawkins?"

My Dad folds his arms and shakes his head. "It wouldn't surprise us, Garry. Lisa has never had good judgment when it comes to boyfriends."

"Her boyfriend in college." My mother sighs. "Then Keith. Plus all the men in between."

"They took advantage of her?" Garry asks.

My Dad raises his brows, shrugs with one shoulder, as though the point is moot. "I don't know about that. But they weren't going to stick around. That was always obvious from the first."

Garry consults the cards in front of him. "But wasn't she with her college boyfriend for three years, and Keith for five? They stuck around for a little while."

"But they didn't stay," my mom points out. "They were always the ones to leave her."

"Garry," my Dad says. "She's thirty-four and not married."

This is a Pronouncement.

"Okay," Garry says with his trademark grin that means nothing. "Let's talk about HEYA for a minute. What, if anything, can you tell us about that?"

"Lisa can have all the big ideas she wants," my mother says. "But she can't get her head out of the clouds."

"Meaning what?" Garry asks.

"Follow-through." My father jumps right in. "Lisa never finishes anything she starts."

Hey! I want to shout. *Don't write me off yet*. Don't they all get that the only reason I'm here is to save HEYA?

Garry picks up a copy of *People* from the desk in front of him. *The* copy of *People*.

Great.

"A few months ago," he says, nodding toward the magazine, "your daughter was a figure garnering the nation's sympathy. Now she's made herself, at best, a laughing stock, at worst, a con artist. Could you ever have imagined such a turn of events?"

I hate Garry Minor. I really, really hate him.

"Her dreams and schemes never turn out the way she expects," my mother says with truly doleful intonation, as if she cares.

"I'm sure there's some explanation to all this," my father adds. "That only makes sense to Lisa."

"And who better," Garry says," to go to for this 'explanation' than to Lisa herself." He turns to me, and the cameras aim straight at me.

"Garry," I say. Calm, level.

"So," he says, "Lisa Flyte. What do you have to say?"

The world watches. Garry watches. My parents watch. My parents. Why on earth do I still let them get to me?

I pick up the magazine from in front of Garry.

I look at the camera. "All kids," I say. "And by kids I mean anyone who has a parent or parents. All kids know what it's like to be embarrassed by their parents."

I chuckle as I hold the magazine up. "Look at this picture. Double chin because no one propped my head up. Drool coming out of my mouth because nobody bothered to wipe it away. Nobody washed my hair."

I run one finger across the front cover. "And my name, in big, bold letters, for the world to see. *This*—" I slap the magazine cover with the back of my hand. "This takes the cake when it comes to being embarrassed by your parents."

I toss the magazine down and smile. "And having them come on national television to say I never picked a good boyfriend? That's pretty harsh, too. But you know what?" I pause, sigh, and fold my hands. "It doesn't matter."

"It doesn't?" This from Garry, who I think was salivating over the promise of a catty family fight on air.

"Not really," I say. "Would you rather a parent who's been in jail all your life, but you don't know why? How about a parent you never see because she works three jobs? A mother you haven't seen since INS deported her, after she carried you all that way from Guatemala? A mother and father you can only dream of having because you've been in foster care your entire life?"

I look at Garry, then my parents on the monitor. They look rigid, desperate not to show any sign of confusion.

"Kids with parents like these," I say, "these are the kids I'm trying to help at HEYA. Not to belittle anyone's problems with their parents, but for me, it's time to step up and look at the big picture."

"You've been working at HEYA for a little over a month," Garry says. "Helping Everyone Young Achieve. A community center in a lower income section of Los Angeles."

"Yes," I confirm. "HEYA lost their corporate funding recently when their dot com backer went bankrupt. My job was to financially stabilize the center."

"Let me remind everyone," Garry says, "that Lisa has been here, at the WNC studios, for the past three hours. She's been sequestered in our green room with no television, radio, cell phone, or internet, while waiting to come on the air."

Huh?

Garry turns back to me. "So why didn't you just give the center some of your Burger Barn fortune?"

"My fortune is not nearly so big as most people think," I explain. "Saving HEYA would take all of it. Then it would be gone in a year or two, and where would they be? Instead, I came up with a sound financial plan to get HEYA to generate and maintain its own working budget."

"It was your job to save HEYA, but you haven't been able to pull it off yet. Correct? And it seems very unlikely that you will, now with all this recent speculation into your activities."

He doesn't even ask about my plan.

"Yes," I answer.

"Then, I have some very good news for you."

I just blink at him.

"Watch this, from earlier today." He swivels his chair toward another monitor behind him. Edna Hawkins pops onto the screen. She stands at a podium, blue velvet curtains behind her. She held a press conference? While I was locked in the green room?

"Hawkins United," her videotaped head says, "has just bought the building across the street from HEYA."

The building whose renovation almost got Pacquito killed? Edna bought them out?

"This will be the new home of HEYA, and it will be signed over to the Community-Based HEYA Trust. My name and Hawkins United's name will never be a part of it. This is a donation, free and clear. Furthermore, this check—" she holds aloft a check in her right hand, "—will be the seed money for the Community-Based HEYA Trust, which will be an internally run operation that will no longer be dependent on sponsorship. The Trust will keep the center open and running as long as there are devoted individuals like these ..." The camera pulls back to reveal Mr. Bennett, Lupe, Edgar and Jimmy flanking the podium. "... who care about the community."

Edna turns to Mr. Bennett and hands him the check. "Thank you." She looks around to Lupe, Jimmy and Edgar. "Thank you all, for everything you do."

The monitor goes dark. That's it. Not a word about me. Or my plan. Or all my hard work.

"When did this happen?" I ask Garry.

"Ninety minutes ago."

I look right at him. He kept me in that room, kept me from the news, so he could spring this on me live. He kept it from me just to get me on the show, when he knew all the time that the only reason I wanted to be on was to save HEYA.

To save HEYA. My eyes fill with tears.

"HEYA," I say. "Gabriel and all the kids. Everyone. They're all saved."

"You knew nothing about this?" Garry asks.

I shake my head and sniff. "No."

"Do you know why she did it?"

"No."

"If that's the case, why did you want to be on the show tonight, if not to be a tandem piece to her announcement?"

"I didn't know. I was still trying to save HEYA myself," I explain. "I wanted to come on the show to encourage the people of Los Angeles to reach out and help." I look at the camera. "And I still do. But I want to encourage everyone, not just people in L.A. So many people, everywhere, need help. Please, find the help centers in your community, and be a part of the helping, even if it's only a very small part. That's something. Donate time, money, books, clothes, blankets, diapers. Whatever your community needs. Just think of how amazing it would be if we all did just one thing to help."

"You want to save the world," Garry observes.

"Don't make that sound like a bad thing," I admonish. "And I'm not after the whole world all at once, Garry. I'm after one starfish at a time."

"Explain that," he says.

"The starfish story," I say. "At least, I think it's a well-known story. I heard it on an NFL commercial once. There are thousands of starfish washed up on the shore of a rocky beach, and a small boy walks along, throwing starfish back into the ocean. A man sees him, goes up to him, and says, 'What are you doing? There are too many starfish. You can't possibly make a difference.' The boy throws another starfish back into the ocean. 'I made a difference to that one.'"

Garry nods. "Touché," he says. He turns to the camera. "And we'll be right back."

I think I'm going to have time to catch my breath during the commercial break, maybe process a thing or two, but it feels like I have barely twenty seconds.

"We're back," Garry booms, then looks at me. "Okay, Lisa, despite your altruistic intentions, there remain many unanswered questions about your recent behavior."

The video of pixilated me plays on the monitor again.

"Why strip for the cameras?" Garry asks.

Deep breath. "Because," I say, "when it comes to the bare-naked truth about me, I'm not ashamed. I have nothing to hide."

"*Nothing* to hide?"

"There are things I wouldn't necessarily choose to discuss with the world," I concede. "Like how I wet the bed in fifth grade. But that was revealed while I was in a coma, so I had no control over that. This," I look at my nude video, "I had control over."

"Do you feel the media has been unfair to you?"

I smile with what I hope is nonchalant elegance. "The media has been *wrong* about me."

"Have they?" Garry asks. He shuffles through papers on his desk as though he's getting ready to incinerate me with verified facts.

"Not about everything, certainly. But I'm not brain-damaged or mentally impaired, for instance. I'm not a fraud. I'm not a con artist."

"So, you deny what Alan Stewart said?"

"Alan Stewart reported what he saw accurately. But the conclusions he drew are incorrect."

"So you *were* naked in Jack Hawkins' office."

"A bra and a skirt," I correct. "And stockings and shoes," I add.

"But you contend you're not having sex with Jack Hawkins?"

I give a little laugh. "Not right this minute."

Garry laughs. "*Have* you had sex with him?"

"Yes," I answer seriously. "But not in his office, not for money, and not to seduce him into pulling off any cons with me."

"Then why?"

I look at Garry and blink. "Because he's really hot." Duh.

Garry lets out one wheezy, smokery bark of laughter. "And?"

"And…" I can't keep the smile from my lips. "It was great."

Garry's chuckle sounds like he's sawing through plywood. "But is there anything more to your relationship?"

The lights beat down on me as I sit there in my gilded trap. I asked to be on the show, yet I cannot say anything of my deal with Jack, or Jack's new line of gear.

But HEYA is saved. That's all that matters.

I turn to Garry to answer him point blank about what else there is to my relationship with Jack. "Not much," I say. "We played Trivial Pursuit once."

"So it's just a fling that has nothing to do with anything? That's a little hard to believe, in light of recent events."

"It makes perfect sense 'in light of recent events,'" I counter. "Sex with Jack is part of my sucking every drop of pleasure out of life that I can. Garry, I almost died a few months ago. For good, lights out. So you better believe that now, when a guy like Jack comes into my life, I'm going to go after him."

"What do you mean, a guy like Jack?"

I make my voice low and kind of dreamy-raspy, like just thinking about Jack is enough to make me come. "A guy who's gorgeous, kick-ass, quiet ... and he's got a good soul. He's the kind of guy women fantasize about." I look right at Garry's craggy face, dream over. "But in the words of Billy Joel, it's just a fantasy."

"Jack Hawkins. Just a sex fantasy in your life. So you don't think it's odd that he hasn't come forward and said anything during all of this?"

Yes I do! How could he be such a jerk? Such a heartbreaker?

"No, Garry," I say, "I don't. Because Jack had nothing to do with my efforts to save HEYA."

"But what about just defending you? Both of you, against these allegations?"

"I don't need him to defend me. He's not my keeper." I lean forward. "Garry, others trumped up this story and got it wrong. It's not incumbent upon anyone smeared to respond."

"You did."

"Because I needed to save HEYA."

"Fair enough. Now that HEYA's saved, what next?"

"RPM," I say. "Rescue Project Money. It's a foundation I'm starting to help people who are behind the eight ball, but trying to help themselves. I'm going to use my Burger Barn Money to make more money to help people and organizations get started in saving themselves. The email address is rescue@rpm.com."

The sawing laugh again. “One starfish at a time, Lisa?”

“Exactly.”

* * * * *

I unlock the front door, triumphant with Chinese take-out in my left hand. I doubt there’ll be the phone calls and accolades like there were in eighth grade when I won The Constitution State's Constitutional Trivia Challenge. But still, the glow of success feels sweet and warm.

But wait. Where are my adoring minions?

As I back through the door, pushing it open with my butt, I look around for the dogs that should be snuffling at me and the cats who should be darting by. I mean, I have Chinese food.

I look around and drop the bag.

Jack.

He walks out of the kitchen, proffering an ice cold Coke.

No. I’m not ready for this yet. I’m not ready.

“I saw your interview.”

I pick up my moo-shoo and put it on the hall table. “Really?” I take the Coke, step out of my heels.

“You were amazing,” he says.

“Yeah, I get that a lot.” I chug down half the can of Coke.

“That’s because—”

“Fuck you.” I slam the can onto the hall table next to the take-out. I keep my voice level. “Fuck you to hell and back. And get out of my house.”

Jack gives me that same Frodo look I got from Keith when he dumped me in the hospital. Desperate, terrified, resolved.

“I know I let you down,” he says. “But you didn’t need

me to save you, Lisa. You did it all by yourself."

"You want me to believe your abandoning me was just another bravery challenge? Is that how you're spinning it? Well, guess what? I didn't want you to save me." A barren chill sweeps across my skin.

"Lisa."

"I wanted you to be *with* me." I stare a thousand daggers right into him. "I just wanted us to be together."

"But ..."

But I don't interrupt him this time, and he's not prepared to go on. He slumps onto the couch. "I wish ..." He stops talking.

Oh, God. This is going to be bad. Both barrels in the face, I can feel it coming. I shouldn't be wearing this get-up. I shouldn't be wearing some classy suit and stockings while having the most devastating conversation of my life.

"I wish ..." His voice is so quiet, but crystal clear. "I wish none of this had ever happened."

"None of what?"

"Everything," he says. "The party, the dance, the entire weekend. I wish we could just wipe it all out."

The hard, spiky frost holding me erect begins to splinter. "The weekend?"

He looks up at me, sad but sure. "All of it."

I'm going to end it, I remind myself. I've known for hours that I would be perfectly clear and end it for good if I ever saw him again. But hearing him say that he'd rather it all never happened stabs me like a blade in the back, sucking out all the air.

Sensing my weakness, he pounces like a hyena. He's on his feet, in my space, hands on me.

He kisses me, and I let my body sink into him. I kiss him back, all wet and hungry and willing. I want every last piece of him I can get.

"What's wrong," he says, still nipping at me, "with just liking each other and enjoying each other?" More kissing.

I give him one last kiss. I pull back, but not out of his arms. "I want more."

He kisses me beneath the ear. "Name it," he rasps.

I pull back further, out of his arms. "Don't abandon me next time life goes to hell in a hand basket, for starters."

"Lisa ..."

"It won't work. You don't have what I want."

"That's a lie."

"A LIE? Are you seriously accusing ME of lying?" I thrust my hands into my hair as though I'm going to tear it out by the fistfuls. "Okay, fine! We'll forget what a liar *you* are about wanting to be my boyfriend. No more lies, just the truth. How's this for the brutal truth? I love you, Jack, and it *kills* me that you don't want to love me back."

Jack jerks back, as if I pulse out radiation poisoning.

Since I can tell he's spooked, I lower my voice. "I wanted you to be with me, Jack. Just *with* me. And you wanted nothing to do with me. You didn't even call." I meet his flaring eyes.

"You've loved before, Jack. You know what it feels like. Just wanting your parents to come home, to *be* home. Not even wanting them to do anything. Just wanting them *with* you. Or, just wanting Luz to be *with* you, no matter who she was married to. You know what I'm talking about."

He shakes his head. "Come on, Lisa. You love me? After one weekend?"

"No, not after one weekend," I say, knowing it's hopeless. He doesn't love me, and he doesn't even want me to love him. "It's been happening all along. I've loved you since ... it doesn't matter." I sigh. "When it counted, then you weren't there. Now, you don't even want to be here."

He says nothing, makes no move.

"I won't do this any more," I say.

"How can you just walk away?" he demands, coming up to me, taking me by the arms. "You know what we have, how good we can be together. Why are you doing this?"

He rips himself away from me, stalks back and forth across the room.

"How can you not want more?" I challenge. "Knowing what we have? How can you not want it all? As much as there is to get?"

He turns to me. "Because I don't want us to keep messing up until we have nothing left."

We stare at each other. "But I want someone who loves me *through* all of the mess ups, Jack. Life is full of them and they never stop."

Jack digs the heels of his palms into his eyes and kicks the couch. "This is so stupid, Lisa." He looks at me. "Don't you get it? We both want to be together. Isn't that all that matters?"

"Then where were you, Jack? Where the *hell* were you? If all that matters is us being together? A few days ago, that was *all* I wanted."

He looks at me, no answer in his eyes. An unreadable gaze because there's nothing to read. His hands lift a fraction away from his thighs as his shoulders give the ghost of a shrug.

Ends not with a bang, but a whimper.

CHAPTER 26

I lie awake and cry into my pillow. Later, I get up to change the pillowcase. Even later, I switch pillows entirely.

What have I done? What what what?

If the world were going to end, wouldn't I run into Jack's arms? He *wants* to be with me. I *want* to be with him. But —

But but but but but!

Okay, so he wants it to be on his terms.

Am I strong enough to do that and not lose myself? Am I crazy? Will I ever be happy? Oh God!

When Jack walked out of my house five hours ago, I wish I'd heard a swell of music to tell me I'd done the right, true, brave, strong thing. I wish I could now move with confidence, satisfied in my pain and loneliness, knowing I'll be the better person for it.

But I heard no music. I know nothing.

Was it all a mistake because I miss him? Or is it better in the long run? Better for whom? What if feelings are really all that matter? But where the HELL are his?

I cry some more. All twelve animals are in the room with me, even Aaron and Christian. Like Cher at the end of *Moonstruck*, I need my family around me. But no lovesick, bread-baking Romeo is going to throw caution to the wind and propose to me right in front of everybody.

Nobody *ever* did that. Just took my side, clearly aligned themselves with me, with everybody watching. Jack wouldn't even do it in private. He's not for me.

But what if I'm wrong! No wonder Ilsa lets Rick make all the decisions at the end. Love is *hard* when it matters.

No wonder I never dared want anything too badly. Somewhere deep inside, I knew what I was doing when I never went after a career that I craved or a love that I burned for.

I always settled and I never suffered.

God damn it. I was so much smarter before I met Jack Hawkins.

But I am not going to let him engineer my downfall. I am not.

I rip off the covers and jump out of bed. "Gotta get to work," I say to the dogs and cats. "Rescue Project Money isn't going to start itself!"

* * * * *

In fact, several people helped get it started. The day after Garry Minor, Mia came over after school to help me set up the RPM office in the second biggest bedroom. Dom, as it turns out, is a tax attorney, and he and Jeffrey invited me to breakfast the next morning so Dom could offer his financial services pro-bono.

A day later, Ethel invited me over for lunch. Ethel opened her front door, ushered me into her kitchen, and sat me down. As I ate my creamed chipped beef on toast, she showed me a gold watch.

"Retirement present," she stated.

"Oh," I said, trying to look interested. But I really just wanted to get back to the creamed chipped beef. Eating meat doesn't count, by the way, when you're someone's guest.

"Best secretary the City of Los Angeles ever did see, back in the day before they all became assistants."

"I bet you were."

"I'll start work tomorrow. I'm the best, and I won't charge RPM a penny." My mouth was too full, so I just smiled and nodded.

When I got home, a sleek, champagne-colored Lexus was preening in my drive. Edna Hawkins stood on my porch.

"Busy, busy, busy," she said in a kind of bitchy lullaby as I loped up to greet her.

"Come on in," I said, pretending she was not a scary person in just so many ways. "Can I get you anything?"

But as soon as Edna saw all the animals rush up to greet me, she stepped back, staying securely on her side of the threshold. "No, thank you. This will only take a minute."

"Okay." I went back out to the porch.

I sat on the glider, but one dubious glance at the dusty seat had Edna posing by the railing instead.

"Were you surprised that I saved HEYA?" Her question was laced with wolfsbane and I wondered what she wanted with me.

"No," I said. "It was a smart business move, extricating you from all the rumors and innuendo and effectively ending the matter."

She tipped her chin to acknowledge my accurate assessment of the situation.

"But," I continued, "your stipulations did surprise me. That your donation was just that. A donation free and clear and you wanted to be attributed no credit whatsoever."

"That was Jack," she said. "All of it was. After Mr. Stewart's unfortunate suppositions, Jack came to see me. He walked right into my office and told me exactly what I would do." She laughed, and for the first time, actually looked into my face. "Up until that moment, I always thought of him as such a hippie. But he was so commanding and fierce. A real Hawkins, through and through. He gave me the notebook you'd made up and explained your plan. It was a good one. A way to set up HEYA." She raised her eyebrows and looked down her nose at me, all bored condescension. "I knew I wasn't throwing my money away." Just so I knew, in the end, it really had been *her* doing, and sound business at that.

For a minute I just stood there, taking it all in. After Alan's TV appearance, Jack went to HEYA and got the notebook. *My green binder.*

I must have just missed him that morning. Jack then got his mother to save HEYA. What did he have to give her in return? Or did she do it because she knew that everything was her fault?

"Why are you here?" I asked Edna. "What's the point in telling me all this?"

"Answer one question for me," she demanded instead.

"Okay."

"Did Jack tell you about Luz?"

My mouth fell open. I shut it. Edna was just so creepy.

"Yes," I answered.

"I knew it!" She clenched both fists as though she was about to play rock, paper, scissors with two fists. "You got to him, Lisa."

"Did I?" I asked, but without much inflection at all.

"Jack actually came to me demanding my corporate money. Something he swore he would never do. Ever. You broke him, Lisa."

"Well," I said, lifting my eyebrows and shrugging, "he left me with a few scratches. I'd say we're even." But really, my gut seized up at the thought that I might have made Jack betray himself.

"Don't get me wrong," she said with a sly smile, "I'm not here to scold you. Quite the opposite. I want to know how you did it." She gave me a withering look. "I don't believe Alan Stewart for one second."

"You want to break Jack? Why?" I stood up from the glider. "Why would you want to do that?"

She pulled herself up to look taller, more imposing. "Not break him completely. We want to be able to work with him, no surprises. To do that, we need to know more about how he ticks, what pushes his buttons."

"We?"

"Frank and I, primarily."

I stood there looking at her, breathing hard. Were parents really this diabolical when it came to controlling their kids?

"You have to go now," I said, ushering her off the porch. "You want to know what pushes his buttons?" I asked as we reached the car. "You do. You're his *mother*."

She gave me a skeptical tilt of one eyebrow. "Hm." She unlocked her car and opened the door. She turned to me. "That's the best you can do?"

"If you want to know what makes him tick, go to his house for Sunday brunch."

"Excuse me?"

"It has to be his house. Go to his house the next time he invites you. Accept an invitation from him."

She got in the car and lowered the window before backing out of the drive.

"I'm very disappointed in you."

"Too scared to try?" I tossed back.

Without blinking, she put up the window between us and drove off.

* * * * *

Despite Edna's downer of a visit, the momentum surging through my life didn't let up. The very next day, in front of TV cameras from news stations all over Los Angeles, a representative from Burger Barn presented me with a $100,000 donation to RPM. The segment got so much airplay you would think I'd exposed at least one boob. But I didn't embarrass myself at all. The presentation itself comprised good cheer and gratitude.

For the first time since that restaurant fell on me, media coverage worked in my favor. Everyone was so anxious to get a piece of my limelight that publicly offered donations poured in. I was becoming so famous for taking checks in flashy news segments that studios and producers courted me with ideas for a TV show about RPM and hard luck cases.

This is where Dolly stepped in, acting as my manager. Her arsenal included the wisdom gleaned from working in the industry for forty years, the moxie of an agent, the *noblesse oblige* of age, and a deep sexy voice that'd give Lauren Bacall a run for her money.

Man, is it ever easy to get a lot accomplished when you have nothing left to lose.

Sure, I'm tired all the time and I haven't turned on the TV in ages, but I don't miss sleep or TV one bit. No time.

Two weeks since Garry Minor and dumping Jack, and I feel like I've done more living than ever before. Embracing my inner publicity slut has been effortless. I'm willing to throw myself out there now, and I don't care what I'm wearing or how my hair looks because none of it matters.

My high profile can help rescue people who really need help. The more media coverage I get, the more people who might watch whatever show we cook up. A large viewing audience will see the stories, and they'll give. That's what I'm hoping, anyhow.

I stare at the phone. Dolly informed me I've just agreed to do *Dancing to the Moon*. Did I really just give America the chance to tell me I suck at dancing? I remind myself that Dolly closed the deal when the show offered a $400,000 donation to RPM.

That's something, anyway.

Plus, now I probably won't do the reality show that'll make me live in a hut in the jungle with some other minor celebrities for a week. Which is good, because I think I'd need shots for that.

Duh nuh nuh nuh.

Manny with the truckload of turkeys for the mission downtown. The smell of poultry drives the dogs crazy as they scramble across the wooden floor, barking all the way. I'm slipping into my shoes as I swing open the door.

"Hey, Man—" I pull up short.

"Hey, Lisa." The dogs rush past me to jump all over him. Jump all over Jack.

"Jack." I let Jack in, and put Fred, Ginger and Pacquito out back with Aaron and Christian. I turn to look at Jack, then head into the hall.

"What do you want?"

"I want to see you."

I shrug. "I guess you can come back to the office." I figure this is the safest place, but I'm not sure why. I walk in and sit behind my desk.

Jack stands in the doorway, one shoulder leaning against the jamb. He looks so good I feel sick inside. Sick and weak and cold. So cold.

"Haven't seen you in class in a while," he says.

I nod and try for a smile. "Yeah, I've already talked to

USC. Everything's just happening too fast for me to stop and learn about it. I'm looking into correspondence courses that meet just one weekend a month. Duke has a good one."

Jack straightens. "Duke?"

"Yeah," I say. "But that's farther than I want to go, even if it is just once a month."

"Oh." He doesn't go back to leaning.

"Meanwhile, I guess I'll hire someone to help me with the money."

Jack nods, but I don't think he's even listening to me. I start shuffling through some papers on my desk.

"My parents are coming to my house for Thanksgiving," he says.

I look up. "That's wonderful, Jack. Really."

Jack nods, looks around the room. Then his eyes settle back on me. "I'd like you to be there, too. Will you come?"

My heart lurches. *Ca-thump.*

"Me? Why?"

He steps into the office. "Because I want us to try again, Lisa."

Ca-thumpca-thumpca-thumpca-thumpca-thump.

I can *not* get carried away. I have to be careful. "Try *what* again?"

"I want us to be together. I want you to give me another chance."

"Another chance to what?" My voice cracks on 'what' and I can feel the tears. I push back out of my chair and speed past him out of the room.

He catches me in the living room. He pulls me into him and kisses me.

Oh, God. Oh, God.

I push away from him. "Jack, stop it. Please, just stop it."

"This is crazy, Lisa. Tell me you don't miss this."

I say nothing.

"I think about you all the time." He moves closer but doesn't touch me. "I want to be with you."

"You're too damn late!" I cry. "Don't you get it?"

"I want to start over."

"No! Jack, I can't just forget that when the world came crashing in, you wanted NOTHING to do with me. Now you want me to just move on like you never did that to me?"

"Lisa, I love you."

"I … I … I ..."

He takes me by the shoulders. "Lisa."

"I don't believe you."

"*What*? You think I would lie? About loving you?"

I shake my head. "I ... I think you're saying what you think you need to say." I try to work it through my brain. "And when you get what you're after, or when it gets hard, you'll be gone."

"How can you think that?"

"How can I *not*?"

"Why can't we get past this?" Jack asks.

"Because, Jack. You've never said you're sorry."

He opens his mouth but shuts it without saying anything. I raise my eyebrows, daring him to deny it.

Nothing.

"I think you regret the way things turned out," I tell him, opening the front door for him. "But I don't believe for a second that you're aware of how awful you were to me. And I'm not going to take that from you or anybody."

CHAPTER 27

"So … how was your Thanksgiving?"

Mia already asked me that when she got here about twenty minutes ago. Maybe she's still in a turkey stupor from yesterday. Very possible. After all, she's supposed to be sorting and answering RPM email, but she just sits at her computer, staring at the screen and pushing the space bar over and over. I don't think I'm getting my fifteen-bucks-an hour's-worth.

"It was wonderful," I say, wondering what's wrong with her. "I was at the mission from the crack of dawn until two, then I came back here and got a lot done. And did you know Velma from Scooby-Doo donated her yellow sweater?"

Mia looks up when I stop talking. "I'm glad. And Mags? Have you heard from her?"

"She called about a half hour ago. She made a billion dollars this morning during the first hour the boutique was open and RPM gets it all."

"Awesome," Mia says. "See? I told you letting her use us to promote her shop would be good for RPM in the long run. She was smart to have her grand opening on Black Friday. Especially since we're getting a piece of the action."

It's true. Mia was right and I was wrong. I didn't want to have anything to do with Mags when she wanted to jump on the RPM bandwagon.

But if exploiting each other for financial gain is the way to sisterly affection, so be it. I know, at least a part of me knows, that I should just forget about Mags. Forever. But I just can't.

I look back to Mia, thankful she's not my sister. Because then I'd probably hate her.

Mia stares right through the laptop in front of her. Her smaller desk is butted up against the smaller section of the L of my L-shaped desk. And since the smaller part of the L is where I've set up my computer, we sit facing each other over our computers as though we're playing Battleship. Still, I can peek around to get a better look. But she actually notices me spying.

"What?" she asks.

"Mia, what's wrong?"

Mia looks back down at the desk and spots a scribbled message about *Dancing to the Moon*. "Did you get on?" she asks, suddenly all excitement and encouragement.

"Yep. They called to confirm Wednesday." God, that seems like a long time ago.

"Cool."

Maybe Mia's having boyfriend trouble. Maybe Rob Yeager—

"Manny told me he saw Jack leaving here the other day."

My head snaps up. "So?" I demand.

Mia shrinks into herself. "It's just that ..." She trails off, bites her lip. But not visibly. She just kind of presses her lips together, but I can tell she's biting them inside her mouth.

Great. I'm intimidating a high school girl. Wonderful.

I make my voice soft and kind. "Sorry, Mia. I can tell something's bugging you. Just tell me." I smile at her. "It's okay."

Good lord. Now I sound like a kindergarten teacher assuring a student that pants-wetting is no big deal.

"Come on," I try again. "Out with it."

Mia scoots her chair over, so we can see each other clearly with no computer screens between us. "You told Garry Minor that Jack was just a fling," she begins.

Oh, God. Am I going to have to do birds and bees stuff? Jesus.

"But you really liked him," she continues.

I assume she means Jack, not Garry Minor. I must remember to warn her about ambiguous pronouns.

"Jack wasn't just a fling," Mia says. She looks around. "He helped paint this room."

Thank you, Mia. Thank you for reminding me that Jack is *everywhere*. I follow her gaze, checking out the pale cobalt walls with natural wood trim.

"So." She stops, all frustrated. "I mean, I know why you didn't tell Garry Minor the truth, but, well, what about Jack? What happened? Why was he here? What did he want?"

I lean back in my chair and look at her. "I don't know," I say. "I really don't. I wasn't thinking about what he wanted. I was thinking about what I want."

"And you want Jack, right?"

"Yeah, but Jack ..." I trail off, confused all of a sudden.

Mia pounces. "What did he *say* he wanted?"

"That he wanted us to get back together."

"Lisa!" Mia is alight with excitement. "What did you say?"

"There is no back, Mia."

Her face falls so suddenly it's like someone turned out the light.

"Mia," I say, scooting closer, "he wants to go back to fun and games, but I can't because I love him and he doesn't love me back."

"You told him you loved him?"

"Yes."

"And he never said he loved you?"

I open my mouth to answer. I close my mouth. I try to think. "Well, he did, but ..."

"But what!?" Mia's eyes are popping out of her head.

I look at her.

But what?

What *had* Jack wanted? Sex and affection without being *my guy*? But he *did* invite me to Thanksgiving with his family. *With his family*. And what he actually said was that he wanted to *try again*.

Start over.

"Oh, God!" I bolt up from my chair with such force that it ricochets into the wall. "Oh, God!" I shout again. "Oh, God, oh, God, oh, God! What have I done?"

I run out into the living room.

"Lisa?" Mia gives chase.

I flop onto the couch as she catches up to me. "Just let me think," I say, clenching my hands to my skull.

What does Jack want?

Did I reject the opportunity of eons by not going to Thanksgiving at his house yesterday?

Did I destroy my life?

His life?

Oh, God!

WHAT HAVE I DONE?

"Lisa?" Mia leans over to try to peer at my face as I rock myself into crash landing position. "What's going on? What did he say when he left?"

My head juts up like a turtle's.

"Lisa? What did he say when he left?"

"Nothing," I answer. "He didn't say anything." My spine straightens, as though I'm a turtle moving right on up the evolutionary scale.

"He didn't say *anything*." I stand. "He still doesn't get it."

"Get what?"

Duh-nuh-nuh-nuun.

The dogs race to the front door.

Ca-thump.

Mia looks at me. I look at her. She scurries to the door. Pausing for a second, she takes a deep breath, then yanks it open.

"Hello," a voice says. A crisp, no-nonsense, female voice.

It's not Jack. My racing heart drops momentum so suddenly it feels like I hit a pocket of turbulence in my chest.

"I'm Tina Chung," the voice continues. "Is Lisa Flyte here?"

Mia looks back at me where I stand dressed in tartan plaid pajama pants. But I took a shower this morning, and I'm wearing a decent long sleeved T-shirt, bra, and clean socks.

"One sec," I say, shuffling across the floor so I can put the dogs out back. When I return to the living room, Tina Chung, well dressed in a taupe business suit, stands there with Mia.

She extends a hand in greeting. "Tina Chung," she reports.

I shake. "Lisa Flyte. What can I help you with?"

"I'm here to get a job," she states. "Can we talk?"

A job? With me? Doing what? I honestly don't care.

I just desperately need to talk about something other than Jack Hawkins. "Come into the office," I offer, leading her back.

Tina settles herself into one of the comfy chairs in front of the big part of the L.

"What's up?" I ask, my gaze drifting to the doorjamb that Jack leaned against just two days ago.

Then Tina surges forward, perching on the edge of the

chair, boring into me with this galvanizing intensity. "You want to take some money and make lots more money for RPM. I'm an investment banker. I can do that for you. I got in the 95th percentile on my SATs and my GMAT, graduated third in my class from Boston University, and first from the UCLA MBA program. I've worked at J.A. Wheeler and Ang for the past eighteen months. I want to retire by the time I'm fifty with enough money to enjoy life to the fullest. To do that, I need more than talent and a good job. I need a platform, a name. Success with RPM can do that for me. I can work for you for four to five years, make you millions of dollars, and get myself the high profile I need. It's a win-win situation."

I'm paying attention now. "Is Wheeler and Ang your first job since your MBA?"

"Yes," Tina answers. "I've done excellent work for them, but I'll never get the recognition I need buried in an investment firm."

I nod, my head spinning. Her dark hair is so thick and lush I can smell her apple blossom shampoo from here. I'm dying to ask her what brand it is.

"Do you know anything about RPM?" I ask instead.

"Just about everything there is to know," she assures me. "But I'll be up front with you, because that is the only way I do business. Helping the poor and the homeless and the downtrodden is not a prime directive in my life."

She said prime directive, like from *RoboCop.*

"My parents arrived from Taiwan with nothing," she continues. "They worked very hard to build a real estate business and make a life for all of us. I believe that hard work and determination can get you the future you want. My goal is to make a name for myself in high finance. To accomplish that, I will need to make truckloads of money for you. Our goals dovetail perfectly. And that," she says, her sharp eyes gleaming, "is the secret to success. Finding the one who can provide exactly what you need."

I smile at Tina. "Exactly."

* * * * *

"Do you see?"

I look over at Ethel. "I, uh, I don't think so." I look back at the wooden filing cabinets lining the wall of the dining room. "Don't you like them?"

"There is no K, Lisa."

"There's not?" I blink a few times, trying to find it. "Did you look everywhere?"

Ethel rolls her eyes. "Believe it or not, yes, I did. When I didn't find it between J and L, I looked to see if you put it somewhere else. You didn't."

"Daaamn," I groan, lolling back my head and stamping my foot. How could I lose K? Stupid, stupid letter. "How many drawers are left over after Z?" I ask Ethel.

"Three."

"Put K in one of them."

"It won't be alphabetical."

"I'll rearrange all the drawers later tonight and put the brass plate on when I get another one." As soon as the words are out, I'm wondering how many I'll have to move. K is in the first half of the alphabet, so I'm looking at pulling out and putting back over thirteen drawers tonight.

She purses her lips, theatrically resigned that this is the best she is going to get.

"Do we have anything to file under K yet?"

"That's not the point."

"You're right," I say.

The point is that now I've got to rearrange a filing

cabinet I screwed up in the first place in time to catch a red-eye to Chicago to do some talk show Dolly set up. "Carry on as best you can," I tell her, then head back to my office. In the hall I see Mal, so I scoop him up and kiss him between his ears.

"Don't cuss, Derek." I can hear Tina through the open door. She doesn't even say the word *curse*, like the word itself is a bad word. "You sound like Lisa, and she's the boss."

"So?" This from Derek who shares the biggest office with Tina. It's the hunter green master bedroom. Jack painted that room, too.

"So, you're not the boss."

"Neither are you, so I'll friggin' cuss if I want to."

But I notice that Derek doesn't actually curse. Those two are going to end up in bed together, I just know it.

I head to my office with Mal.

"What are you looking so giggly about?" Dolly taps away at the laptop on her small desk in the corner of my office.

I sit down, pushing back to prop my feet on the desk so Mal can stretch out on my lap. "Derek," I say. "I was so brilliant to hire him. Just as ambitious as Tina, and just as competitive. They're outdoing each other to see who can make the most money for RPM."

"Well," Dolly says, "until they get down and dirty, they have to channel all that sexual energy into something."

"Dolly!"

"Oh, please. By the way, when does the Christmas special tape?"

My feet thunk to the floor, and Mal darts away. "Don't you know?" I squeak. "You're supposed to be my agent!"

"Manager." She levels me with a haughty look. "Of course I know. But do *you* know?"

"Oh," I say, trying to remember what day it is. "Next Thursday?" Total guess. "I have to be at CBS by 5 a.m.," I add, just to make it sound as if I know what I'm talking about.

"Very good," she says, clearly impressed. She gets up to leave.

"Where are you going?"

"Sweetheart, it's two o'clock."

Two o'clock? Already? I didn't even have breakfast yet. "Oh," I say. "See you tomorrow."

"Love ya."

"Love ya back." Man. How did it get to be afternoon so fast? I have a billion things to do.

I swivel to the computer to catch up on email. Mia will be ticked off if she gets here and I haven't gone through all she sorted yesterday. I quickly type in my password, realizing that I'm scared of my teenage assistant. Tapping my foot, I click my INBOX.

My foot stops tapping.

TO: lisaflyte@RPM.com

FROM: jackhawkins@intothewild.com

SUBJECT: For Lisa

Oh. My. God. Jack has *never* emailed me. Never ever.

I open the email. But it's not just one email. I scroll down, starting at the bottom to read through a series of emails between Jack and Mia.

Lisa, this is for you. Jack.

Jeez, it sounds like he's about to stab me in the throat with a pair of scissors. I look up to the top of the email. There is an attachment. But before looking at it, I continue reading through the exchange between Jack and Mia. Next is Mia.

Is this a hoax? How do I know you're really Jack Hawkins?

Jack's reply: Is this Mia?

Mia: Yes. And that's not proof.

Jack: I helped you and Lisa paint her house. Wash got

his tail in the paint, and when it comes to belting out Bonnie Raitt, neither of you can sing worth a damn.

Mia: Fine. I'll forward your email to her.

That's it. I look at the dates and times of the emails. Jack sent the first one at 5:42 a.m. yesterday. Mia replied after school yesterday at 4:15 p.m. Their back and forth finally wrapped up at 5:24 p.m. yesterday.

And Mia never let on. I was in and out of the office yesterday as she sat at her desk organizing the day's email, but she never said a word.

I look to the top of the screen. The attachment. It's an MP3. A heartfelt apology from Jack? A snippet about us from some radio show? I can't imagine.

I get up and close the door to my office. Then I make sure the volume on my computer is low enough that only I'll be able to hear it. I open the attachment.

With the first riff of guitar strings, I catch my breath. "Joey," by Concrete Blonde.

The heart-wrenching lyrics rip into me with their desperate struggle to salvage messed-up love.

I can scarcely breathe. Is Jack asking me to come back? Again? Is he trying to confess something? Explain something? Or did he just send me a song he thought I'd like? And if so, why? Why why why why why?

The song ends, making it easier to hear my heart pounding.

The silence of the computer makes my skin prickle. Jack sent me a song. Jack sent me a song? Are we in middle school? I slap my hand hard onto the top of my desk, making my palm sting.

I suck on my throbbing flesh. Is he sending me a message in a language he knows I'd appreciate? Does he get points for choosing THE BEST SONG EVER?

I don't know I don't know I don't know I don't know.

* * * * *

Two days later and I still don't know. But I want to know. Ever since Jack sent the first song, I've been trolling my inbox like a hungry shark looking for stranded divers. True, getting "Joey" was weird, but somewhat mysterious and powerfully appealing. The next day Jack sent "Only You" by Yaz.

Then "Don't Stop Believin'" by Journey.

Don't stop believing? Don't stop believing what, Jack? What are you trying to say?

I need another song. I open my inbox for the fourth time in the past sixty minutes. And here it is. I breathe for what feels like the first time all day.

TO: lisaflyte@RPM.com

FROM: jackhawkins@intothewild.com

SUBJECT: Something else for Lisa

And it has an attachment. I open the file. No text, just the attachment. And not an MP3 this time.

A video file.

I click it open.

Dah nah nah nah nuh nuh nah na na na na…

The opening notes trill through the room as the black and white sketch work of the music video unfolds on screen. "Take On Me," by Ah-ha.

How did Jack *know*?

I had an Ah-ha poster hanging by my bed all through junior high. Well, all the way up until I went away to college.

Okay, I took it to college but was too embarrassed to hang it up when I saw that all my roommate's posters were prints of classic art. Cezanne, for cryin' out loud.

I haven't seen this video in ages.

I watch it twice through. Okay. Jack is throwing down the gauntlet. He's asking me again to take him on, to take him back.

I think.

How dare he? He already asked me to take him back in person, and I said NO. Does he think I'm just going to forget the I-said-I-wanted-to-be-your-boyfriend-then-abandoned-you part?

Because of some stupid video?

What kind of life would that be?

Would we date in shameful secret, but he'd take me to a Bruce Springsteen concert to make up for it?

As if!

With Hulk-like rage coursing through my blood, I surf the net, find the song, download it, send it. "Dirty Little Secret" by The All-American Rejects. Take that, Jack!

Wait. What have I done?

I sent Jack a song. We are arguing through songs. Still, pre-teen mating rituals aside, I stare at the monitor, my heart pounding. What will he do? Actually write me an e-mail this time?

Ten minutes and nothing. Good. By the time he sends me something back, if he even bothers, I won't care anymore. I am a very busy and important person, so tomorrow, this won't even matter.

CHAPTER 28

I rake through my email again, looking for a message from Jack I might have missed. I scour every folder available.

Nothing.

Nothing.

Nothing.

Noth—

"I knew it!"

I jump out of my chair, my heart lodged in my neck. "Jesus, Mia!"

She puts a cup of Starbucks on my desk and sits across from me. "Any more emails from Jack?" Her eyes positively dance.

"Aren't you supposed to be in school?" I take the lid off my coffee cup and blow on the foam.

"That's what you're doing, right? Looking for email from Jack? What's he been sending you? You never talk about it."

I take a sip. "Then why are you asking me about it?"

"Because I caught you red-handed, so you can't deny that you care."

"Is that why you've been bringing me coffee before school? So you could catch me reading email?"

"What does he say?" She's leaning so far over my desk

she's practically horizontal. "They're songs, right? From the eighties, I bet."

I put the cup down and stare at her.

"That's what I would send if you were mad at me." Then she just looks at me, still all smiles and bright eyes, and I think she's actually vibrating.

"So?" she demands.

"So, what?"

"So ... has he apologized for being such a jerk?"

"No."

"Oh." She dims forty watts. "Does it matter?" She gets a little brighter. "If you guys really like each other? Love each other?"

"I ... I'm pretty sure it does." I look right at her. "Honestly, I think he just gets in these moods where he wants a girlfriend. Not just sex, but maybe some affection, too. But he doesn't want it to last. He doesn't want it to be part of his real life."

"You're wrong about him," Mia hefts her backpack onto her shoulder. "You have to be."

"Or what?" I call to Mia's back as she heads off to school. But I can hardly blame her for having romantic delusions about me and Jack. Not when I watch Tina and Derek as if they're characters in a Thursday night sitcom.

I look back to my inbox and the phone rings.

I look at the caller ID. HEYA. I haven't talked to any of them since the day they kicked me out. "Hello?"

"Lisa? Good. It's Lupe." She stops talking.

"It's okay, Lupe. Everything going good at the center? That's all that matters."

"Yeah, it is. I just called to see if ... I know you said on Garry Minor that there was nothing between you and Jack, but, well, it was so weird that day. When Jack stormed in here and took the book. Then, Edna Hawkins saving our butts. Now this. It has us all worried. I know we shouldn't be, but what if ... I don't know. None of us do. We just thought you might know something."

"Know something about what? Lupe, what are you talking about?"

"The press conference. It doesn't have anything to do with us, does it?"

"Press conference?" I look up to see Dolly coming into the office. "Dolly, do I have a press conference today?"

"Nooo!" Lupe yells through the phone.

"What?" I say to Lupe.

"Not *your* press conference. Jack's. The press conference he's having with his mom and the shoe company this morning. They're kicking off the Southern California Conference of Business Leaders."

My pulse kicks up a notch. "Lupe, what the hell are you talking about?"

"Into the Wild is joining up with Hawkins United. They're planning some big merger with a sneaker company and we were just wondering if it had anything to do with us."

My blood starts pounding faster than the spin cycle of a Whirlpool, making my speech stilted, jerky, demanding.

"Who's doing the merger?"

"Into the Wild."

"But who are they doing it with? What sneaker company?"

"I don't know. Sampson, or something like that."

"Sawyer?"

"That's it."

Noooo!!!!

"What time is the press conference?" I ask.

"Nine o'clock."

"What?" I screech. "Where?"

"The Sheraton downtown. In the Macy's Plaza."

I pocket the phone and run to the front door. It's 8:36. I have 24 minutes to make it downtown in morning rush hour traffic. I grab my keys, and I'm off.

What is Jack about to do? Is it all my fault? Why else would he merge with Sawyer and join Hawkins United? He must have sold his soul to his mother in order to save HEYA.

I tear out of the driveway, zipping around cars like I'm playing Atari with a joystick. I want to call Jack's cell, but I cannot take my hands and eyes away from driving for even a second. I get to the metro station, park illegally, and tear down the giant escalators. I don't even stop to buy a ticket as I head for a train just pulling in.

Goddamnit! Evil, hateful Edna! Leave it to that BITCH to blackmail Jack just because he wanted to fix a mistake that was totally her doing in the first place!

I try to use my cell. No signal on the subway.

This must have been Jack's plan all along, but he didn't tell me.

Jesus, Jack.

Why?

Whywhywhywhywhywhy?

I would have figured out something else to save HEYA. I would have used all my own money and started from scratch to help others if I'd had to.

I never, NEVER would have sacrificed Jack for anything. Especially not for money.

Oh, God! That must have been why he was sending me those songs. He wanted me back so he would have someone beside him as every hope and dream he ever had disintegrated before his eyes.

And I ignored him. I'm making him go through his

worst nightmare all alone.

The train slows, pulling into the 7th Street station. As soon as the doors swish open, I'm off, heedless of all the commuters. I race up the sliding escalator stairs two at a time, emerging directly across from The Macy's Plaza. I dodge across the street, making cars stop for me.

In seconds, I'm in the Plaza, skidding down the stairs to the mezzanine level. The twinkling white lights strung throughout the corridor sparkle off the speckled tile, paving the way to the entrance of the hotel.

I'm here. I made it.

Hotel personnel stand at the door checking press identification. But I look so totally un-press-like in my beat up jeans and long sleeved T-shirt that I squeak by.

I'm in.

I scan the lobby. A fancy placard on an easel announces that the SCCBL Press Conference is in the banquet room to my left. I veer towards it.

Oh, man. The doorway is clogged with people focused on the front of the room. My gut seizes up. It must have started. I race to join the throng and start working my way through. I can't see anything.

My eyes dart around frantically until I spot a garbage can just inside the door. It's polished and expensive looking with a sloped lid that discourages miscreants from climbing up onto it. But up I climb anyway, balancing precariously so that I can see everything.

The vast hall is set up with round banquet tables at which various business-attired men and women sit with pastries and coffee in front of them. Reporters and photographers stand wherever they can at the back of the room, and some even sneak in to stand between tables.

At the front of the room on an impromptu stage sits a

long rectangular table skirted with white linen. A peachy-mauve curtain is somehow erected behind the stage.

Jack is going to sacrifice everything in front of a peachy-mauve curtain?

Edna and Frank sit in two chairs to the left of an empty chair at the center of the table, and some guy I don't recognize—must be the Sawyer dude—sits to the right of the empty chair. Then Jack steps up onto the stage.

Jack.

Jack in a dark suit and green tie takes the empty chair. There they all are: Frank, Edna, Jack, Sawyer Guy. Flashes go off as the room hums with the buzz of anticipation.

I don't know what to do.

Should I shout? Make a scene?

I check my cell again. Still no signal. So that's out as a way of letting Jack know I'm here.

I slide carefully off the trash can, press myself against the back wall. I'll work my way around the room by staying plastered to the wall but inching forward. I'll be inconspicuous as I sidle toward the stage. I start my slide but halt when Edna clears her throat.

"We will each read a brief statement," she announces in her expertly modulated, cosmopolitan voice. "Then we will take any questions that either our fellow business leaders or the representatives of the press may have." I can positively hear the ingratiating smile.

The room falls silent, flashes still wink.

"Today," Edna begins, "Jack Hawkins, CEO and founder of Into the Wild, will announce his company's merger with the Sawyer Sport Shoe Company. They will sign papers to that effect. Then Hawkins United will absorb the newly formed powerhouse. Jack?"

She turns toward Jack. It's his turn. He's on. Oh, God.

Whatever he is about to say, I know it will rip him apart. Big, fat tears roll down my face.

Jack puts his elbows on the table, moving toward the microphone in front of him. “I will not sign those papers and Into the Wild will not merge with anyone.”

What?

Shocked gasps.

And then I feel it. The hope, the power. I don’t know what Jack has up his sleeve, but I know that voice. He is in complete control.

“What?” The guy from Sawyer and Frank echo each other’s budding outrage.

“Excuse me, Jack?” Edna, of course.

Jack looks at her, then turns back to address the room.

“The only reason I’m here is to tell the world that I’m in love with Lisa Flyte.”

!!!!!!!!!!!!!!!!

“What?!” All three of them this time. The outrage blossoming into full bloom.

“I love her,” Jack says into a thousand flashing cameras. “Totally. Completely. And definitely madly.”

“Jack, you mean—” Frank, sounding almost scared.

“You can’t do this!” The guy from Sawyer, looking disgusted.

Jack turns to him. “*You* outsource to poverty-stricken children in Thailand for three cents an hour, so you can just shut up.”

“Jack,” Frank begins, “there are serious repercussions. Our business—”

Jack turns to him. “Your business will recover. My life won’t. Not if I can’t get Lisa back.”

Edna focuses icy fury on him. “You—”

“I’ve used every trick I’ve ever learned from you to get

what I want. Thanks, Mom."

Edna pulls back, considers this for a second. Then, with the barest hint of a nod, she appears to decide it's all right.

"This is just an asinine attempt to manipulate the market and increase the value of your stock!" calls a voice from the crowd.

Really?

I look around, spotting the short, dark-haired reporter with a chip on his shoulder. I hate him.

"My company isn't publicly traded, Sherlock."

Jack is so damn kick-ass.

"Increase your market share, then!"

Jack almost visibly brushes off this comment.

"Irrelevant. None of our so-called competitors come close to doing what we do. We have our own market."

Calm. Confident. Damn sexy.

"So you set up this whole thing just to get us here to report that you love Lisa Flyte?" A different reporter, this one with a sallow complexion and beer gut.

Jack tips his head in the guy's direction. "Look at it as the chance to get the story right this time."

"Or an opportunity to cash in on her fame and up your own profile. Isn't this just a ploy to market Into the Wild?" This time, the reporter wears purple high heels that match her nail polish. I definitely hate her.

"By admitting what an awful boyfriend I turned out to be?"

"This makes no sense," another reporter calls.

"I knew there was a chance you wouldn't believe me," Jack concedes. "Why should you? You've gotten everything about her wrong so far. But I don't care. I need only one person to believe me."

"Now that's an interesting question, Jack." This time it's

Alan Stewart, emerging from a crowd against the back wall. "Why should we believe you? Why? You had your chance to confess your love weeks ago, but you hung Lisa out to dry, instead. Now, you haven't got a penny to your name, not since buying up every share you could of your company once we all jumped ship. And we're supposed to believe that suddenly you love a famous rich girl? I think we need some convincing. You set up this press conference to let the world know you love Lisa. So, why Jack? What's so special about Lisa? Convince us she's the one for you."

Silence.

Uh-oh.

A few call from the room, "Yeah, Jack. Why do you suddenly love her?"

"Why?"

"Yeah, why?"

Oh, God.

Then Jack laughs, a smile breaking across his face.

Oh, no! What's he going to say? *You got me. I don't really love her.*

"I love her," he says, "because she wants to see a flea flicker on third and inches."

Huh?

"What?" the first reporter squawks. "Nobody in their right mind would do a flea flicker on third and inches."

"I know!" Jack laughs. "Nobody ever does something like that. Though it would be a pretty smart play. But that's the point. Lisa wants to see it just because it's so unexpected. It wouldn't be boring. And that's what she loves. Finding the excitement in every possible second."

I start moving more toward the center of the room, more toward Jack.

"How many inches?" lilts a sassy reporter with dark

roots.

I stop moving. Jesus. My love story is going to end up in *Playgirl*.

Jack looks at her, giving her his full attention. "A flea flicker is a trick football play that nobody ever calls when you only need a few inches to get a first down."

"So," the woman asks, "what are you saying? That Lisa doesn't understand football and that's why you love her?"

"She definitely knows football," Jack says, "and she likes to watch it naked. I love that, too."

My mouth drops open.

"And I love that she loves to eat."

Jack. Jack, Jack, Jack, Jack.

"And I love that every time we see an animal in the woods, she's sure it's lost its mother and she wants to help." He laughs. "I love the way she dances, like she wants to use her body to touch every inch of space around her. I love that she gets all teary when she's describing the first episode of *Murphy Brown* that stars Colleen Dewhurst. I love that she took the smallest bedroom in her house. I love that it was never about the money. I love that she can't help loving her family. I love that she can back up any point she's making with a quote from *Quantum Leap*. I love that she never kowtows to anyone, not even to my mother."

By this time, I've moved so far toward him that I'm standing alone in the center of the room where everyone can see me.

Jack looks right at me. "And I love that she loves me."

He's searing into me with those damn cobalt eyes, and I cannot move.

The room pulses with silence.

"Nice," I finally say in a scratchy voice. I swat away a tear. "You get full marks for the grand romantic gesture."

He doesn't move. He just keeps looking at me.

Nobody in the whole room breathes.

"But you swept me off my feet before," I say. What am I saying?!?!?! Shut up shut up shut upshutupshutup!!! "Then you dropped me."

Jack never stops looking right at me, like there's no one else in the room. "You were right, Lisa. Physical courage and emotional courage are completely different. I can do one as easily as flicking a switch. But the other? I couldn't handle it. I froze. I left you. I'm sorry."

My mouth opens.

Jack waits to see if I'm going to say anything, and when I don't, he says, "Lisa." His voice is soft, but so strong, gliding across my skin like an ocean zephyr. "You suffered because I was a coward, and I am so sorry I hurt you. I can hardly believe that I did that to you. I don't want to be that guy. Not ever again."

I stand there, staring at him.

"Lisa, you lacked a certain kind of courage, or thought you did, so you worked on it. I'm working too, doing the things that terrify me most. Things I suck at. But I will not let you down ever again."

He leans forward, right shoulder leading. "I'm asking you to have the guts to give me another chance."

I'm speechless, like I'm watching a movie, waiting to see what happens next.

He pins me with a look so hot I gasp. "Lisa, can you fly this plane?"

My breath puffs out in a kind of laugh, breaking the spell of my glazed-over silence. In a rush, I realize everything is real. A line from a freaking movie, but at last, the story is about me.

"Yeah," I say. "I can fly it. I'm the best there is."

He smiles at me from the stage, a smile that's anchored

deep in those eyes of his. "Yeah," he says. "You really are."

Then he pushes back his chair and stands up. Without missing a beat, he steps onto and over the table. Flashes go wild all over the room.

Jack is coming for me, walking right up the aisle at me. He's not stopping. Or slowing down.

He sweeps right into me and kisses me.

And I'm ready for it.

He's here, and it's real, and I can't get enough.

Jack Jack Jack Jack Jack.

Jack breaks the kiss, leans into me and kisses me again, then rests his forehead against mine. "Lisa."

I blink at him through the barrage of flashes. It tingles through me, this strange and amazing and wonderful sensation of standing here with Jack. For the first time since I've known him, I feel like I am really *with Jack.*

"Jack," I whisper, leaning into him. "Jack."

He smiles, the really good kind where his eyes crinkle. "Let's get out of here," he whispers back.

I take a deep breath, look around. Impossible, but I'm ready. "Okay."

I see a hint of a smirk. "I've got a plan."

And we take off. He leads me full speed back up the aisle toward the stage. We leap onto and over the table, through the curtains. Edna follows as Frank tries to hold off the reporters on the other side.

Edna hands Jack a set of keys. "5B."

Jack flashes her a grin and tells her, "That way." He points down the hotel corridor toward the kitchen doors. Then he leads me along the curtain, wrapping us both in its folds as the reporters break through.

Edna runs toward the kitchen and shrieks at her imaginary quarry. "Stop! Get back here, you filthy whore!"

The reporters chase her down.

Jack and I sneak out from our cover, head back through the curtain, and race right down the center aisle of the banquet room. We make it out of the hotel and dart down the mezzanine.

My feet pound across the speckled floor as we race along under the twinkling lights. An impromptu chase finally gets underway behind us, but we're across the mall and in the elevator to the parking garage before any media people can catch us.

As the elevator doors close us in, Jack pushes the button for four, three, five, six, two and seven. Then he turns to me, grabs me by the face, and kisses me.

When the elevator stops at two, Jack hustles me off and calls the elevator right next to the one we were just on. Then he pushes the call button for the elevator that's on its way down to get our pursuers.

In another second, we're safely inside our new elevator. "Lisa," he says. He kisses me again. "I love you."

I smile. "I love you back." I sink into his arms. "Did you really use all your money to buy the shares from the employees?"

He laughs. "I don't have that kind of money! I used the trust fund I said I would never touch." He stops laughing and pushes back to look at me with brilliant blue intensity.

"I've learned a thing or two from you about using corporate money to do good." He strokes his thumb across my cheek. "And a few of the employees stayed or came back, keeping or re-buying their shares."

"Peg?"

"Never even thought of leaving. Holding down the fort as we speak."

The elevator stops and the doors open. Jack grabs my hand, and we're off, across the floor of the parking garage and into one of its dark corners.

"This is Brenda and McGraw from Into the Wild," Jack says, introducing me to two people waiting by two motorcycles. They both wear skin-tight body armor and nothing else.

"Hey," I say in way of greeting.

"Thanks, guys," Jack says to them, as he rips off his jacket and tie. "They're close behind. Lisa, take off your clothes."

In an instant I catch on and start to strip. Brenda and McGraw put on our clothes over their body armor. In less than a minute, they're dressed. Then they each slap on a helmet with a darkened visor as Jack and I get into the clothes they had waiting for us. Jeans and a green T for him, sleek black leggings and a snug turquoise hooded sweatshirt for me. Brenda and McGraw hop on the motorcycles and speed off across the garage.

"Thanks," I call softly to the retreating roar. They stop to rev their engines at the top of the exit ramp, waiting for their pursuers. Well, *our* pursuers, really. Mine and Jack's.

Jack watches me zipping my turquoise hoodie and smiles. "Your eyes look fantastic." He kisses me. "Come on."

Before I can even think, he's pulling me toward the edge of the garage. Toward the railing. As in, four stories above the zipping traffic of 9th street.

But there's a space in the railing. A staircase?

More of a fire escape, really. The narrow steps zigzag down the outside of the parking garage. We're just climbing onto them as our pursuers burst off the elevator in time to spot Brenda and McGraw disappearing down the ramp. The reporters and security people scatter to chase them down.

Jack heads down the stairs first, clattering like a monkey along the bent ladder-thing. I gamely follow, my knees in my throat, looking at nothing but each step in front of me. When we reach the ground, Jack takes my hand and looks around. Nobody takes the slightest notice of us.

"It's a great day," I decide, smiling up at him.

"It is," he agrees.

And just like that, we start walking, hand in hand, through downtown L.A. Up and across, over the glittering sidewalks, in the shadows of the tall buildings. And as we go, we talk. About everything.

He asks me about RPM, tells me how cool I am.

I ask him how Thanksgiving went with his family. His mother was astounded that he'd cooked.

But we don't just talk as we walk. Jack touches me, too. He puts his hand on my neck, trails fingers down my back. Stuff like that. I think we're on Third, maybe Fourth, when Jack stops walking and looks up. The tall glass towers of the Bonaventure Hotel rise up before us.

Jack looks at me. "I checked in this morning. Have the room key and everything."

"Everything?" I ask softly.

"I've got you."

Like I said, a really great day.

THE END

Also by Geralyn Corcillo

Novels

Queen of the Universe

Catch a Falling Star Spring 2016

Short Stories

"Jane Austen Meets the New York Giants"

"All Summer on a Date"

"Miss Understanding in the Ballroom with the Wrench"

"Random Acts of Violet"

About the Author

Geralyn Corcillo taught high school in Watts and South Central Los Angeles. But deciding she needed an even tougher job, she chose to write. She won a few contests, hit the *New York Times* Bestseller List with her first short story, and got a screenplay produced. *Miss Adventure* is her first novel.

Geralyn Vivian Ruane Corcillo is a native of Scranton, Pennsylvania and now lives in North Hollywood with her husband Ron, a guy who's even cooler than Kip Dynamite.

Acknowledgements

Thank You:

Leonard W. Kingsley, the greatest literary manager on the planet and in my heart

Marlo Thomas, for giving me my first big break

Matt Wheeler, for everything

OCC, for making me believe I could do it

Debra Holland & Kitty Bucholtz, for lighting my way

The Ruane Family of Chinchilla, Pennsylvania: Pat, Gloria, Marianne, Mike, Marice, Grady, and Pepsi

And now …

A sneak peek at Geralyn Corcillo's latest romantic comedy novel,
Queen of the Universe
Available on Amazon

Can a charismatic TV writer convince a reclusive handyman to become her show's leading man in time to save her career?

Chapter 1
LOLA

"I need a sexy man!"

I fling the script to the floor hard and clench my teeth. Suppressing a growl, I suck in a deep breath. I swivel to Brian, pinning him with a look that could ice Pluto. "Why haven't we found him yet? You're supposed to be the damn casting director!"

He opens his mouth to answer but I plow over him.

"Don't these agents get it?" I burst out of my chair and head toward the windows. Spinning back to Brian, I clench my fists so hard I'd be bleeding if I had fingernails worth anything. "I don't want some buff model who thinks stubble makes him look like a tough guy. For God's sake, Wendy Hunter is playing Celeste. Wendy Hunter! Do they think they can just send us *anyone*? What's wrong with these clueless agents?!"

My heart flips into hyperdrive as I consider that my future might be in the hands of these brainless freaking bloodsucking agents. Agents!

I throw myself back into the roomy upholstered chair behind my desk. I didn't actually choose this particular office chair in order to catch me mid-meltdown, but it totally does the job. I jam one sneaker to the floor to keep from careening backwards and then I lean toward Brian. "I need a man who exudes raw, dangerous sexuality. Sam Destry, the dark, brooding bounty hunter who lives next door to Celeste. Sexy is just what he … is. Your job is to find him. Where is he?"

"He's out there." Brian is bent over the camera, removing the SD card. He straightens up and looks at me. "And possibly coming in this afternoon." He sits down at his laptop and inserts the card.

I lean back, resting my elbows on the arms of the chair. "You need to step up your game," I tell him. "Cameras roll in just over two weeks and they can't roll until we cast Sam. I don't care if you have to cruise Santa Monica and pick up every guy you see and drag him in here to read."

Brian finishes typing with a flourish. I swallow, knowing some incredibly lame auditions just uploaded to the main server. Where Tom will see them.

"One of the guys we're seeing later plays Hamlet in an all-nude production," Brian offers. "Long, lanky, brilliant, AND brooding."

I snatch the bottle of Evian off my desk and thump it against my palm. "Sam does not have three hours of nudity to win over an audience. *Off the Beaten Path* takes up forty-four fully-clothed minutes, once a week. And Sam's not even the lead!" I uncap the bottle of water. "We need a man who can melt a woman's bones with his very presence." I take a long drink.

"Or a melt a *man's* bones," sings Ray as he sweeps into the office. He fans a set of head shots across my desk with panache. "These are your afternoon guys. Good luck. I'm off."

"Off?!" I slam my hand onto my desk. "It's eleven a.m. Go back to your desk, sit down, and do your damn job."

"Can't," he trills, totally blowing me off. "Dentist. Gotta keep this smile killer."

"During AUDITIONS?! Get back to your desk and get me a Mocha Frappucino double whip. With caramel!"

"Yeah, that's what you need. More caffeine. And sugar."

"Ray!"

"You said I could go today at eleven because you'd be—"

"Oh, shut up and get out. Go if I said go and just be back here by one!"

"Don't forget—"

"Go! And you better come back with Starbucks if you value your life."

"Yada yada yada." And with that, Ray strolls out of the office, already texting as he goes.

My phone jingles quietly. Ray was texting *me*? I glance at my phone.

... forget about Sam for the next hour ...

"Rrrr!" I toss my cell on the desk, in no mood for Ray's namaste crap. I need to find Sam!

Brian watches me as he pops the SD card back into the camera. "Lola, you've been in the business, what? Twelve, thirteen years?"

"Fourteen," I correct.

"Yeah, and you don't have the reputation as the writer who saves shows for nothing. Now that you've got your own series to run, I'm betting you'll do your magic."

"I'm no miracle worker. I'm just like every other writer with a pilot on the chopping block."

Brian barks out a laugh. "You *dress* like every other TV writer," he says. "But jeans and a Green Lantern T-shirt don't change the fact that you look like you could be the love child of Jessica Lange and Marilyn Monroe and you got two Emmy nominations before you were thirty."

"Neither of which I won," I say evenly. "And Jessica Lange is in her sixties. So thanks."

"I totally mean *Tootsie* Jessica Lange."

"Whatever."

Does Brian seriously think flattery can work on me? He's not even good at it. All he's doing is reminding me that I peaked in my twenties. And that I am no longer in my twenties!

My phone starts to buzz and play a song as it vibrates across my desk. *Baby, did you ever wonder? Wonder, what ever became—*

"Hang on," I say to Brian as I slide my thumb across the screen of my cell and press it to my ear. "Tom."

"Lola!"

My neck muscles tighten. Tom's big sunny greeting. Doesn't mean a thing. His salutations are always over the top, no matter what he's about to say. But they never go anywhere, so I like letting his echoing words just hang there for an empty second.

"Tom," I say again. "What's up? We're in the middle of auditions."

"I'm having a meeting with Wendy in a few minutes," he announces, as if I've just won a brand new car. Once again he stops talking, but no applause and squeals of joy fill the gap.

"Fantastic!" I smile hard enough to edge out the knot in my stomach. I'm not ready for Wendy to stick her oar in and start making waves. Not until I've locked down Sam.

"She wants to see the auditions we've got so far for Sam," Tom tells me. "America's favorite actress is anxious to know who her new leading man will be."

"Perfect," I agree with gusto, flying right into the jaws of the beast. I pray that Tom stays true to form and backs off the second he realizes he's not the fly in my chardonnay. "I'm really depending on Wendy's take. Her insight into her craft is unparalleled. Ask her to look especially keenly at the second and fourth auditions from this morning. But you know, it was such a good crop, I'm sure Wendy is going to adore every one of them."

"Well," Tom says, slipping into his schoolmaster voice, "I'll mention what you said. But Lola, that's not really her job."

I bite my lip and catch my breath as if I'm going to say something but think better of it, channelling the appropriate chagrin through the phone.

"Lola," he continues, more fatherly now, even though I'm three years older than his preposterously inexperienced thirty-two, "Wendy Hunter doesn't come with a multi-million dollar price tag because she's so willing to help out the crew."

The crew? I created the damn show and he's calling me *the crew*? Like superstar diva Wendy Hunter is the reason I get to work on this show, and not the other way around!

I decide to control the churning in my blood before everyone on the crew is out of a job. One. Two. Three.

I give a little laugh. "*Au contraire.* We're here to help Wendy sparkle more brightly than ever. It's our job to give her whatever she needs because when she shines, the show shines, and the network shines."

"I'm glad you feel that way. Because what she needs right now is someone to play Sam to make her shine off the charts."

Okay, gloves off. "No, not *someone*. She's Wendy Hunter. She needs the perfect guy. And Brian and I are closing in."

"She's getting nervous. And she's not the only one."

"It's not nerves, Tom. It's adrenaline. The kind that rushes through you just before your finesse forward sinks a three-pointer and wins the game at the buzzer."

A few minutes later when I tuck the phone back into my pocket, I notice Brian staring at me. "You despised guys two and four. You said guy two reminded you of a sunflower wearing pedal pushers. Whatever *that* means. But it wasn't good."

"Wendy Hunter ... " *wants everything until you tell her that she might like it*. But I can't help but notice the dewy glow in Brian's eyes. "Wendy Hunter isn't just a wonderful actress and an excellent judge of acting talent. She's also an amazing communicator. She'll look at two and four and she'll make Tom understand that we haven't found Sam yet and we need to keep looking. I'm not going to risk the casting of Sam just because Tom Glenn wants to sign off so he can leave early for a Duran Duran reunion concert on Friday."

"I hear you," Brian agrees. "But it can't be good to mess with the studio exec's weekend." He clears his throat. "So, maybe, uh … maybe, since Wendy is going to be on the lot anyway, maybe she can come to a few auditions this afternoon, give some input, and help speed things up."

I stand up like Wesley at the end of *The Princess Bride*, trying to strike a sense of menace. "I don't need input." I look right at Brian. "Nobody knows how to cast Sam better than I do. I created the guy."

Brian looks away and I walk toward the windows. I stare

down at the empty parking lot below. “He's what Celeste wants,” I say quietly, “but can never have.”

“Maybe Wendy—”

I shut my eyes and command myself not to react. “There's no point to involving Wendy until I've found the guy I want.” I try to make my voice sound almost blasé. “All we've seen so far are models and bodybuilders.” I take a deep breath and speak clearly. “I don't want any of them.”

I open my eyes as an old blue pick-up parks in front of the building. I move closer to the glass, scarcely believing what I see.

A man looking to be in his thirties gets out of the truck and strides across the pavement. Scuffed boots, worn jeans, rangy build. He looks dark and dangerous, cool and wild.

It's Sam.

My Sam.

I can't breathe. “I want *him*.”

www.ingramcontent.com/pod-product-compliance
Lightning Source LLC
Chambersburg PA
CBHW030551180626
46816CB00005B/1503
* 9 7 8 1 6 2 6 7 8 0 0 7 1 *